THE DIARIES OF AVA WREN

INCLUDES

AVA AND PIP
AVA AND TACO CAT
AVA XOX

Carol Weston

sourcebooks
jabberwocky

Published by Sourcebooks Jabberwocky, an imprint of Sourcebooks, Inc.
P.O. Box 4410, Naperville, Illinois 60567-4410
(630) 961-3900
Fax: (630) 961-2168
www.sourcebooks.com

Library of Congress Cataloging-in-Publication data is on file with the publisher.

Source of Production: Worzalla, Stevens Point, Wisconsin, USA
Date of Production: May 2016
Run Number: 5006719

Printed and bound in the United States of America.
WOZ 10 9 8 7 6 5 4 3 2 1

PRAISE FOR *AVA AND PIP*

"Through Ava's diary entries, Weston perfectly captures the complexities of sisterhood...a love letter to language."

—*The New York Times Book Review*

"Ava Wren makes reading and writing so much fun, she deserves a T-O-P-S-P-O-T on your bookshelf. This charming diary will inspire shy kids, young writers, and even reluctant readers. Y-A-Y for A-V-A!"

—Dan Greenburg, author of The Zack Files series

"With her engaging voice, jaw-dropping wordplay, and tales of good people making not-so-good decisions, she casts the perfect spell. A big W-O-W for *Ava and Pip!*"

—Julie Sternberg, author of *Like Pickle Juice on a Cookie*

"Will have readers cheering."

—*Booklist*

"Just enough conflict to keep the pages flying, with the comfortable certainty that it will all work out."

—*School Library Journal*

"You're gonna fall head over heels for the new book by our very own advice columnist Carol Weston."

—*Girls' Life*

"The charming story covers writing, sisterhood, and events that occasionally, says Ava, are 'making me feel like P-O-O-P.'"

—*Yale Magazine*

"Weston deals with family dynamics and creative challenges in realistic, emotionally honest ways."

—*Shelf Awareness*

"A witty, warm, wonderful story… As with all good books, I was both eager to find out, and reluctant to have it over, noting with sorrow the dwindling pages."

—Neil Steinberg, columnist at the *Chicago Sun-Times*

"Young readers will be enchanted with this endearing story about two very different sisters and their journey to find their voices."

—*Pittsburgh Post-Gazette*

"Such a wonderful book. It's so gratifying to see a child devour a book."

—Laura Ingraham

"Filled with funny wordplay, this clever story will grab anyone who has ever felt overlooked."

—*Discovery Girls*

"YAY!"

—Jon Agee, author of *The Incredible Painting of Felix Clousseau* and *Go Hang a Salami! I'm a Lasagna Hog!*

Contents

AVA

and

Pip

CAROL WESTON

sourcebooks
jabberwocky

for kids who are shy,
and for kids who are not,

and

in memory of
Christopher Joseph Todd
who loved books

DEAR NEW DIARY,

You won't believe what I just found out.

Fifth grade started today, and my homeroom has three Emilys but only one Ava, so at dinner, I asked Mom and Dad why they named me Ava.

Innocent question, right?

Well, Dad answered: "We like palindromes."

"Palinwhat?" I said.

"Palindromes," Dad replied, passing the salad. "Words that are the same backward and forward."

"Like M-O-M," Mom said.

"And D-A-D," Dad said.

"And P-I-P," Pip chimed. Apparently she knew all about this. "And H-A-N-N-A-H," she added. That's Pip's middle name.

My full name is Ava Elle Wren. When people ask what the L stands for, they expect me to say Lily or Lauren or Louise, but I say, "It's not L, it's E-L-L-E."

I thought about P-I-P, H-A-N-N-A-H, A-V-A, and E-L-L-E, and stared at my parents. "You chose our names because of how they're spelled? Wow." Then I noticed how you spell "wow" (W-O-W).

And suddenly it was as if I saw the whole world—or at least the Whole World of Words—in a brand-new way.

My parents' names are Anna and Bob (A-N-N-A and B-O-B), and they are word nerds.

"Why didn't you tell me before?" I asked.

"You never asked," Dad answered.

"When did you tell Pip?"

"A while ago," Mom said, "when she asked."

Pip looked at me and shrugged. "At least we didn't get named after Nana Ethel."

Pip is twelve—for one more month. She talks at home, but at school, she is extremely shy. Pip was a preemie, which means she was born early. Since our last name is Wren, which is the name of a bird, Mom and Dad sometimes call her Early Bird.

When Pip was little, they worried about her a lot. To tell you the truth, they still worry about her a lot. They also pay way more attention to her than to me. I try not to let it bother me...but it kind of does. I'm only human.

"Guess who was the first woman in the world?" Pip asked.

"Huh?" I replied, then noticed how "huh" (H-U-H) is spelled.

"Eve," Pip said. "E-V-E!"

Dad jumped in. "And guess what Adam said when he saw Eve?"

"What?" I said, totally confused.

"Madam, I'm Adam!" Dad laughed.

"Another palindrome!" Mom explained. "M-A-D-A-M-I-M-A-D-A-M."

"A whole sentence can be a palindrome?" I asked.

"Yes." Dad pointed to Mom's plate. "Like, 'Ma has a ham!'"

Pip spelled that out: "M-A-H-A-S-A-H-A-M."

I put down my fork, looked from my S-I-S to my M-O-M to my P-O-P, and started wondering if other people's families are as nutty as mine. Or is mine extra nutty? Like, chunky-peanut-butter nutty?

A-V-A

DEAR DIARY,

It's wayyy past my bedtime, and I'm hoping Mom and Dad won't barge in and tell me to turn off my light. But something's been keeping me awake.

After dinner, Pip and I played Battleship. We usually like sinking each other's carriers, cruisers, submarines, destroyers, and battleships. It's fun. She'll say, for instance, "B-8." And I'll say, "I can't B-8 because I'm 10!" Or I'll say, "I-1." And she'll say, "No, you didn't! The game isn't over!"

Tonight I was about to sink Pip's last ship when I said, "I-4." But Pip said, "I-quit."

"You can't quit!" I protested.

"I can and I did!" she said and stomped off to her room.

That made me so mad! I hate when my big sister acts like a little sister! I hate when she's a sore loser!

Once, after a teacher conference, I overheard Mom and Dad talking about Pip's "social issues" and how they wish they could help her "come out of her shell."

Well, sometimes I wish I could take a hammer and break Pip's "shell" into a million zillion pieces. What if she *never* comes out? What if she grows up to be a sore loser quitter with no friends and a hundred cats and only me to talk to?

Thinking about Pip drives me crazy. Here's why: I always end up feeling mad at her *and* bad for her all at the same time!

The problem is that sometimes her problems turn into *my* problems. Like when I have to clean up after a game of Battleship or Clue or Monopoly by myself. Or when I have friends over and Pip doesn't come out of her room. Or when I walk into the kitchen and Mom and Dad suddenly go all quiet because they were in the middle of talking about her.

I know Pip isn't shy on purpose, but it still gets me mad.

AVA, ARRRGGGHHH

DEAR DIARY,

Whenever I start a new diary—like I'm doing this week—I end up accidentally writing something totally embarrassing that I would never want *anyone* to see. Then I put my pen down and bury the diary in my dresser drawer.

So far in my life, I've started seven diaries and finished zero. It's like there's a dead diary graveyard underneath my underwear!

Today in language arts, Mrs. Lemons asked us what we read this summer. Well, my family reads big books for fun—they even reread and *rereread* them. But long books intimidate me.

Long words (like "gigantic" and "intimidate") don't scare me, just long books.

Here's how I pick books:

1. I look at the front and back covers.
2. I check to see if it's about a regular kid with normal problems (not superscary or supernatural problems).
3. I read the first page so I can hear the "voice" and how it sounds.
4. I peek at the last page to see how long it is.

If there are too many pages, forget it, I put the book back. In *short*, I like *short* books.

Mrs. Lemons also asked us when we read. A lot of kids said, "Before bed," but one girl, Riley, said, "On the bus," and one boy, Chuck, said, "If I read on the bus, I'd barf. I get bus sick."

Mrs. Lemons said, "How about you, Ava?"

"Sometimes I read before bed," I said, "but sometimes I write." I did not add that when I was little, I thought I was a great writer because I could write my whole name before Elizabeth and Katherine and Stephanie could write theirs. (Pip burst my bubble by pointing out that Ava has only three letters and theirs each have nine.)

"It's good to keep a journal," Mrs. Lemons said. "And, Ava, your handwriting is excellent."

"It used to be terrible," I confessed. "In first grade, Mrs. Quintano said I didn't even hold my pencil right."

I don't know why I blurted that out except that it was true. In first grade, I erased more than I wrote, and I collected erasers— pink rectangle ones and colorful ones shaped like cupcakes and rainbows and sushi.

Now I like pens more than pencils, and I have a favorite pen. It's silver with black ink and is the kind you click, not the kind with a cap. Dad bought it for me at the Dublin Writers Museum, and I am using it right now. I think of it as my magic pen, and I like to imagine that it has special powers and that I can write anything I want with it—anything at all!

Dad is a real writer. He's a playwright—which is spelled playwright, not *playwrite*. He works at home writing plays and tutoring students.

Mom has a regular job—she runs the office of a vet named Dr. Gross who is more grumpy than gross.

At the end of class, Mrs. Lemons asked one last question. She said, "What do you want to be when you grow up?" Everyone said things like "President," "Ballerina," "Doctor," "Actor," "Fireman," "Rock star," "Comedian," "Chef," and "Fifth-grade teacher." Maybelle (my best friend) said, "Astronaut," and Chuck said, "Championship boxer."

I was the only person who said, "I don't know."

AVA WITH A FUZZY FUTURE

Friday Night

Dear Diary,

We had the first spelling test of fifth grade today and I got a 100. So at dinner, I said, "I got a 100 on a spelling test."

Dad said, "Great," but I could tell he was mostly concentrating on cutting up the chicken. Mom didn't really hear me either. She was talking about an operation Dr. Gross did on a dog that ate a rock.

I decided to tell a dog joke, so I said,

"Question: What does a dog eat at the movies?

Answer: Pup corn!"

I was going to point out that P-U-P is a palindrome and that popcorn goes P-O-P P-O-P P-O-P, but since no one laughed, I didn't.

And okay, I realize my joke was lame, but couldn't Mom and Dad have laughed a little?

Sometimes it feels like they don't quite see me. Or hear me. It's like I'm not even at the table.

Maybe *I* should go eat a rock.

A

Dear Diary,

Pip was on the sofa with her freckly nose in a book. "You read that book last week!" I said.

She said that when she first reads a book, it's to find out what happens, but when she rereads a book, it's like being with a friend.

Here's what I did not say: "You need *real* friends!"

Instead, I went to the basement and opened a few old boxes. In one, I found a bag of plastic animals that Pip and I used to play with. I picked out a lion cub and took it to the kitchen and put it in a jar and covered it with corn oil. Why? So it would be a lion in oil.

Get it? L-I-O-N-I-N-O-I-L is a palindrome! And I came up with it all by myself!

I put the jar on the windowsill and am waiting for M-O-M and D-A-D and P-I-P to find it and figure it out. They are going to love my little L-I-O-N-I-N-O-I-L!

AVA IN ANTICIPATION

AT SCHOOL

DEAR DIARY,

Our librarian, Mr. Ramirez, knows I'm big on words. "Ava, you like to write," he said. "You should enter the Misty Oaks Library story contest."

"I don't think so," I said.

"Why not?"

"Because I won't win."

He frowned. "Well, you definitely won't win if you don't enter. Why not give it a shot?"

I wanted to say, "A shot? I'm not a doctor." But I just listened as he explained that the story had to be four hundred words, the title had to include the name of a living creature, and the deadline was October 12.

"I'll think about it," I said. And I have been. A lot. Maybe too much.

If I won a library contest, Mom and Dad would be proud of me for sure, so I'm trying to come up with ideas.

Like, what if I write about two crazy cats that are losing their minds? I could name them Nan (N-A-N) and Viv (V-I-V) and call the story:

SENILE FELINES

Get it? S-E-N-I-L-E-F-E-L-I-N-E-S is a palindrome!
Pretty smart, right?
>^..^<   >^..^<

A-V-A A-V-A

9/8
BEDTIME

DEAR DIARY,

I read what I wrote yesterday, and OMG, what a stupid idea!

Good thing no one ever sees what I write in here except me.

To tell you the truth, I'm getting tempted to bury this diary underneath my underwear!

The reason I came up with the crazy cats idea is that Mom is always saying how sad it is when old pets get "put down." Yesterday, some lady realized that her beloved cat, Whiskers, had gotten so rickety, he could no longer drink or eat and that "his time had come."

Mom says the worst part of her job is when a person walks in with a pet and walks out without one. The second worst is when someone gets the pet back, good as new, and Mom hands them a bill for a thousand dollars, and the person faints on the floor. (That almost happened to the lady with the rock-eating dog.)

Anyway, instead of writing any sad sagas (S-A-G-A-S) about ancient cats, I might write about glamorous rats: star rats (S-T-A-R-R-A-T-S). Who knows? With my magic pen, I might even win!

X-O-X
A-V-A

9-9
(A NUMBER PALINDROME)

DEAR DIARY,

So far, no one has spotted my L-I-O-N-I-N-O-I-L.

AVA, ACTUALLY

DEAR DIARY,

This might sound dumb and immature, but I'm sitting in bed crying. Two little drops just fell on *you*!

At dinner, I said, "I got another 100 in spelling." I wasn't expecting a bunch of high-fives or a confetti parade or for them to dance around the room or phone Nana Ethel. But couldn't they have said, "Way to go"? Or, if they wanted to be nutty, "Yay, Ava, Yay" (Y-A-Y-A-V-A-Y-A-Y) or "Atta girl" (A-T-T-A girl)?

Dad said, "Ava, you're on a roll," and Mom said, "Now please pass me a roll." Dad laughed at her not-that-funny joke, then Mom and Dad and Pip started talking about rolls and Pip's art class and a calico kitten named Fuzz Ball who got hit by a car and operated on and now has just three legs but still scampers around just fine.

And I can see how all of that is wayyy more interesting than a 100 in spelling, but I still wish that what mattered to me mattered to them.

After dinner, I remembered my palindrome project, so I said, "Hey, did anybody notice my little lion?"

Mom, Dad, and Pip stared at me blankly, so I hopped up to show them. But it wasn't on the windowsill! I looked all around, and it was *nowhere* to be found! I came back and said, "I put a lion cub in a jar next to the cactus." Dad and Pip looked at me like I had three noses, but Mom said, "Oh, sweetie, I threw it out. I thought it was garbage." And she didn't even apologize!

I stomped upstairs to write in you, but I left my magic pen in the living room and I didn't want to go back down, so now I'm writing with an old pencil. That's how I feel anyway: like a stubby yellow pencil covered with teeth marks with a worn-down eraser and a broken point that no one even cares about.

AVA FEELING AWFUL

Dear Diary,

One nice thing about keeping a diary is that it never interrupts or changes the subject or thinks your jokes aren't funny or that you're boasting or whining. And it's not a writing contest, so there's no pressure. A diary just lets you be honest. And I appreciate that.

I also appreciate that Dad made a big Irish breakfast with eggs, sausages, baked beans, mushrooms, and scones.

Ava the Appreciative

Satur~~day~~ Night

Dear Diary,

Maybelle invited me to dinner, but I was with our neighbors Lucia and Carmen. They're fourth-grade twins, and they don't dress exactly the same, but they always wear the same color. Today it was pink.

Maybelle said they could come too, so Dad drove the three of us over.

At dinner, which was a cookout, Maybelle's parents asked me lots of friendly questions. Maybelle told them about the writing contest and even said, "Ava can spell anything!"

Maybelle's dad said, "Spell *anything*!"

I said, "A-N-Y-T-H-I-N-G," and everyone laughed.

After dinner, we all went for a walk. We didn't need flashlights because the moon was almost full. When it was just me and Maybelle, I told her about my oily lion palindrome project and how my mom threw it out. Maybelle looked sad for me, but then Lucia and Carmen caught up with us so she changed the subject. She said, "I like the moon more than the sun."

"What do you mean?" Carmen said.

"You can't look directly at the sun," Maybelle explained. "But you can look at the moon all you want. And it changes!"

"I like when it's bright and there are no clouds," Lucia chimed in. "Like tonight."

"Moon shadows are cooler than sun shadows," Maybelle added.

Well, I started waving my arms in the air, and my shadow started waving its arms on the ground. It was all stretched out in front of me, long and skinny. Maybelle, Lucia, and Carmen started waving their arms too, and soon we were all jumping up and down—and so were our long skinny shadows.

Maybelle said, "The moon is 240,000 miles away."

Lucia looked surprised, but I'm used to Maybelle being a math wonk and coming out with random facts.

"Another thing I like," Maybelle said, "is that you don't have to worry about moonscreen or moonglasses."

"Hey, I brought moonscreen!" I blurted. "Smell!" I squeezed a pretend blob onto everyone's palm.

"Lemon lavender!" Maybelle said.

"Gingerbread spice!" Lucia said.

"Strawberry shortcake!" Carmen said.

"Grape with a hint of honeysuckle," I said, and then at the exact same time, we all went "Mmm!" (M-M-M).

"I also brought moonglasses!" I said and handed out pretend pairs.

"I'm putting mine on top of my head," Maybelle said. "The movie star way."

"Me too!" Lucia said.

"Me three!" Carmen said.

"Me four!" I said, and we laughed.

"What's so funny?" Maybelle's dad asked.

"The man in the moon!" Maybelle said, and we all kept walking and laughing with our moonglasses on top of our heads, in the dark but not-too-dark.

I wish we could have walked for hours.

And I wish my family liked to laugh and have fun together.

AVA IN THE MOONLIGHT

Dear Diary,

I told Mom how fun last night was, and instead of saying, "That's nice," she said, "You should have invited Pip." Well, that made me mad because it's not my fault that Pip doesn't have real friends!

AVA IN THE MORNING

DEAR DIARY,

Mr. Ramirez just asked how my story was coming along.

My story? What story? I didn't tell him that I don't have a character or a plot or even a first sentence.

At least I have a magic pen.

O-X-O
A-V-A

9/17
8 P.M.

Dear Diary,

After school, I went to Dr. Gross's and waited for Mom. She was really busy, so I had to sit in the waiting room. After a while, I said, "I'm bored."

Mom said, "Shhh."

She hates when I say, "I'm bored."

I hate when she says, "Shhh."

I also hate being quiet. Pip is the Queen of Quiet. She's even quiet when she goes up and down stairs while I, according to Mom, sound like "a herd of elephants."

In school, Pip can go a whole day without saying five words. Last year, Lacey, a loudmouth girl with thick bangs and thick eyeliner, teased her and called her "Pipsqueak." It made Pip even quieter!

I don't know why Pip is so quiet. She just is. It's like she has permanent stage fright—and she's not even an actress.

I realize it must be hard for her, but does she realize that it's hard for me too?

Pip and I don't look that much alike (I have longish brown

25

hair and brown eyes and no freckles, and she has medium red hair and green eyes and tons of freckles). We also don't act alike (I talk fast and a lot, and she barely talks at all, and I write a lot, and she draws a lot). To be honest, I'm glad most people don't know we're related. It can be embarrassing when kids find out we're sisters. They say, "You mean the short pretty girl who never talks?" or "You mean the weird girl who eats lunch by herself?"

Pip isn't weird. She just has no life. Hardly anyone besides me even knows that deep down, she's normal. And nice—well, except when she's bratty.

One thing I like about having a big sister is she tells me stuff about when I was little. Like, she says I used to call "marshmallows" "marshmelons." And once I had a tick on me and called it a "ticket." And once I got us both in trouble because instead of a lemonade stand, I wanted to have a flower shop, so I cut all of Mom and Dad's tulips so we could sell them. (Oops!)

Anyway, while I was waiting in the waiting room, I started thinking about how Dr. Gross does *cat* scans on *cat*s and *lab* tests on *Labs* (Labrador retrievers). And I came up with an unbelievable four-word palindrome: Step On No Pets (S-T-E-P-O-N-N-O-P-E-T-S).

I was really proud of myself, and I told Mom I was going to make them a sign. I even started digging markers out of her drawer. But Mom said, "Not now, Ava! Can't you see I'm trying to finish up?"

I said, "Okay." But it was *not* okay. It was not one bit okay! In fact, it made *me* feel stepped on.

At five, Mom made sure all the animals were happy. There were lots of cats and dogs, two birds, two hamsters, one ferret, and a green basilisk lizard that would probably be walking on water if it weren't stuck in a tank at Dr. Gross's. Mom and I locked up, and I asked where the lizard came from. She said Central America and started telling me about a famous palindrome about a Central American waterway: "A man. A plan. A canal. Panama" (A-M-A-N-A-P-L-A-N-A-C-A-N-A-L-P-A-N-A-M-A).

"H-U-H," I said, and wondered how many other kids have word-nerd families and silent siblings and moms who sometimes seem like they care more about other people's pets than their own daughter.

AVA ALL ALONE?

Saturday, bedtime

Dear Diary,

I found a two-word note from Pip on my desk. It said: "Wanna talk?"

I do, but her lights are off, and she gets mad when I wake her up.

Ava in Suspense

DEAR DIARY,

Pip and I were on the floor in her room doing Word Scrambles. I asked what she wanted to talk about, but she said she changed her mind.

I said, "That's not fair!"

She shrugged.

Dad shouted up from the kitchen, "Who wants a Sunday sundae?"

A Sunday sundae is my favorite dessert, so I shouted, "Meeeee!" and ran downstairs.

While Dad was sprinkling nuts on our ice cream, I told him about the contest. Big mistake! He said I should definitely submit a story.

I told him my ideas about S-E-N-I-L-E-F-E-L-I-N-E-S and S-T-A-R-R-A-T-S.

He asked, "Does the 'living creature' have to be a palindrome?"

I said, "No," and started feeling small.

"Then think big," he said. "You'll come up with something. You have a facility with language."

"H-U-H?" I asked palindromically.

"A way with words." He smiled. "Be patient. You'll find your voice."

Dad says the best writers have a "voice," which means their words flow naturally, and you can recognize their style, and it's almost as if you can "hear" them reading to you.

I wish I had a "voice."

I wish I had a subject!

I guess I should be glad I can write about anything. Anything at all. Anything in the whole wide world! Anything alive!

But what should I write about? Princesses or presidents? Lions or lionfish? Friends or enemies? Frenemies??

Blank pages can be scary.

And I'm *not* patient.

"A way with words"? Right now I feel like shouting: "Away with words!"

AVA THE ANXIOUS

Dear Diary,

Pip's door was open a crack, so I said, "Pip, c'mon, tell me the thing you were going to tell me."

"It's not a thing," she said. "It's a person." Then she said she was going to bed, but that tomorrow we could do some more Word Scrambles.

AVA IN MYSTERY

9/27
MORNING

DEAR DIARY,

Not only have I not *found* my voice, I've *lost* my pen!! The silver
one Dad brought me back from Ireland!

Last night when we were running errands, Dad said that even
though Ireland is not a big country, four Irish writers got the
biggest prize a writer can get: the Nobel Prize.

I couldn't bring myself to tell him that I lost his—*my*—
prize pen.

Until now, I hadn't even told *you*, my diary. I just stopped
writing for a week. But *not* writing did *not* make me feel better.

Well, here I am, back again. I'm using a plain pen with the
name of a boring bank on it. And I'm worried that I'll never
be able to write anything good again—let alone anything
prize-worthy.

AVA, AVERAGE

9/29
ALMOST DINNERTIME

DEAR DIARY,

I barged into Pip's room and said, "I know two transportation palindromes."

Pip said, "You have to learn to knock!"

I went back out and knocked, and Pip said, "Who's there?" so I said, "Ava," and then barged in and said, "I know two transportation palindromes."

She looked up and said, "K-A-Y-A-K and R-A-C-E-C-A-R. Duh."

I sighed and sat on her bed. "What are you doing?" I asked. The answer was pretty obvious because there were pants and tops everywhere.

"Trying on clothes."

"Aren't you going to tell me your secret?"

"No."

"Pleeeease." She didn't answer, so I said, "Just answer me this: is the 'person' a boy?" Pip blushed a little, so I said, "I knew it!"

She got pinker and said, "Don't tell anyone, okay?"

"Okay," I said.

"Not a word!" she said.

"Not a P-E-E-P!" I agreed. "But, Pip, if you have a crush, you have to tell me who it is."

"No, I don't," she said. "That stays secret."

AVA AGAIN

DEAR DIARY,

What if I'm stuck? What if I have writer's block? I have no pen, no voice, no words, *no no*thing! And my story is due in eleven days.

Dad says I'm too young to have writer's block. He got it once after a theater critic wrote a bad review of one of his plays. Dad had worked hard, and the actors had worked hard, and the director and stage manager and costume and set and lighting designers had all worked hard, and then a reporter sat down and didn't like the show and said so. People stopped coming, and the show closed early, and it was sad for Dad.

For a while, he started moping instead of writing.

That was no fun for him—or for us, either!

It helped a little when Dad's brother, Uncle Patrick, sent a note that said,

"The play was a great success but the audience was a disaster."

Oscar Wilde

Dad taped it on the wall by his desk, and it's still there.

I wish someone would write me an encouraging note.

Today, Mom and Pip started planning Pip's birthday. She invited six seventh-graders to a slumber party. I think Mom's hoping the party will fix Pip's "social issues."

Here's what I love about slumber parties:

1. Staying up late
2. Raiding the refrigerator
3. Sleeping in sleeping bags
4. Doing Mad Libs

This will be Pip's first real slumber party ever! She usually tries hard to stay off everyone's radar (R-A-D-A-R). I mean, if someone next to her sneezes, I bet she doesn't even say, "Bless you."

It's as if Pip thinks people will bite—like the mean dogs Dr. Gross sometimes has to take care of. The ones that when they're hungry, the assistants open the cage door just a crack, put in the food really fast, and shut the door again before they snarl or nip or worse.

For Pip's party, Mom offered to bring party pets, including a one-eyed owl from the wildlife refuge center.

Pip said, "Mom, I'm not in second grade!"

I think Mom forgets how old Pip is because Pip doesn't act her age and I'm two and a half inches taller. (We just got checkups.)

Unlike me, Pip never keeps a diary. She's not a writer; she's a drawer.

Wait, that makes her sound like a piece of furniture! I mean, she's an artist—she likes to draw and sketch.

Questions:

Do artists ever get artist's block?

And *do* I have writer's block?

At least I have you. When I write in you, it's not for a prize or review or grade or anything.

I've decided to stop thinking about the dumb contest.

Who cares about it anyway? Even if I entered, I'd probably lose. I'm excellent at losing things.

AVA, BLOCKED

DEAR DIARY,

I got a 100 on a spelling test but didn't even mention it.

AVA AGAIN (AGAIN)

Dear Diary,

Yesterday, I asked Maybelle if she ever noticed that her name starts with *Maybe*.

"*Maybe*," *Maybe*lle said and laughed. I think she must have, but then I'd never noticed that my family's names are all palindromic.

Last night, Maybelle *slept over*, and this morning we *overslept*. She was supposed to be at a soccer game at ten sharp, but she forgot!

She's lucky—her mom didn't even get mad.

Today I wanted to ask my mom to help me think up story ideas, but she was busy with Pip. They were ordering helium balloons and a gigantic strawberry cake that says "Happy Birthday, Pip." Now they're talking about what to put in the goody bags and what kind of pancakes to make on Sunday—blueberry or chocolate chip.

To tell you the truth, I'm getting sick of the whole subject. I know they don't want Pip's party to be a dud (D-U-D) and they want it to be really fun, or at least fun enuf (F-U-N-E-N-U-F). But Mom never makes a big deal about my birthdays.

And that's not fair. She's my mom too!

AVA, AN AFTERTHOUGHT?

DEAR DIARY,

Pip came home from school *sobbing*. During first period, a girl told her that something came up and she couldn't go to Pip's party. During second period, a second girl told her the same thing. During third period, a third girl also said her plans had changed. In gym, when even Isabel, who lives three houses away, offered a lame excuse, Pip made her tell her what was going on. Isabel did, but that got Pip even more upset.

What she found out is that this new kid, Bea, who has long straight blond hair, is having a boy-girl party on Saturday—the first boy-girl party of seventh grade!

Pip said it wasn't fair that everyone was going to Bea's party when she'd known them longer and invited them first. Then she ran to the girls' room and hid out and ended up being late to science, and her teacher was giving a pop (P-O-P) quiz, so he gave her a zero.

Poor Pip! She's never gotten a zero before. She usually gets nothing but straight As because she's so smart and hardworking (even though she never participates).

Now she's in her bedroom doing an extra-credit science project to make up for the zero. She just came out with puffy eyes and said she hates the new girl's guts.

I said, "Me too."

Pip called Mom at work, and Mom offered to call Isabel's parents or the new girl's parents, but Pip begged her not to and said it would only make everything worse.

I feel so bad for Pip. Even though I was getting sick of hearing about her party, I never thought she'd have to cancel it!

I wish I could help.

AVA THE ANGRY

I don't know what to write!

I still don't know what to write!!

I STILL don't know what to write!!!

DEAR DIARY,

I told Mrs. Lemons I have writer's block and asked if it's curable. She said, "Ava, sometimes you just have to get out of your own way. I know you can write a wonderful story—no—lots of wonderful stories!"

I mumbled, "Thank you."

Chuck, the boy who wants to be a boxer and who gets bus sick, added, "Ava, you stress out too much. Who even cares if you submit a dumb story or not?"

I mumbled, "I do."

AVA, IN HER OWN WAY

Dear Diary,

Yippee! I have a story idea! And it might help Pip feel better too! Wish me luck. I have only three days.

Dad and I went to the copy shop to buy paper, and I confessed to him that I lost my pen. Dad didn't get mad at me because he could tell I was already mad at myself. He said that even great writers lose their pens from time to time and offered to buy me a new one.

I went up to the display and tried out scented pens and glittery pens and fountain pens and pens with feather tops and pens with gold ink and pens with erasable ink. Finally I picked out a pen with turquoise ink. It's cool, but it does not feel magical and obviously does not have "the luck of the Irish."

On the way home, Dad told me the names of the four Irish writers who won the Nobel Prize: Yeats, Shaw, Beckett, and Heaney. He said I should read their books someday. I said, "Are they short?"

Dad laughed. The book he is now rereading is a thousand pages long! It's called *Ulysses* and is about one day in the life of one person in Ireland.

Dad started talking about "sloppy copy" (messy first drafts) and said, "Writers have to write and rewrite till they get it right." He also said writers have to let their words "sit and marinate" so they can return to them with "fresh eyes."

When Dad is in the middle of writing a play, he sometimes invites actors to come over to read the lines out loud in our dining room. This helps him figure out what works and what doesn't. Sometimes the actors come back a month later to read the same old play with brand-new changes.

Well, I can't let my words sit and marinate! I barely have enough time to "cook" them up in the first place!

Speaking of cooking, for dinner, we ordered in Chinese. (Actually, we *ordered* in English, but we got Chinese food.) Dessert was pineapple rings and fortune cookies, and I am taping my fortune here:

Hard work without talent is a shame,
but talent without hard work is a tragedy.

Was that message meant for me?? I haven't been working very hard lately.

This weekend, while stupid Bea has her stupid boy-girl party and Pip quietly turns thirteen, I plan to write and write.

Here's my title:

STING OF THE QUEEN BEE

Get it? "Queen Bee" as in *buzz buzz* and "Queen Bee" as in popular girl. That's a homonym. "Bee" can also mean contest as in "spelling bee." And of course "bee" sounds like "Bea," as in mean-awful-new-seventh-grade-girl.

Titles are my specialty.

AVA THE AMBITIOUS

DEAR DIARY,

I spent all afternoon writing, and it felt as if I were in another world. I totally lost track of time! Suddenly Mom said, "Get dressed," because we were going to the Kahiki for Pip's birthday.

The Kahiki is Pip's and my favorite restaurant. It is Polynesian and has big bubbling aquariums, flaming spicy meatballs, and steaming drinks that come with little umbrellas and overflow like gentle volcanoes.

Well, tonight Pip didn't eat much, and I could tell she was trying not to think about the giant seventh-grade boy-girl party that was going on right then.

Dad looked at all the food on our plates, and next thing you know, he started talking about rotten potatoes.

He said that in the middle of the 1800s, almost all the potatoes in Ireland went rotten, and there were "political problems," and a million people starved to death, and another million left the country.

Obviously, this was a terrible tragedy and not "the luck of

the Irish." But if Dad's great-great-grandfather had *not* gotten on a boat to Boston, he would *not* have met my great-great-grandmother, and there'd be *no* Dad, *no* Pip, and *no* **me**.

I would *not* have been born!!

Mom would have been born, but she would have been just a random lady named Anna, not my M-O-M—which is very strange to think about!!

Anyway, we were about to order cake for dessert, but Pip said, "I hate when waiters sing to me." Personally, I *love* when waiters sing to me.

We drove home, and Mom, Dad, and I sang to Pip in our kitchen. She blew out the candles, and we ate some of the gigantic strawberry birthday cake. (Mom had canceled the balloons.)

It was pretty pitiful. Mom tried to liven things up by telling us about a boxer dog who ate his owner's underwear. "His *boxers?*" I asked, and Mom said, "No, it was a pair of pink panties!" I thought that was funny, but Pip looked like she couldn't care less about what kind of undies the dumb dog ate.

Dad tried to liven things up by saying that thirteen is a special number because if you rearrange the letters in "ELEVEN PLUS TWO," you get "TWELVE PLUS ONE." I thought that was funny, but Pip looked like she wasn't in the mood.

At least she got a lot of presents—way more than I ever get!

Mom and Dad gave her a watercolor set and a cell phone, and I gave her *Great Expectations* because the main character's name is Pip. (It was Mr. Ramirez's suggestion.) Unfortunately,

Pip already has that book, so now it's like I haven't given her anything!

A

PS Psssst: Pip doesn't need presents anyway. She needs friends— and maybe for her crush, whoever he is, to like her back. Is that asking for a miracle?

Dear Diary,

Maybelle came over, and we took turns walking around backward and blindfolded while the other person gave directions on where to go. Then we polished off Pip's strawberry cake—bit by bit and bite by bite.

After Maybelle left, I spent all day writing. Dad said to think BIG, but a bee is small. I wrote the story by hand, then typed it on our computer. I had to check the word count over and over and kept adding and subtracting words as if I were working on a math problem, not a library story. Finally I put a moral at the end, the way Aesop does after his fables. If you include everything from the title to the moral, the story comes to exactly four hundred words.

I'm handing it in tomorrow, on the due date. Dad congratulated me for meeting the "deadline." I said I didn't like that word. *Deadline* makes writing sound dangerous. Which it isn't, 'tis it (T-I-S-I-T)?

I printed out an extra copy and am stapling it here:

Sting of the Queen Bee
by Ava Wren, Age 10

Once upon a time, there was a new girl in school. Her name was Bea. She was mean and she was a thief. She didn't steal erasers or candy or key chains. She didn't steal money or clothes or jewelry. She stole other people's friends.

She did it without even thinking, because she wanted to have as many girls as possible in her group. If someone didn't have many friends of her own, it made Bea extra happy to steal them for her clique, which she called her hive. She didn't care about the girls themselves—she just cared about how many she could get.

In the middle of middle school, Bea had more friends than anyone in seventh grade. But deep down, she felt lonely. She knew she was not a nice person. She knew she was evil, selfish, and rude. And she knew nobody liked her for her. They liked her because her family had a pool and her freezer was full of Popsicles.

One afternoon, Bea and her so-called friends were at her pool when a queen bee—a real queen bee with a teeny tiny crown—was buzzing around looking for flowers. Buzz! Buzz! It landed right on Bea's big nose. The bee stared at Bea; Bea stared at the bee. Then it flew off toward the other girls and listened to their conversations. It was surprised! The girls were whispering and saying that Bea was a friend stealer and a queen bee!

"A queen bee?" the queen bee said to herself. "I'm the only queen bee around here!"

It buzzed straight back to Bea's big nose and stung her twice with its stinger. It wanted to teach Bea a lesson. And it did! Ouch! Ouch!

Bea's nose got red, sore, swollen, and bigger than ever. She put a giant Band-Aid on it and spent two days at home watching TV and feeling very sorry for herself.

Meanwhile, the other girls went back to school, and since Bea wasn't there, they hung out with all the old friends they had dumped—all those loyal girls who'd been kind since kindergarten. Everyone forgave everyone, and everyone got all their friends back.

As for Queen Bea, she learned her lesson: you can't be a friend thief and get away with it.

Moral: There's no shortcut to true friendship.

AVA THE AUTHOR

DEAR DIARY,

I wonder who else in school knows about the contest. No one is buzzing about it. (Get it? Buzzing??)

I keep picturing myself getting good news and telling Mom and Dad, "Now I won!!" (N-O-W-I-W-O-N).

A #1 AVA

DEAR DIARY,

Another 100 on another spelling test.

AVA WHO GETS AS ON FRIDAYS

Dear Diary,

In language arts, Mrs. Lemons said that good writers notice things, and today, while Pip and I carved a jack o' lantern, I noticed that Pip has fewer freckles in the fall than in the summer and that they are lighter now too.

"Wanna play the Homonym Game?" I said. It's when we make sentences with words that sound the same but mean different things, like NUN and NONE, and CHEWS and CHOOSE, and HAIR and HARE. And BEE and BEA and BE.

Pip said, "Not really," but since she didn't say "no," I started. I said, "The FAIRY took a FERRY."

"She had to BURY a BERRY," Pip replied halfheartedly.

"BUT a bee bit her BUTT!"

"They DISCUSSED it with DISGUST," Pip said, then added, "I don't want to play anymore."

"Oh c'mon," I pleaded. "The tennis star hoped to CRUSH her CRUSH!"

Pip squinted at me and said, "I'm not telling you who my crush is, and I'm not playing anymore."

Well, of course that meant I wasn't either.

On the one hand, I feel sorry for Pip. On the other, her bad moods are annoying!

AVA THE ANNOYED

DEAR DIARY,

I asked Pip to tell me her Homonym Joke.

"Why?"

"Because I want to write it in my diary."

She sighed as if telling me her joke was a big fat favor. Finally she said: "Why is six afraid of seven?"

"Why?"

"Because seven ATE nine."

I jumped around repeating, "Because 7-8-9!" a couple of times, but Pip rolled her eyes. That got me mad, and I ended up shouting, "Why can't you ever just be happy?!"

Of course, that got *her* mad, and she stomped off and shut her door—which made me wish I'd shut my mouth.

AVA THE ANNOYING?

DEAR DIARY,

Lunch was fish sticks. I saw Pip eating alone in the corner, but I sat with my friends.

We talked about the contest. Maybelle didn't enter because she's better with numbers than words. (She just joined Mathletes.) One of the Emilys wrote about zombies, and Mr. Ramirez had to break it to her that zombies are not living creatures. (Duh.) Matthew wrote about a fire-breathing dragon, but dragons are not living creatures either, and besides, he came up with only eighty-three words.

Riley wrote a love story about her pony. All she ever talks about is her pony. Some girls are boy-crazy, but Riley is pony-crazy.

The only other submission I know about in the fourth and fifth grade category is from a dweeby boy named Alex. He wrote about an earthworm named Ernie.

I feel sorry for the judge who has to slog through a story of a BORING worm that goes BORING in the dirt. (Homonym alert!)

At least my story has a beginning, middle, and end, as well as a plot twist. (*Buzz! Buzz!* Ouch! Ouch!)

I told Dad that I wrote about a mean queen bee, and he said that sounded clever. But he smiled in a way that made me wonder if it also sounded dumb.

Should I have given my four hundred words to Dad to fix? Too late now! I also thought of having Mom take a look, but she was always online or busy with Pip. Besides, Mr. Ramirez said we were supposed to write our stories "without any outside help," and that "getting assistance would be inappropriate."

Well, I'm crossing my fingers and hoping to win. If I win, it might be like a small step to becoming a real writer.

Ava the Appropriate

DEAR DIARY,

Question: Do I even want to be a real writer?

AVA THE AMBIVALENT (WHICH I'M PRETTY *SURE* MEANS *UNSURE*)

10/21
AFTER DINNER

DEAR DIARY,

After school, I went to the vet's, and I got to *pet* some *pets*. A yellow lab named Butterscotch started wagging his tail the second he saw me. His owner goes away a lot, and Butterscotch always carries a stuffed-animal fox in his mouth. I also pet Panther, a black kitten with a pink nose. He started purring before I even touched him.

Poor pets! They deserve wayyy more attention than they get!!

I liked hanging out with the animals, but I *really* wanted to hang out with Mom. I even said so, but she said, "Ava, shhh. I have piles of files to get through before we have to pick up Pip."

"Fine," I said. But it wasn't fine. Sometimes it seems as if Mom cares more about Pip than about me. Pip, her precious firstborn. Here are three pieces of evidence:

1. Mom always buys Pip her favorite snacks (like pretzels and mangoes), but doesn't buy me mine (like grapes and cheddar cheese).
2. Mom gives Pip an allowance, but I have to take the garbage out for nothing.

3. Mom praises Pip's sketches more than my writing—not that I ever show her my writing, but still.

I didn't even tell Mom that I got another 100 in spelling (or that I got a 79 on a math quiz).

Since I didn't want to accuse Mom of playing favorites, I said, "Sometimes it seems like you care more about animals than about me."

She looked surprised. "What makes you say that?"

"Do you even know what I've been working on?"

"Dad said you entered a writing contest."

"That's right," I said, hoping she'd ask about my story. I was thinking of showing her a copy and telling her that I want to get first prize.

But all she said was: "See? I pay attention." Then she went back to her computer.

Question: *does* Mom like Pip more than me??

Well, at least writing all this down is making me feel a little better. Even though I still miss my magic pen.

Ava the unAppreciated

DEAR DIARY,

The phone rang. Our caller ID said, "Misty Oaks Library," so I picked up and said, "Hello."

"Hello. This is Mrs. White at the library. May I please speak to Ava Wren?"

Since she was being formal, I said, "This is she." Pip made a face because "This is she" sounds so dorky.

"I'm calling about the contest. Congratulations! Your story received an honorable mention."

I didn't know what to say. I didn't want to get *mentioned*—honorably or dishonorably. I wanted to win. I wanted to be the ONE who WON!

Mrs. White said my entire family was invited to a 6 p.m. reception on October 28 with "punch and nibbles." She said a famous author, Jerry Valentino, was the judge and would be there.

I was tempted to say, "I've never heard of him, so how famous can he be?" But I thanked her, stuck a note on Dad's computer that said "10/28 6 p.m. Library," and shoved my turquoise pen to the bottom of my backpack.

Obviously, it's *not* a lucky pen, let alone a magic one.

AVA, ABOVE AVERAGE BUT NOT AWARD-WINNING

DEAR DIARY,

I told Dad about the phone call, and he congratulated me. He also said that before Mrs. White got married, her name was Miss Bright, so now her full name is Wendy Bright White. ☺

At dinner, I *mentioned* my honorable *mention* but didn't make a big deal of it because:

1. I didn't come in first.
2. Why bother?
3. When Pip is bummed out, it doesn't feel right to act as happy as a lark.

Mom congratulated me, then said, "I wonder how many submissions they got." Well, that made me wonder if the only reason I even got an honorable mention is that not very many people entered. And that made me upset inside.

Pretty soon we all went back to talking about regular stuff (except Pip who went back to not talking).

I wish Pip felt sunnier. Living with her these days is like living with a rain cloud.

That's a simile.

A simile, according to Mrs. Lemons, is when you describe something using "like" or "as."

If I say, "Pip is quiet as a mouse," that's also a simile, because I'm comparing Pip to a mouse.

I don't think Pip would appreciate any of my similes.

AVA WREN, *NOT AS HAPPY AS A LARK*

DEAR DIARY,

Maybelle came over with ginger cookies from a batch that she and her mom had baked for a game.

We painted our nails orange and let them dry, and then we wet our fingers and made whistle-y sounds by rubbing them around the tops of our water glasses. We also slid down the stairs on a bath mat. It was fun until I landed on my butt. Owwww! Owwwwch!

I can't complain though because:

1. It's embarrassing to talk about your butt.
2. Mom and Dad might say I'm old enough to know better, or
3. Mom and Dad might not say anything at all.

Here's what worries me: What if I broke my butt? Can butts get broken? Like arms and legs? And hearts?

AVA THE ACHY

Dear Diary,

Brace yourself because I have a *lot* to tell you. I'll start with the good part, then get to the BAD part.

When Dad and I arrived at the library, Mr. Ramirez asked Dad if he was working on a new play. Dad said, "Yes, but tonight is all about my daughter." He put his arm around me, and it was half-sweet, half-embarrassing.

Soon everyone sat down on folding gray chairs. None of the Emilys were there and neither was Chuck or Matthew (the boy who wrote about dragons). But Riley (pony girl) and Alex (earthworm boy) were. Alex is the kind of boy who burps without saying, "Excuse me," but tonight he was dressed up and on his best behavior. There were kids from other schools too. Everyone was sitting in the room with the high ceilings and high bookcases. Mom and Pip were "on their way."

Mrs. (Bright) White had on a black scarf dotted with pumpkins. She introduced the famous-ish author, Jerry Valentino. He was tall and skinny and looked like he'd forgotten to comb his hair. He said that when he was our age, he loved libraries:

"the smell of books, the wooden tables, the peace and quiet." He said his family was "loud and noisy," so as soon as he could, he got a library card. It took him "many years and many rejection letters," but when he was twenty-nine, he published his first children's book.

He lifted it in the air. It was called *Campfire Nights*.

On the cover were three boys and a giant bonfire. I couldn't tell if they were roasting hot dogs or toasting marshmallows, but it was the kind of cover that if you judged a book by its cover, you'd want to buy it. For a second, I pictured myself as a famous-ish author talking to a roomful of kids and lifting a book in the air.

Judge Jerry said there were many "outstanding" submissions and that it had not been easy to choose winners. "We'll start with best story by a fourth- or fifth-grader," he said. Riley and I kept sneaking peeks at each other. I think we each thought the other had come in first.

"This year's winning story," Judge Jerry announced, "is about the underground adventures of an earthworm."

What?! I couldn't believe it! Ernie the Earthworm snagged first prize? Top spot (T-O-P-S-P-O-T)?

"Alex Gladstone's writing is so detailed," Judge Jerry continued, "I could smell the moist dirt! Alex, come tell us what inspired you to set your story deep in the bowels of the earth."

Bowels of the earth? Earth bowels?? Eww!!

Alex stood up. He was wearing a navy jacket and maroon tie and looked even dweebier than usual. Judge Jerry lowered the microphone and Alex breathed into it. I felt almost sorry for him because you could tell that he hadn't expected to have to talk.

After a *lot* of breathing, Alex said, "Whenever I go fishing, I feel bad for the worms, so I wanted to write a worm story with a happy ending." Everyone clapped, and Judge Jerry handed him a certificate and a shiny pen in a velvety box. I was jealous, even though I knew it was pathetic to be jealous of a worm-obsessed fourth-grader.

Judge Jerry raised the microphone and said, "The next two stories were so good that I am honored to award two honorable mentions." He started reading a passage about a pony's "trusting brown eyes," and I wanted to barf because it sounded as if now even Judge Jerry had a crush on Riley's stupid pony.

Riley strutted to the podium as if she were accepting an Academy Award. Her parents were there and so was her sister. Mom and Pip still hadn't arrived, and I kept thinking: "Where are they?"

When Judge Jerry asked Riley what inspired her, she said, "Ponies and horses are my favorite living creatures—besides people."

I thought, "Oh puh-lease!" but everyone clapped, so I fake-clapped.

"The second honorable mention," Judge Jerry continued, "goes to Ava Wren who wrote 'Sting of the Queen Bee.'" My heart was beating really loudly, but no one else seemed to hear. I looked around again for Mom and Pip. Where were they??

"Don't you love that title?" Judge Jerry asked. "It's a *double entendre*, which is French for 'double meaning.'" (I didn't know that.) "I admire Ava's wordplay and vivid imagination," he continued, "as well as her sense of humor and understanding of social dynamics. Furthermore, her depiction of the villain is both whimsical and believable. Or should I say, 'BEE-lievable'?" He laughed at his own wordplay and invited me up. Dad gave my shoulder a little squeeze, and I stood up and walked to the front of the room. I must have been nervous because it seemed like it was a long, long way from my seat to the podium even though obviously it wasn't.

Judge Jerry met my eyes. "Ava, what inspired you?" he said and lowered the microphone.

Well, I couldn't exactly talk about how I'd wanted to get back at the seventh-grade bully who'd ruined my sister's birthday, so I said, "I enjoy observing older kids," and hoped I didn't sound like a spy.

"Wonderful!" Judge Jerry said. "Keen observation is an important tool in every writer's toolbox."

Everyone clapped, and for a second, I thought I spotted Mom in the back of the room. But I was wrong. She really had missed my big moment.

I sat back down next to Dad feeling one-third proud, one-third mad at Mom and Pip, and one-third worried about them, when the library door creaked open.

In walked not Mom, not Pip, but...Bea! Queen Bea!! With her family!!!

Bea was the *last* person I expected to see! Really! I was Ava the Astonished! And she arrived just seconds after Judge Jerry had exclaimed over my "BEE-lievable" villain!

I'd assumed that writing wasn't dangerous, but was I wrong? Dead wrong?

What if Bea finds out what I wrote? And why, oh why didn't I think of that earlier??

I'd tell you what happened next, but my hand is about to fall off. (Figuratively, not literally.)

To be continued...

AVA THE AFRAID

DEAR DIARY,

So here's what happened: when Bea walked into the library, I tried not to look nervous, scared, or petrified. She saw me and smiled as if she recognized me from our middle school. I did *not* smile back!

Well, the first prize in the sixth- and seventh-grade category went to a boy from an all-boys' school. His story was about a *penguin* with a *pen*, and Judge Jerry said it illustrated "the extraordinary power of words." The boy stepped up but did not say a single solitary word, let alone any extraordinary powerful ones. He just got redder and redder (R-E-D-D-E-R and R-E-D-D-E-R) until he sat down again.

"The next honorable mention," Judge Jerry announced, "goes to seventh-grader Beatrice Bates who wrote a story called 'Bookshop Cat.' Bea, come on up!" She hopped up, and he welcomed her on stage and asked what inspired her.

She flicked her long blond hair behind her ears and leaned into the microphone and said, "I'm a cat person, and my parents are book people. They own a bookshop."

I looked at Dad, and he was smiling. Clearly he had *not* put two and two together. Why would he? Nobody realized that the villain in my story was standing in front of our very eyes, basking in the library limelight. I couldn't believe Bea-Bee the two-faced was attempting to come off as a decent person! What a little faker! Everyone (except me) clapped until she sat down, all full of herself.

If only people knew what she was really like!!

Judge Jerry gave the last honorable mention to an eighth-grader named Charona who has lavender braces and wrote "a humorous story" about a timid turtle named Timmy who wouldn't come out of his shell. Charona was there with her parents, grandparents, and even a teacher.

Finally it was time for "punch and nibbles." A photographer told us "winners" to smoosh together and say, "Stories!" with a big cheesy "eeeeez" at the end. Guess who plunked herself right next to me and started smiling away? Bea! I fake-smiled as well as I could.

Outside, I may have looked happy, but inside, I was worried. If Bea found out about my story, would she punch or nibble *me*? Bea bruises and Bea bites were something I did not want!!

Mrs. (Bright) White tapped the microphone and said, "Thank you all for coming, and don't forget to pick up your free copies of this year's *Winning Words*." She pointed to a big stack of sky-blue booklets, which were really just colored paper that got printed on and folded over and stapled in the middle. I started praying that the booklets included only the stories that won-won, *not* the stories that got mentioned-mentioned.

"Every story is in here," Mrs. (Bright) White continued, "so you're in for a treat. Congratulations again to all our winners and their proud families."

My heart sank to my belly button. A *treat*? If Bea read my story, I'd be dead *meat*!

I looked over at Bea. She was talking with her parents and brother. He's in eighth grade and has sandy hair and is new in school too (duh). He has as many freckles as Pip and is the kind of boy who's cute if you're the kind of girl who notices. Which I'm not.

Riley's mom asked if she could take a picture for us, and Dad handed her his camera. But it was APPARENT that I was with just A PARENT. Where *were* Mom and Pip?

I get that Pip's favorite place is home-sweet-home (which she's turning into home-sour-home). But they'd told me they were coming!

Riley's mom took pictures anyway, and I tried my best to real-smile, not fake-smile.

Soon I started wondering if we were all taking this contest too seriously. Judge Jerry was making it sound like we were destined to be the next J. K. Rowlings or Judy Blumes, but c'mon, we're just a bunch of kids writing about worms and ponies and bees. Were we like those sports teams where everyone gets a shiny trophy, even if she can't catch a fly ball to save her life?

When Dad and I finally got back to our sweet-and-sour home, Pip and Mom were there. Pip said she'd gotten stomach cramps at the last minute, and Mom said she hadn't wanted to leave her alone. I didn't ask Pip whether it was because of her "stage of life" or her allergy to people. I was just sorry she'd missed the reception and mad that because of her, Mom had too.

Now I'm wondering if, deep down, Mom was a tiny bit relieved that her favorite daughter wouldn't have to listen to a bunch of people clapping for her *other* daughter. Or maybe Mom thought Pip had something serious—like appendicitis? Or that going to the reception didn't matter much because it was just a dumb kid contest, and Dad showed up and besides, I didn't really win?

Secret: it *did* matter!!!

Here's my new worry: What will happen when Bea reads my story? Will *Bea bea*t me up? Or turn all of Misty Oaks Middle School against me? I wish I'd never entered the stupid contest!

I wish my writer's block had blocked me for real!

AVA IN AGONY

DEAR DIARY,

No Bea stings in school. No Bea bites either. Maybe Bea threw away her *Winning Words*, and my little story won't get me in big trouble?

As for my library booklet, I was going to put it on Mom and Dad's bed, but I didn't want to get disappointed if they didn't like it—or didn't read it.

Besides, since Dad saw Bea on stage, what if he figured things out and instead of being proud of me, started asking questions?

I decided to stash the booklet under my underwear in my dead diary graveyard.

Then I changed my mind again and put it in Pip's room by a sketchpad with a note that said: "For Your Eyes Only, see page 8." I'd meant to show it to her when I first wrote it.

Speaking of Pip, she's hardly *speaking*. She brought a book to dinner, but Mom made her put it away.

I wish Pip weren't so moody, or should I say, bad-moody?

I also wish I didn't care. But when she gets down, it gets me down. Her moods are contagious—I'm like a sponge for bad feelings.

AVA THE SPONGE

DEAR DIARY,

Bea passed me in the hall today smiling as though we're besties. I half-smiled back because I didn't know what else to do.

Does this mean I can relax? Because when I see Bea, I still feel very jjUUmmPPyy.

It's insane! At school, I worry about Bea, and at home, I worry about Pip!

Tomorrow is Halloween. Maybelle came over, and we played Hangman. I won with "gypsy" because Maybelle wasted five guesses on the regular vowels, A-E-I-O-U.

Afterward, we microwaved marshmallows. At first, it got messy because we nuked them too long. Then we got the hang of it, and we even invented variations like adding jelly beans and chocolate chips.

We also planned our Halloween costumes: we are going as yellow-and-black-striped bumblebees. (*Not* queen bees!)

Tomorrow I am not going to think about anything except candy. Candy. Candy. Candy. Candy. Candy.

Sweet!

AVA WITH AN APPETITE

10/31
HALLOWEEN

Dear Diary,

Halloween can also be spelled Hallowe'en because the *e'en* stands for "evening." Dad said it's from All Hallows' Eve—which is the night before All Saints' Day, which is when ghosties go floating around. (Not really.)

Pip is staying home tonight to help Mom give out candy.

I invited Pip to trick-or-treat with me and Maybelle. Mom didn't even have to ask. But I didn't beg her or anything. If Pip wants to be antisocial, that's her problem, not mine. I mean, it's not my fault that she's not *outgoing* and doesn't like *going out*.

Observation: all year long, parents say, "Don't eat too much candy," but on October 31, no one cares.

Here's my two cents on that:

1. Y-A-Y
2. M-M-M

AVA IN COSTUME

Dear Diary,

Today's date and time would be a number palindrome (111111) if you left out the dash and dots, which no one does, so never mind.

I reread what I wrote yesterday: "If Pip wants to be antisocial, that's her problem, not mine." But that's not totally true, is it? When one family member is sick or stressed or writer's-blocky, it affects everybody. Or *infects* everybody.

Like right now, I feel like saying, "Hey, Pip, did you read my story?" or "Hey, Pip, want to watch a movie?" But she'd just say something gloomy, so I'm being as quiet as she is. We're like *two* mice!

I feel bad for Pip, but I also feel like yelling at her again!!

Last night after trick-or-treating, I was going to show her my bag of candy, including some palindromic Milk D-U-Ds and Blow P-O-Ps, but I didn't want to make her feel worse about missing a fun night. Later, Mom went in, and they talked for a long, long time. That made me mad, because I'd set aside five red licorice sticks—Mom's favorite—but I fell asleep before she came to say good night.

Things are too quiet around here. Personally, I don't like living in the House of Silence. We're the Wrens! We're supposed to be singing!

AVA WREN, SONGBIRD

11/1
SUNDAY NIGHT

DEAR DIARY,

Dad gave us snack money, so Pip and I biked to Taco Time, which is four blocks away. We rode past the yellow, orange, and red trees, and I tried to remember the last time we even went. We used to go every week!

The first time was last spring. Dad was tutoring a high school junior, and Pip and I were starving, so he handed us $14 and said, "Take care of each other." And off we went—all by ourselves.

Today when our tacos came, I saw a Toyota out the window, so I said, "A Toyota!" (A-T-O-Y-O-T-A). Pip was supposed to reply, "A Toyota's a Toyota!" (A-T-O-Y-O-T-A-S-A-T-O-Y-O-T-A), which is our family's new inside joke. But she didn't.

"You okay?" I asked.

"Why wouldn't I be?" she said. And I realized that the person I really wanted to yell at is Queen Bea. Just thinking about that girl drives me 100 percent *crazy*!

Pip must have read my mind, because she said, "Hey, Ava, I meant to tell you, I liked your story."

"Really?" I tried to sound casual.

"Yes. It was funny. And I know you meant well." I waited for her to say more about my way with words or how she was glad I'd trashed her archenemy. "But I wonder what Bea Bates is going to think," she continued. "She might freak out. She *is* a real person, after all."

Well, that made me so nervous, I forgot to hold my taco properly, and the beef and sour cream insides came sliding out and plopped onto the table and some splattered onto my lap.

Did I really pick a fight with a popular seventh-grader? How could I be so dumb?

"Maybe she won't read it?" I said. "At school, she always smiles at me."

Pip shrugged.

AVA THE DOOMED

DEAR DIARY,

I passed Bea in the hall this morning, and she did *not* smile at me. She gave me an odd look.

I spent the rest of the day trying not to panic.

In language arts, I finally got a little distracted because Mrs. Lemons was talking about "perspective" (which she said is like "point of view") and was going over spelling words (including the bonus word "throughway"). She said there are many ways to pronounce "ough," and on the board, she wrote:

1. "oo" as in thr*ough*
2. "oh" as in th*ough*
3. "uff" as in en*ough*
4. "off" as in *cough*
5. "aw" as in *ough*t and
6. "ow" as in b*ough*

I said, "That's so cool!" at the same exact time that Chuck said, "That's so complicated!" Everyone laughed. Even Mrs. Lemons.

At home, I wanted to tell Dad about the "ough" thing, but he and Pip just went out to buy groceries.

Probably pretzels and mangoes.

EY•VUH

11/2
A LITTLE LATER

DEAR DIARY,

The phone rang, and instead of checking caller ID, I picked up like an idiot. I thought it would be Dad, and I was going to ask him to buy some grapes.

"Hello," I said.

"Is this Ava?"

"Yes…" My heart started doing flip-flops because I thought I recognized the voice.

"It's Bea. Bea Bates."

I didn't know whether to hang up, apologize, defend myself, or say, "Wrong number."

"Hi," I mumbled.

"Hi," she repeated. Why had I picked up? Pip never picks up! She lets the machine take messages unless it's Dad or Mom or me.

"First of all," Bea began, "I don't have a big nose."

I was torn between saying, "I don't know what you're talking about" and "Poetic license." Dad says writers get a "poetic license" when they exaggerate to make a point.

"Second, I don't have a pool or a lifetime supply of Popsicles."

I kept quiet.

"And third, I am not rude, but your story was."

"Rude?" I repeated, which meant that so far, all I'd said was: "Yes," "Hi," and "Rude?" I'd heard of one-liners, but never one-worders. Bea was making me as tongue-tied as Pip!

"Why did you write about me like that?" she asked.

"My story isn't about you! It's about a girl with a big nose and a big pool…" Suddenly I was glad no one was home, because I didn't want Dad or Mom or Pip to hear me trying to defend my story.

"Named Bea? Who's new? Ava, don't insult my intelligence."

I went quiet again. I didn't want to insult her intelligence, but I didn't want her to insult me either.

"You know what? Maybe you're right," Bea continued. "Your story is *not* about me. But you should think twice before you set out to ruin someone's reputation."

"Well, *you* should think twice before you set out to ruin someone's birthday!" I blurted, surprising myself. "My sister still hasn't gotten over it!"

"Excuse me? How was I supposed to know your sister was having a party that day?" Bea asked. "I barely knew she existed! If she or her friends had said something, I could've invited her. No big deal. So blame Pip, not me."

"Wait. You're saying it's *Pip's* fault you stole her friends?!"

"Stole her friends?! Ava, you're in fifth grade, right? When you're my age, you'll realize that friends aren't objects you can steal. I'm friendly, so I have lots of friends. Your sister is unfriendly, so she doesn't. To be honest, when I first met Pip, I thought she was a snob because she keeps to herself so much."

What?! Did Pip really come off as a *snob*? Do some people think she doesn't talk because she thinks she's too good for them? "You shouldn't say mean things about someone you don't know!" I said and started pacing around our living room with the phone at my ear.

"You shouldn't *write* mean things about someone you don't know!" she shot back. "And I'm *not* a queen bee. *You* are a drama queen!"

"Me?"

"You! What was my big crime anyway? Throwing a party? Because *yours* was jumping to conclusions and writing a malicious story."

I stopped pacing and quickly looked up "malicious" on Dad's computer.

The dictionary said "intending to do harm."

Whoa. Had I *intended* to do harm? I felt dizzy. My Queen Bee story was supposed to be about kindness, but was the story itself *unkind*? Was *I*? I was starting to feel like a rotten potato.

"Ava? Are you still there?"

"Yes," I said, and mumbled "I'm sorry" into the phone.

"Sorry you wrote what you wrote, or sorry I found out?"

"Both," I replied before realizing that was *not* the best answer.

"Well, you *should* be! How would you feel if I wrote a story about a mean fifth-grader named Ava?"

"Bad."

"Exactly. And for your information, when you write something down, it doesn't go away. It's not like talking on the phone."

I nodded, but since we *were* talking on the phone, I forced myself to say, "Okay."

"But don't you see? That's my point: it's *not* okay. From now on, whoever reads your story at school will think less of *me* or less of *you*." I hadn't thought of it that way and slumped into Dad's chair. "For the record," she continued, "I had to read your story three times just to be sure I wasn't being paranoid."

I pictured Bea reading 400 x 3 = 1,200 of my words. If it had been a regular story, I would have felt incredibly proud. Instead I felt like a potato with mold all over it.

How many other copies of *Winning Words* were out there for me to worry about. Forty? Fifty?

I went upstairs and into Pip's messy room, holding the phone to my ear. The sky-blue booklet was on her desk, and I picked it up.

"I finally asked Isabel about it," Bea was saying, "and she explained everything. I just wish she'd said something then! Or that your sister had! I gave that party to make friends, not enemies."

I carried *Winning Words* into my room and stuck it in my dead diary graveyard where it could keep my underwear and my Loser Words company.

"Ava, are you even there?"

I said, "Yes," but didn't know what else to say because I was starting to see things from Bea's side. I was about to mumble "Sorry" again when she said, "My aunt said I should call you, so

I did. But that's it. We're done. I just wanted to give you a piece of my mind."

I pictured myself holding a piece of Bea's mind, which was a pretty disgusting image, to tell you the truth.

Bea hung up and I did too. But I wished I'd apologized better.

I also wish I *weren't* alone in the house anymore, because right now I'm feeling alone in the world.

AVA, ALONE AND APOLOGETIC

11/2
BEDTIME

DEAR DIARY,

Dad and I were sitting on the sofa. He picked up his big fat thousand-page book. "What if James Joyce had written about two days instead of one day?" I asked. "Would *Ulysses* have been two thousand pages long?"

He laughed and said he wanted to read *my* story. I said I misplaced it. He said, "Really?" like he didn't quite believe me. I said, "Really" because it was sort of true: I'd *placed* it where it would be *miss*ing!

To be honest, I don't like being less than honest with Dad. I mean, I wish I could just tell him everything and have him hug me and tell me it's all going to be okay.

But what if he got disappointed in me instead? Or thought everything was *not* going to be okay? I don't think I could take it.

Anyway, Dad went back to reading, and I wrote Bea an apology note in my very best handwriting.

I'm going to deliver it tomorrow before homeroom.

Here's what it says:

Dear Bea,

I really am sorry. I was just trying to help my sister.

Ava

It's late, and I hope I can fall asleep.

Asinine Ava

PS I *swear* "asinine" is not a *swear* word. It means really foolish and idiotic.

DEAR DIARY,

I slept terribly. I dreamed a vicious bee with a tiny tiara was buzzing around my head and would not buzz off.

At breakfast, I was exhausted. Dad opened the fridge and said, "No melon, no lemon" (N-O-M-E-L-O-N, N-O-L-E-M-O-N). Then he said, "Aha!" (A-H-A) and picked up a shriveled olive. "An evil olive!" (E-V-I-L-O-L-I-V-E). Then he bit into a banana.

Mom said, "Yo, Banana Boy!" (Y-O-B-A-N-A-N-A-B-O-Y). "It's too early. Besides, I have a headache. And I already took one lonely Tylenol" (L-O-N-E-L-Y-T-Y-L-E-N-O-L).

Pip and I looked at each other, and I thought: no wonder Pip doesn't talk much in public. When it comes to conversation, our parents are very peculiar role models.

I told my family I had a nightmare, but didn't say it was a night*bee*.

"I'm sorry," Dad said, then added, "I guess I'd better not tell you girls about what I'm working on."

"Why not?" Pip asked.

"Because it would give you both bad dreams!"

96

"Tell us!" Pip and I said, right on cue. Then we both said, "Jinx!"

Dad smiled and said, "You know how there are lots of books about vampires?"

"Yes," Pip said.

"Well, the first good one was *Dracula*, and I'm trying to turn it into a play for kids. It was by an Irish writer."

Mom leaned her head on her hand in a tired way, while Dad explained that the author, Bram Stoker, got the idea from a church in Dublin. The church was so dry and cool inside that the bodies in its crypt barely decomposed. They looked alive even though they were dead!

For a second, I pictured Little Bram Stoker as a ten-year-old in a navy jacket and maroon tie telling a contest audience how inspiring it was to observe a bunch of non-rotting corpses.

Mom looked up. "Really, Bob? You're telling our daughters about corpses first thing in the morning?"

Dad shrugged, but the funny thing is, I didn't mind hearing about the creepy, well-preserved corpses because it gave me "perspective." I mean, at least I'm—

AVA, AWAKE AND ALIVE

AFTER SCHOOL, IN THE LIBRARY

DEAR DIARY,

Before homeroom, I walked down the school hall and up to Bea's locker, which I'd noticed was close to Pip's. I looked both ways, slipped my note in, and ran. Instead of my phone number, which she obviously had, I wrote my locker number next to my name.

An hour later, I noticed a corner of a yellow piece of paper sticking out of my locker. I could feel every one of my nerves jingling, but I reached for the note and opened it up. The handwriting was bad, but I deciphered it and here it is:

> Ava,
>
> Meet me at my Locker after Seventh period
>
> bea

I was tempted to write her a note back saying I had a dentist appointment, and I thought: How am I going to survive until seventh period?

Well, you know how time can go fast or slow? Today *time* took its *time*! All the minute hands on the wall clocks seemed stuck, and I kept trying to figure out what I should say to Bea.

When the bell finally rang after seventh period, I went to her locker. I stood there like an idiot and watched the entire school rush by, nice kids and mean kids, nice teachers and scary teachers, and even Principal Gupta, who is strict, and Nurse Abrahams, who is sweet. (I wanted to call out, "Nurse Abrahams! Help! Help! S-O-S! S-O-S!")

It was almost time for math when Bea showed up. "Have you thought about what you did?" she asked.

"Yes." She looked at me, waiting for more. "I was trying to help my sister, but what I wrote wasn't fair, and I'm sorry. I apologize again."

She stared at me for a while then said, "You should have left me out of it. And there are better ways to help your sister. Tell you what, Ava, why don't you meet me after school in the library?"

Another meeting? I didn't want another meeting!

The bell rang, and I mumbled, "Okay," and ran to math. I didn't want to be late because Mrs. Hamshire gets mad when kids are late. And she's scary even when she's not mad.

After math, I called Dad and said I was going to the library after school and would get home a little late.

Dad loves libraries, probably even more than Mrs. (Bright) White + Jerry Valentino + Mr. Ramirez combined. So he didn't say, "The library? I forbid it!" He said, "Okay."

So I didn't say, "Dad, if I never make it home, I love you, and blame Bea Bates!" I just said "Okay" back.

Well, it's now 3:05, and I'm in the school library, and Bea is nowhere in sight, and I feel like an inchworm. (That's a sad simile.)

Outside, the branches are blowing every which way. Inside, it feels hot and stuffy.

I'm waiting and waiting and trying to stay calm. The custodian is emptying the waste paper baskets and scraping gum off from under the desks.

Did Bea tell me to stick around just to torture me? Did she mean *today*?

I got out my pleasure-reading book but kept rereading and *rereading* the same page, and it was *not* a pleasure. I took out my spelling notebook and tried to study bonus words, but I couldn't keep my mind on them.

One was "libel," which means writing something "unfavorable" about a person. Well, I now realize that if you LIBEL someone, you're LIABLE to get into big trouble.

Questions:

1. Are my days numbered? My hours? My minutes?
2. Where is Bea??
3. What does she want with me anyway???

AVA IN ANGUISH

11/3
BEDTIME

DEAR DIARY,

At 3:10, Bea came racing in. Mr. Ramirez looked surprised to see Bea (a seventh-grader) heading straight toward me (a fifth-grader).

Suddenly Bea was looming over me all out of breath with a yellow pad and pointy pencil.

"Are you going to write a mean story about me?" I asked. The words came tumbling out.

"What are you talking about?" Bea sat down. "I'm not here for revenge. I'm here to help you help your sister."

"I don't get it," I said. If I were Bea, I'd hold a grudge for a year. Or for life.

"Ava, I've been thinking. You did a bad thing for a good reason. And it does stink about Pip's party. But it's not too late to make things better for her." She pulled a scrunchie off her wrist and put her blond hair into a ponytail. "She can't go through middle school not talking, right? Being painfully shy must be painful."

I was about to defend Pip, but I realized that Bea wasn't attacking her. So I sat there speechless, which is way more Pip-y than Ava-y. Finally I said, "I still don't get it."

"This may sound weird," Bea began, "but when I grow up, I want to be an advice columnist."

"For real?"

"For real. Whenever I pick up a magazine, I turn to the advice column first."

I wasn't sure what to say. I'm not used to seventh-graders confiding in me about their life goals. And not one kid in homeroom had said, "Advice columnist."

"My aunt says I have a lot of common sense, and that that's very *uncommon*," Bea continued. "So look, you want to help Pip, and I want to help people, so maybe we can figure something out."

"Maybe…" I said.

"My big brother used to be really shy, and I helped him. I mean, he's still a little shy, but not as shy as he used to be."

"Huh," I said, remembering the sandy-haired freckled boy at Misty Oaks Library.

"Last summer at camp," she said, "I made a lot of friends on the first day, but it took him weeks to get to know people. He said I was 'the opposite of shy' and asked how I did it. Well, that got me thinking."

"Oh," I said. Bea had turned me back into a one-word wonder.

She met my eyes and said, "Tell me about Pip." I didn't know if I should or not, but Bea had just told me about her brother, so next thing you know, I heard myself telling her that Pip likes big books and small animals and that she's artistic and smart and pretty, but "too quiet for her own good."

Bea said, "Let me sleep on this and let's meet tomorrow. Same table, fifteen minutes before school starts."

I couldn't believe we were scheduling another meeting. It was like we were grown-ups or something.

Now I'm in bed. I told Mom and Dad to wake me early because I had to work on a language arts project. They didn't question that, and it wasn't a total lie anyway because Bea and I want to try to help Pip use the English language.

Funny how some parents ask about every detail of their kids' lives, and some don't.

Question: Mom and Dad *over*protect Pip, but do they *under*protect me?

AVA ALL ANTSY

DEAR DIARY,

I got to the library on time, and Bea got there a few minutes late. "You have really good handwriting, right?"

"Right." I almost told her that my favorite letter in cursive is a capital Q because of how it looks a little like a fancy 2: *2*. I did *not* almost tell her that when I was little and my family needed me to be quiet, they'd sometimes give me a page of Os that I would turn into Qs (regular Qs, not cursive *2*s), and that this was my idea of a good time.

"My handwriting's terrible," Bea said, and luckily I did not blurt, "I know" or "I noticed" or "You can say that again." "Tell you what," she continued. "I'll talk, and you write."

"Okay." I dug out my turquoise pen, and Bea handed me a piece of yellow lined paper. She also got out a small spiral notebook that looked pretty worn, and then she started dictating. Well, I was concentrating so hard on spelling and neatness that I hardly even noticed what I was writing. I wanted all the dots on my *i*'s to match, and I didn't want them to be bubbles, hearts, or daisies because I wanted Bea to think I was mature.

When I got to the last word of her "four pointers," she took the paper back.

"Perfect!" she said. She borrowed Mr. Ramirez's scissors and cut the paper into four strips. It felt like we were doing an arts and crafts project.

"Here's the first assignment," Bea said as she handed me a yellow strip. The handwriting was mine, but the words surprised me:

WEEK ONE:
SMILE AT ONE NEW PERSON EVERY DAY.

"If all goes well," Bea stated, "in just one month, we can get your sister to go from a Before to an After."

"Really?" I said and tried to picture Old Pip turning into New-and-Improved Pip. I couldn't see it. "It might take at least five weeks," I said and looked over the strips. "Mind if I add a fifth pointer?"

"Not at all," she said. "I made these up last night, though I guess I have been thinking about them for a while."

I wrote out, "Week Five: Ask someone a question each day. Listen to the answer," because I like when people ask me friendly questions.

"Good one!" Bea said, which made me feel good. She even scribbled it down in her own little notebook.

"Are you going to tell Pip that you want to be an advice columnist and she's your first guinea pig?"

"Second," Bea corrected. "Ben was the first, remember? But he wasn't a guinea pig, and neither is Pip. They're more like the timid turtle in that contest story, the one who wouldn't stick his head out."

"Timmy," I said, though I wished she hadn't mentioned the contest.

"Right!" Bea said. "And, Ava, we're not doing this for my *future*. We're doing it for Pip's *present*."

"That's a homonym," I said, then wanted to kick myself. Since it was too late, I kept talking. "PRESENT like 'now' and PRESENT like 'gift.'"

I hoped Bea wouldn't think this was a strange thing to say. It *was* a strange thing to say.

Questions:

1. Why, oh why does my brain work this way?
2. Can I blame B-O-B and A-N-N-A?

Speaking of palindromes, Bea said she liked my name. Since I did *not* want to be speaking of palindromes, I just said, "Thanks."

She said there was a book in her family's store about an actress named Ava Gardner. "That Ava had three husbands, all famous. Frank Sinatra, a singer, Mickey Rooney, an actor, and Artie Shaw, a musician."

"So she wasn't at all shy," I said.

Bea laughed. "What were you reading when I came in?" She reached across and flipped over my book.

"*The Witches*," I said.

"I love Roald Dahl!"

"Me too."

Funny how I'd assumed Bea was a witch and she'd assumed Pip was a snob. I guess people can't help but judge books by their covers and people by their looks.

At school, kids get made fun of if they're dweeby or fat or funny-looking. But even when a girl is cute, like Bea or Pip, some people still think bad things.

I started feeling a little guilty for having assumed that Bea was a jerk and for thinking not-nice thoughts about Alex Gladstone just because he's dweeby and burps out loud.

"Does your bookshop really have a cat?" I asked, because I didn't want to dwell on my shallowness.

"Yes. His name is Meow Meow. He's orange with stripes. He wanders around with his tail in the air, and he knows which customers are cat people and which aren't."

I told her about some of the cats Dr. Gross takes care of, like Fuzz Ball with the three legs and purry Panther with the pink nose. I didn't tell her about Whiskers, since he's dead. And I didn't tell her that Dr. Gross was a grump.

"Does he ever take care of monkeys?" Bea asked, sort of randomly.

"No monkeys, no goldfish," I said. "But he once removed a tumor from a mouse named Stuart Little."

Bea laughed again. "Okay, here's the plan: I'll stop by your house at 4. All you have to do is make sure your sister's alone. Agreed?"

"Agreed," I said, because Pip's always alone.

AVA THE AGREEABLE

107

DEAR DIARY,

At 4, Pip and I were in the living room. I was having big problems doing decimals, and she was having no problems doing fractions. I casually said, "Bea's coming over."

"Bea?" Pip said. "Did you say *Bea*?"

"Remember 'Sting of the Queen Bee'?"

"Uh, *yeah*."

"Well, Bea thought it was mean that I thought she was mean."

"Wait, wait, wait! You *talked* to her? To Bea Bates?"

I told Pip that Bea called and said she hadn't known Pip was having a party.

Pip stared at me, and I wondered if I'd been a total traitor.

"And you believed that little phony?" Pip said.

"I did. I do." I looked at her. "I know I called her a thief, but now I think she's the opposite. She's a very giving person."

"Oh, Ava! *You're* a very gullible person!" Pip threw her book down and started stomping around the room.

Since Aesop says honesty is the best policy, I told Pip the truth.

"Bea said she helped her brother 'come out of his shell' and now she wants to try her method on you."

"Are you kidding?! I don't need her help! Or her *method*!" Pip said "method" as if she were saying "poison" or "booger" or "throw up." I didn't say anything, and Pip said, "Seriously, Ava, thanks a lot! I bet she's just looking for a new way to humiliate me!"

"I don't think so."

"What's she planning to do anyway? Sprinkle me with popularity powder?" I could tell that Pip was mad, but also a tiny bit curious.

"She isn't planning to *do* anything. She has tips for *you* to do. Pointers." I didn't mention all our meetings or our five-week master plan.

"Thanks, but no thanks. I do not need a personality transplant."

I wanted to shout, "Yes, you do!" But I just sat there and didn't say another word.

At 4:05, I started wondering if Bea was even coming. "Where's Dad, anyway?" I asked.

"Upstairs, putting new wallpaper in the bathroom. He said he had to repaper it and then he looked all happy, because, you know, R-E-P-A-P-E-R. You know what? I'm going to go help him." She started walking upstairs.

"No! Stay here!" I said. "I'll give you M&M's." I still had some from Halloween.

Pip hesitated. She can never resist M&M's. Especially green ones and Minis.

The doorbell rang.

Pip stood frozen in place like a statue. It rang again. I waited. Pip waited. It rang one more time. "Well," Pip finally said, "aren't you planning on opening the door for Bossy Bea, your new best friend?"

I did, and Bea burst in holding a bike helmet. "Hi!" *Bea* was *bea*ming. "How's it going?" she said, walking right in. "Pip, I hope Ava told you I'm sorry about your birthday. I had no clue we were both giving a party on the same day."

Pip didn't say anything, but since she usually doesn't, I couldn't tell what she was thinking.

"Want some gum?" Bea said and offered us some pieces.

"What flavor?" I asked.

"Lemon lime," she said. I took a piece, but Pip didn't.

"Pip," Bea began, "Ava says you're a good student and good artist, but that you're a little shy."

Pip glared at me, and I basically died.

"I was thinking," Bea continued, "that you should take another look at the other kids at school. They're not Olympic athletes or famous musicians or anything. Most are just regular." Now Bea turned to me. "So that's why Ava and I think you could put yourself out there a little more."

When Bea said my name again, I could feel Pip's eyes burning a hole in my head. I wondered if she felt as if we were all playing Battleship, and Bea and I had found her hiding place and were ganging up on her with torpedoes.

I didn't want to upset her, and I felt bad that she was being even more speechless than usual, if that's possible.

Finally Pip started talking. "Listen, Bea, thanks for the apology but—"

"My brother used to be shy," Bea jumped in. "Pip, I think I can help you too. Just give it a try?"

Pip looked cornered. She had obviously not been expecting this pep (P-E-P) talk. Should I have prepared her? Warned her?

"Give *what* a try?" she said.

"Your first assignment."

Pip frowned. "I have enough homework."

"C'mon. Just let me explain?"

Pip shrugged, but it was obvious that she was listening.

"Okay, every day this week," Bea began, "all you have to do is smile at one person you don't usually smile at. It can be a teacher. Or a cashier. Or someone's mom or dad."

Pip didn't say anything, so Bea kept going.

"It can be someone next to you in line, or someone you'll never see again. Or even someone who looks like he or she could use a smile. I'll stop by next week, and you can tell me how it went."

"That's it?" Pip said.

"That's it."

"Just smile?"

"Well, you could try to make a little eye contact too."

Pip looked at me, and our eyes made a little contact. Hers were saying, "Ava, I might have to chop you up into tiny pieces."

"You don't have to be someone you're not," Bea reassured Pip. "Just seven little smiles is all we're asking."

She handed Pip the strip of paper. Pip looked at it suspiciously, as if it really had been dipped in poison or boogers or throw up. I knew she recognized the handwriting—and besides, the turquoise was a dead giveaway. I hoped Pip wouldn't be too mad that I'd opened our home to a girl whose guts, one month ago, we'd both decided we hated.

"Mind if I get a glass of water?" Bea asked. We went to the kitchen, and she got herself a glass. "Thanks," she said and put it in the sink. "I'll be back in a week."

After she left, Pip said, "Who does she think she is, anyway?"

"I don't know," I said, hoping Pip felt at least a teensy bit flattered. It wasn't every day that a popular seventh-grader dropped by.

AVA WITH HOPE

DEAR DIARY,

Pip didn't say anything about Bea's visit, so I didn't either. Not to her or anyone.

After dinner, I put a small pile of green M&M's on Pip's desk. I'd been saving them up. I also wrote her a joke:

Question: Why did the worker at the M&M factory get fired?

Answer: Because he kept throwing out the Ws.

She didn't say anything about the M&M's or the joke, and since I was bored, I decided to clean my room. I was still looking for my missing pen.

Well, I kept putting things away and did not find the pen. But at least I found the top of my desk!

AVA WITH ABUNDANT M&M'S

11/7
SATURDAY AROUND NOON (N-O-O-N)

DEAR DIARY,

"Abundant" was one of the bonus words on yesterday's spelling test. After the test, we had to switch papers with the kid next to us and grade each other's. Chuck got a 65. He said spelling doesn't matter because of spell-check. I said that wasn't true, because spell-check can't always help you (and I wrote this part down) "fined yore miss steaks." He studied my words and smiled.

For homework this weekend, Mrs. Lemons gave us an assignment to write about something we read and say what we learned from it. I thought about my lost magic pen and the moral, "No use crying over spilt milk," and I asked if I could write about an Aesop's fable. She said sure.

But which one?

"The Milkmaid and Her Pail"? Naa. Meh. Nuh-uh. (Is that how you spell those words?)

"The Ant and the Grasshopper"? Maybe. I could write about how people (not just ants and grasshoppers) should plan ahead.

"The Tortoise and the Hare"? Maybe. I could write about

how people (not just turtles and bunnies) should strive to reach their goals.

I started thinking that I'm *not* good at planning ahead and setting goals. Then I realized that it was okay because I'm only in fifth grade. And then I watched an origami video and started folding paper flowers.

AVA, AESOP FAN

11/7
AFTERNOON

DEAR DIARY,

After reading (and rereading) a bunch of fables, I decided to write about "The North Wind and the Sun." It's about a bet between the wind and the sun on who can make a traveler take off his coat first. The wind blows and blows as hard as it can, but the more it blows, the more tightly the traveler holds on to his coat. Then the sun takes a turn, and instead of using all its might, it just shines and shines warmly and normally. Next thing you know, the traveler removes his coat. The moral? "Kindness wins where force fails."

Here's what I think: when I wrote that Queen Bee story, I thought I was being *kind*, but I was really being *blind*.

Here's what else I think: you can't force people to change, but you can help them try. Like, Bea and I aren't *forcing* Pip out of her shell, but if she does the assignments, maybe she'll inch out on her own, step by step.

Speaking of Pip, this morning I saw her smile! Our postman rang the doorbell and handed her a bunch of letters. Instead of just taking them silently, she smiled and even said, "Thank you."

The postman's eyes got big, and he said, "You're welcome." Then he shot *me* a look that said, "I didn't know your sister could talk."

That may not sound like much to you, Diary, but to me it felt like a mini miracle.

AVA THE AMAZED

Dear Diary,

Dad said he got an email from Misty Oaks Library and that the story contest winners have been posted online.

"All of them?"

"All of them," Dad said.

"Even the honorable mentions?"

"Of course," Dad said. "So I finally got to read your story, Ava. And I liked it. It was like a fable."

More like a libel! I thought and felt bad all over again that I'd based Queen Bee on Real Bea. Dad said, "Mom will want to read it too."

"Did the library email the parents of all the kids who won or got mentioned?"

"I bet Mrs. White emailed everyone in town!" Dad said. "Or at least everyone with a library card."

I felt so wobbly I had to sit down. I used to like picturing people reading my story, but now I just want the story to go away.

AVA

Dear Diary,

Nobody said anything about my story today. Maybe I'm going to get off easy after all?

At dinner, Dad asked, "What's an eight-letter word that if you keep taking one letter away, it will still be a word all the way down until it's just one letter?"

Mom, Pip, and I had no idea what he was talking about, so Dad got out eight index cards and wrote one letter on each. They spelled S T A R L I N G. Suddenly I understood what he meant, and I went first. I took away the L so it was STARING. Pip took away the A so it was STRING. Mom took away the R so it was STING. I took away the T so it was SING. Pip took away the G so it was SIN. Mom took away the S so it was IN. And I took away the N and it was...drum roll please...I!

STARLING, STARING, STRING, STING, SING, SIN, IN, I! Cool, right? But then I started getting attacked by questions.

1. Did I commit a SIN?

2. Will I get STUNG?
3. Will everyone soon be STARING at *me*?

AVA...VA...A

11/10
BEDTIME

DEAR DIARY,

Nothing bad happened today either, so I showed the word-bird trick to my language arts class. They liked it.

Chuck had a trick too. He made a boxer's fist and wrote M, E, A, and T under his knuckles so his fist said MEAT. Then he lifted his pointer finger, so his fist said EAT. He put it down, so his fist said MEAT again. Then he lifted two fingers, and his fist said AT. And then he opened up his whole hand and inside, he'd written JOE'S. He said, "Get it? EAT MEAT AT JOE'S!" (Maybe he should be a comedian instead of a boxer.)

Speaking of words, tonight, my family played a game of Boggle, and we added a new rule: double points for palindromes.

When I was really little, Mom and Dad used to give me points for one-letter words (like A or I) and two-letter words (like AN or IN). That made Pip mad because her words had to be at least three letters.

Now that I'm almost eleven, mine do too.

Well, I found S-E-E-S and E-Y-E and G-I-G and S-O-L-O-S and T-O-O-T. But so did everyone else, so those got crossed out. Mom and Dad both found L-E-V-E-L, so they canceled each other out. I got double points for B-O-O-B, which Pip thought was funny. And Pip got double points for B-I-B. I was tempted to tease her about being a baby with a B-I-B and P-U-L-L-U-P diapers, but when Pip acts babyish, it's worse for everyone. Plus, I'm trying to be *kind* of *kind*—like the sun. I'm on a kindness kick!

To tell you the truth, I'm also glad that Pip didn't yell at me (or tell on me) after Bea's visit. It's strange, but we're both sort of pretending it never happened.

During the game, Mom said, "Ava, I read your story at work today. I even showed it to Dr. Gross. We thought it was clever."

For a second, I felt really good. Then I remembered what I'd written, and I felt more like a big balloon soaring high in the air that gets pricked and makes a bunch of farty noises and becomes a deflated crumple of shriveled rubber, lying splat on the ground.

Mom changed the subject anyway. "And, Pip," she said, "Dr. Gross said you've grown up a lot and have a beautiful smile."

Well, Mom's boss never says anything nice about human beings, particularly children. He's better with animals, particularly furry ones. (Mom says he's not that great with reptiles.) Whenever Pip and I go to Dr. Gross's clinic, he looks at us suspiciously, as though he thinks we might turn off the lizard lights or open the birdcages or let the dogs loose. Every so often, he'll act nice and show us an X-ray of a rabbit or a dog tick under a microscope. But mostly he's a grump. Mom says Dr. Gross complains that it's hard to be a vet because regular doctors have to know about just one species but vets have to know about a lot of species.

Anyway, I figured it out instantly: Pip must have given Dr. Gross one of her smiles. And it must have worked!

AVA, ASTUTE

11/11 (A PALINDROME DATE)
AFTER SCHOOL

DEAR DIARY,

The doorbell rang. I put down *Charlotte's Web* (which is short), and Pip put down *A Tree Grows in Brooklyn* (which is long), and we let Bea in.

"Hi, Ava! Hi, Pip! How'd it go this week?" she said.

Pip stared at Bea as if she were deciding whether or not to smile at her. But Bea just started taking off her gloves, scarf, jacket, and bike helmet.

"It's ccccold out!" she said, and for some reason, that seemed to warm Pip up.

We talked a little about the wind and rain, and then Bea plunked herself on the sofa. "Want some gum?" she asked, and Pip and I each took a piece. It was raspberry mint, which is my favorite after bubblemint.

"So who'd you smile at?" Bea asked Pip with a smile.

"A few people."

"A few? Or seven?"

"Five."

"Well, spit it out…"

I imagined Pip spitting (yuck!), but Pip started to answer. "Let's see, on Thursday, I smiled at Ava's friend Maybelle. On Friday, I smiled at the gym teacher, but I don't think she noticed. On Saturday, I smiled at our postman. And on Monday, I smiled at my mom's boss, and he actually told our mom."

"Positive reinforcement!" Bea said, and I wondered how positive she was going to feel once she found out that our stories had gotten posted online.

"On Tuesday," Pip continued, "I smiled at a girl, Nadifa, who just moved here from Somalia. She smiled back and sat by me at lunch. But it was a little awkward because neither of us knew what to say."

"No one ever died of awkwardness," Bea said. "Overall, how did it feel?"

"Overall, pretty good," Pip admitted.

"You think you can keep smiling this week and do a whole new assignment?"

"Depends on the assignment," Pip said.

"Here it is. When you see your reflection in a mirror, I want you to say, 'You are totally awesome!'"

"No way!" Pip said.

"Yes way. But don't worry, not loudly! Mostly just say it to yourself. Or say it in your head. It'll boost your confidence."

"My confidence?" Pip repeated. "No. Sorry. I can't. I really can't."

"Yes, you can! You can do anything!"

"I'd feel too stupid." Pip looked at me for backup, but I stared straight down at my shoelaces.

125

"Never question your life coach," Bea said. "It may sound weird, but it works. Instead of letting shyness conquer you, you have to conquer it!" She handed Pip the second strip of yellow paper.

Pip looked at me and read the words aloud:

WEEK TWO:
EVERY TIME YOU SEE YOUR REFLECTION, TELL YOURSELF, "YOU ARE TOTALLY AWESOME!"

She rolled her eyes, so Bea added, "If you'd rather give yourself a specific compliment, like 'I draw well,' or 'I'm good in school,' that would be okay too."

Pip shrugged, and Bea shrugged back, so I shrugged too.

"I'll try," Pip said softly, and I wanted to jump up and down shouting, "Y-A-Y!"

"Great," Bea said. "Okay, same time next week!" She started putting back on her gloves, scarf, jacket, and bike helmet, and then got on her bike and rode off.

When she was out of sight, Pip said, "Seriously, Ava, why couldn't you have just minded your own business?"

I didn't know whether to say, "I don't have a business," or "C'mon, it's kind of working," or "Can't you see I have worries of my own?"

So I pulled a Pip—I kept quiet.

AVA, AGITATED

11/11 (STILL A PALINDROME!)
BEFORE DINNER

DEAR DIARY,

I heard Pip talking in her room, so I slowed down by her door.

Here's what I heard: "You are totally awesome."

I thought that was funny (H-O-H-O-H-O-H) and was tempted to call Maybelle. But I decided not to, even though Maybelle and I usually tell each other everything. (In first grade, she was the first person I told when I got lice, which Pip says I called "head lights.")

Thing is, if I tell Maybelle about what's going on, Pip might kill me, and I'm big on life. Besides, I'm also trying to be a kinder, better person.

I'm glad I can at least tell you that I am—

AVA THE AMUSED

DEAR DIARY,

Mr. Ramirez just said, "I read your story online, Ava. The link went out to all the regional schools and town libraries." He also told me that Mrs. (Bright) White nominated it for a nationwide contest for a book called *Kids' Eye View: Short Fiction by Young Writers*.

"Why?" I asked, though he probably expected me to say W-O-W or Y-A-Y.

"Why? I imagine she liked it! And if your story becomes part of a collection, that brings recognition not just to you, but to the entire Misty Oaks School District."

Here's what I did *not* say:

1. "I wish you'd never told me about the stupid contest."
2. "Help! I wrote a mean story about a nice person!"
3. "My stomach hurts. Can I go see Nurse Abrahams?"
4. "Am I really a 'Young Writer'?"

Here's what I did say: "Did she nominate other stories too? Like 'Bookshop Cat'?"

"No, just yours," Mr. Ramirez answered.

"I don't think I even want to win," I mumbled, imagining all my words on the loose in cyberspace.

"Why not?"

I didn't answer, but I wondered if he would figure it out. After all, he'd been there when Bea and I had our meetings and made the Pip Pointers.

AVA, ASHAMED

FRIDAY THE 13TH
BEDTIME

DEAR DIARY,

I do not believe that unlucky things happen on Friday the 13th. I believe that bad and good things happen all the time. Sometimes they just do, and sometimes people do dumb stuff or smart stuff that makes them happen or not happen.

I also doubt one pen is luckier than another. And I know pens can be replaced and don't really and truly have magical powers. But I still wish I hadn't lost the pen Dad gave me. When I wrote with it, it felt as if Dad were right there helping me or, I don't know, rooting for me.

Anyway, Mom said Nana Ethel has laryngitis and "lost her voice."

I said, "I hope she finds it."

Mom didn't laugh.

I'm still hoping I can find my voice. I know it didn't get "lost" like my pen, but is it the kind of thing you can find—ah-ha! (A-H-H-A)—like a four-leaf clover? Or is it something you have to discover little by little?

Yesterday, Dad was helping a high school senior write his essay for college. They were in the dining room reading out loud. It

130

started out like this: "I feel fully prepared to undertake rigorous academic challenges."

I thought that sounded good, but Dad said, "Can you put more of your personality in there, Taylor? Let them hear your voice." He even added, "Kids think about how they look, but not how they sound."

The whole voice thing still confuses me. I know it's more than tra-la-la-la-la, but what is it?

Being a writer is way more complicated than I ever thought.

To tell you the truth, I started feeling a little *overlooked* as I *overheard* Dad tutoring Taylor. Dad was so full of en*courage*ment, and I don't think he gets that I need extra *courage* too. And that a little attention would go a long way.

Bea and I have been encouraging Pip with the Pip Pointers, but I wish Mom and Dad realized that I could use some advice too.

Do they need Parent Pointers??

AVA, ABANDONED?

Dear Diary,

We went to The Great Wall for dinner. It was raining, and I said I liked the sound of the raindrops on the sunroof.

"*Rain*drops on the *sun*roof," Dad repeated. "That's almost a poem."

When we sat down, we ordered egg rolls and dumplings, and I looked at the menu and said, "Wonton? Not now." Then I spelled it out: W-O-N-T-O-N-N-O-T-N-O-W.

Pip said, "Good one, Ava!"

Dad laughed, and I liked that they appreciated my wordplay. It made me want to keep playing with words.

Pip went to the bathroom, and I followed her. I wanted to ask her how things were going with her crush, but she was blabbing away about how she and Nadifa are going to be lab partners. (*Blab* partners??) Well, Pip was so busy talking about science experiments that she didn't notice that Mrs. (Bright) White walked in behind her—and *between* us.

Mrs. (Bright) White didn't notice me either, and I didn't say anything because it's awkward to see a librarian outside of a library. Especially in a bathroom!!

What was really awkward was what happened next.

Pip marched up to the mirror, fluffed her red hair, smiled, and proclaimed, "You are totally awesome."

Mrs. (Bright) White said, "Excuse me, are you talking to me?"

"No!" Pip replied, all flustered. "I thought you were my sister!"

"Your sister?" Mrs. (Bright) White turned and saw me hiding in the doorway. "Oh! Hello, Ava!" She looked back at Pip and said, "I quite agree: Ava *is* awesome." She smiled and added, "And how nice that you two get along so well."

Pip and Mrs. (Bright) White went into separate stalls, and when they came out, they washed their hands side by side like it was no biggie. I just stood there wriggling, because I was not going to pee with Mrs. (Bright) White in the room!

They left, and after a minute, I left too.

Guess what? Mrs. (Bright) White was at our table talking to Mom and Dad! She was telling them that she sent my story to the publishers of *Kids' Eye View*. "I think it has a real chance in the fifth-grade category," she said.

Mom and Dad smiled, and I tried to. But as Pip knows, sometimes even a *little* smile takes a *big* effort.

AVA, AWKWARD

11/15
LATE SUNDAY AFTERNOON

DEAR DIARY,

After breakfast, I went to Maybelle's. Maybelle's mom congratulated me about the writing contest, and I mumbled thank you. I still hadn't told Maybelle about the Pip Pointers or my Queen-Bee-Real-Bea worries.

We went to her backyard, and she said, "Want to trim my hair?"

I said, "I've never trimmed hair before."

"Yes, you have," she said. "Remember when we gave haircuts to all of Pip's Barbies?"

Actually, I still feel kind of bad about the time we pretended we had a barbershop. It was a long time ago, but Pip got really upset when she saw all the yellow Barbie hair on the floor of our basement. Mom and Dad got mad too, so it's something I try to forget. But when you try to forget something, you usually remember it extra.

"We didn't exactly do a great job," I reminded Maybelle.

"That's true," she admitted. "But we're older now. And how hard can it be to trim hair?" She lifted a strand of her hair and examined the ends. "The thing is, at my mom's salon, they always cut off way too much."

She handed me scissors, and I objected a little more, and she said, "C'mon. Just snip off half an inch."

I protested, but she begged, so I started: *snip, snip, snip.*

(Funny: *snip, snip, snip* backward is *pins, pins, pins.*)

I was nervous but not *pins*-and-needles nervous, so I kept doing it, cutting Maybelle's hair. At first it came out a little slanty: the right side was longer than the left. I said this out loud, and Maybelle said, "Just even it out."

I tried, but then the left side was longer than the right. "That's okay. You can fix it," Maybelle said, so I tried. I was getting a little worried though. What if I kept evening it out until there was no hair left? Fortunately, that didn't happen. But all in all, I ended up cutting about *four* inches—not half an inch. And it still wasn't completely even.

"I'm sorry!" I said.

She said it was okay, and I blurted, "Want to trim my hair?" I don't know why I said that, because I didn't even need a haircut. But before I could take it back, Maybelle said, "Sure."

Next thing you know, she was behind me chatting and snipping.

"I meant to tell you," Maybelle began, "the other day in school, Pip smiled at me."

"Really?"

"Really. And in the lunchroom last week, I saw her sitting with a new kid, *laughing.*"

Well, next thing you know, I told Maybelle everything. When you're not *facing* someone *face-to-face*, it's easier to spill your guts. (Yucky expression.)

Thing is, I needed to talk, and I knew I could trust Maybelle with my secrets—I was trusting her with sharp scissors at my neck!

When I was done explaining everything, she said the Pip Pointers sounded cool and not to worry too much about my Bee-Bea story getting read by too many people.

"I hope you're right," I said, feeling better. I was tempted to tell her about Pip's crush, but resisted. Besides, I didn't want to distract her. "How's it going back there?" I asked.

"I'm just trying to even it out."

A little later, I said, "Almost done?"

"Almost."

For a few minutes, things were quiet. Then she said, "Oops."

"What??"

"Nothing."

"Nothing?" I knew it was *not not*hing, but I didn't want to add another worry to my list of worries.

"I'm on the finishing touches," Maybelle said. "Hold still."

"I'm trying!" I said, even though I was also trying to take my mind off my head, which is as hard as it sounds.

"Done!" Maybelle finally announced, sounding apologetic. She ran inside to get a mirror. I looked at all the curled wisps of brown hair on the grass. Mine was a little darker than hers.

When she came back, we checked each other out, front and back. We both looked worse instead of better, and we knew it.

"Is your mom going to be mad?" I asked.

"No. She hardly ever gets mad."

I felt a pang of jealousy, but a little bit of relief too. "Good," I said, because I would hate having a friend's mom mad at me!

"Is yours?" Maybelle asked.

"She might not even notice," I had to admit, and Maybelle looked a little sad for me.

"You know what we need?" she said.

"What? Hats? Wigs? Brown bags?" I was trying to be funny.

"Moonglasses!!" she pronounced and dug into her pockets. She brought out two pretend pairs and put hers on the movie-star way. I did too.

"Look!" she pointed up. "The moon! And the man in the moon!"

We looked, and in the middle of the blue sky, surprise! There was a big round white moon. That made me feel a little better— it was like the moon was watching over us or something.

"Is it really 24,000 miles away?" I asked.

"Multiply by ten!" Maybelle laughed. "*240,000* miles!"

AVA WITH ALTERED HAIR

DEAR DIARY,

Mom and Dad went to a party and told Pip and me to "look after each other."

Pip asked about my hair, and when I told her, she said, "It'll grow back."

"I know," I said and nuked some alphabet soup.

I've liked alphabet soup ever since I was a baby. I used to eat it at room temperature in a high chair. I even have a poster next to my bed of a can of Campbell's alphabet soup. It's by Andy Warhol and is called P-O-P art.

If Pip keeps drawing, maybe she can make P-I-P art.

Tonight, all Pip made was a mess. She poured herself some Lucky Charms, and then her cell phone buzzed—practically a first. It said: "Nadifa." Pip jumped up and—*unlucky* for her—spilled the *Lucky* Charms.

On the floor was a pink puddle of soggy shamrocks, pots of gold, shooting stars, rainbows, and mushy hearts.

"Smooth!" I said, but Pip just picked up her phone with one hand and a sponge with the other. Last week, she might have cried over spilt milk. Today she mopped up and kept talking.

"Tomorrow? Sure!" Pip said into the phone. "I love ice-skating!"

I stirred my letters, looking for words and keeping myself company. It's not that I expected Pip to include me. But I didn't expect to feel left out.

AVA WITH NO APPETITE

11/17
BEDTIME

DEAR DIARY,

Dad told me he'd googled "Wren Misty Oaks" and three of his plays popped up. "So did 'Sting of the Queen Bee,'" he said. "There are two writers in town now!"

"I never thought my story would show up online," I mumbled, quiet as Pip.

"Well, no need for modesty. The more people who see your work, the better." He put his arm around me. "Maybe it'll go viral!"

"Like a virus?" I asked.

Dad laughed, but I didn't.

I wished I could tell him that even though "Sting of the Queen Bee" got an *honorable* mention, it's making me feel like a *dishonorable* person!

No, worse. It's making me feel like P-O-O-P.

AVA, AILING

DEAR DIARY,

Yesterday, Maybelle's mom took her to get a real haircut, a "bob" (B-O-B), and today at school, everyone kept saying how adorable she looks. I tried not to feel jealous.

My math teacher, Miss Hamshire, stopped me in the hallway. Most kids refer (R-E-F-E-R) to her as Miss *Hamster*. She has beady eyes and big glasses, and no one likes her except Maybelle, because Maybelle loves math and Miss Hamshire loves kids who love math.

Miss Hamshire said, "Ava, I read your story on the school website. I hope it's not based on any fellow students." She peered down at me, her beady eyes all googly and magnified.

I started sweating, because I had a feeling that my math teacher had put 2 + 2 together.

"I wonder what Mrs. Lemons thinks," she said.

"Mrs. Lemons likes me," I blurted, which was moronic because Miss Hamshire hadn't said she didn't like me. She'd just hinted that she didn't like my story.

After school, Bea came over. Her hair was in a braid, and she asked about my hair. I told her, and she offered to try to straighten it, but I said, "No thanks." I mean, just because Bea is good at giving advice doesn't mean she's good at giving haircuts, right?

She turned to Pip and said, "How'd Week Two go?"

This time, Pip seemed happy to answer. "I won't give you a day-to-day play-by-play. But whenever I saw myself in a mirror or a window, I did what you said: I gave myself a compliment. Fortunately, only one person caught me—not counting Ava."

"And I don't count," I joked, then realized that this was starting to feel a teeny bit true.

"Did you also keep smiling at people this week?" Bea asked Pip.

"Mostly at myself," Pip answered.

"Well, that's part of the whole point. But keep smiling at other people too. Not 24/7, and not when you don't feel like it. But sometimes, when you can."

"I'll try."

"Good. So you ready for your third assignment?" Bea pulled a folded strip of paper from her pocket and read it aloud.

WEEK THREE:
SAY HI TO SOMEONE NEW EVERY DAY, KID OR GROWN-UP.

"That's it?" Pip asked.

"That's it," Bea said.

"That doesn't seem so hard."

"It's not."

I almost pointed out that "It's not" sounds like "It's snot," but

I didn't. Funny how Pip has to tell herself to speak up and I have to tell myself to shut up. Just because something pops into my head doesn't mean it should leap from my lips.

Bea looked at Pip. "Two weeks ago, it would have seemed harder."

"You're probably right," Pip said.

"I *am* right," Bea said with a twinkle, and somehow it didn't sound conceited.

The phone rang. It was Mom. Pip answered and started talking, so I walked Bea out to her bike. "How'd you get so good at helping people feel more confident anyway?" I asked. It's not like she went to Advice Columnist School or Life Coach Academy.

"At my old school," Bea replied, "the whole sixth grade was pretty clique-y, and a lot of girls put me in the middle of their fights. I didn't like it, and there were a lot of stupid rumors. So I talked to my aunt a lot—she's a psychotherapist. She's expensive, but she always talks to me for free."

I started wishing I had an aunt who was a psychotherapist. But I don't, and even if I did, I couldn't picture myself talking about my troubles.

"I also just hung out at the bookshop a lot," Bea continued. "Me and Meow Meow. I read a ton: novels, magazines, and books with quotes."

"Quotes?"

"Quotes. You know, like, 'No one can make you feel inferior without your consent.'"

"Who said that?"

"Eleanor Roosevelt. And, 'The only way to have a friend is to be one.'"

"Who said that?"

"Ralph Waldo Emerson."

"You know a lot of quotes?"

"I guess. Oprah Winfrey said, 'Being angry with other people hurts you more than it hurts them.'"

I thought about how angry I'd been at Bea before I'd even met her. "The only quotes I know are the morals of Aesop's fables."

"The morals?"

"Yeah. Like, you know 'The Mouse and the Lion'? It's about a big lion that spares a little mouse, and later, when the lion gets captured by hunters, the mouse saves him by gnawing through the hunters' net."

"What's the moral?"

"No good deed, no matter how small, is ever wasted."

Bea nodded. I think we were both aware that we were doing Pip a good deed, but only I was aware that deed (D-E-E-D) is a you-know-what.

I started thinking about the moral of my Queen Bee story: "There's no shortcut to true friendship." Then I thought I'd been *right* about friendship, but *wrong* about Bea.

I wished I could tell her that I was worried that my BEE-BEA story was turning into a BB gun, but I couldn't.

Besides, Bea's visits aren't for me. They're for P-I-P.

AVA, AWARE

11/18
MIDDLE-OF-THE-NIGHT

DEAR DIARY,

I just got out of bed and turned on my lamp. I hope Mom and Dad don't notice and tell me to turn if off and go to sleep, but there's something else I want to tell you.

In gym we combined classes and this lady came to teach us yoga. She talked about "breathing" and "balance," and it was actually pretty calming. Then she said to pretend we were trees.

First, we stood on our right leg and lifted our left foot in the air and raised our arm-branches and wriggled our finger-leaves and tried not to fall. Then we switched and stood on our left leg and lifted our right foot in the air and raised our arm-branches and wriggled our finger-leaves and tried not to fall.

It was hard!

Most of us couldn't help wriggling and jiggling, and some of us (including me) kept putting our feet down so we wouldn't keel over. A few of us did fall!

Only Chuck had no problem standing perfectly still. I bet he could have stood there like a tree all day long. He's either extra coordinated...or part egret?

Well, the yoga instructor told us to form a circle, stand on one leg, hold hands, and make a "group tree." (She should have said "forest.") I was in between Maybelle and Alex, and as I reached for their hands, I started to giggle, but the instructor said, "No giggling, and please close your eyes."

Next thing you know, we were all in a circle with our eyes shut.

"Some of you are still swaying, like trees in a breeze," the instructor said. "But notice how you are holding each other up and supporting one another. Be aware that you can trust each other, and know that you will not let each other fall."

The amazing thing was: she was right! All of us (except Chuck) kept wobbling, but not one kid fell! Not one! Alex and I almost fell, but we both "supported" each other and even shared a teeny tiny half-smile.

Right now, under my covers, I'm thinking that even though my plate is chock-full of worries, and even though Pip can sometimes be annoying, I'm glad that Bea and I are helping her.

She's my sister, after all, and I'm not going to let her fall.

AVA WREN, YOGA TREE

DEAR DIARY,

Lunch was meatballs. Maybelle and I were standing in line right behind Pip, and I was starving to death (poetic license). Pip said hi to the lunch lady, and while I paid for my meatballs, the lunch lady, who is very bubbly, said, "Ava, I read your story about the bee! Good for you!"

I said, "Thanks," even though her "*Good* for you!" made me feel *bad* for me.

Well, Maybelle and I followed Pip into the lunchroom, and I don't know what Pip was thinking, but as she walked by two seventh-grade boys, *she said hi*. One was tall and skinny with curly hair, and the other was stocky with a starter mustache. Neither one answered—they just sort of looked through her.

Pip didn't even notice. She kept heading toward a corner table where Nadifa and Isabel were saving her a seat. The two boys were sitting next to Loudmouth Lacey. She's the girl with thick bangs and thick eyeliner who was mean to Pip last year.

Okay, I think this is a metaphor, not a simile, but let me put it this way: if middle school were an ocean, Lacey would be a barracuda and Pip would be a minnow.

Anyway, here's what happened. Lacey began making squeaky sounds, like, "Pipsqueak, squeak, squeak, squeak," and then the boys started doing it too!

At first, I couldn't believe my ears, but I stopped and listened, and it was true: all three of them were squeaking. Lacey was the loudest.

Maybelle and I were just yards away, and I was tempted to throw my meatballs at them. But what would that help?

Then things got worse.

Lacey took the rubber band out of her ponytail and twisted it around her tongue and lisped, "Look! I'm tongue-tied! I'm tongue-tied!" Mustache Boy cracked up, and soon all three of them were laughing like hyenas.

Personally, I couldn't take it anymore! How dare they make fun of Pip? I was glad she was at the other end of the lunchroom, and I was thinking how brave she had been to follow Bea's step-by-step advice and get herself "out there"—and how I should try to be brave too.

I started walking, step by step, toward their table.

Maybelle said, "Ava, no!" but it was like their table was a magnet and I was a paper clip. My heart was pounding, and my *sneakers*, instead of walking me safely away, were heading toward the *squeakers*. Suddenly I was standing in front of them, staring into the taller boy's eyes. I looked at him, human being to human being, and said, "Why can't you leave her alone?"

"What's it to you?"

"She's my sister!" I shouted, which surprised all of us, especially me.

Mustache Boy laughed, and Lacey lisped, "Sheeth her thith-ter!" But the tall boy was listening, I could tell.

"Give her a break," I said. "She's shy, but she's a good person." Mustache Boy snorted, and Lacey squeaked, and I added, "And being a good person is a good thing." I couldn't believe I added that.

I looked at Maybelle, and her mouth was flopped open. Other kids were listening too. Even Chuck. I wondered what would happen if a fight broke out. Would he jump up and defend me using his boxing and balancing skills?

The taller boy nodded at Lacey as if to say, "Let's stop," and Lacey made a face and mumbled, "Whatever." Then she stuck her hand in her mouth and slid the slimy rubber band off her tongue and shot it at the window, saliva and all. It struck the glass and fell onto the floor.

Mustache Boy shrugged, and they all stopped squeaking.

I just stood there, shaky as a one-legged yoga tree. I was trying not to drop my tray.

Maybelle got me to sit down, but I couldn't eat. I looked toward Pip. She and Nadifa and Isabel were all facing the wall. I was glad they had missed everything.

Funny, even as I write this, hours later, I'm still a little shaky. But I feel proud of myself too. Like, maybe for once, I blurted out the right thing.

AVA THE ADMIRABLE?

Friday Lunch Period, in the Library

Dear Diary,

"Principal Gupta wants to see you."

These are six words you do *not* want to hear.

Since Principal Gupta never wants to see me, for a tiny second, I thought it might have to do with my standing up to the Squeakers. Maybe she was going to give me a bravery award?

But Mrs. Lemons wasn't smiling. And as I walked down the hallway and got closer and closer to Principal Gupta's office, I felt more and more sure that I was in trouble.

I knocked on her door, and she said, "Come in. Sit down."

I did, and I saw a blond lady sitting in the other chair. The blond lady looked familiar. I had definitely seen her before. But where?

Uh-oh! At Bates Books! And Misty Oaks Library!

"Ava, I'd like you to meet Mrs. Bates."

My heart went plunging down one of my legs and landed on top of my big toe. (Poetic license.)

"How do you do?" I said as politely as I could, but it came out kind of high-pitched.

Mrs. Bates eyeballed me as if she'd expected the malicious Ava Wren to be taller and tougher. "I've been better," she answered.

Principal Gupta said, "Ava, Mrs. Bates just read 'Sting of the Queen Bee.'"

My throat got all tight.

"I did," Mrs. Bates confirmed. "And frankly, I felt a little stung by it myself. I can't say I appreciated your portrayal of my daughter as an evil, selfish, rude friend-stealer."

I felt about as slimy as Ernie the Earthworm, so I apologized and said, "It was a mistake." I was tempted to mention Pip's ruined slumber party but decided not to, because Mrs. Bates hadn't asked what had *inspired* me.

"I liked 'Bookshop Cat,'" Mrs. Bates said, "and thought others might find it charming. So this morning I sent our customers an email with a link to the library contest site. Within the hour, two people emailed back asking me about Queen Bee, the nasty new seventh-grader. One even took it upon herself to telephone."

I sat there staring at the dark green rug. It had a bunch of crisscrossing vacuum lines in it. My eyes were prickling, and I had a lump in my throat.

"I'm all for free speech," Mrs. Bates continued, "but not when it's hurtful or damaging. At Bea's last school, she had to deal with a number of mean and jealous girls and their nasty rumors, and I don't want her to go through that again. That's why I came over to put an end to this."

"I wish I could press Undo," I mumbled.

"Speak up," Principal Gupta said.

"I wish I could press Undo," I repeated, a little louder.

"I wish you could too," Mrs. Bates replied. "Ms. Gupta, perhaps you can remove Ava's story from the school website? I assume that wouldn't be considered censorship?"

"Under the circumstances, I think it would be fine."

Principal Gupta phoned her tech person while I sat there like a criminal. I started feeling smaller and smaller, and it was all I could do not to burst into tears.

I thought: I wish my parents were here. Then I thought: no, I don't. And to be honest, that made me feel even worse!

"I'm not sure if Bea even knows about your story," Mrs. Bates said.

"She does," I said softly. "She and I already made up."

"Really? Well, I shouldn't be surprised." She nodded. "My daughter has a very forgiving nature. More so than I." Did that mean that Mrs. Bates was going to stay mad at me forever? "Bea is wise beyond her years, and she has a heart of gold."

I wondered what my heart was made of. Pebbles? Dirt? Mud? I was still afraid I might start bawling.

"Mrs. Bates," Principal Gupta said, "I feel certain that Ava has grown a lot because of this unfortunate experience. Would you say this is true, Ava?"

"Yes!" I said and threw in a couple more "I'm sorry"s. There was a silence, so I asked, "Would it be okay if I went back to language arts? I mean, if I'm not getting suspended?"

"It's okay with me," Principal Gupta said. Mrs. Bates gave a nod too, so I stood up and backed out of the room, closing the door behind me.

In the hall, I was starting to breathe full breaths again when a seventh-grader I'd never met before said, "Are you Ava Wren?"

"Yes."

"Bea Bates is a nice person," she said. "She did not deserve what you did to her."

"I know," I said and kept walking.

"What's with the weird hair anyway?" she called.

I hurried back to class wishing Thanksgiving were *this* week instead of next week.

AVA WHO WROTE A BUNCH (INSTEAD OF EATING LUNCH)

Dear Diary,

I don't know how Pip survives without talking. She may think talking is hard, but *not* talking is so much harder.

I wish I could talk to my parents the way some kids do. Or the way Bea talks to her aunt.

This afternoon, Maybelle and I sat in the library near Pip, Isabel, and Nadifa. Nadifa's hair is even shorter than mine, and she wears two earrings in one ear and one in the other.

Maybelle and I were playing I Spy. Here's what I spied with my little eye: Pip said a quiet hi to Bea's freckly brother! And Ben said a quiet hi back!

Questions:

1. Is Ben her crush??
2. Does Pip know that Ben is Bea's brother?
3. Does Ben know his mother hates my guts?
4. Does Pip have any idea about all the drama going on?

After the bell rang at the end of the period, I got up the nerve to talk to Mr. Ramirez. Since my story is no longer on the school website, I asked if he could ask Mrs. (Bright) White to take it off the town library website and also take it out of the running for the anthology. He said, "Why don't we call her together?"

I wanted to say, "Can't you just do it?" but he punched in her number. I was hoping a machine would pick up, but Mrs. (Bright) White said, "Hello," and Mr. Ramirez handed me the phone. I had no choice but to talk!

"Hello, this is Ava Wren, and I'm sorry," I said, apologizing to my third grown-up in one day. I admitted that I should have given more thought to my stupid story before handing it in and said, "I wish you could just make it all go away."

Mrs. (Bright) White said she couldn't "just make it all go away," but that she could remove the story from the library site. "May I ask why?" she said, and I had to tell her that I'd based Queen Bee on Real Bea in a not-nice way. "Well, that's a shame, Ava," she said. "When you have talent, you owe it to yourself and others to put it to good use."

I felt like a puppy who'd piddled on the carpet, but I said, "If you have a contest next year, I'll submit a story I can stay proud of." I hadn't expected to say that.

"All right, it's a deal. I'm looking forward to reading it already." It was funny that Mrs. (Bright) White was looking forward to reading a story I hadn't started thinking *up* or writing *down*. "And I'll notify the publisher that the author of 'Queen Bee' wishes to withdraw her story."

"Thank you," I said and added some more "I'm sorry"s for good measure.

Believe it or not, after I hung up, Mr. Ramirez apologized to *me*. He said, "Ava, I'm sorry this all got so out of hand and that we didn't discuss your story in the first place. In my day, kids could show poor judgment and their mistakes didn't go on their permanent record."

"This is going on my permanent record?!" I asked, horrified.

"No, no. I just mean, in the age of the Internet, you have to be extra careful. Mistakes can follow you around." I pictured my mistakes swarming after me like stinging bees.

I nodded, glad that at least Mr. Ramirez knows I'm *not* a bad person—I'm just a person who did a bad thing.

AVA WHO DOES *NOT* WANT HER MISTAKES TO FOLLOW HER AROUND

DEAR DIARY,

Hi from the *high*way.

Dad and Pip and I are driving back from shoe shopping. Dad and Pip are up front, and I'm in the backseat—with you.

Bea called this morning and said, "Sorry about my mom."

I said, "It's okay." I told Bea that my runaway story had been taken off the school website and library website and that Mrs. (Bright) White had submitted it to be in a book, but I'd asked her to un-submit it.

"Wait. Why?"

"Because I want my story to disappear!"

"Wait a sec, Ava," Bea said. "I'm glad people in Misty Oaks won't be reading about the evil new seventh-grader named Bea, but I don't care if kids in Alabama or Alaska do. If you can get it published, you should."

"I don't know…"

"Well, *I* know. If Mrs. White thinks your story is good enough to get into a collection—"

"But it's *not*—"

"Never say no to yourself, Ava! Let other people do that for you. Because who knows? They might say yes."

I wondered if she'd gotten that from a quote book. "Too late," I said. "I already told her to withdraw it."

"So un-tell her! Let's un-tell her together! C'mon, we're biking to the library right now! I'm picking you up in five."

With Bea, there was no point in even protesting, and minutes later, we were pedaling to Misty Oaks Library.

I was hoping Saturday was Mrs. (Bright) White's day off, but she was at her desk wearing a cream-colored sweater speckled with maple leaves. I asked if she'd withdrawn my story, and she said she was "just about to do so."

"You can keep it in if you want," I said.

"Really?" She met my eyes. "What made you change your mind?"

I turned toward Bea. "Remember Bea Bates?" Bea took off her helmet, and her long blond hair came tumbling out.

"Of course! Hello, Bea. I love Bates Books, and I liked your 'Bookshop Cat' story—especially the bit about the fluffy orange cat who plays favorites among the customers. The competition among seventh-grade entries is quite stiff and…"

"Mrs. White," I said, "Bea thinks I should keep my story in the running."

"Really? May I ask why?"

"Bea is a very encouraging person," I said and looked over at her. Bea stayed quiet and gave me a smile.

"Well then," Mrs. (Bright) White said, looking at us in turn. "We'll simply leave everything alone and wait to see what the editors decide."

I thanked her, and we left. But here's the funny thing: I still don't know if I want my Queen Bee story to go into a book...or to just go away.

AVA, AMBIVALENT BUT WITH NEW SHOES

DEAR DIARY,

This morning, Bea came over and asked Pip if she'd been saying hi to a lot of people.

"Not a ton," Pip answered and looked at me. I could tell Pip was thinking of spelling out N-O-T-A-T-O-N, and hoped she wouldn't. I didn't want Bea to know how strange our family is!

I nodded to Pip, as if to say, "Don't," but then I was afraid Pip might tell me not to nod—and spell that out too: D-O-N-T-N-O-D.

Bea said, "I just mean: did you talk to someone new every day?"

"Yes," Pip said and mentioned the lunch lady, a substitute teacher, and a bus driver. She did *not* mention that some of her someones were boys, and that two did not smile back (in the lunchroom) and one did (in the library).

She also did not mention Ben by name. Is that because he's a boy or because he's Bea's brother? Or does Pip still not know? I'd thought of telling Pip, but since I wasn't sure if that would help or backfire, I didn't.

"Great job!" Bea said to Pip, and we snacked on pretzels.

After a while, Bea checked her cell phone and said, "Gotta go. My parents are waiting for me because we're going to my grandparents' for Thanksgiving. I hope I don't get *ill* in *Ill*inois—get it?"

"Got it!" I said, surprised by her wordplay. "You won't!"

Bea handed Pip a fourth assignment.

WEEK FOUR:
COMPLIMENT ONE PERSON EVERY DAY—ON ANYTHING AT ALL.

After Bea left, I asked Pip if she still thought Bea was bossy. Pip thought about it and said, "Yes, but somehow I don't mind."

"Same," I agreed. Because Bea isn't really bossy. More like bold and encouraging and generous.

And she likes us—and we like that!

I went into my room and scooped up two handfuls of Mini M&M's then went into Pip's room with both hands behind me. "Pick a hand," I said.

Pip pointed. I opened my right hand and dumped the Minis into her palm.

"Yum!" she said. "Lucky guess!"

"Actually," I said, "lucky is having *me* as a sister!" I opened my other hand and showed her that it was also full of Minis. And I spilled those chocolates into her palm too.

AVA THE ADORABLE

Dear Diary,

I found another Pip note in my room. It said, "I know I'm lucky." At first I was confused, then I realized she wrote it after I told her she was lucky to have me as a sister.

Well, even though it's just four little words and not a bouquet of roses, four words from Pip are a lot.

I was going to throw the note away, but instead I'm taping it right here.

I know I'm lucky.

AVA THE ANGELIC

11/26
THANKSGIVING MORNING

DEAR DIARY,

As soon as we woke up, Mom said, "Kids, we have a lot to do before everyone gets here. Give me a hand in the kitchen."

Pip said, "Okay."

I said, "I don't mind helping, but I need both my hands." Mom didn't react, so I added, "I'll give you a hand if you promise to give it back." She still didn't crack a smile. (Do people crack smiles? Or only eggs?)

I wondered if Mom thought I had a bad attitude when I was just trying to be funny.

Finally I said, "What do we have to do?"

"Set the table for seven," Mom said. "With cloth napkins."

AVA WITH AN ATTITUDE?

11/26
THANKSGIVING NIGHT

DEAR DIARY,

I'm as stuffed as our turkey was, but I'm confused too. My feelings are all jumbled.

Nana Ethel and Aunt Jen and Uncle Patrick flew in early, and everyone gave everyone *huge hugs*.

When Uncle Patrick and Aunt Jen got married, Pip and I got to be flower girls. Aunt Jen didn't want to change her name to Jen Wren, so she kept her own name, which is Jen Honoroff, which sounds like On or Off, which makes Pip and me laugh.

Anyway, Nana Ethel, Mom's mom, asked Dad how his writing was going. Dad said, "Oh, you know, this morning, I took out a comma, and this afternoon, I put it in again."

Uncle Patrick said, "Oscar Wilde!"

Dad said, "Bingo!" which is a weird word. (It's not like kids go around saying, "Bingo!")

Dad and Uncle Patrick both love talking about Irish writers. Uncle Patrick once told me about a bunch of monks who wrote one of the first books ever—the Book of Kells. Instead of paper, they used calfskin. Instead of ink, they used ground-up rocks and gems!

When Dad started preparing the turkey, Uncle Patrick asked, "Is the FOWL FOUL?"

Dad smiled and said, "The NOSE KNOWS." Then he asked Uncle Patrick to hand over some herbs.

"You're running out of THYME," Uncle Patrick said. "TIME to get some more."

Dad said, "Homonym jokes are NOT ALLOWED. At least NOT ALOUD."

They were playing the Homonym Game! I thought Pip and I had made it up, but I guess not. Dad once told me that his father was the original word nerd and "pun pal" of the family. So maybe *he* invented it?

"No one BEATS your BEETS," Uncle Patrick said.

Pip must have decided to use one of her compliments, because she said, "You guys are funny. Ava and I like homonyms too."

I was surprised, but Uncle Patrick looked *really* surprised. His bushy eyebrows shot up and practically met in the middle. I think he'd forgotten Pip could talk.

Next thing you know, he was asking Pip about her sketches and schoolwork, and she was answering, and they were having a normal-ish back-and-forth conversation. She even showed him her "portfolio," and he called her work "very accomplished." She showed him two book covers she drew for English, and he said, "You've always been such a good reader."

Well, I wanted him to know that I'm a good writer and I thought about showing him *Winning Words* or telling him about the *Kids' Eye View* competition, but forget it, no way. I also thought of showing him my spelling tests, but I didn't want to seem desperate. And since I hadn't told Mom and Dad about all my 100s, I didn't see how I could tell Uncle Patrick.

Still, it was *not* easy listening to him praise Pip to the skies.

Who knew that Pip would keep on soaking up all the attention whether people are worried about her or proud of her?

To tell you the truth, it's making me feel upside down.

ＡＶＡ (A-K-A A-V-A UPSIDE DOWN)

Dear Diary,

Thanksgiving is over and I'm still mad.

For starters, I did way more cleanup than Pip. I took out tons of garbage—turkey bones and yam peels and pumpkin cans—and *I* got treated like garbage! Well, not garbage exactly. More like Cinderella before the fairy godmother part. No one asked about my life or realized that I deserve some credit for the fact that Pip was blabbing away about hers.

I wanted to invite Maybelle over, but there's some prehistoric rule that Thanksgiving is only for families.

While Pip was at dinner chitchatting with our relatives, Mom kept asking me to refill glasses and clear away dishes. I could tell she didn't want to interrupt Pip. Pip would say something, and Uncle Patrick or Aunt Jen or Nana Ethel would say something back, and it was like a jolly little ping-pong game was going on while I was running around being "helpful."

You know what? I'm sick of being helpful!

Have Bea and I created a monster? Pipenstein?

I wish I could talk about all this because, not to use a bad word but...#-A-M-M-I-T-I-M-M-A-D.

At dinner, I started to feel like a volcano full of hot simmering lava.

At least I can get my feelings out in you. For a few minutes, I couldn't find you, and I thought I was going to lose my mind. (Lost: one pen, one diary, one mind...)

AVA FULL OF LAVA

Dear Diary,

I'm at a desk in the library looking over bonus spelling words like "nuisance," "stomachache," and "invisible."

Some kids think bonus words are a "nuisance" that give them "stomachaches." But I love bonus words. What I hate is feeling "invisible."

Oh! Pip just walked in! She's sitting near the water fountain with Nadifa.

Ben is three tables away. I wonder if he noticed her.

Whoa! He did! He's staring at her!

I don't think she sees him though.

Wait! She definitely sees him!!

I can tell because she looked right at him then turned away and started looking everywhere *except* back in his direction.

Oh! Oh! He's getting up! He's walking toward her! He's a few feet away! He's at her table! He's sitting down!!

OMG!! I have to check this out close-up!!

I'm back. I went to get a sip of water so I could eavesdrop. Here's what I heard:

Ben said hi. And Pip said hi back. Then Pip said, "I like your sweater."

Well, I couldn't believe it. And I *didn't* believe it. Because I don't think Pip likes his sweater. I think she likes *him*!!

AVA WREN, SPYING AGAIN

12/2
AFTERNOON

DEAR DIARY,

Bea came by and asked, "How was Thanksgiving?"

I was about to grumble a bit, but Pip chimed, "Great," and offered her a slice of leftover pie.

"Pip's Pumpkin Pie," I said, because last week Mrs. Lemons said alliterations are when a bunch of words start with the same sound.

Bea got a funny look, and then Pip said, "'*Desserts*,' I stressed," (D-E-S-S-E-R-T-S-I-S-T-R-E-S-S-E-D), which is a palindrome. I could tell she was about to launch into our parents' peculiar passion for palindromes, but fortunately Bea complimented Pip's pie and asked, "So how'd it go? Did you compliment people this week?"

"I complimented my dad's turkey," Pip said, "and my uncle Patrick's jokes and my aunt Jen's earrings. And it all went really well."

"Just fantastic," I mumbled and tried to remember the last time anyone complimented me.

"How about in school?" Bea asked.

"I complimented Mr. Ramirez's holiday book display. And a boy's sweater."

"A boy?" Bea asked, eyes wide.

"A boy!" Pip giggled.

Was she going to name names?

Pip turned to Bea, "Should I tell him I like him?"

Bea considered the question. "It's usually better to *show* not *tell*. At least that's what real advice columnists say."

"*Show* not *tell*? How do I do that?" Pip asked.

Bea said, "Just talk to him and smile and stuff. He'll figure it out. He'll be able to guess, and you won't have to spell it out."

"Our family likes to s-p-e-l-l stuff out," I was thinking. But I didn't say that. I didn't say anything. Just call me Ava the Absent.

"The problem," Bea pointed out, "is that once you put stuff in words, you can't take it back."

"I guess," Pip said.

"I know," I almost added because, well, duh!

"Pip," Bea said, "I was going to say that you've come out of your shell like a snail or a turtle. But I think you've come out of your cocoon like a butterfly."

"Me?" Pip asked.

"You!" Bea answered.

I sat there trying not to feel jealous of Pip Hannah Wren, Center of the Known Universe.

"What's my next assignment?" Pip asked.

"To ask people questions, at least one per day. And to listen to their answers."

"I can do that."

"Good. Because it's your last assignment." Bea handed over the final strip of yellow paper. "Ava came up with this one," she added.

I wasn't sure if I even wanted credit or not. I mean, I know I'm supposed to be happy for Pip the Butterfly, but I'm also frustrated for—

AVA THE ANT

Dear Diary,

Over 2,500 years ago, Aesop wrote a fable called "The Ant and the Chrysalis." "Chrysalis" is an excellent spelling word and the story goes like this:

One hot day, an ant came across a chrysalis that was near its time of change. The ant felt sorry for it because it was imprisoned in its shell. The ant thought, "Poor you. I can scurry anywhere and you can hardly even wriggle!" Later, the ant came back to the same spot, and the chrysalis was gone. The ant was puzzled, but suddenly he saw that he was being shaded and fanned by the gorgeous wings of a beautiful butterfly. The butterfly called down, "No need to pity me, little ant!" And with that, he flew far, far away.

The moral: "Appearances can be deceiving."

Question: Is Pip nearing her "time of change"? And did she really become a butterfly while I'm still a bug?

Ava (and Aesop)

DEAR DIARY,

After lunch, which was chicken fingers, I saw Bea at her locker, so I went over to say hi. The taller Squeaky Boy stopped by and also said hi. I looked up at him, and he looked down at me, and then he said, "Hey, kid," in a not-mean way. When he left, Bea said, "You know Josh?" So I spilled the story about Lacey and the Squeaky Boys, which, come to think of it, sounds like the name of a terrible band.

"Wow," Bea said. "You're braver than I thought."

"Or dumber?"

"No, Ava. Braver. You're a risk-taker."

"Me?"

"You," Bea said, and suddenly I did feel a little extra brave.

AVA WREN, RISK-TAKER

DEAR DIARY,

I like thinking of myself as a risk-taker, so I decided to take a risk. I mean, it always helps to pour my thoughts out into you, but somehow I knew I had to talk to Mom directly. So I went to see her, my insides as fluttery as if they were crawling with ladybugs. (Gross simile.)

When I got to Dr. Gross's, Mom was busy as usual. At least Butterscotch was thrilled to see me. So was a *sh*aggy *sh*eepdog named *Sh*ep who just got *sh*ampooed for fleas. And so was a calico cat named Fever whose owner is always dropping him off for "observation" even though Dr. Gross keeps telling her that Fever is fine. (Fever once got his tail caught in a drawer, so now he has just a short nub because cat tails don't grow back; only chameleon tails grow back. Mom says Fever's owner feels guilty because it was her fault the file drawer was open.)

Anyway, I waited as patiently as I could, but at 5:05, I passed Mom a note. It said, "Mom, we have to talk now."

I knew the conversation would be awkward, but as Bea once told Pip, no one ever died of awkwardness.

Mom glanced up, and from her expression, I swear, I think she was afraid I was going to ask her to explain puberty. (*Hellllo!* I'm a kid. I don't even have B-O-O-Bs!)

"What is it?" she asked.

When Pip and I were little, whenever we got fussy, Mom would say, "Use your words." Well, as Wilbur found out in *Charlotte's Web*, even a few words can make a giant difference. And I'd been saving up a humongous pile of words—so it was time for me to let them out.

"It's me!" I said. "Me! I'm here and I matter!" Next thing you know, it was like a dam inside me had broken. I couldn't stop talking. "Mom, you pay way more attention to Pip than to me. You can't even deny it!"

Mom sat there as silent as the Old Pip. "It's true!" I said. "You favor her! You always have! Sometimes you act like she's as fragile as an old canary. Other times you act like she can walk on water, like that dumb lizard. Maybe it's the whole getting born early thing, but that was a long time ago, and Pip is a big girl now!"

"You're taller."

"Oh, Mom, that is *so* not the point! She's thirteen! She's a teenager! And she's not as small as she used to be. Not as quiet either—in case you haven't noticed."

"I have noticed. I'm proud of her."

I took a deep breath so I wouldn't explode into a billion boiling lava bubbles all over the walls and ceiling. "You should be proud of me too because I've been helping her. And I am *totally awesome!*" It came out much louder than I meant, so I was glad the waiting room was end-of-the-day empty. No dogs on leashes or cats in boxes or upset pet owners.

"I *am* proud of you, Ava."

"You don't even know what I'm going to say!"

"Okay, go on." For once, I had Mom's full attention.

"First of all, will you admit that you favor Pip?"

"No. I love you both equally!"

"I didn't say 'love,' I said 'favor.'" Mom stayed quiet, so I did too.

Finally she said, "If it sometimes seems that I favor Pip—and I'm not saying I do—I suppose it may be because I worry more about her. She's older, but she struggles more than you do. She's our Early Bird, and she still doesn't really fly." She met my eyes. "Can you keep that to yourself?"

"Yes," I said, because it doesn't count that I'm telling you, my diary.

"I can see how this might have felt unfair, and I'm sorry," Mom continued. "Maybe you and I should have talked about it sooner. But I never meant to favor her, just protect her, encourage her. I wish she could be more like you: friendly and fearless." She looked up. "Is there any chance you could take it as a compliment that I *don't* worry about you as much as I worry about her?"

"Depends," I replied. "Is there any chance you could start noticing me more?"

"Absolutely." Mom smiled softly. "What's 'second of all'? And what did you want to say?"

I liked that she'd been listening and that she thought of me as friendly and fearless. "Well, you know my story about the new girl—"

"Yes, I tried to email it to Nana Ethel today, but for some reason, it wasn't online anymore…"

I told Mom that the girl who gave the party turned out to be a very nice person, and that appearances can be deceiving. I also told her that I had to apologize to the girl's mother, and the principal took the story off the school website.

My voice caught a little when I said all this, because I was remembering that in Principal Gupta's office, first I wished my parents were there and then I was glad they weren't.

Since Mom was looking right at me, I added, "Pip has her struggles, but I have mine too."

Mom's eyes got a little shiny when I said that.

"If I tell you something else, will you keep it to yourself?" I asked.

She nodded, so I told her about the five assignments and how when Bea started *coming over*, Pip started *overcoming* her shyness. I didn't tell her about Pip's crush, but I did tell her about Loudmouth Lacey and the Squeaky Boys. Mom looked pained during that part, but I said I stood up to them.

"C'mere, Ava," she said. "You've been a super S-I-S, haven't you?" She gave me a big hug, and I pictured myself as a hero in a book: Ava Wren to the rescue! "And Pip *has* been more extroverted lately," she added.

I didn't want the subject to switch back to Pip quite so fast, but I said, "Extra what?"

"Extroverted. Outgoing. Talkative. Last week, she told me she participated in class."

Mom said Pip had told her that a substitute teacher called on her and she'd answered. "A lot of the regular teachers have stopped trying to call on her," Mom admitted.

"She participated? That's incredible," I said.

"Ava, *you're* incredible!" Mom said and looked right at me. "Thank you for what you're doing. And for telling me about it. I'm sorry I let work and other things get me so distracted."

"Thank you for listening," I answered. Then I think we both felt a little embarrassed about all the thank-yous, even though it's nice to be thanked and Thanksgiving wasn't that long ago. "Mom, can you *not* tell Pip that I told you about Bea? She'll probably tell you herself sometime. And don't mention the Squeaky People either. It would just hurt her feelings. Plus, one of the boys might not be as bad as the other."

"I hear you," Mom said, and I felt like she really did hear me. "We'll both keep quiet. Mum's the word."

"M-U-M," I said.

Mom looked up and stroked my hair. "Hey, you could use a haircut, don't you think?"

"Sure," I said, like it was no big deal.

AVA THE ASTOUNDED

12/4
AFTER DINNER

DEAR DIARY,

It snowed today! Big fluffy flakes that didn't stick.

Three weeks till Christmas. Four till my birthday.

January 1st is a new year *and* a number palindrome (1-1) *and* the day I turn eleven (also a number palindrome).

I was thinking about what to give my family and I thought: maybe I've already given them pretty good gifts. Pip needed to get a life, and I helped her get one. And now, not only is Pip happier, but Mom and Dad seem happier too.

Dad's in the next room humming.

Is "hum" an onomatopoeia? Mrs. Lemons says those are words that are spelled the way they sound. Comic book examples are "pow," "bang," and "wham." Animal examples are "meow," "buzz," and "quack." A cereal example might be "snap," "crackle," and "P-O-P."

I went into Pip's room and asked, "Pip, do you think you and I are word nerds, like Mom and Dad?"

"Yeah, we can't help it," Pip said. Then she told me that in Spanish, she learned that "*Yo soy*" (Y-O-S-O-Y) means "I am"— which means other languages have palindromes too.

I told her that I knew a word that was eight letters and had only one vowel.

"In English?"

"Of course in English."

"How can that be?"

"It just is."

"Give me a clue."

I made a fist and pointed right at my bicep, but she didn't get it. So I said, "It's hard to guess. It's STRENGTH."

She nodded like she was impressed.

I told her that in the library, Mr. Ramirez lectured everyone about the Internet. He said we should *not* give out personal info, *not* believe everything we read online, and *always* be respectful of others. "Think before you click," he kept saying. "Fortunately," I said, "he did *not* say what inspired him."

AVA THE INSPIRING

12/6
AFTERNOON

DEAR DIARY,

This morning, Pip and I got haircuts, or in my case, a hair-fix. I got a B-O-B, like Maybelle.

On the way home, a flock of Canada geese honked in a V above us, and Pip turned to me all serious and said, "Do geese see God?"

I said, "What are you talking about?"

She spelled it out: "D-O-G-E-E-S-E-S-E-E-G-O-D?"

"Good one!" I said.

After lunch, Maybelle, Lucia, and Carmen came over. The twins were both wearing red, and we started playing a four-person card game of "I Doubt It." But then Carmen had to go home. Lucia didn't want to stop, so she said, "Think you can get Pip to play with us?"

I said, "I doubt it," and everyone laughed. But it occurred to me that Pip hadn't acted like a sore loser for a long time and hadn't been hiding in her room as much either. So I knocked on her door and asked her to play with us, and she said, "Sure," and took Carmen's place. And instead of us doing Pip a favor, Pip was doing *us* a favor. Which was nice, to tell you the truth.

When she sat down, Lucia said, "You're in seventh grade, right?"

Pip nodded.

"Don't the seventh- and eighth-graders have a dance coming up?"

Pip said, "Yes," and blushed a little.

"Are you going?" Maybelle asked.

"I don't know," Pip said.

Maybelle sneezed and Pip said, "Bless you," and I started thinking I should write Ben a note telling him that Pip likes him and asking if he likes her. But then I thought: nah, it's better to think twice (or three times!) before putting some things in print.

A-V-A WITH A B-O-B

12/1
AT 7:12

DEAR DIARY,

In the library today, I went straight into Spy Mode—A-K-A Keen Observation Mode.

Pip and Ben were on opposite sides of the room, sneaking peeks at each other. I kept watching them watch each other, and soon only two minutes were left in the period.

I wanted to jump up and shove them together. It was time for one of them to make a move!

Suddenly Ben stretched, stood up, walked toward Pip, and said, "Oh, hey, hi," as if he'd bumped into her by pure accident.

"Hi," she said, barely looking up.

Neither of them said another word. I wanted to shout, "Talk! Talk! Talk about music or sports or TV! Or the weather! Or anything at all!"

But it was like they had *talker's block*.

At last, Ben said, "I like your watch. What time is it?" This was a funny question since there was a wall clock right by the door.

Pip said, "1:59. Thanks. I got it for my birthday."

They fell silent again.

His eyes landed on her book and he said, "*Great Expectations.*"

"Have you read it?" Pip asked.

He said no, and Pip told him there was a character in it named Pip.

From the corner of my eye (not that eyes have corners), I could see Mr. Ramirez starting to take giant steps toward them. I knew he was going to ask them to "pipe down," which is how he says, "Be quiet."

Well, I couldn't let him ruin the moment, so I looked straight at him, human being to human being. And just like that, Mr. Ramirez stopped in his tracks. It was as if he read my mind and decided to do a good D-E-E-D and let Pip and Ben talk (or at least try to).

"Some of my friends are going to the dance on Friday," Ben finally stammered. "Are you?"

I thought P-I-P might P-O-P, but she stayed M-U-M.

Then she said, "I haven't really thought about it," which I knew was not true.

Then they both went quiet again! They were M-U-M as mummies!

I wanted to jump up and say, "Don't believe her! She *has* thought about it, and she's dying to go with you, you, you!"

The bell started to ring, and Ben managed to mumble, "Maybe we could go together."

Pip looked up and said, "K," very softly, and their eyes met for a split second, and then Ben went back to his seat.

Well, neither of them said another word, but I knew that

inside, they were both all melty. And I felt sort of proud of them, and proud of myself too.

If Pip's life were a book, this would be the start of a whole new chapter! And I helped her turn some important pages!

AVA THE ALTRUISTIC

DEAR DIARY,

Mrs. Lemons asked us to do some in-class creative writing, and instead of worrying or getting blocked, I just wrote and wrote as if I were writing in you.

I got so inspired that I wrote a three-page story called "Invisible Girl." It's based a little on me and a little on Pip, but not quite on either of us. The first line is: "Once there was a girl who could disappear at will." I read the story out loud, and my whole class liked it, including Chuck, all three Emilys, Pony Girl Riley, and of course Maybelle.

Tonight when Dad tucked me in, I showed him "Invisible Girl," and he laughed at all the right parts. "Ava, this is good!" he said. "I like it even more than the other one."

"Thanks."

"You're a real writer," he said. "You have the gift of gab."

I said, "The gift of what?"

Dad said there's a castle in Ireland, and millions of tourists climb its tower, lean over backward while a guard holds their legs, and kiss the Blarney Stone so they can get the "gift of gab" and become better talkers.

"Is that a G-A-G?"

"No, I'm serious."

"Is it scary?"

"No, it's fun!"

"Is it germy?"

Dad laughed. "Life is germy."

"So why didn't you take Pip?" I asked.

"County Cork is a long way from Misty Oaks!" he said.

"I think she's figuring out how to talk anyway."

"I think you're right," Dad replied. He ruffled my hair, and I knew Mom must have told him about our conversation. I thought he was going to say, "Good night," but he said, "Do you sometimes feel that way?"

"What way?"

"Invisible."

My eyes stung, and the tip of my nose got all tingly as though I'd had too much wasabi on my sushi. I blinked a few times then said, "Sometimes. Maybe. A teeny bit." I didn't want to hurt Dad's feelings, but then again, he was asking about *my* feelings.

Dad nodded. "Ava, I'm sorry. Next time I'm talking too much or joking too much or reading too much, speak up, okay? If Mom and I get sidetracked with work or Pip, just talk to us. Don't wait for an invitation. I want to know what's important to you and what's upsetting you."

"Okay," I said and blinked some more. "Dad?"

"Yeah?"

"I got another 100 in spelling. That's all I ever get. Nothing but 100s. The kids in my language arts class think I'm a genius because I can spell words like 'genius.' And 'invisible.' They're rooting for me to get every word right for the rest of the year. Even this boy Chuck who can't spell to save his life and wants to be a championship boxer." I was talking way too fast, but the words came flying out. "Dad, I'm the best speller in the entire grade. I'm, like, a *great* speller!"

Dad kissed me on the head. "You know something, Ava? You're a great daughter too."

I smiled. "It's good I never kissed the Blarney Stone."

"What do you mean?"

"You once called me a 'chatterbox.' What if I never stopped talking?"

Dad laughed. "You're a talker, but you know how to listen too."

He was about to turn off the light when I asked, "Can I write for a few more minutes?"

"Sure." He glanced at my diary and added, "Hey! You're almost out of pages, aren't you?"

"Yup," I said.

He left, and I wrote down our whole conversation. Then I heard his footsteps and a knock on the door. "It's getting late," he said, poking his head in. He added that in *Ulysses*, James Joyce coined the longest palindrome in the Oxford English Dictionary.

"H-U-H?"

"Tattarrattat. T-A-T-T-A-R-R-A-T-T-A-T. It means 'knock on the door.'"

"Can I write that down?"

"Okay, but then lights out in one minute."

"Okay."

"And by the way," Dad said, "I meant what I said."

"About 'lights out in one minute'?"

"About you being a great daughter."

AVA (WITH AN AWW)

Dear Diary,

Bea asked if we could meet at her bookshop instead of our house. She said her parents like her to make herself "useful during the holidays" by unpacking boxes, shelving books, helping customers, and wrapping presents. December is their busiest season.

"Okay," I said, even though I was *not* dying to run into her mom.

After school, Pip and I walked to Bates Books, and on the way, we passed Loudmouth Lacey. She actually squeaked—but just once. I pretended not to hear, and I think Pip really didn't hear, which, in its own weird way, might be lucky. (Maybe she'll always have minor "social issues"? Maybe Lacey will too??)

At the bookstore, I saw Mrs. Bates. At first I wanted to pretend I didn't notice her, but Pip said hi, so I had to say something. I thought of Pointer #4 and said, "I really like your bookstore. It's so cozy."

Mrs. Bates looked surprised. "Why thank you, Ava. Having a bookstore was my dream ever since I was your age. Of course I didn't know what a challenge it would be."

She laughed like we were old friends.

Bea came over and motioned for us to follow her to the back, so we did. She said she had something for us. I thought it might be gum, but she handed us two night-light pens that glow in the dark! If you click the tips, they light up! You could use them to write in the middle of the night if you woke up and didn't want your parents coming in!

When Bea handed me my pen, she said, "Ava, 'Sting of the Queen Bee' was *not* my favorite story in the world, but if you keep writing, someday maybe we can sell your book right here at Bates Books." She pointed to a bottom shelf. "We could shelve it next to E. B. White's."

I liked imagining my name on a bookstore book. I began picturing a kid picking up a book by Ava Elle Wren, and maybe even looking at the front and back and skimming the first page and seeing what it was about and how it sounded and how long it was.

I also started wondering if the pen Bea gave me might feel magical. Then I realized that, magic or not, it was wayyy cooler than the library pen Alex got for his Ernie the Earthworm story because it was proof that Bea and I really had become friends after all.

"Does your mom know you're giving me this?"

Bea said, "Yes."

"Did she say anything?"

Bea looked like she was deciding how to answer. "She said you're a 'young writer with a lot to learn.'"

I couldn't argue with that, and I was glad Mrs. Bates called me a "writer," just as Dad had. Lately I have been thinking about *becoming* a writer, but in some ways, maybe I already *am* one? All I do is write! Well, write and spell.

Bea turned and said, "Pip, you deserve a fancy pen too because you completed all five assignments."

Pip thanked her and clicked the little light on and off, on and off.

"How'd the questions go this week, anyway? Did you talk to anybody good?"

"As a matter of fact…" Pip began.

Just then I saw a blur of orange. Was it the tip of a tail? I remembered hearing about Meow Meow and blurted, "Was it a cat I saw?"

"Great one!" Pip said. "W-A-S-I-T-A-C-A-T-I-S-A-W!" I didn't respond, and Pip said, "Ava, that's an amazing palindrome!"

"Palinwhat?" Bea asked.

"Palindrome," Pip said. "A palindrome is the same backward or forward. Like P-I-P. Or A-V-A."

"Wow," said Bea.

"Or W-O-W," Pip said. "Our parents Bob (B-O-B) and Anna (A-N-N-A) named us Pip (P-I-P) and Ava (A-V-A)," she continued, "and now we're all four word nerds!"

For the first time in my life, I wanted to tell Pip to shhh, be quiet, pipe down, and *shut up*. Was I going to be sorry I'd helped Pip find her voice? Was Bea going to think our whole family was bonkers?

"But what are ya gonna do?" Pip added merrily. "Sue us? S-U-E-U-S?"

Right then, I swear, I wanted to evaporate. I actually *wanted* to be invisible.

But Bea just laughed and said, "My dad is weird about words too." She said he was into alliterations, and that her parents' names are Bill and Beth, and they named their kids Ben and Beatrice. "Hey, Pip, have you met my big brother Ben Bates, my BBBB?"

Out of nowhere, her BBBB appeared, holding a striped orange cat. At first, no one said anything. Then the cat meowed twice and jumped to the floor.

"That must be Meow Meow," I said.

"It is," Ben and Bea replied at the exact same time. Ben turned to Pip, and their eyes locked. I have to say, Pip looked extra pretty, and for a tiny second, I pictured them married with two freckled toddlers, one boy, one girl.

Bea was staring at them too. "I guess you two *have* met," she said.

Pip and Ben stayed M-U-M, and I figured it might help if their younger sisters weren't standing there breathing on them.

I scooped up Meow Meow and gestured for Bea to follow.

As we walked away, Bea whispered, "So the boy Pip had a crush on is...*Ben*?" I nodded and hoped she wouldn't mind that I hadn't told her earlier.

"They do have a lot in common," she said.

"True," I said and listed three things:

1. Freckles
2. Shyness
3. Totally awesome sisters

Bea smiled. "Think they'll go to the dance together? Ben's still a little shy."

"I know they will," I answered.

"Huh."

"H-U-H," I spelled out, then suddenly noticed a copy of "Bookshop Cat," framed and hanging on the wall. "Your story!"

"Yeah, my aunt framed it."

"The psychotherapist?" I'd never said that word aloud before.

"Yeah," Bea replied.

"Cool," I said and asked, "Bea, did Ben read my story?"

She shook her head. "He wanted to, but he couldn't find it online. So he asked me if I had the library booklet, and I said yes, but that I'd torn out your story and fed it to the shredder."

"And had you?" I said, surprised.

"The day I read it. Turning your dumb-head story into confetti made me feel better."

"You mean, even future advice columnists are human?"

"Yup." She laughed, so I did too.

AVA THE AWESOME

DEAR DIARY,

Mrs. (Bright) White called to say my story didn't get picked for the anthology after all. "That's okay," I said. To be honest, I was more relieved than disappointed.

Someday I hope I'll write a story that is so good, I'll *want* it to get published. And even framed!

Could that happen? You never know!

Hey, I just noticed something: *know* backward is *wonk*.

AVA WREN, WORD WONK

12/12
SATURDAY NIGHT

DEAR DIARY,

Last night, I was folding origami snowflakes and snacking on grapes when Ben came over to pick Pip up for the dance. She looked happy, and I felt happy for her—which, trust me, is way better than feeling annoyed by her or sorry for her or worried about her.

After they left, Dad took me to buy a new diary at Bates Books because this one's almost done. (Obviously!) I'm pretty proud of myself for finishing it—and not burying it in my dead diary graveyard.

I think Dad's proud of me too.

Funny how I haven't been scared of blank pages lately. I like writing in them about...*everything*! And while I miss my magic pen, I like my new pen. So long as I have something to write with, I'm okay. It's when I have an idea and don't have a pencil or pen or marker or crayon or keyboard that I go a little nuts.

Anyway, when we bought the diary, Mr. and Mrs. Bates were both there. They were talking about decorating their shop windows, and I offered to make them one hundred origami snowflakes. "Would you?" Mrs. Bates asked. "We could put them in the children's section."

I said "Sure," and that's what I did the whole time Pip was at the dance. It felt like "penance," which is one of this week's bonus words. It means making up for messing up. As I folded and folded, I pictured my snowflakes decorating their cozy bookstore.

Observation: when you buy books online, it's not cozy, there are no homemade decorations, and a cat never comes by to rub your legs.

This morning, when Pip woke up and came downstairs, I asked how the dance was, and she said, "Really fun." Mom, Dad, and I exchanged a look.

I said, "Did everyone have fun?"

Pip said, "Everyone except Isabel."

"Why not Isabel?" Mom asked.

"Because both her parents chaperoned."

Mom and Dad laughed. Then Mom said, "I'm going to get a manicure later. You girls want to come?" Well, that was an absolute lifetime first, so we said sure.

At the nail salon, the lady said, "Pick a color." Instead of picking out a polish by color, like a regular person, I kept turning over the little bottles to read the names. I didn't want to pick "Blushing Bride" or "Nude Attitude" or "Pinking of You" or "Gold Digger." I finally settled on "Life's a Peach." Mom liked "Life's a Peach" too, so now she and I match.

Back home, I was passing Pip's room, which is a total disaster area, and on her desk, I noticed the five yellow strips of paper crinkled up. I poked my head in and asked if I could have them.

"What for?"

"I don't know, to tape into my diary."

"Why?" Pip looked at me as if I were a kook (K-O-O-K).

"Souvenirs," I said, but to tell you the truth, they might come in handy someday. Like, what if I ever have to be a head life coach instead of a junior life coach? Or what if I ever need a Friendliness Refresher Course?

Pip shrugged and handed over the strips, and here they are, all taped in:

WEEK ONE:
SMILE AT ONE NEW PERSON EVERY DAY.

WEEK TWO:
EVERY TIME YOU SEE YOUR REFLECTION, TELL YOURSELF, "YOU ARE TOTALLY AWESOME!"

WEEK THREE:
SAY HI TO SOMEONE NEW EVERY DAY, KID OR GROWN-UP.

WEEK FOUR:
COMPLIMENT ONE PERSON EVERY DAY—ON ANYTHING AT ALL.

WEEK FIVE:
ASK SOMEONE A QUESTION EACH DAY. LISTEN TO THE ANSWER.

When she gave them to me, she said, "Just so you know, I'm never going to turn into a big ol' blabbermouth."

"Good," I said, "because if you turned into a big ol' blabbermouth, I'd have to pretend we weren't related."

After I said that, I realized that I used to sort of pretend we weren't related anyway, and I felt kind of ashamed about that.

Maybe the Pip Pointers and all my trials and tribulations have helped me be a better person too?

AVA, NEW AND IMPROVED

DEAR DIARY,

Ben texted Pip to ask if he could come over to borrow her copy of *Great Expectations*. Lamest excuse ever! His parents own Bates Books! And I bet he could have downloaded it!

Pip said, "Sure," then went crazy cleaning her room and giving it a makeover. She even put her stuffed animals into a giveaway bag (poor things!). She left only one on her bed: a goldfish named Otto (O-T-T-O). She named him for the goldfish in *A Fish Out of Water*. (My favorite P. D. Eastman book is *Sam and the Firefly*, which is about a firefly that makes words that get people into and out of trouble.)

Anyway, when Pip was cleaning up, guess what she found under her bed?

No…

Guess again…

No…

Nope…

My Irish pen!!! The one Dad gave me!!!

Y-A-Y-Y-A-Y-Y-A-Y-Y-A-Y-Y-A-Y!!!

I went running around the house jumping for joy, happy as a lark. (Question: are larks happier than wrens or starlings?)

Dad was happy too. He said, "A good writer should have a good pen."

Then he told me the expression "The pen is mightier than the sword." So I told him *sword* scrambled is *words*. He laughed and gave me a hug.

Pip said, "You should take better care of your pens, Ava. A lot of good things happened because of stuff you wrote."

"A few not-so-good things too," I mumbled.

"True," she replied. "But more good things." She was blushing, and I wondered if someday she'd tell me more about you-know-who who, just then, rang the doorbell.

I'll say this: I love having my magic pen back, but what I like most about it is that Dad gave it to me. And that he thinks of me as a writer, a real writer.

You know what else? Just as Pip found my pen (which in some ways wasn't 100 percent lost), I think I may have found my voice (which in some ways may have been inside me all along).

The key might be to know, in your heart and your head, what you want to say and how you want to say it, and then to just trust that it will come out *right* if you *write* and *write* and *rewrite* and *rerewrite*.

AVA, ASPIRING AUTHOR

PS Has my pen been under Pip's bed ever since we played Word Scrambles on her floor? That was in *September*! (I know because I left the blank page in my diary.)

12/19
AFTER DINNER

DEAR DIARY,

We hung up our holiday wreath. It has pinecones and a red bow and smells like Christmas.

At dinner, I mentioned that I got another 100 in spelling. Dad said, "You're unstoppable!" Pip joked, "GO, AVA, OG!" Mom said, "Great job, honey!" then added, "Can you spell veterinarian?"

I said, "V-E-T-E-R-I-N-A-R-I-A-N."

She said, "W-O-W," so I asked if they knew how to spell the longest word in the English language.

Mom said, "I don't even know what the longest word is."

Dad said, "Antidisestablishmentarianism?"

Pip said, "Supercalifragilisticexpialidocious?"

I said, "*Smiles*—there's a *mile* between the first and the last letter."

Mom and Dad laughed. And the funny thing was: that joke wasn't even that funny. So I told them a funnier one:

"Question: What does a fish say when it swims into a concrete wall?

Answer: Dam!"

They liked that one, so I figured this was a good time to show them what I'd made this morning. I'd found another lion and put it in a jar and added corn oil. It didn't come out as cute as Slimy Simba I, but Slimy Simba II was still cute. I held it up and asked, "Who can guess what this is?"

Dad looked confused.

Pip asked, "W-A-S I-T-A-C-A-T-I-S-A-W?"

"Close!" I said, because it was a palindrome and a feline. "Any other guesses?"

"A-H-A!" Mom said. "I know. It's a L-I-O-N-I-N-O-I-L!"

"Bingo!" I said just to be funny.

"I'm putting this on the windowsill," I announced. "Don't anyone throw it out." I looked straight at Mom.

"Wouldn't dream of it," she said. Later, as we were washing dishes, Mom said, "Ava, we still have a little time, but you and I should start planning your birthday, don't you think?"

"Sure," I mumbled with a shrug. But inside I started doing a happy dance.

AVA THE APPRECIATED

PS Pip just slipped two pieces of paper under my door. One is a sketch of me writing in you. It makes me look much older than ten. I look eleven at least. Maybe even eleven and a half. The other is a note. It says:"If there were a contest for Best Sister, you'd get First Prize."

You know what? I'm taping that right on my wall!!

DEAR DIARY,

I hope I never lose my long-lost pen again. I hope I don't lose the one Bea gave me either.

I'm going to end this diary now, on a palindrome date at a palindrome time. I'll even throw in a palindrome sentence that Dad told us. It is perfect for today, the first day of winter, but it's a *word* palindrome (not a letter palindrome). Here it is: "Fall leaves after leaves fall."

Cool, right?

Well, it's late, so I'd better catch some ZZZZZZZZs.

Wait, I just remembered: I wanted to end this diary with a moral.

First I was considering "Families and friends *count*—and a few even *spell*." But that's not really a moral.

Then I was considering "When you lose something, you find something," because I lost my pen and found my voice. But that's too fortune-cookie-ish.

Then I came up with a moral that's a little *sappy* and a little Ae*soppy*. Ready? Set? Here goes:

Moral: Helping others helps you too.

X-O-X-O-X
ABSOLUTELY AVA

Psssst, it's past midnight, and I just clicked on my new night-light pen. I wanted to see what it's like to write in the dark. Answer: totally awesome! My pen is shining a bright little beam onto my letters and words and putting them all in a spotlight—where letters and words belong!

I've been thinking a lot about pens lately—my Irish pen and my turquoise pen and my light-up pen—and how any pen can be a special pen. Or a power pen. Or a magic pen!

In one of my favorite picture books, *Harold and the Purple Crayon*, what's special isn't really the crayon. It's Harold's imagination. And the author's!

Funny, when you stop and think about it, it hardly even matters what kind of pen you use—or lose! What counts is what you write and think and not the color of your ink. (Hey, that's a poem!)

Anyway, the main reason I got up is that I have been thinking a lot about everything, backward and forward, and I have two things to say:

1. My family *is* seriously nutty. Maybe even extra-chunky-peanut-butter nutty. But they're mine, and I'm not going to trade them in. Not P-I-P. Not M-O-M. Not D-A-D. We're the Wrens, after all. And you know what they say about birds of a feather. (They stick together!)

2. I want to write a book someday. A book that kids my age can read and reread and even *reread*. That is my goal, and I'm putting it in ink right here right now: when I grow up, I want to be an author and write a book—a short one. I've been thinking that it could be about a good kid who does a bad thing and sometimes feels invisible, but who helps her sister find her voice and ends up finding her own. H-U-H. Maybe it could be a diary…

HERE, IN ORDER OF APPEARANCE, ARE THE PALINDROMES IN THIS BOOK:

AVA

MOM

DAD

PIP

HANNAH

ELLE

WOW

ANNA

BOB

HUH

EVE

MADAM I'M ADAM

MA HAS A HAM

SIS

POP

PUP

LION IN OIL

NAN

VIV

SENILE FELINES

SAGAS

STAR RATS

XOX

YAY

ATTA

MMM

STEP ON NO PETS

A MAN A PLAN A CANAL,
    PANAMA

KAYAK

RACE CAR

PEEP

RADAR

DUD

FUN ENUF

'TIS IT

NOW I WON

TOP SPOT

REDDER

A TOYOTA'S A TOYOTA

NO MELON NO LEMON

AHA

EVIL OLIVE

YO, BANANA BOY

LONELY TYLENOL

SOS

REPAPER

M&M

PEP

NOON

SEES

EYE

GIG

SOLOS

TOOT

LEVEL

BOOB

BIB

PULL UP

HOHOHOH

AHHA

WONTON NOT NOW

POOP

REFER

DEED

NOT A TON

DON'T NOD

AKA

#AMM IT I'M MAD

DESSERTS I STRESSED

MUM

YO SOY

DO GEESE SEE GOD?

GAG

TATTARRATTAT

WAS IT A CAT I SAW?

SUE US

KOOK

OTTO

XOXOX

AND HERE ARE 15 BONUS PALINDROMES:

DOG DOO? GOOD GOD!
NEVER ODD OR EVEN
A NUT FOR A JAR OF TUNA
LIVE NOT ON EVIL
MY GYM
PARTY BOOBY TRAP
REWARD DRAWER
SPACE CAPS
HE DID, EH?
BORROW OR ROB
LLAMA MALL
MADAM, IN EDEN I'M ADAM
NOT A BANANA BATON
ABLE WAS I ERE I SAW ELBA
and
IN WORDS, ALAS, DROWN I...

AVA

and

TACO CAT

BY

CAROL WESTON

sourcebooks
jabberwocky

To the cats in my life,

cuddly and otherwise:

Rosie,

Smokey,

Pokey,

Lilac,

Chanda,

Slate,

and

Mike

Dear Brand-New Diary,

I'm really worried. At dinner tonight, Mom said that right before closing, a man came into the clinic with an injured cat. He'd found him shivering in a tree! The cat was scrawny and scared and his neck had a gash and his left ear was bitten up. The man got the cat down and took him to the nearest vet—which was Dr. Gross.

"Poor cat!" I said.

"Is he going to be okay?" Pip asked.

"I don't know," Mom said. "Dr. Gross stitched him up and gave him antibiotics. If he makes it through the night, we'll call the shelter in the morning."

"*If!?*" I said.

Mom nodded. "I think a coyote got to him."

"What's his name?" Pip asked.

"No idea. But he's neutered, so he's not feral." Pip and I know that "feral" means wild, and "neutered" means he can't make baby cats. But does Mom know that stories about hurt cats and dogs make me sad?

"What does he look like?" I asked.

"He's honey-colored," Mom said. "But his right leg and paw are white, and he has a white zigzag above his nose."

"Awww," I said, trying to picture the cat's sweet little zigzag.

"No chip or collar or anything?" Dad said.

"No identification at all," Mom said.

Soon Mom and Dad and Pip were talking about other things, including dinner, which was stuffed eggplant—*blecch*! (Dad just started a terrible tradition of "Meatless Mondays." Fortunately, tonight he also made plain bow tie noodles for me.)

Well, I couldn't stop thinking about how lonely that cat probably felt all by himself in a cage at Dr. Gross's. I wished we could go check on him. But no way would Mom agree to go back to work after she'd already come home and put on her slippers.

I was trying to imagine what it must have been like for the skinny cat when the coyote started attacking him. He must have known it was life or death. He probably thought he was a goner for sure! It was lucky he was able to scamper up that tree, but then he must have been too afraid to come back down! And maybe too weak? I bet he was starving as well as stuck and petrified! Poor little thing!!

Suddenly my nose and eyes started tingling. I blurted, "May I be excused?" but it was too late! Teardrops fell right onto my bow tie noodles.

"Are you *crying*?" Pip asked, surprised.

"Oh, Ava." Mom met my eyes. "I'm sorry I brought it up."

Dad gave my hand a squeeze, and I ran upstairs and splashed

water on my face. I don't know why I was getting so upset about a lost honey-colored cat. But I was. I *am*.

It's just so sad to think of him all alone in a cage instead of a home.

Ava, Upset

DEAR DIARY,

After dinner, Pip came and knocked on my door, which was nice of her. She's been easier to talk to now that she's an official teenager. I think it's because she's been coming out of her shell instead of staying scrunched up inside it.

Anyway, she said, "Want to do another page?" so I said sure. Pip and I started making a book on the third day of winter break when we both got bored at the exact same time. I'm the author and Pip is the illustrator.

I'd wanted us to write *A Duck Out of Luck*, but I couldn't come up with a plot. Then I suggested *A Goose on the Loose*, but I couldn't come up with a plot for that either. Finally we decided to make an alphabet book because alphabet books don't have plots. I said it could be about animals, but Pip said it should be about fish.

Pip is constantly doodling fish. Her favorite stuffed animal is an orange fish named Otto. She named it Otto for two reasons:

1. O-T-T-O is a palindrome. It's spelled the same backward and forward, like A-V-A and P-I-P and M-O-M and D-A-D.

2. Otto is the name of the fish in *A Fish Out of Water*, which was the first book Pip read all by herself. (She has now read about a bazillion books.)

So far, our book is two pages long. It's called *Alphabet Fish*, and these are the two pages:

A is for angelfish.

The shy little angelfish has fins like wings.
Shh! It is hiding among weeds, rocks, and things.

and

B is for bumblebee fish.

If you found this fish, would you name it Bumblebee?
It doesn't buzz or sting, but it's black and gold, you see.

Pip has already made a list of the twenty-six fish she wants us to do. C was supposed to be for clown fish, but I thought about the lonely injured cat and said, "C should be for catfish." Pip agreed and drew a cute catfish with pointy whiskers.

I'm going to sleep now. I hope the lost cat is already asleep.

What I really hope is that he makes it through the night!

AVA...ALMOST...ASLEEP

PS If I cross my fingers for luck, will they stay crossed while I'm asleep?

12/29
MORNING

DEAR DIARY,

In three days, I turn eleven. If I could ask for any present in the whole wide world, I would ask for a pet. But a real pet this time—one with fur.

Whenever I beg for a cat or a dog or even just a gerbil, Mom always says she has enough pets to worry about. She once admitted that the main reason she applied for her job as office manager for Dr. Gross was because the clinic is near our house—*not* because she adores animals.

I can't believe I've been alive for over a decade and have never had a real pet. I've never even had a bunny! Or a turtle! Or a frog!

The only pet Pip and I ever had was a goldfish named Goldy Lox, and we loved her, but she was not exactly Little Miss Personality. (I'm not even sure she was a she!)

Maybelle once had a frog. And last Christmas, she got one of those kits of chrysalides that turn into butterflies. This year, she got a makeup set, a manicure set, and beads for making bracelets. I don't get why so many girls in our class (including my BFF!) all of a sudden want to wear makeup, nail polish, and jewelry.

Maybelle even got a *sports bra* for Christmas. When she showed it to me, I almost fainted on the floor. But I tried to act like it was no big deal.

Later when I told Pip about Maybelle's sports bra, I pointed out that boob (B-O-O-B) is a palindrome and that bras seem like booby traps. I also mentioned that "booby trap" spelled backward is "party boob." Pip said I was being an immature idiot.

Pip thinks she's very mature because she is in seventh grade (I'm in fifth), and she has a boyfriend, Ben. He's our friend Bea's brother, and right now Bea and Ben are both in Chicago.

Our family is not going away on vacation. Mom says we're having a "staycation" in Misty Oaks.

I think "staycation" is a dumb word.

The reason we're not going anywhere is because we don't have a lot of extra money.

We aren't rich, but Mom and Dad say it's better to be *enriched.* That's why Pip takes art classes.

Mom and Dad have offered me writing classes, but I'd rather write just in you, my diary, because then I can write down all my secrets and private thoughts, and no one but me ever reads them.

So far in my life, I have started eight diaries and finished one. The one I finished last week is on my bookshelf. The other six are in my dead diary graveyard, underneath my underwear.

Here is a private thought: I *still* feel bad about what happened to Goldy Lox. Two years ago, I did not take good care of her. I accidentally overfed her, and she did not grow bigger and bigger like Otto in the picture book. She floated to the top, sideways and dead. I wanted to give her a proper burial, but Mom flushed her down the toilet. When I started to cry, she said, "Oh, Ava, it's only a fish." Which was true.

But she was *our* fish.

AVA ELLE WREN, STILL JUST TEN

DEAR DIARY,

Outside, some of the trees have snow on their branches.

Inside, Dad made snowman pancakes just for me. That's when he places three round pancakes in a line (not a stack) and adds chocolate chip eyes to the top one.

"Can you make me a cat pancake?" I asked.

"I can try," he said, and he did try, but the tail and legs blobbed together, and the pancake looked more like an amoeba than a cat.

I said, "Do you know the Aesop fable 'The Cat and the Fox'?" Dad knows I like to read short fables more than long books, probably because (1) they are about animals, and (2) they give you a lot to think about in just a few pages.

He said, "Remind me." So I did. I said:

A fox is bragging to a cat that he knows a ton of ways to save himself from hounds. The cat says he knows only one and asks the fox to show him more. The fox sticks his snout in the air and says, "Maybe someday if I'm not toooo busy." Just then, a pack of hungry hounds comes bounding toward them, barking furiously. The cat escapes by racing up a tree and says, "This is my one and only trick. Which of yours are you going to use?" But while the fox is thinking and thinking, the hounds attack.

Dad asked what the moral was. I said: "It's good to have a plan." Then I confessed that I was still worrying about the honey-colored cat who escaped up the tree, and I wished I had a plan.

When Mom came downstairs, I asked her if she'd called Dr. Gross.

"Ava, he's not in at this hour," Mom said. "And I haven't even had my coffee yet."

Dad handed Mom a mug of coffee and mumbled, "You think the cat will have to be put down?"

Hello! I know what "put down" means! It's a euphemism for "kill"! (I know what *euphemism* means too. It's a nice way of saying something not nice. It's also an extremely advanced spelling word.)

"Depends on his condition," Mom said.

I stood up so fast, my chair fell over. "You can't kill him!" I said.

"Sweetie," Mom replied, "Dr. Gross is not in the business of killing animals. He does everything he can to *save* animals. But if the cat isn't going to get better…"

"Please don't kill him!" I felt like Fern in *Charlotte's Web* when she tells her father not to kill the runty newborn piglet. (Note: Mr. and Mrs. Arable love their daughter Fern very much, so they let her keep the piglet, and she names him Wilbur.)

"I'll call you when I get to work," Mom said. "And now I'd like to change the subject. Have you thought about what you want for your birthday?"

Without missing a beat, I said, "Yes. I want a cat. I want *that* cat!"

A-V-A Who Wants A C A T

Dear Diary,

Mom didn't call, and when I couldn't stand it anymore, I called her even though she doesn't like to be "interrupted" at work.

"Did he make it through the night?" I asked.

"Yes, he did. He's a tough old boy."

"Can I visit him?" I could feel my heart beating extra fast.

"Actually, the man from the shelter just came and picked him up."

"*No!*"

"Ava, that's *good* news. They'll try to find a home for him."

"I want him to live in *our* home! And not all cats get adopted! You always say people like kittens best—and he's a scratched-up grown-up with ears that don't match."

"Honey, we've been through this. At the end of a long day, the last thing I want to do is deal with pets."

"It's *pet,* not pets! Singular, not plural. And you won't have to. *I'll* do everything! Besides, dogs need to be walked, but cats just sit around purring all day."

"Ava, it's a moot point, so you might as well save your breath.

That cat's been stitched up and sent on his way. He's not here anymore. I'm sorry."

"Where is he?"

"At the rescue center."

"What 'rescue center'?"

"I have to get back to work now," Mom said, sounding exasperated. But she didn't get that *I* was exasperated too!

We hung up, and I looked up "rescue center" on Dad's computer. Guess what? The Misty Oaks Rescue Center is pretty close to Taco Time, our favorite place for lunch!

Ten minutes ago, one of Dad's students showed up. Besides writing plays, Dad tutors reading and writing and helps high school seniors with their college essays. When the teenager rang the doorbell, Pip was coming downstairs. She had slept right through breakfast, which she never used to do. I decided to ask Dad if he'd give us money for lunch.

Dad said okay because he likes having a "quiet house," which is "impossible" when we are "underfoot."

Pip is now zipping up her winter boots. Here's what she and Dad don't know: I have a plan. A BIG one!

AVA ON A MISSION

12/29
3:33 (A NUMBER PALINDROME!)

DEAR DIARY,

Pip and I went to the rescue center! It's a brick building with an old bike stand near the entrance.

We parked our bikes, and I almost stepped in something warm and brown and gooshy. I told Pip to be careful, and she looked down and said, "Dog doo? Good God!" (D-O-G-D-O-O-G-O-O-D-G-O-D). That made us both crack up because "Dog doo? Good God!" is an extremely funny palindrome.

Inside, behind a counter, a lady with a high ponytail told us that if we wanted to visit the cats, we had to be accompanied by someone at least eighteen. She looked like she was around eighteen herself! Pip got nervous and whispered, "We should leave," but I convinced her to stay so that we could people-watch—and animal-watch!

I wanted to know why someone lucky enough to have a pet would decide to give him or her up. Pip and I sat down and started observing, and soon we had answers.

- A man in a suit came in with a barky dachshund and said

he and his wife had a newborn baby and couldn't keep their noisy dog.

- A woman with dark purple fingernails came in with a pit bull with claws painted the same color and said her new landlord had a "no dogs policy."
- A hippie-ish couple came in with five black-and-white kittens and said their tuxedo cat had seven kittens and they could keep only two.
- A boy and his mom came in with a bunny they called Peter Rabbit, and the mom said the boy turned out to be allergic, and the boy said, "And, it poops all over the place."

It was sad, really. All these people coming in with furry animals and leaving with empty pet carriers and droopy leashes.

Next thing you know, a family with four kids showed up and said they wanted to "pick out a dog."

Ponytail Lady left to take a lunch break, and a bald bearded guy took her place. He told the parents that if they wanted a "companion animal," they had to fill out an application form. I started talking with the oldest kid, and Pip started talking with the youngest kid and told her she liked her yellow mittens, and suddenly a lady with a little ring in her nostril came and invited their family to meet the dogs.

When the lady with the nostril ring said, "Right this way," I made a face at Pip and hopped right up. Pip hesitated, but then she hopped up too! We tagged along as though we were Kid #5 and Kid #6!

The family was so excited about getting a dog that they didn't notice us sneaking in behind them. And the lady with the nostril ring was so happy that someone was *adopting* a pet rather than dropping one off that she didn't either.

The family followed the signs for dogs and turned left. Pip and I followed the signs for cats and turned right.

Soon we were standing in front of cages and cages of cats! It was like a wall of cats!

Each cat had a food bowl, water bowl, litter box, and soft cloth. Some were asleep, but most were wide-awake. One poked his nose out, and another poked his paw out, and another twitched his ears. There was an old white cat and an old black cat pacing back and forth, back and forth. I wondered if they were senile felines (S-E-N-I-L-E-F-E-L-I-N-E-S), which is a palindrome I came up with recently. Then I felt bad for wondering that. Poor cats!

On the cages were clipboards with pieces of paper. They said things like "indoor cat" and "outdoor cat" and "finicky eater" and "not good with other cats." One said "gentle with children." Another said "may require time to warm up to new people."

"Where's the one that got hurt?" Pip asked. We both knew that we needed to find him before someone found us!

"I'm *looking*!!" I said. And I was! I was searching and searching for the honey-colored cat. I did not want to fall in love with the wrong cat by mistake!

Pip spotted a sign about "adoption options." It said that if you couldn't provide a "forever home," maybe you could provide a "foster home." She read it out loud and said, "Think we can talk Mom and Dad into letting us have a cat for a month?"

"I don't want a cat for a month!" I said. "I want a *forever* cat! And I want the one we came to find!"

But where was the cat with the bitten-up ear and soft white zigzag?

We walked down the hall and entered a second room filled with nothing but kittens. Observation: the only thing cuter than a wall of cats is a wall of kittens! The room smelled a little tiny bit of cat pee (kitten pee?) but I didn't even mind because the kittens were *seriously* cute—probably because they were so *unserious*. One was swatting a ball. Another yawned a big yawn, and then started closing its eyes and flopped over—fast asleep on its food bowl. Another was napping *inside* its litter box. Each cage had one toy and two or three (or even four!) kittens, and most were licking each other and playing and tumbling. One fluffy gray kitten stood on its hind legs and put out a front paw as if to high-five me. It was hard not to fall head-over-heels in love—but I resisted because I'd made up my mind about which cat I wanted to save.

Pip pointed out a sign that said: "Please adopt kittens in pairs." She looked at me and said, "I wish we could."

Just then a short lady with a long braid walked in. "Hello, girls." She was carrying a cage and must have assumed we were allowed to be there.

"Hello," we chimed and followed her back to the room with the grown-up cats.

The volunteer placed the cage on top of a row of other cages. "This yellow tabby arrived this morning," she said, adjusting the clipboard. "Got himself into quite a scuffle, poor fella."

Pip and I walked over to the yellow tabby. He looked at me with big, sad, round green eyes. He was like a skinny lion cub with a white Harry Potter zigzag above his nose. His right leg was also white, as if he'd broken it and was wearing a cat cast. And the tip of his tail was white, as if he'd dipped it into paint.

Pip and I both knew this was the cat we'd come to find! I looked at him and he looked at me, and I wished I could adopt him right then and there!

"He's a bit skittish," the lady said.

"Scottish?" Pip said.

"Skittish," the lady repeated. "Frightened. You know, a scaredy-cat. But who can blame him? He's been through a lot."

"How much does he cost?" I asked.

Pip stared at me, eyes wide.

"Kittens come with a small price tag—unless you take two," the lady answered. "But older cats are free. We *want* them to find good homes."

"Can I put this one on hold?" I asked.

"That's not our policy." She smiled. "But you may spend a few minutes with him to see if it would be a good fit. And your parents can fill out an application stating that they understand that pet ownership is a big commitment and responsibility." We did not mention that our parents were not with us and didn't even know we were there. "Cats can live fifteen to twenty years," the lady continued, "so we always check references. But if everything goes smoothly, you can take him home today. I bet he'd like that."

She gave the cat a smile, and the cat gave me a blink, and I wished I *could* promise him a forever home.

"Would you like me to go over this with your parents?" the lady asked. Pip and I exchanged a look and said, "No!" at the exact same time.

I wanted to say, "Jinx!" but instead mumbled, "Thanks anyway." Then Pip and I hurried off and raced downstairs and out of the building.

Outside, we started biking the three blocks to Taco Time. Pip was just ahead of me.

"He neeeeeeds us!" I called up to her.

"If we get to keep him," Pip shouted back, "we could name him van Gogh."

"Van Gogh?"

"Because of his ear!" she shouted. Pip has a poster of van Gogh sunflowers and once told me that when van Gogh couldn't sell any paintings, he got so upset and unstable that he cut off a piece of his ear and mailed it to a woman. Or something.

Well, I did not want to name our cat after a depressed artist with mismatched ears! So I said so—or shouted so.

"You have any better ideas?" Pip shouted back.

I considered saying, "Dandelion!" because then we could call him Dandy. But the cat's fur was more *lion*-colored than *dandelion*-colored. I also considered saying, "Honey," but he was a tough tomcat so that wouldn't work. I shouted, "Not yet."

Pip and I got to Taco Time and parked our bikes. I was trying and trying to come up with the perfect name, but I couldn't think of one. We ordered and our tacos arrived, and soon I was staring at mine and suddenly it occurred to me that the hurt cat was the exact same color as my...taco!

"I've got it!" I said a little too loudly. "Taco!" I couldn't believe what my brilliant brain came up with next. "No! Wait!" I said. "His name is... *Taco Cat!* T-A-C-O-C-A-T! It's a palindrome!"

"That's genius!" Pip said, and I could feel myself beaming. "But you'll never be able to convince B-O-B and A-N-N-A." To be funny, Pip spelled out our parents' names.

"Never say 'never,'" I said.

I will now stop writing because my hand is about to fall off. (Figuratively, not literally.)

AVA WREN, FUTURE CAT OWNER?

AFTER DINNER, WHICH WAS STEW

Dear Diary,

Pip's boyfriend texted Pip a photo of a big lungfish in the Shedd Aquarium. She texted him back a photo of the little catfish in our ABC book. Then Ben texted her a whole *school* of fish. From the face she made, you'd think he'd sent her a box of chocolates.

I just looked up "school of fish," and here are ten more good expressions:

1. A kindle of kittens
2. A prickle of hedgehogs
3. A troop of monkeys
4. A band of gorillas
5. A pride of lions
6. A leap of leopards
7. A tower of giraffes
8. A zeal of zebras
9. A flamboyance of flamingos
10. An exaltation of larks

A bunch of people is called a *crowd*, but there's no expression for a bunch of wrens—besides *flock*.

If I could invent one for my birthday, I'd invent "a wonder of wrens."

Wonderful Ava Wren Who Wants Wonderful Taco Cat

DEAR DIARY,

Pip and I made a drum fish and an electric eel. The electric eel, I'm sorry to report, is pretty ugly.

Funny that some things are *pretty ugly*, but nothing is *ugly pretty*. This is my eel poem:

E is for electric eel.

The electric eel looks like a worm or a snake.
Beware, beware of the shock it can make.

I wish I could *shock* my parents and tell them that we *are* adopting a cat, instead of having to ask (or beg).

AVA, ASKING ABOUT ADOPTING AN ANIMAL

12/30
RIGHT BEFORE DINNER

Dear Diary,

Pip and I didn't know whether to tell Mom and Dad that we went to the rescue center. We didn't want to lie, but we also didn't want to get in trouble if they found out.

Finally I decided to spill all to Dad. A few weeks ago, Mom and Dad both said I should speak my mind. Besides, my birthday is in two days, and parents don't ground kids right before their birthdays, do they?

While Dad was paying bills, I got out thirteen index cards and wrote one letter on each. When I finished, I made a fan out of them so Dad could see it was a palindrome: W-A-S-I-T-A-C-A-T-I-S-A-W.

"Was it a cat I saw?" Dad read. "Good one, Ava!"

"Dad, Pip and I *did* see a cat," I said. "We went looking for that injured cat Mom told us about. And we *found* him!"

"What do you mean 'found' him?"

"At the rescue center."

Dad looked more puzzled than mad. Maybe now that Pip is a teenager and not as shy as she used to be, he doesn't object to our doing some things on our own?

Weird that Pip is old enough to be independent and wear a bra and have a boyfriend!

I don't want to be independent or wear a bra or have a boyfriend. I just want Taco Cat!

I told Dad all about him, even his name.

"T-A-C-O-C-A-T? That's clever." Dad laughed. "But, Ava, you know Mom doesn't want a pet."

"I know." I wanted to add that it's not fair that Mom gets to spend all day with tons of animals when we don't even have one. "But I almost wish we had a mouse problem," I said. "Like, an *explosion* of mice."

And that's when I got an idea. An amazing idea. It was so amazing, I decided to call Maybelle and ask her to come over and help me with an "art project." (Dad said we could have a short after-dinner playdate since it's still vacation.)

But when I called Maybelle, she said, "Zara asked if she could sleep over, and I said okay and now we're about to have dinner. Can she come too?"

"I guess," I mumbled, surprised that Maybelle was having a sleepover with Zara, a girl who had just moved to Misty Oaks in September. Since when did my best-friend-since-first-grade have sleepovers with anyone besides *me*? To be honest, the thought of Maybelle and Zara having dinner together or even microwaving marshmallows made my stomach lurch.

Next I called my neighbors, Carmen and Lucia. I could hear Carmen asking her mom in Spanish if they could come over. Their parents are from Peru. Carmen and Lucia are twins and they each have a Paddington Bear. They say their bears are twins from Peru too.

I wish I could speak Spanish. I wish I were bilingual instead of just lingual. People say I have a "way with words," but I know only one language—so far.

I went into Pip's room. She was illustrating our F page:

F is for flying fish.

This lucky fast fish has wings and can fly.
When mean fish swim close, it jumps ten feet high.

"Pip," I asked, "do you know how to draw mice?"

She made a face and said, "Duh."

"Good," I said and told her my amazing idea—my amazing *plan*. She said it sounded dumb—but she got right to work.

AVA THE AMAZING

DEAR DIARY,

Six people in one bedroom is pretty squooshy, but we sat in a circle: Pip and me, Carmen and Lucia, Maybelle and Zara. Pip showed us all her life-size drawing of a model house mouse. It had dot eyes, round ears, short whiskers, a curly tail, and (I don't know how Pip does this) kind of a cute personality. I gave everyone a pencil and scissors, and in the middle, we put a stack of paper, erasers, and a pencil sharpener.

"Why are we making paper mice?" Carmen asked. She and Lucia were both wearing green. They don't dress exactly the same, but they always wear the same color.

"Because my birthday is the day after tomorrow and I want a pet cat." I said that I wanted to show our parents how practical a cat could be.

"Practical?" Maybelle asked.

"Like, what if we had a *mouse invasion*?"

"I don't get it," Zara said. She crossed her legs, but not the crisscross applesauce way. She crossed them yoga style, feet on top. I wondered if she thought mouse-making was immature. Was it? "What are you going to do with all the mice?"

"Put them all over the furniture," I said. "First thing tomorrow, before our mom and dad wake up."

Zara looked like she didn't quite get it. (Confession: I didn't quite get what she was doing on my bedroom floor.) She shrugged and said, "I once had a pet guinea pig."

"In Peru, people *eat* guinea pigs," Carmen replied.

"Ewww!" Zara said.

"They roast them on spits," Lucia added.

"Did you ever try one?" Zara asked, squinching her face.

"They're yummy with garlic and lemon," Lucia admitted, looking sheepish. (Note: *sheepish* is a funny word. No one ever looks cattish or doggish or guinea-piggish.)

"What happened to your guinea pig?" Carmen asked.

"My cousin got to keep it when I had to move in with my grandparents," Zara answered, putting down her scissors.

It was strange having this new girl in my room. Were we supposed to ask about her family? Or *not* ask? After an awkward moment, Carmen said, "We once had pet mice."

"All they did was multiply!" Lucia added.

"It was disgusting!" Carmen said.

Pip wasn't saying much of anything. She was being as quiet as she used to be. Probably because of Zara.

I decided to tell the Aesop fable "The Country Mouse and the City Mouse." The twins like it when I tell fables, so I even spiced it up a little:

A country mouse invites a city mouse for dinner, but there's nothing to eat besides a little pile of beans. Then the city mouse, who is snobby, invites the country mouse to come dine with him. The two mice sneak into a fancy banquet hall and are about to dig into delicious leftovers—everything from lobster to banana splits. But no sooner do they start nibbling at what's left of the feast, than a hungry cat and giant barking dog chase them into a hole.

"That's it?" Zara asked.

"What's the moral?" Lucia asked.

"It's better to eat beans in peace than lobster in danger," I said.

"Or maybe it has to do with making new friends?" Zara said.

"I don't think so," I said because I didn't, and because I didn't like that Zara was making friends with *my* friends.

"You know what?" Maybelle said. "We're making *suburban* mice!"

"I just made three *blind* mice!" Carmen said. "Look!"

Lucia looked, then quickly erased the eye dots from three of her mice. "Me too!" she chimed, and they both started humming "Three Blind Mice."

Did Zara think the twins were being babyish?

Maybelle said, "Did you know that if you hold your nose, you can't hum?"

"Really?" Pip said.

"Really!" Maybelle said and told us all to start humming "Three Blind Mice." We did, even Zara. Maybelle raised her arms as if she were conducting a symphony. "On your marks, get set, go!" she said and held her nose, so we all held our noses. She was right: Our mouse-making factory fell silent! You can't hum and hold your nose at the same time!

After we'd made many, many mini mice (alliteration alert!),

Pip got out *Alphabet Fish,* and Zara started asking questions. I know asking questions is *consider*ed *consider*ate, but she was asking a *lot* of questions. She asked why we were making a book (because we felt like it), and why it was about fish (because Pip likes fish), and if we'd ever made a book together before (no), and if Pip took art classes (yes), and if I took writing classes (no), and what G was going to be for (goldfish).

She said, "G could be for guppy."

I said Pip and I had already decided that G was going to be for goldfish.

Zara said, "Guppy sounds cuter." I looked at Maybelle to see if she thought Zara was being a bossy busybody, but Maybelle was admiring Pip's illustrations. "And I like the title *Something Fishy,*" Zara added.

"The title is *Alphabet Fish,*" I replied in a firm voice. Carmen and Lucia exchanged a worried look. "And G is for goldfish," I stated, "in honor of our pet goldfish who died." I almost told her that we'd named her Goldy Lox because LOX and LOCKS are homonyms: "lox," like smoked fish, and "locks," like the blond hair of the girl with the three bears, so it was a funny punny name. But I didn't want Zara to ask any more questions.

Soon Maybelle's mom came to pick up Maybelle and Zara so they could have their stupid sleepover. Maybelle's mom said she could drop the twins off too, "no problem."

But it *was* a problem because when everyone climbed into the same car, talking and laughing, I felt a twinge of loneliness. (Actually, a few twinges.)

By the time I went back upstairs, Pip was in bed with a book, and I knew she wouldn't want to talk. So I got in bed too and started writing in you.

I wish Taco Cat were here to keep me company.

AVA, ALONE WITH A MOUNTAIN OF MICE

12/30
MIDDLE OF THE NIGHT

DEAR DIARY,

I just turned on the light-up pen that Bea gave me, the one her parents sell at their bookshop. I wanted to double-check that my alarm was set for 6:45 a.m. so I could sneak down and do what I had to do.

I was also curious about how you say a "bunch of mice," so I looked it up. Guess what? It's a "*mischief* of mice"!

AVA THE MISCHIEVOUS

12/31
6:55 A.M.

DEAR DIARY,

I did it!

You know how in *Goodnight Moon*, there's a mouse peeking out on every single page? That's how it looks downstairs! There are mice everywhere! On chairs and on the sofa and bookshelf and floor and windowsill and coffee table…you name it, I put a mouse on it. I even put two in the fridge!

Now that it's (almost) daytime, a teeny tiny part of me wonders if this whole plan is dumb. Or if Mom will get mad.

Oh well, too late!

As Dad says when he's quoting Shakespeare, "What's done, is done."

In fifteen minutes, Dad and Mom will wake up and see my mischief of mice. (My *mess* of mice?) I put one on Dad's desk with a note that says, "All I want for my birthday is T-A-C-O-C-A-T. I will take excellent care of him. Pleeeeeeeeeeeeeeeeease."

The "please" might have even more e's. I didn't count.

I keep thinking about Taco Cat. I hope we can get him and that no one else adopts him first. I'm not too worried because

Mom says kittens are more popular than cats, especially "cats with issues." (According to Mom, mismatched ears are an "issue," even though mismatched eyes are considered a good thing, spelled *heterochromia*.)

Poor Taco! He probably feels so lost and alone!

I remember once when I felt lost and alone.

I was about three, and Mom and I had gone shopping in a giant department store. I don't know if Mom got distracted or if I did, but suddenly the high heel shoes next to me did *not* look familiar. I looked up, and the lady next to me was *not* my mother! I burst into tears. Where was my mom? Would I ever see her again??

The lady with the high heel shoes took me to a security guard and next thing you know, a loudspeaker announcement said: "Will the woman who lost her daughter please report to the information desk?" I stood there with a bunch of strangers for what felt like a really long time until finally Mom came *clip clip clipping* over. I guess the security people could tell by my expression that she was not a kidnapper, and Mom swooped me up and took me home.

I wish I could swoop Taco Cat up and take him home.

I'm really tired, but I'm trying to stay awake until it gets light outside. It's already officially New Year's Eve, which means it's almost New Year's Day—and my eleventh birthday! A new year and new age!

I'm practically falling asleep though. If I were a cat, I would have conked out in my food bowl.

Maybe I'll go back to sleep for just five more minutes and get up when Mom and Dad get up.

AVA IN ANTICIPATION

12/31
NEW YEAR'S EVE MORN

DEAR DIARY,

I slept until 10:30! I did not mean to do that! I meant to wake up hours ago so I could see Mom and Dad's reaction!

Not only did I oversleep, but just now, I banged my funny bone. It was not one bit *funny*!

Mom must already be at work. She says vets work all the time because animals get sick all the time. Dr. Gross works every day except Sunday, and even on Sunday, someone has to go to the clinic to feed and check on all the animals.

Question: Did Mom and Dad like my mice?

Bigger question: Will they let me have a cat??

Time to find out!

AVA, AWAKE

Dear Diary,

I opened my door and saw a trail of mice. It went all the way from my room to Dad's desk! One little mousie after another! I figured this *had* to be a good sign.

"Did you find them all?" I asked Dad.

"Good morning, Sleepy Head," he said. "Yes, I think we did."

"Even the pair in the cheese drawer?"

"You put mice inside the fridge?"

"Just two," I said *sheepishly* (but not mouseishly). "What did Mom think?"

"Actually, she thought it was funny. She knows this means a lot to you."

"Really?"

"Really. You did a good job of expressing yourself."

I said thanks, and Dad told me a story about when he and Mom were housesitting when they were newlyweds. They bought a little bag of fancy chocolate-covered almonds and left them on the kitchen counter. In the middle of the night, they heard a loud clattering and were afraid burglars had broken in. So they went downstairs and turned on the lights. No one was there, but the bag of chocolates was empty, and on the kitchen floor, they saw itty-bitty mouse droppings! The cat burglars were...a *mischief of mice*!

I laughed and planned to tell that story to Chuck in school. He is pretty much the only fifth-grade boy I talk to, and we like to make each other laugh. I've known him even longer than I've known Maybelle, because in kindergarten we sat next to each other on the bus on an apple-picking field trip.

"So can I get Taco Cat for my birthday?" I asked Dad straight out.

Dad pushed back his big brown chair and did not say no. He said, "Want to run some errands? You and Pip went through a lot of paper last night."

I said, "Sorry," even though I could tell Dad wasn't mad. He likes it when Pip and I do "creative projects" together.

"What do you think: Great Wall or Taco Time?" Dad asked.

"Taco Time! Should I wake up Pip?"

"At your own risk," Dad said because lately Pip has been waking up grumpy. I took the stairs two at a time, and with each giant step, I could feel myself coming up with a brand-new plan.

"Pip!" I said, knocking and barging in at the same time. "Get up!" I started talking a mile a minute.

Pip opened her eyes and listened. "It'll never work," she said, sounding like the big brother in *The Carrot Seed*. The one who doesn't believe in his little brother's little seed and says, "It won't come up."

"You should be more optimistic," I said.

"You should be less annoying," she said.

But here's the thing: she's getting dressed, so I think she *is* willing to give my plan a try.

AVA, FULL OF PLANS

12/31
1:30 P.M.
AT THE RESCUE CENTER!

DEAR DIARY,

At Taco Time, Dad asked if I knew how to spell "quesadilla" and "guacamole." I spelled both words, no peeking and *no problema*. So far in fifth grade, I've gotten nothing but 100s on all my spelling tests. English is by far my best subject. (I stink at math, which is Maybelle's best subject, and I'm only okay at gym, which is Chuck's best subject.)

After lunch, Pip told Dad that we wanted to take him "on a field trip." Dad looked suspicious, and I stayed quiet (M-U-M). Pip was saying everything exactly as we'd planned. "The rescue center is really nearby," she casually remarked.

"The rescue center?" Dad made a face, then said, "Oh, why not?"

Pip gave me a little kick under the table, so I gave her a little kick back. We both know that deep down, Dad is a mushball when it comes to us kids. And deep down, maybe he likes cats as much as we do.

While we were walking the three blocks, Dad started rambling about how writers and cats are natural companions. He said that James Joyce wrote about cats, and so did Charles Dickens and

Mark Twain. He said Ernest Hemingway left money in his will for his cats in Key West, Florida, "and some were polydactyl."

"Polywhat?" I said.

"Polydactyl. It means having extra toes." Dad said that most cats have five toes on their front feet and four on their back, but "mitten kittens" are born with extras.

"H-U-H," I said, because our family likes spelling out palindromes. I was trying to picture "mitten kittens" and trying to picture myself as a famous writer known for her children's books and her faithful furry feline friend, Taco.

"T. S. Eliot," Dad added, "wrote cat poems that got turned into the Broadway musical."

"*Cats*," Pip said.

I thought about T. S. Eliot and said, "If you take the S away, his name backward is T O I L E T."

Dad laughed. Pip said, "Dad, it's mostly your fault we're word nerds!" (which is true, even though Mom must have agreed to name us P-I-P H-A-N-N-A-H and A-V-A E-L-L-E).

Anyway, we're now at the rescue center. Ponytail Lady said that before we could go upstairs, Dad had to fill out a form. So when Dad started writing, I did too.

Gotta go! Here comes Nostril Ring Lady!

AVA, ABOUT TO SEE ANIMALS

DEAR DIARY,

Nostril Ring Lady escorted us upstairs, past the barking dogs, and into the cat rooms. Then the short lady with the long braid came in and said, "I remember you girls!" I asked if our cat was still there, and she winked and said, "He's been asking about you." She was carrying a cage with a *kindle* of kittens.

Dad and Pip and I stayed in the room with the older cats, and at first, I didn't see Taco anywhere. I looked and looked, but…no Taco. What if she was wrong? What if someone *had* adopted my yellow tabby? We kept searching and searching.

Suddenly I noticed a cage on the floor in the corner. And there he was! I saw his green eyes and taco-colored fur and jagged ear and white leg and little zigzag. He was looking right at me! It was like he was *waiting*—just *waiting*—for me to recognize him. Our eyes met and my heart melted!

I sat on the floor, put my face near his cage, reached in, and tried to pet him with my fingertips. He seemed nervous and was still skinny, but not as skinny as when I first saw him.

"Dad," I said. "I found him! He neeeeeeds us." I reminded

Dad for the quintillionth time that Taco was all I wanted for my birthday—and that my birthday was *tomorrow*.

Pip said, "Dad, let's just do it. Let's get him!"

"We have to talk to Mom," Dad said, which meant he was at least considering it. Then he looked into Taco's big sad eyes and whispered, "Buddy, this might be your lucky day."

AVA, FULL OF HOPE

DEAR DIARY,

Believe it or not, we are in the car outside Dr. Gross's clinic waiting for Mom! She's getting off early because it's New Year's Eve. When she walks out, Dad and Pip and I are going to surprise her and drive her straight to the rescue center!

In my almost eleven years in Misty Oaks, I'd never once been to the rescue center, but this will be my *second* time today and my *third* time this week!

Dad said not to get our hopes up, but of course our hopes are up. Mine are sky-high! They are as high as Mount Everest, which Maybelle once said is over 29,000 feet high and the highest mountain in the world.

While we sat in the car, Dad told us that Mom is the only person in Dr. Gross's practice who doesn't have a pet. I knew that Dr. Gross has a dog named Cowboy, and the front desk lady and her partner have three cats (one has just one eye), and one of the technicians has a ferret, and another has a canary, but I did not know that *everybody* has a pet except Mom.

Right now, Pip and I are in the backseat, and while I'm writing, Pip is illustrating my H poem:

H is for hammerhead shark.

The great hammerhead shark is a scary beast.
If it saw you at sea, it would think: What a feast!

It is almost 4:30 p.m.
In seven and a half hours, at midnight, I will be eleven.
In one hour, will I have a cat?
Gotta go! Here comes Mom!!

AVA WITH FINGERS CROSSED

New Year's Eve Night

Dear Diary,

Mom said yes!!!
   I have a cat!!!
   His name is Taco!!!
   ❤❤❤❤

AVA

1/1
MY ~~BIRTHDAY~~ NIGHT

DEAR DIARY,

Last night, I woke up and it was pitch-black outside. I wasn't sure if the glittery Times Square ball had or hadn't dropped, or if it was or wasn't my birthday. Was it a new year? Was I a new age: 11 on 1/1?

All I knew for sure was that Taco was 100 percent *mine*!

I have a pet cat!!!

We brought him home in a cat carrier, but Mom said we had to keep him in the bathroom the first night. That didn't seem very welcoming, but Mom said that when a cat is not "accustomed to a new environment," it's best to take things slowly, and that Taco would feel safest in a "small, confined space." I was so glad we'd actually adopted him—and bought canned food and pet bowls and kitty litter—that I didn't object.

Right before I went upstairs, I told Taco that he was the best birthday present in the whole wide world. He still seemed scared (skittish?), so I didn't pick him up, but I petted him and told him I'd be back first thing in the morning.

Well, this morning, he was curled up on the bathmat. He'd

eaten some food and used his litter box and even covered his P-O-O-P with sand, which cats do. Mom said these were all "good signs." She showed me how to scoop out his dried doodies and shake off the sand and flush the P-O-O-P down the toilet. I told Pip it reminded me of the game we used to play by Nana Ethel's creek called "Panning for Gold." Pip said I was crazy, but I knew she remembered Panning for Gold as well as I did. (I like that we have a lot of the same memories.)

Anyway, Mom and Dad had said they'd take me and my friends out for pizza for my birthday, but I didn't want to leave Taco alone that long. So I called Maybelle and Bea and Carmen and Lucia and invited them to come here instead.

Bea and Ben had just gotten back from vacation, and she said she'd be right over. She's two years older than me, but we became friends last fall. That's when she and I came up with the five Pip Pointers to help Pip shake off her shyness.

Well, everyone got to meet my new cat—but not in the way I was hoping.

I'd pictured Taco taking turns climbing onto their laps, purring and kneading. Kneading is what cats do when they press their little paws against you one at a time, left and right, right and left. Mom said that newborn kittens knead and purr when they nurse because that's how they tell their mother to stay still. Grown cats knead and purr mostly when they are relaxed and happy.

Taco did not knead or purr at all.

What happened was this: We all stood by the bathroom door. Bea and Pip were on tiptoe, Maybelle and I were in the middle, and the twins were crouching down (dressed in matching yellow). The plan was for me to open the door a crack so everyone could peek at Taco, asleep on the bathmat. I did—but Taco dashed out! He made a beeline (cat line?) for the sofa! And he's been hiding underneath it ever since!

All anyone saw was a flash of fur!

Before I could stop them, Carmen and Lucia raced after him and got on their stomachs and started groping under the sofa. Not only did Taco *not* come out, he *hissed* at them! He even grumble-growled! It was a strange, low, unhappy sound.

Mom said we needed to let him get comfortable on his own terms. She also said that adult cats don't meow to other cats, they meow only to people, usually to "ask for food or water or space."

Well, we let Taco have some space while I opened birthday presents. Maybelle gave me a rainbow-colored beaded bracelet that she'd made just for me. The twins gave me a gold picture frame (which I like) and a fuzzy pink jewelry box (which I don't). Bea gave me a book of funny cat photographs from her parents' shop. Pip gave me a scarf. And everyone sang, "Happy Birthday!" and ate pizza and cake.

Now that I'm eleven, I wonder if I seem a lot older than the twins, who are in fourth grade. I also wonder if I seem a lot younger than Bea and Pip, who are in seventh. Am I growing up at the right speed?

I can hardly believe I'm eleven. I won't be a palindrome age again until I'm twenty-two!

AVA WREN, BIRTHDAY GIRL

1/2 (WHICH LOOKS LIKE ONE-HALF BUT MEANS JANUARY 2) SATURDAY 11:30 A.M.

DEAR DIARY,

This morning Pip and I were playing Battleship. I was trying to locate her submarine and said, "B-7?"

She said, "BELIEVE."

I said, "BEWARE!"

She said, "BEHOLD!"

I said, "BEHAVE!"

She said, "BEEHIVE!"

We both laughed, and she said, "Ava, come with me to Bates Books."

I said I wanted to stay with Taco. But Pip pleaded—and even offered me a pack of bubblemint gum. I knew she was hoping to run into Ben since Bea and Ben's parents own the bookstore and Pip hadn't seen him since vacation started. Finally I said okay—if we made it quick.

We bundled up and off we went, but Ben wasn't there and neither was Bea. Their fluffy orange and white cat, Meow Meow, was, and he rubbed against us, his tail high in the air. He is as sweet as a…Creamsicle!

Guess who else was there? Chuck! He looked different because he'd gotten a haircut and maybe gotten a little taller since last week? (Is that possible?) He also had a Band-Aid under his chin—the tan kind, not the cartoon character kind.

Mrs. Bates was helping him find a book about a boxer. She's good at helping kids pick out books. When Chuck saw me, he came over, so Mrs. Bates started helping Pip instead. She was telling her about some "new YA paperbacks." YA stands for young adult. (Confession: I don't think of Pip as a Young Adult. I think of her as a Big Kid.)

Well, I told Chuck about our new cat, and he told me a joke:

Question: Why did ten cats jump off a bridge?

Answer: They were copycats.

He expected me to laugh, but I said, "That's not funny. That's sad." I was picturing a soggy bunch of forlorn felines.

He said, "Ava, it's a *joke*, and besides, cats have nine lives!"

I rolled my eyes, and he asked what I was going to buy. I said, "A pen," and he helped me pick out a striped pen covered in orange and black velvety cloth with a tiger's head.

"What's a cat's favorite color?" he asked.

"What?"

"Purrrrple!"

This time I did laugh, and I also poked him in the ribs and he poked me back. I asked what happened to his chin (he tripped), and then he said he had to go because his mom was waiting for him.

Pip was still "browsing," so I found a coffee table book about cats in paintings and took it to an alcove with giant pillows. The origami snowflakes I'd made for Mrs. Bates last month were still on the walls. Meow Meow came and stretched out by my feet, and even though I wanted to check on Taco Cat, I felt happy with Meow Meow, waiting for Pip and looking at colorful cats.

I've liked Bates Books since I was little, even before Bea and Ben switched into our middle school.

It's true that I like short books, not long books, and that I am not an "avid reader" like Pip. But I really like bookstores—especially cozy ones with fluffy cats.

If I ever had to be stuck—stranded!—overnight somewhere and I could pick where, I would definitely pick a cozy bookstore.

I could see how a kid might *think* she'd want to spend the night in a candy store, but that would get boring and you'd end up with a stomachache. A rescue center might sound fun, but that would get noisy and you'd feel sorry for the animals. And a zoo or an amusement park would definitely get creepy at night.

But a bookshop, if you kept all the lights on, could be nice.

And you wouldn't get bored. Even if you were locked in for *hours*! Plus, if you got lonely at night, you could read *Goodnight Moon* or *Owl Moon* or *Many Moons* or *Kitten's First Full Moon* or any bedtime book, even one without a moon or a cat. And if you got tired of reading, you could look at pop-up books and coffee table books.

I started thinking about words on screens versus words in books. Like, with texting or Facebook, you can read what people are thinking *right that very second*. But with books, you can read what people took *ages* to think about. Some authors take years and years to write a book that a reader can gobble up in hours, which, for the reader, is a very good deal.

Paintings are like that too. An artist works on them for a long time, but you can enjoy them in a short time.

Anyway, even though I was enjoying looking at cat paintings with Meow Meow, after a while I wanted to check on my own cat, so I showed Pip my favorite pages then said, "Let's go."

Pip said okay, and she bought two books and I bought my pen and we went home.

Guess what? We hadn't missed a thing because Taco hadn't come out from under the sofa!

He still hasn't!

Dad said we need to be patient. Mom said you can't rush a cat.

Since Dad had told Pip and me about writers and cats, I told Dad and Mom about artists and cats, and the book I'd been looking at. I said that Goya painted spooky cats, and Picasso painted pointy cats, and Renoir and Cassatt painted soft, cuddly cats. I also said, "If Pip drew Taco, it would be a drawing of a sofa." Everybody laughed.

AVA, AMUSING

DEAR DIARY,

Maybelle invited me over after lunch, but I was positive Taco was going to come out and I didn't want to miss the big moment, so I said I couldn't. What I didn't know was that Taco was planning to spend the *whole entire afternoon* under the sofa!

At night, when we're asleep, he creeps out and eats and uses the litter box. But during the day, all he does is hide. I've been getting on the floor and lifting the flap of the sofa to check on him. It's like lifting a curtain, except there's no show.

At least he doesn't hiss or grumble or growl. He just stares. And sometimes backs away.

I want Taco to be happy, but I wish he'd hurry up about it!

AVA, IMPATIENT

1/3 (WHICH LOOKS LIKE ONE-THIRD BUT MEANS JANUARY 3) SUNDAY MORNING, STILL IN BED

DEAR DIARY,

Next to my bed, along with my diary, I always have *Aesop's Fables*, and I just dog-eared the cat fables.

Isn't that funny: *dog*-eared the *cat* fables?

I also reread "Belling the Cat." Here's how it goes:

A bunch of scared mice come out of their holes to have an emergency meeting. They are trying to decide what to do about a hungry cat that won't stop sneaking up on them. Finally a young mouse says he has solved the problem. "We should put a bell on the cat," he states, "so we can hear it coming." The mice all think this is a great idea—until a wise senior citizen mouse says, "And which of you would like to put the bell on the cat?"

The moral: "It's easy-peasy to *have* a great idea, but that's just the beginning."

My great idea was to adopt a grown-up, scratched-up, funny-looking cat.

What if it wasn't a great idea? What if it was a horrible idea?

AVA, AGGRAVATED AESOP ADMIRER

DEAR DIARY,

Maybelle called this morning to invite me to go with her family to the circus and dinner in the city. I knew that would take all day so I said I'd better stay home because Taco was bound to come out.

Maybelle said, "Really? You sure?" She sounded disappointed.

When I hung up, I peeked under the sofa, and Taco wasn't even there! I looked all around the living room and downstairs, and he was nowhere to be seen. I searched upstairs and finally found him under Mom and Dad's bed. I told Mom and Dad everything, and they said to call Maybelle right back and tell her I changed my mind.

I did, but it was too late! Maybelle said she was sorry, but her parents had bought an extra ticket and wanted her to invite someone, and then Zara called, so she invited her.

"It's okay," I said, even though of course it wasn't. When we hung up, my throat was so tight, I could barely swallow. Why hadn't I said yes to Maybelle?

Pip could tell I was upset and suggested we work on *Alphabet*

Fish. She said her art teacher, Ms. Richichi, says doing something creative always helps you feel better.

Well, Pip and I worked on two pages, and it helped a little, but only a little. I think Pip might be more into this fish book than I am. Still, I did "I is for icefish" and:

J is for jellyfish.

The jellyfish looks like a clear parachute.
Do you think it's ugly or do you think it's cute?

Taco, by the way, is not ugly or cute. He is…invisible.

Confession: I'm actually glad school starts up again tomorrow even though that will mean waking up early and having home-work. I miss seeing Maybelle and Chuck. And I like English—though I'm not sure how I'll feel about it now that Zara and Maybelle have started hanging out. (Did I used to think that *Zara* was invisible?)

I am about to go to sleep. I wish Taco were next to me, purring.

But he's not. I don't know where he is. I'm alone and trying not to be furious at myself for being too dumb to go to the circus. Am *I* a clown??

Sometimes at night, it's hard not to think bad thoughts. Like: What's wrong with me that all I wanted for my birthday was an injured old scaredy-cat? And what's wrong with Taco? Is he a D-U-D?

Grrrrrrrrrrr.

While we were brushing our teeth, Pip reminded me that our next page is "K is for kissing gourami." As a joke, I asked if she'd ever kissed Ben. She spat into the basin and said, "No!" Then she quietly added, "Not yet anyway."

I have to say, I am shocked. I can't picture Pip kissing anyone.

Then again, last year I could hardly picture Pip *talking* to anyone!

AVA, ASTONISHED

1/4 (WHICH LOOKS LIKE ONE-QUARTER BUT—OH NEVER MIND!) 2:30

DEAR DIARY,

First day back in school! I'm in the library, by the big window.

Homeroom was fun. People were talking about their vacations, and even though ours was a "staycation," I got to tell everyone about Taco Cat.

Lunch was *not* fun. Maybelle sat next to me wearing a string necklace with a M on it, then Zara sat down wearing a string necklace with a Z on it!

At first, I thought they'd each gotten it for Christmas. Then I wondered: what if it *wasn't* a coincidence? Had Zara copied Maybelle? Was she a copy*cat*?

Just to be nice, I said, "I like your necklaces."

Zara said, "We got them yesterday! We got matching bracelets too." She put her hand out and dangled her bracelet. Maybelle put her hand out and dangled *her* bracelet. I wished I were at least wearing the rainbow bracelet Maybelle had beaded for my birthday, but I wasn't, so I kept my hands down.

They high-fived each other with their dumb dangly bracelets, and I felt like Taco: I wanted to run away and hide.

Worse, they were talking about the circus—the ringmaster and tightrope walkers and miniature ponies and jugglers and acrobats. They said two kids from the audience got to help a clown spin some plates.

"We loved that!" Zara said.

Well, I did *not* love the way Zara was saying "we" about Maybelle and her. Maybelle and I are supposed to be the "we"!

For once, I was glad that lunch period was ridiculously short. I don't think I could have sat there one more minute fake-liking their matching stuff and hearing about the oh-so-fun circus I'd stupidly missed.

When it was time for English, Maybelle and I sat down and Zara sat right next to us.

Mrs. Lemons began a unit about haiku. Haiku are poems that started in ancient Japan. They're pronounced "hi coo" and are made of three lines: five syllables, seven syllables, five syllables. Mrs. Lemons said they're often about the natural world— "seasons, plants, and animals"—and the best ones use imagery and "give readers something extra" to think about.

She gave us an example of a haiku that a poet named Basho wrote way back in the 1600s:

OBSERVED BY DAYLIGHT,

THE FIREFLY IS ONLY

A SIMPLE INSECT.

275

Then she asked us to write one in class and one for homework.

Since Mrs. Lemons once taught us that onomatopoeias are words that are spelled the way they sound, I tried to be extra creative. I wrote:

THE CRIES OF CATS ARE

ONOMATOPOETIC:

HISS, GROWL, MEOW, PURR.

We went around the room reading our haiku aloud. Maybelle's was about constellations, Chuck's was about icicles, and Riley's was about her pony (of course). Well, since you are my diary, I hope it doesn't count as boasting if I tell you that Mrs. Lemons *loved* my haiku. I swear, she wanted to marry it! (L-O-L)

Chuck liked it too and said, "I bet Ava even spelled 'onoma-towhatever' right!" Everyone laughed.

Except me. I just smiled.

AVA, WHO WRITES HAIKU

PS Writing haiku is more fun than writing fish rhymes.
PPS Writing in you is also more fun because a diary is like a really good friend who is always there and always listens and never goes off with anybody else.

DEAR DIARY,

Taco Cat came out in the open today!

At least that's what Dad said. When Pip and I came home, Taco was back under the sofa, and all we could see was the tippy tip of his tail. Pip tried to lure him out with a phone charger cord, but he wouldn't come. I tried to coax him with yarn, and he started reaching for it with his front paws, but the phone rang and he went back under again. (It wasn't even a real phone call! It was a telemarketer!!)

After a gross "Meatless Monday" starring sweet potatoes and tofu (which Pip and I used to call Toe Food), I kneeled down by the sofa and lifted the flap. I was remembering how Bea and I had helped Pip come out of her shell with our Pip Pointers. They included making eye contact, saying hi, paying compliments, and asking questions. So I looked right at Taco Cat, said hi, told him how handsome he was, and asked about his stitched-up ear.

Taco did not say hi back, but he did blink at me. Twice. And I think he appreciated my attempt at human-feline communication.

Still, his behavior is frustrating! It makes *me* want to growl.

Mom said she is going to bring home some cat treats and that might help.

I thought about this for a while then announced that we could set up a reward drawer (R-E-W-A-R-D-D-R-A-W-E-R). I said we could put treats in there for us too, like licorice for her, M&M minis for Pip, and bubblemint gum for me.

Mom said the drawer should be just for Taco, but that maybe she'd bring home a cat brush too.

Anyway, after being excited about getting Taco, then disappointed by how much he hides, I am hopeful again. Dad says I'm keeping the faith.

Is keeping the faith like believing in happy endings?

A lot of kids' books have happy endings, but Aesop's fables mostly have morals.

Tonight, I got in my pajamas and tried to write the homework haiku. For a long time, I just looked out at the full moon, hoping for inspiration. Finally, I saw the old moon in a new way, so I started counting syllables on my fingers and wrote:

THE FULL MOON TONIGHT

IS CAUGHT IN HIGH BRANCHES, BUT

IT WILL FIND ITS WAY.

AVA WREN, PATIENT POET

DEAR DIARY,

All of us were having breakfast (except Taco), and Dad said, "One of the best things about being a grown-up is morning coffee."

For some reason, I counted that out, and I said, "Hey! That's a haiku!"

Mom said, "A haiku?"

"It's 5-7-5!" I repeated the sentence aloud: "One of the best things / about be-ing a grown-up / is morn-ing cof-fee."

Dad smiled but said that even though it was the right number of syllables, I couldn't call it a "real haiku" any more than someone can read a phone book onstage and call it a play. "There's math, and then there's poetry."

I said, "Number one, *phone books* are only in old movies. And number two, I know about real haiku." I told him Basho had written over a thousand of them.

Pip said her Spanish teacher told her a Spanish palindrome: *Anita lava la tina* (A-N-I-T-A-L-A-V-A-L-A-T-I-N-A). It means: Anita washes the tub.

I said, "W-O-W."
Mom said we'd all better hurry up or we'd be late to school.

Ava Wren, Haiku Expert

DEAR DIARY,

In school, we read our haiku aloud, and Mrs. Lemons said, "Ava, that is a real haiku!"

I felt proud—until I noticed Zara whispering to Maybelle. They were wearing their stupid matching bracelets.

Is Zara trying to take Maybelle away from me? Is she succeeding??

At the end of class, I decided to talk to Maybelle. But Mrs. Lemons said she wanted to talk to *me*, so I had to stay behind while Maybelle and Zara walked out together.

Mrs. Lemons asked if I thought Pip might want to make a poster of my moon haiku to hang in the hallway. She knows Pip is artistic because Pip used to be in her class.

I said I'd ask then tried to catch up to Maybelle and Zara. But I didn't see them anywhere! It made me feel all alone even though there were kids everywhere. It just hurts when your old friend makes new friends.

Back home, Pip said sure to illustrating my moon-in-a-tree haiku, so she got out thick poster paper and we started working quietly at the kitchen table.

Guess who came creeping over? Taco Cat!

I thought he was finally going to say a proper hello! And I liked his timing because I needed a cat cuddle. But all he did was sniff my sneakers—then dart inside an empty grocery bag.

Did he come out of his shell only to disappear into a bag??

Doesn't Taco know by now that I'd never try to hurt him? And why is everyone, from my cat to my BFF, running away from me?

Well, Taco didn't stay in the bag long, and when he emerged, I said, "Cat's out of the bag!" which was funny if I do say so myself. Pip half-smiled, but I could tell she was deep in the world of her drawing. That happens to me sometimes too: I start writing and lose track of everything else.

AVA, AUTHOR, NOT ARTIST

I wrote another haiku:

JANUARY SNOW

FLAKES FLOATING FLYING FALLING

WHISPERING WINTER

AVA, ALLITERATING

Dear Diary,

Pip wanted to work on *Alphabet Fish*, but lunch was fish sticks and dinner was mahimahi (weird word), so I said I'd had enough fish for one day.

She said, "Oh, c'mon!"

I said, "You're my sister, not my boss!" She looked a little mad and a little sad, and that made me feel a little bad (especially since she had illustrated my moon haiku), so I scribbled a quick K rhyme:

K is for kissing gourami.

The kissing gourami do just as they please.
They kiss all day and don't care who sees.

When I handed it to Pip, she didn't say anything, but I swear, she blushed a little.

After dinner, I was struggling with my math homework and getting very distracted by Taco. He'd found a fly in the living room and was chasing it all around. It was as if he'd completely forgotten Dad and I were there. Dad and I gave each other a smile because Taco was finally making himself at home. But then Taco caught the fly with both paws, and we exchanged a frown because, well, it was disgusting that Taco ate a fly up as if it were a Raisinet!

Oh, that reminds me: Dad told me a math joke.

Question: What did the math teacher say when he was offered cake?

Answer: "I prefer pi."

Get it? I-P-R-E-F-E-R-P-I.

(H-O-H-O-H-O-H)

Pi, according to Maybelle, is a special specific number that starts with 3.1415 and never stops. Maybelle's family actually celebrates Pi Day each March 14. They make pie!

Anyway, I told Dad a math joke too.

Question: Why should you never argue with a ninety-degree angle?

Answer: Because it's always right.

Maybelle was the one who told me that joke.

Is she telling jokes to Zara now?

Sometimes I wish I had a remote control for my brain so I could change the channel and not think about things I don't want to think about. Is that one reason Pip likes books so much? Because she can just enter another universe and stay there as long as she wants?

AVA, WHO LIKES PIE MORE THAN PI (AND SOMETIMES WANTS TO CRY)

DEAR DIARY,

Taco let me pet him! I was on the sofa, and he came and sat on the armrest under the lamp. I started petting him gently, and he didn't make a run for it. He stayed there—for at least thirty seconds.

I was so happy, *I* felt like purring!

Taco still hasn't purred, but Mom said he is "learning to trust us."

At dinner, which was drumsticks, Dad said that today Taco jumped onto his desk, stepped on his keyboard, and typed some pretend words.

I said, "Maybe Taco wants to be a writer too!"

Pip said, "He could go by T. C. Wren. And his books could be shelved next to E. B. White's."

I said, "I wonder what the E in E. B. White stands for."

Dad said, "Elwyn."

Pip and I looked at each other, stupefied (which is a bonus spelling word that means shocked, not stupid). We said, "Elwyn?!" and then, "Jinx!" and then spent the rest of dinner trying to think of other kids' book authors who use the initials of their first names. I came up with J. K. Rowling. Mom and Dad and Pip came up with:

- J. M. Barrie, who wrote *Peter Pan*
- A. A. Milne, who wrote *Winnie-the-Pooh*
- J. R. R. Tolkien, who wrote *The Hobbit*
- P. L. Travers, who wrote *Mary Poppins*
- C. S. Lewis, who wrote *The Lion, the Witch, and the Wardrobe*
- E. L. Konigsburg, who wrote *From the Mixed-Up Files of Mrs. Basil E. Frankweiler*
- S. E. Hinton, who wrote *The Outsiders*

Believe it or not, Pip has read all those books!

When authors use initials instead of names, readers don't know if a woman or a man wrote the book. But that shouldn't matter anyway, as long as the book is good.

I wonder if I really will be able to write kids' books someday. I hope so!

A. E. WREN

PS Here are the first names, in order, of all those authors: Joanne, James, Alan, John, Pamela, Clive, Elaine, and Susan. (No offense to E. B. White, but Elwyn is the weirdest name in the bunch.) PPS Zara is a weird name too.

Dear Diary,

Today was a bad day.

At lunch, I sat with Maybelle, and naturally Zara came rushing over with her red tray and grilled cheese. Maybelle asked about Taco, and Zara said, "I thought its name was Paco." (She said "it" not "he," and "Paco" not "Taco.") "*His* name is *Taco Cat*," I said and explained that palindromes, like T-A-C-O-C-A-T, are spelled the same backward and forward. I also said that I'd gotten to pet him for almost a minute. Well, I could feel Zara looking at me as if I had a gnat on my nose, and I realized how lame that sounded— like my cat is an antisocial loser. And I'd even exaggerated!

Finally I decided to just go ahead and admit that it's hard because I'd wanted a cat and now that I have one, it's not like we hang out.

Zara said, "In my old school, I'd wanted a boyfriend, and when I got one, we didn't hang out either."

Maybelle laughed, but I didn't see what that had to do with *anything*.

Sometimes Zara says zany things. Maybe that was her way of

saying boys notice her. Which they do. Because she's new. And prettyish. And a little flirty.

When boys talk to her, she sometimes lights up and laughs. They sometimes do too! (Even Chuck!)

I don't understand flirting. How to do it or why you'd want to. Question: Am I a *tom*boy with a *tom*cat?

"Your mom's a vet, right?" Zara asked.

"She manages the practice of a vet named Dr. Gross," I answered. "She does bookkeeping and deals with clients." Zara didn't say anything, and it was strange, feeling as if I had to defend my mom. "Sometimes she comes home with sad stories," I said and started babbling. "Like, about dogs who eat rocks or socks. Or lunatic bunnies who don't like being cooped up. Last month, a lady dropped her dog off for a shot and she didn't come back to pick him up! She *abandoned* him!"

I expected Zara to ask what happened because that's what people do when I tell pet stories. But Zara said, "Oh, so she's not actually a vet."

That bugged me, and when Zara switched from pets back to boys, things got worse. She said Pip and Ben make a "cute couple" and asked if they'd kissed. Pip hadn't liked when *I'd* asked that, and I knew she'd *hate* that other people were talking about them.

Zara even asked who I like. I said I didn't have a crush (because I don't) but added that I have friends who are guys (because I do). To give an example, I added, "Like Chuck." I might have smiled a tiny bit because I was remembering three dumb jokes he'd recently told me:

Question: How do you make a hot dog stand?

Answer: Take away his chair.

Question: What's brown and sticky?

Answer: A stick.

Question: What did the dog on the roof say?

Answer: "Roof!"

Well, Zara said, "I can find out if he likes you."

"Of course he likes me," I said. Then I added, "But not *that* way!" Suddenly Zara was standing up, and I realized that she was going to talk to Chuck—and ruin everything! "Wait, no, no, don't *ask* him!" I blurted. "He and I are friends, just friends, and that's all we want to be!"

I looked at Maybelle for backup, but she was talking to Emily Jenkins, who had just put down her tray.

"Ava, relax," Zara said, "I'm just trying to help."

I sat there, frozen, while Zara bounded over to Chuck. I wanted to go after her, but it was like I was stuck to my chair. And the thing is, I wasn't even 100 percent sure if Zara was butting into my life to cause trouble, or if she was, as she put it, "trying to help." Does she meddle on purpose, or does she just not think about things? (Do I think *too much* about things?)

When Zara reached Chuck, he looked surprised. He was sitting with Aidan, Jamal, and Ethan (who are all good at sports), and she leaned in and started talking to him. Suddenly he turned and stared at me, wide-eyed. I wanted to disappear! Moments later, she bounded back. "He says he has to think about it," she reported and smiled as if she'd done me a favor!

Next Zara lowered her voice and asked, "Do either of you have a pad?"

I was about to say, "No!" but Maybelle said, "Let me check." And then (you won't believe this!) Maybelle dug into her backpack and unzipped a cosmetic case and handed Zara what I guessed was a little wrapped-up pad.

"Thanks," Zara said. "I'll be right back."

When she was gone, I said to Maybelle, "You got your period?!" She said no but that she and her mom had had a big talk, and her mom said that Maybelle might want to start carrying pads in case she or a friend ever needed them. Which I guess Zara did. (!!!)

"Whoa." I couldn't imagine ever having a conversation with my mom about that stuff—though maybe someday Pip will explain it all to me. Right now, whenever Mom and Pip talk about growing up, I just walk away.

I was also surprised Maybelle hadn't told me her mom had given her pads. We usually tell each other everything—even though some things take longer to come out than others.

"You and Zara are becoming pretty good friends," I mumbled because I couldn't bring myself to say, "Don't let her come between us!" or "I liked things the way they were!" or "You and I were friends first!" or "Why are you so nice to someone who keeps minding everybody *else's* business?"

Maybelle shrugged, and Zara came back, and we headed

toward class. I had to stop at my locker to get the rolled-up poster, and instead of waiting, they kept going, which made me feel even worse than before. I watched them walk away, and they were so close to each other that the sides of their backpacks bumped together.

Seconds later, I walked in and handed Mrs. Lemons the poster. I'd written the haiku in big, neat letters, and Pip had made the trees look like hands and the moon look like a shimmering golden ball.

Mrs. Lemons said she wanted to share my haiku with Mr. Ramirez and Mrs. White, the school librarian and the town librarian. I always think of Mrs. White as Mrs. (Bright) White, since she was Miss Bright before she married Mr. White. Mr. Ramirez, by the way, just got engaged to his boyfriend who teaches history at a private school. When he told us, everyone said, "Invite us to the wedding!!!" and he said he wished he could but it was going to be just family.

Anyway, Mrs. Lemons said that Mr. Ramirez and Mrs. (Bright) White had arranged for our fifth-grade classes to have a two-day writing workshop. She said that on January 26 and 29, Jerry Valentino, the children's author who had judged the library contest, was going to come with "writing tips and hands-on exercises."

I said, "Cool," even though that was the library contest that had gotten me into so much trouble.

Meanwhile, I had to find a seat. I looked around, but Maybelle and Zara were sitting together in front of Riley and the three

Emilys, and there were only two empty seats left. One was next to Chuck. Usually that would be fine, but he glanced at me then quickly looked away, which he never does. So I decided to sit by myself in the back.

I felt like I was in Siberia (wherever that is).

For a second, I wished we were all still in fourth grade, when we had assigned seats and rotating jobs like snack helper and line leader, and our teachers walked us everywhere, and we were the oldest in the school, and math wasn't hard, and friendships weren't fragile, and nobody ever tried to elbow her way into my life without an invitation.

AVA, ALL ALONE

PS I looked up Siberia. It's a freezing cold place on top of Russia. (Well, in *northern* Russia.)

DEAR DIARY,

Pip and I just finished "L is for lionfish." Lionfish are beautiful but poisonous.

Zara is pretty and poisonous.

I was going to ~~confront~~ call Maybelle, but I thought, "What if she's *with* Zara?" so I didn't. (I changed "confront" to "call" because "confront" sounds unfriendly, and Maybelle is my friend.)

Mom brought home cat treats, a cat brush, and yellow tulips. Problem: When no one was looking, Taco nibbled at the tops of the tulips, so now all the petals have tiny bite marks.

(I thought it was cute, but Mom didn't.)

Taco let me brush him with the new brush and Mom kept me company and said that it's not easy training cats.

"What do you mean?" I asked.

"Most dogs can be bribed, but most cats can't," she said. "Can you picture a cat shaking or rolling over or playing dead?"

"I guess not," I admitted, but then told her the Aesop fable "The Thief and the Housedog," which goes something like this:

In the middle of the night, a thief came to break into a house. The housedog started barking and barking, so the thief tossed him two big, juicy steaks. But the dog was no fool. He said, "You can't bribe me! You're not my master and this is not my dinnertime. In fact, I'm going to bark louder than ever."

Mom smiled. "What's the moral?"

"If someone tries to bribe you, beware," I said.

Mom said that I could think of cat treats and dog biscuits as "rewards" and "incentives" and ways to "show love" and "encourage behavior modification"—and not just "bribes," since real bribes are bad and illegal. She also said that Dr. Gross's technicians often give pets treats after they squirt goo in their eyes or shove pills in their mouths or do procedures that are no fun.

It was nice talking to Mom, and inspiring too. In fact, I could feel myself coming up with a plan.

At dinner, we talked more about cat treats. Pip said she'd heard about a cat that got trained to use a toilet bowl instead of a litter box. Mom said toilet-training cats is challenging. Dad said potty-training *us* wasn't "a piece of cake" either. I said, "Can we change the subject?"

Dad laughed and taught us all a new word: ailurophobia. It means "fear of cats."

AVA, WHO IS NOT AILUROPHOBIC

DEAR DIARY,

Last night right before bed, I put my new plan into action. Even though cats are not easy to train, I thought Taco might be easy to *tempt*. I decided to try to lure him into my room using treats as bait. I was tired of Taco playing hard-to-get!

Remember how Dad used our paper mice to make a bee-line—a mouse line!—from my bedroom to his office? Well, after everyone had gone to bed, I opened the new bag of treats, spilled some into my hand, and placed them one by one in a line from the top of our stairs to the foot of my bed.

After I turned out my light, I tried to stay awake to see if Taco would come into my room. I even made believe I was on a safari in Africa. I pretended my bed was a jeep, and it was a moonlit night, and I was staying up late to spy a lion or leopard (or maybe a *pride* of lions or *leap* of leopards).

I kept my eyes peeled for as long as I could…but I must have fallen asleep.

I just woke up and guess what? Taco Cat is not in my room, and neither is the trail of treats! When no one was looking, he must have snuck in and eaten them all up, one by one!

Believe it or not, I consider this progress.

Ava the Astute

PS It's cool that cats can see in the dark—well, unless it's totally pitch-black.

DEAR DIARY,

The bonus words on today's spelling test were *catastrophe* and *cataclysmic*. Both start with *cat* and mean when something truly terrible happens.

Chuck used to tease me about all my 100s on spelling tests, but we haven't talked to each other since Zara talked to him about liking me. I know that's not a *cat*aclysmic *cat*astrophe, but it feels like one!

I miss our little looks. Like, whenever something funny happened, we used to look at each other. Today, when Riley said something about her horse, I wanted to sneak a peek at Chuck, but I knew I might feel dumb if he saw me looking at him. And what if he *didn't* see me looking because he *wasn't* looking back? That might feel even worse!

It didn't help that Maybelle and Zara were both wearing their string necklaces today and also matching sky-blue nail polish. I tried not to care, but I couldn't help but care, especially when I heard them giggle together. I started feeling sorry for myself, and then I started getting mad at myself for feeling sorry for myself.

It is *not* easy being eleven!

After school, I asked Maybelle if she wanted to sleep over. She said she had "plans." I mumbled, "Okay," but felt as if I'd swallowed an ice chip. I mean, if she had mathletes or a dentist appointment, she would have just said so. We stood there for an awkward moment and it was as if Zara were standing right between us.

I said "Bye" and walked home with Pip, and she made me work on *Alphabet Fish*. M was supposed to be for "minnow," but Pip wanted to change it to "mudskipper" because mudskippers have eyes that stick out on the top of their heads, like aliens, and she said they'd be more fun to draw. I said, "Whatever," because I didn't care whether M was for minnow, mudskipper, or...Moby Dick.

After a few minutes, I handed her a mudskipper rhyme and also:

N is for nurse shark.

If you were sick and this shark called nurse
Took care of you...you might get worse!

Confession: I was thinking of Zara when I wrote that. If Zara had never moved to Misty Oaks, she would never have moved in on my friendships with Maybelle and Chuck!

Is Taco my new friend? Maybe. But he could be a lot friendlier!

AVA, ALIENATED (THAT'S HOW IT CAN FEEL WHEN
YOUR FRIENDS AREN'T BEING FRIENDLY.)

DEAR DIARY,

You know how they say to think outside the box? Taco *pooped* outside the box.

And it was my fault!

We were watching TV and I used the downstairs bathroom. Afterward, I shut the door behind me and completely forgot that we're supposed to leave it open so Taco can go in and out and use his litter box whenever he wants. Just now I remembered that I'd closed that bathroom door *hours* ago! I went down to open the door but...too late! There were two little poops right next to the door. Cat scat! (Scat is a fancy way to say P-O-O-P—or poo or doo or dung or manure or feces or excrement.)

Poor Taco! He'd obviously tried to be a good boy! He could have pooped *anywhere*. And cats prefer to bury their P-O-O-P and not leave it out in the open for everyone to see.

I got a bunch of toilet paper, picked up the poops, dropped them into the toilet, and flushed.

I'm glad Taco didn't pee outside the box. That would have been way harder to clean up.

Cleaning up the P-O-O-P was surprisingly easy—not that I want to go into the pooper-scooper business.

Here's what I've been thinking: Most dogs are trainable and protective and loyal and friendly and fun to take on walks (which is good). But when you take your dog on a walk, you have to take a plastic bag with you and deal with the doody (not good). You're expected to just *stand* there while your dog is crouching and straining as though it's nothing. And neither you, nor your dog, are supposed to act embarrassed even though you're in public. If your dog has diarrhea, you're still supposed to clean it up. And if there's no garbage can in sight, well, you're supposed to just carry the P-O-O-P (or diarrhea!) around in your plastic bag until you find one.

Yuck!!

I think cats are more dignified—but then, I'm more of a cat person than a dog person.

AVA, CAT PERSON KID

PS I was brushing my teeth and left the water running. Taco jumped up, stuck his head under the faucet, and starting lapping at the water. It was cute. But it was *not* dignified!

PPS I'll admit that if a stranger wanted to break into your house, a dog might be a handier pet than a cat. Like, there are *watchdogs*, but no *watchcats*. A dog might also be handier if you accidentally spilled food on the floor.

Dear Diary,

Dad made a big Irish breakfast: eggs, bacon, sausage, baked beans, mushrooms, tomatoes, and scones.

I asked Maybelle to come over, but she had "stuff to do." She said I should come over Monday after school.

Monday feels far away, but I said, "Okay," and decided that that's when I'd ask her what Zara has been saying about me.

Mom just took clean clothes out of the dryer to fold, and when the laundry pile was all toasty warm, Taco hopped on top and settled in with his legs tucked under him. He looked like a hen sitting on eggs and seemed pleased with himself.

Mom and I smiled as if we were sharing an inside joke. I was glad Mom didn't shoo Taco away or make a remark about cat fur on clean clothes. She even turned to Taco and said in a singsongy voice I'd never heard before, "Are you finally making yourself at home? Yes, you are. Yes, you are."

It was sweet, to tell you the truth.

AVA AND TACO AT HOME

Dear Diary,

Dad and I were making Sunday sundaes, and I told him I wished Taco would jump on my bed and snuggle with me and purr.

Dad said, "Be patient. Rome wasn't built in a day."

I was about to ask, "How many days was it built in?" but instead said, "He's had *ten* days!"

"And he *is* warming up to us," Dad pointed out. We both looked at Taco. He'd found a patch of sunshine on the kitchen floor and was grooming himself: licking his five-toed paws and "brushing" his mismatched ears.

He might have sensed that we were talking about him because he lifted his head and looked right at me.

"Who's a good boy?" I said and got on the floor and puckered up as if to give him a kiss. He sniffed my lips and sneezed a little cat sneeze. That made Dad laugh—and *that* made Taco scamper off.

Since Maybelle was (supposedly) busy, Pip and I texted Bea to see if she wanted to come over. She texted, "Can Ben come too?" Pip liked that idea, so we texted back, "Sure."

Now Bea and Ben are *both* about to walk in. Pip is nervous, I can tell. She just put on lip gloss. Lip gloss! Next thing you know, she'll be wearing eyeliner! Or cologne!

She has also been cleaning her room. She said she's almost done.

I said "almost" is an unusual word because all its letters are in alphabetical order.

I also said that my initials are in alphabetical order and hers aren't.

She said, "Who cares?" I said that if my first name were her *middle* name, she'd be Pip Ava Wren and her initials would be P. A. W.—like "paw." She rolled her eyes as if she had way more important things to think about—like brushing her hair and getting ready for you-know-who.

A. E. W.

DEAR DIARY,

There wasn't enough snow to make snowmen, so Pip, Ben, Bea, and I made snowkids. Pip and Ben kept making happy faces at each other, and their gloves kept touching. Well, Pip and Ben's snowboy turned out way cuter than Bea's and my snowgirl. Pip can draw *and* sculpt! At the last minute, I said they should give their snowboy freckles, so they dotted him with Apple Jacks. Unfortunately, the "freckles" looked like chicken pox. (Fortunately, no one blamed me.)

Back inside, we all made hot chocolate and ate peanuts. (We aren't allowed to have peanuts in school, so we always stock up at home.) Pip showed Bea and Ben *Alphabet Fish*—because she's proud of it and we're up to "P is for porcupine fish." We also talked about Meow Meow, Taco Cat, and even long-lost Goldy Lox. It was fun talking to an eighth-grade boy.

Ben told us a joke he'd heard:

Question: What's the difference between a dog and a cat?

Answer: When a dog has a wonderful master who feeds him and grooms him and cleans up after him, the dog thinks, "He must be

God!" But when a cat has a wonderful master who feeds him and grooms him and cleans up after him, the cat thinks, "I must be God!"

We laughed, and then Pip went to play a computer game in the living room.

Bea and I went to the kitchen, and I put my hot chocolate cup in the sink and said, "Bea, can I ask you for advice?" Bea is the only person I know who wants to be an advice columnist when she grows up.

"If it's about Taco," she said, "I don't have any Pet Pointers. I know some cute cat videos though. And we stock tons of cat books at the shop because Americans own, like, a hundred million cats."

"It's not about Taco," I said, a lump in my throat. "You know that new fifth-grade girl, Zara?" Bea listened, and I told her that Maybelle was always busy with Zara, and that Zara had asked Chuck about me, and now things were awkward between us.

"I think you and Maybelle will always be friends," Bea said reassuringly. "And with Chuck, maybe if you try to act the way you used to, things will go back to how they were." I didn't say anything, so she added, "It might feel forced at first, but no one ever died of awkwardness."

I nodded, remembering when she'd told Pip that no one ever died of awkwardness. Who knew *I'd* be asking Bea for advice months later?

Taco Cat pitter-pattered in and rubbed against our shins. I think he was actually inviting us to pet him.

"You know what Taco likes?" I said. "To be brushed."

I got out his brush, and Bea and I took turns brushing him.

"Meow Meow loves when we brush him. He purrs up a storm."

"Taco never purrs," I said.

"Really?" Bea looked surprised.

"Well, not yet anyway. He's very independent. Even for a cat."

"Meow Meow is the opposite. She's very affectionate—but a little needy sometimes." Bea smiled. "We don't mind though."

I didn't think I would mind either. (I mean *I'm* a little needy sometimes!)

Ava, Whose Cat Does Not Purr

PS Is having a cat that doesn't purr like having a dog that doesn't wag its tail? Will he ever purr? And will he ever realize that I don't even want to be his master—just his *friend*?

PPS Bea and I went on Dad's computer, and she showed me an amazing video of a cat playing Jenga. I think the cat was gifted or something.

1/11 (PALINDROME DATE)
IN BED

DEAR DIARY,

After school, I went to Maybelle's—just me. It started out fun. We made popcorn (P-O-P-P-O-P-P-O-P) and played Slow Down/ Speed Up. It's the game when one person starts doing something, whether it's jumping jacks or juggling marshmallows, and the other says, "Slow down!" or "Speed up!" The person has to do whatever she's doing really slowwwwly or lightning fast. When Carmen or Lucia play it with us, they say, "*¡Más lento!*" or "*¡Más rápido!*" And in the summer, we sometimes go outside and do slow and fast cartwheels.

Today, I was happy to be playing with just Maybelle (and not Zara). We started making necklaces with her beads, but after a while, I couldn't hold in my questions anymore. So I asked straight out: "Did Zara say anything about me, like, behind my back?"

Maybelle looked guilty and as if she didn't know if she should answer.

Which was an answer right there.

"What did she say?" I pressed.

Maybelle folded her legs up and put her chin on her knee.

I could tell she didn't want to report their conversations, but maybe I was sort of cornering her.

She sighed, and we both looked at our beads instead of at each other. "She thinks," Maybelle finally began in a quiet voice, "that you're kind of a teachers' pet."

My mouth flopped open. Even though that may not be untrue (which is a double negative), it was *not* what I expected to hear.

Still, I decided I could live with that. I mean, it's a fact that Mrs. Lemons likes me. And I like her back. But for what it's worth, not *all* teachers think I'm special. I annoy Miss Hamshire. She acts like I'm bad at math on purpose.

Well, it turned out that Maybelle wasn't done! While I was contemplating Zara's first complaint, Maybelle came up with a second.

"Zara also says that your primary topic of conversation is your cat."

That made me mad! Of course I talk a lot about Taco Cat! I was desperate for a cat, then I got one, and we've had him only eleven days! What does Zara expect me to talk about? Carpet cleaners? Climate change?

I was trying to decide whether to defend myself when Maybelle said that Zara also wonders why I haven't let her meet Taco yet.

What?!?

"I haven't *stopped* her from meeting him," I said.

"She says you've never once invited her over even though she helped make the paper mice."

I wanted to shout, "Oh puh-lease! Zara doesn't have the right to jump feetfirst into my whole life!" But I didn't. I just mumbled, "She can meet him."

"Now?" Maybelle asked, which made *me* feel sort of cornered.

I shrugged and said, "I guess." Then I wished I hadn't, because suddenly Maybelle was speed-dialing Zara and inviting her to hang out at my house! Next thing you know, Maybelle's mom was driving Maybelle and me to my house and picking up Zara on the way as though that had been the plan all along! I couldn't believe it!!

Even Dad looked surprised when he opened the door and there we were, all three of us. We walked in and searched all over for Taco and finally found him sleeping in the corner of Mom's closet, by the slippers.

Zara said he was handsome.

I said that cats spend most of the day sleeping—about eighteen hours.

Maybelle said, "That's three-fourths of the day! Humans sleep only one-third of the day." That was a very Maybelle thing to say. (She can do fractions in her head.)

Zara said that sloths sleep even more. "They sleep more than any other animal in the animal kingdom."

Zara had brought a ping-pong ball for Taco to play with, and he chased it around and even let her pet him. At first, I thought Taco was being a traitor. But I told myself not to feel that way. The problem though, is that it's hard not to feel whatever you're feeling, even when you try to talk yourself out of it.

Taco wanted to keep playing, and he pressed his little white zigzag against Zara's shin. She laughed and said, "He's giving me a head butt!" For a second, I thought she was calling my cat a butthead! Then I realized that this was in *my* head.

Anyway, Maybelle said that in 1963, France sent the first cat ever into outer space. "Her name was Felicette."

"Really?" I said.

"*Oui,*" Maybelle said. "A lot of animals went into space. Dogs, monkeys, mice, turtles, even newts and fruit flies."

"Newts?" Zara and I said at the exact same time.

She gave me a little smile so I went ahead and gave her a little smile back, which was nice of me. Then we both said "Jinx" at the same time.

"Did the cat live?" I asked Maybelle.

Maybelle said the cat went up for fifteen minutes and "came back famous."

Zara said, "Cool." She was petting Taco and he was letting her. "What a good cat," she said. I appreciated her appreciation, even though I was glad Taco did not choose that moment to purr. But then Zara said something I did *not* appreciate. She said, "I wonder who he used to belong to."

"What do you mean?" I said. Obviously, I think of Taco as *mine*, not as some hand-me-down stray.

"I mean, did you look for Lost Cat signs?"

"No…" I said and wondered whether we should have.

"My stepfather once had a dog that got lost," Zara continued. "But it had tags, and we put up signs, and the person who found him gave him back."

"Taco didn't have tags and we didn't see any signs," I stated in a way that I hoped made it clear that this conversation was over.

Soon Maybelle and Zara left, and I felt irritated that Zara had come over at all. I hugged Taco close and was glad that he was mine, and that he's Taco *Wren*—not Taco Smith or Taco Jones or even Taco Bell!

AVA ELLE WREN, OWNER OF TACO CAT WREN

PS Dinner was a revolting concoction of kale, quinoa, and mushrooms. Ugh! Why can't we have Taco Tuesdays instead of Meatless Mondays?

DEAR DIARY,

I had the scariest dream!

A gigantic elephant was trying to barge into my room. I locked the door, but the elephant started getting in anyway. I was really scared and didn't know where to hide, and I hoped it would not get in and trample or squash me!

When I woke up, I thought: What the heck was that about? Had I read something scary before bed? Was my nightmare inspired by an Aesop fable about elephants?

But no, I hadn't. And I doubt Aesop wrote about elephants in ancient Greece.

I doubt Basho wrote about elephants in ancient Japan either.

My mind was all over the place, and then I remembered the expression "an elephant in the room," which means the upsetting thing no one is talking about.

Right now what's upsetting me is what Zara said about Lost Cat signs. I have to admit: it didn't even occur to me to look for Lost Cat signs—let alone round up my friends to make Found Cat signs. And even if I *had* made Found Cat signs, I probably wouldn't have posted them in plain sight. I would have posted them in closets and behind doors!

Should I talk to Mom or Dad about this?

I wish Zara had kept her mouth zipped!

AVA, ANGRY

DEAR DIARY,

Question: What if someone out there *is* looking for Taco Cat?

I don't even want to think about that.

I could think about Chuck, but he and I haven't said a word to each other in six days.

I could think about Maybelle because she's coming over again tomorrow. But what if Zara thinks she's invited? She isn't!

Sometimes I wish I could just turn off my brain.

AVA, AGITATED

Dear Diary,

Maybelle came over, and Dad built us a fire in the fireplace while we made banana milk. That's when we put bananas and ice cream and ice in a blender. (Taco hates when we use the blender.) We also made a snack of banana slices topped with dabs of chunky peanut butter. (Dad and Mom both bought bananas so we have way too many.) Anyway, Maybelle and I took off our shoes and warmed our toes by the fire, and I decided to tell her that I'd been worrying.

"About what?"

"About what Zara said about Lost Cat signs and also"—my voice caught—"about Zara wanting to steal you away." I looked into the fire, which was crackly and smoky-smelling and yellow-orange with a little blue and purple too. Then I looked at Maybelle and added softly, "I don't want you to dump me."

"Ava, I would never dump you," Maybelle said. She sounded a teeny tiny bit annoyed. "And I didn't get mad last fall when you started spending time with Bea."

"True," I said, feeling embarrassed and bite-size.

"Besides, didn't you once tell me that Bea said people can't *steal* friends, they can only *make* friends?"

"Yes," I admitted, impressed that Maybelle remembered.

"Zara is new," she continued, "and it seemed like she could use a friend. And you weren't around much because you had just gotten Taco."

I nodded, trying to be understanding, but I still wished Zara hadn't zeroed in on *my* BFF. "Doesn't Zara ever get on your nerves?" I asked. "She says really random things."

"Everyone says random things," Maybelle said, and it occurred to me that while Zara can be insensitive, maybe I can be *over*sensitive. "And you don't have to like her just because I like her."

"I don't *hate* her…" I said quietly. "But I like when it's just us."

Taco Cat came padding over and I reached down to pet him. Instead of running away, he stayed still. I went to get his brush, and Maybelle and I took turns brushing him and brushing him.

You are *not* going to believe what happened next!

Brace yourself because this is BIG!

Taco Cat was lying there, letting us brush him by the fire for like, three minutes, and then, out of the blue, I heard a rhythmic sound, a soft gentle *rumble bumble rumble bumble*. It was coming from *him*! He was purring!

And purring!!

And purring!!!

He remembered that he had a little purring motor inside him, and he turned it on!

Maybelle and I kept brushing him, and we kept looking at each other and smiling.

"It's the first time he's ever purred!" I whispered. "I'm glad you're here with me."

"Me too," she whispered back. "You think purring is how cats say, 'I feel happy'?"

"Or 'I feel safe'?" I said.

"Or 'Thank you'?" she said.

"Or 'I love you'?" We kept brushing and brushing, and Taco kept purring and purring. "My mom said cats also communicate by blinking. It's their way of blowing a kiss."

"Don't some cats communicate by killing mice and birds and leaving them on doorsteps as tokens of affection?"

"Do they?" I asked, horrified.

"Maybe not in winter," Maybelle said.

Taco kept purring away, and I hoped he would never bring me a dead mouse or chickadee valentine.

"Some big cats purr too," I said. "Lions and tigers roar, but cheetahs and pumas purr."

"Zara's pet guinea pig used to purr," Maybelle said.

We kept listening to Taco Cat's *rumble bumble rumble bumble*, and I was glad that Maybelle was *here* to *hear* it (homonym alert), even if she did bring up Zara.

It's funny how some big events really are newsworthy. Like when rockets go into space, or athletes beat world records, or presidents get elected.

But some big events are kind of small. Like when your cat

comes out in the open or finally purrs. Or when a shy person opens up like a flower bud. Or when two best friends clear the air.

Later, as Maybelle was putting on her winter coat to go home, she said, "Ava, Zara is my new friend, but you're my old friend and my best friend. And that's a much bigger deal."

AVA, A #1

DEAR DIARY,

I'm glad Maybelle and I talked yesterday. And maybe Zara really did need a friend. Like Taco did. And maybe Maybelle needed someone to talk to about bras and growing-up stuff, especially since she doesn't have a sister and it's possible that I have been a teeny tiny itty bitty eensy weensy bit cat-consumed.

Zara doesn't have sisters or brothers either. She never even talks about her parents—just her grandparents.

I am trying to be mature about everything—which is not particularly easy. (Maturity may not be my strong suit.)

By the way, Pip got jealous that Taco purred for Maybelle, and not her, so I told her that next time Taco settles under a lamp or by the fire or in a spot of sunshine, she should tiptoe over and brush him softly. (Usually, Pip and Taco play runaround games. She chases him around the living room or they play a game we call Bat and Bite. It's when Pip jiggles a ribbon and Taco bats it and bites it!)

Last night, I let Pip feed Taco. We'd gone to the Great Wall for dinner (the squid came with tentacles, yuck!), and when we came home, I forgot to feed Taco. It was the first time that ever happened! Well, he rubbed my shins and also gently bit my ankle to remind me, but by then I was upstairs and about to get in bed, so I told Pip she could feed him. Pip was happy, and this morning, she told me that when Taco heard her open the bag, he came running!

Here are three sounds Taco loves:

1. A can of cat food being opened
2. A bag of cat food being shaken
3. A bag of cat treats coming out of the R-E-W-A-R-D-D-R-A-W-E-R

Here are four sounds Taco hates:

1. Dad grinding coffee
2. Mom using her hair dryer
3. Me using the blender
4. Mom or Dad vacuuming

AVA, AWARE AND OBSERVANT

PS We got fortune cookies after dinner. Pip's said, "You have a yearning for perfection." Mine said... well, I'll tape it here:

Declare peace every day.

Dear Diary,

In the library, Mr. Ramirez said he liked my cat and moon haiku, and that when Jerry Valentino comes to our school in ten days, a reporter from the town newspaper, the *Misty Oaks Monitor*, is going to "cover" the workshop.

"Cover?"

"Write about it," he explained, then added, "Zara said you and your sister have been working on a picture book called *Something Fishy*."

"*Alphabet Fish*," I corrected, only half-surprised that Zara had blabbed about—and retitled—our book.

But for once, maybe it was good that Zara had meddled, because I blurted, "Do you think Mr. Valentino could *critique* it?" I'd never used that word, but it was a bonus word on today's spelling test. It means to "evaluate or read critically."

"Maybe…" Mr. Ramirez said, taken aback. "Is it short?"

That was funny because that's always the first thing I want to know about a book. "It's mostly pictures," I said.

"I don't see why not," he said. "It wouldn't be fair to ask him to read a student novel, but a short book, sure."

"We haven't quite finished."

"Can you have it ready by next Friday?"

"Yes," I said even though I didn't know how Pip would react to a deadline.

"Don't sacrifice quality for speed," he cautioned.

"We won't," I said. And then, even though I haven't been all that into *Alphabet Fish* lately, I started daydreaming. I was giving the book to Mr. Ramirez, who was giving it to Mr. Valentino, who was giving it to an agent, who was giving it to an editor, who was giving it to a publisher, who was giving it to the factory people who turn floppy pages into hardcover books, who were giving it to librarians and bookstore owners and reviewers and bloggers who were all telling regular readers about it. In my mind, our ABC book was on its way to being a bestseller! In my mind, Pip and I were about to be a world-famous writer-artist sister duo!

I tried to remind myself of the Aesop moral: "Don't count your chickens before they are hatched." But it was hard not to start counting. In fact, I started picturing a basket of eggs and a half dozen baby chicks hatching out of shells, their tiny beaks first, *peep peep peep, cheep cheep cheep.*

One two three
four five six…
Chick chick chick
chicks chicks chicks…

AVA IGNORING AESOP

DEAR DIARY,

I told Pip that Mr. Ramirez said he would give our book to Jerry. I even mentioned that we might turn into a world-famous author-illustrator team.

"Dream on, Ava," Pip said, but I bet she has been daydreaming too. She once told me that while she would *not* want to be famous, she *would* like to be an artist.

I handed her:

Q is for queen triggerfish.

The queen triggerfish is big and bright;
It changes colors and sleeps at night.

Then I casually mentioned that we had to finish by next Friday.

"What??!" Pip said, her voice rising. "Ava, we still have ten letters to go!" She was freaking out, but I think she was also getting extra inspired because next thing you know, she was drawing an elaborate border of shiny golden crowns for the Q page and telling me to get to work on "rainbow trout."

I am now going to bed. I'm going to leave my door wide open in case Taco Cat decides to visit. Lately, when Pip and I have been writing or drawing, he'll plunk himself on top of our picture book as if asking to be petted—or maybe saying, "I dare you to make me move."

Pip says it's annoying. Me, I never mind putting down my pen and picking up my cat. I love that he's becoming more affectionate!

Ava, Affectionate

PS Chuck and I have gone over a week without talking. Bea said I should try to act normal with him, but how can I when we haven't been sitting next to each other? Is he avoiding me? (Or does he...*miss* me a little too?) I can't believe Zara caused so much trouble with one stupid question! Arrrggghh!

Dear Diary,

Here are my latest poems:

S is for seahorse.

With a kangaroo's pouch and a horse's head,
The dad carries the babies and makes sure they're fed.

and

T is for trumpetfish.

The slow trumpetfish is straight as a stick,
Hiding in branches is its very best trick.

Speaking of hiding, Taco Cat isn't hiding as much as he used to—except when he finds a bag or box or wants to take a catnap. It seems like he'd rather keep us company than keep his distance. When we watch a movie on TV, for instance, he'll sit near us, almost as if he's watching too.

Sometimes he even follows us into the bathroom. (This morning I heard Pip say, "Taco, get out! I need privacy!")

When Mom or Dad drives into our garage, or Pip comes home from art class, Taco pricks up his ears and goes trotting over to the back door to say a quiet hello.

He doesn't like when we play Boggle though. When anyone shakes the letters, he takes off. So that's another sound he abhors. (And "abhors," which means "hates," is another six-letter word with all its letters in alphabetical order.)

Personally, I think Taco can't really change his inner nature, which is that he is a bit of a scaredy-cat.

I wonder if Zara can't change her inner nature either, which is that she's a bit of a blabbermouth.

I once read an Aesop fable about how it's hard to hide your inner nature. It's called "The Cat and the Maiden," and it goes like this:

The gods were arguing about whether a living creature can change its nature. Jupiter, the king of the gods, said yes, but Venus, the goddess of love, said no. To prove his point, Jupiter turned a cat into a beautiful maiden. A man fell madly in love with her and proposed. At the wedding, Jupiter said to Venus, "Look how lovely she is. Who would have thought that she used to be a cat?" Venus said, "Watch this!" and tossed a squeaky mouse into her path. No sooner did the bride see it, than she pounced upon it. The groom was horrified! And Venus said to Jupiter, "See? You can't change who you are."

Well, not to argue with Aesop or anything, but I don't agree that you are who you are. Maybe in *some* ways. But not in all ways. I mean, I think people and cats *can* change a little bit, if they want to and they try.

Like, Pip and Taco are both a lot less timid than they used to be. Right now, Pip is at Isabel's, and Pip never used to go to other kids' houses. As for Taco, maybe he will always seem aloof and like he's planning his escape. But he is settling down a bit and trusting us. And I'll say this: his ready-to-run personality makes his "cat cuddles" extra sweet. >^. .^<

AVA, NOT ALOOF

DEAR DIARY,

Dad and I were in the car running errands, and I asked him if we should have put up Found Cat signs.

"Ava, we didn't *find* Taco. We *adopted* Taco."

I told him that Zara had asked if I knew who Taco belonged to before us.

Dad patted my knee. "I doubt Taco thinks he ever belonged to anyone. I bet he thinks *we* belong to him. We're the ones who feed him, right?" I nodded. "Maybe he thinks *he* owns us!"

We talked about how pets aren't property, and I told him Ben's jokes about cats versus dogs. Dad told me that in ancient Egypt, cats were revered as gods, mostly because they killed the mice and rats that were spreading disease and eating up all the grain.

AVA, OWNED BY TACO GOD

PS Maybelle is coming for a sleepover. Y-A-Y! First time in a long time!!

Dear Diary,

Maybelle brought a laser light with her. It made a red beam, and Taco chased it everywhere, even up walls. (We were careful not to flash it in his eyes.)

Pip was in the kitchen illustrating the V rhyme she made me write:

V is for viperfish.

The viperfish has sharp teeth and shines its own light,
It swims deep down by day but less deep at night.

Pip is worried that we won't finish in time, but after dinner, I told her to come outside with Maybelle and me, and she did. The three of us bundled up and went to look at the stars. Maybelle started talking about life in outer space and that French space cat. I said that in science we learned about "inherited, acquired, and learned" traits. For instance, if Taco hadn't had certain private parts snipped off, he could have had kittens, and some of his kittens *might* have been taco-colored (inherited), but none of them would have been born with a bitten-up ear (acquired) or able to play Jenga (learned).

This morning, Taco found a diamond of sunlight and lay down on his side. Maybelle joked that it was a "rhombus" of sunlight and said he looked like "a breaded pork chop." That made me laugh, but I have to admit that if Zara had said the exact same thing, I might have wanted to punch her face. (Not that I would have.)

I said that when Taco sits with his paws tucked in, he looks like a golden loaf of bread.

The twins came over (wearing orange sweatshirts), and we played Slow Down/Speed Up. Pip and Maybelle were eating cereal, and when Carmen said, *"¡Más lento!"* they lifted their spoons in slow motion, and when she said, *"¡Más rápido!"* they shoveled cereal into their mouths, spoonful after spoonful. It was funny—but I was glad Mom and Dad weren't watching.

Sometimes I wish I really could slow down time because I like being a kid. Especially when everyone is getting along.

Does *growing* up mean *growing* pains?

Actually, I think Pip likes being thirteen more than she liked being my age, eleven. She used to be moodier and more *temperamental* (a hard bonus word because of the "a" between "temper" and "mental"). Now she's happier—which is better for her and for us. But she still has her moments! And she's been stressing about finishing the fish book on time.

Taco was sitting in the living room with his left paw stretched out in front of him. Maybelle said, "He looks like the king of the beasts."

I said, "Or the prince of the beasts."

Lucia asked, "Has he purred yet?"

Pip said, "Yes! For me and Ava and Maybelle!"

We told Carmen and Lucia to go up to him very slowly and brush him very gently. And sure enough, instead of bolting, Taco let them brush him. After a long, long while, he even turned on his *rumble bumble rumble bumble* motor and started purring and vibrating. Lucia pressed her ears against his side and he didn't run away!

"*Más rápido,*" Lucia whispered, and then, "*Más lento.*" But Taco didn't speed up or slow down. He kept purring at his very own speed.

AVA, WHOSE CAT IS PURRRRRFECT

DEAR DIARY,

I'm really worried about Taco!! After Maybelle and the twins went home, Dad and Pip went to a matinee, and I noticed that Taco started acting strange. His bathroom door was open, and he was going in and out and in and out. He was also crouching as if he had to pee but couldn't. His little behind was all quivery, and he looked at me with his big round eyes and gave a melancholy meow as if to tell me something was wrong. It seemed like he was even trying to pee *outside* his litter box, which he never does.

I went into the bathroom and saw a couple of tiny pink drops on the white bath mat. I didn't want to get Taco in trouble, but I thought I'd better tell Mom.

But she wasn't home! I remembered that she'd gone out for a walk with our neighbor, Mrs. Farris. I called Mom on her cell phone, but then I heard her phone buzzing in her purse—she'd left it on the kitchen counter!

Taco looked up at me—but not with a love-blink, more like an anxious expression. I was trying to figure out what to do—stay with him or get help—and decided to put on my coat and boots and run to the park and find Mom.

At first I couldn't find her anywhere. Then I saw her way ahead, so I ran and ran and caught up to her.

Mom seemed surprised to see me. I told her about Taco, and I don't know what I expected her to say, but I did not expect her to say, "Ava, we need to get Taco to the clinic *immediately*."

"But it's Sunday!"

"Let's hurry home. I'll call Dr. Gross, and you get the cat carrier. We have no time to lose!"

We said good-bye to Mrs. Farris and ran back. Mom called Dr. Gross, and I got Taco into his carrier and held him on my lap as Mom drove. Mom and I both kept telling Taco things like, "Don't be scared," and "Dr. Gross is going to take care of you."

Now we're at the clinic, which would normally be closed. If regular people have a Sunday emergency, they have to drive to the animal hospital twenty-five minutes away. But Dr. Gross told Mom he'd meet us here.

It's strange to be sitting in the empty waiting room. It's hardly ever empty. Mom said I could watch the "procedure," but I was afraid to. I knew it would be better for me to write in you.

Writing always helps.

I'm actually writing with the "magic pen" Dad gave me, the silver one from the Dublin Writers Museum in Ireland, the one I almost lost. I barely use it anymore because I don't want to lose it again. But I grabbed it for luck, just in case.

Taco may need all the luck he can get!
Why is it taking so, *so* long? I don't like this!

AVA, AGONIZING

1/17
BACK HOME WITHOUT TACO!

DEAR DIARY,

Poor Taco Cat has to stay at the vet's *without* us! He's back in a cage! On the drive home, Mom said that because there was blood in his pee, they have to be sure he doesn't have a "urethral obstruction" which can be "extremely serious in a male cat."

Mom always sounds different when she talks about animals.

She said Dr. Gross remembered Taco because of his "distinctive coloration" and the "lacerations" on his ear. He gave him an "antibiotic injection," "anti-inflammatory medication," and anesthesia. And Taco conked out, which meant that at least he couldn't feel anything. Mom said Dr. Gross did a "bladder radiograph" and "urine analysis" and blood tests too, because he had a UTI.

"UTI?"

"Urinary tract infection," Mom said.

"Is that bad?" I asked.

Mom looked somber. "In some cats, it can be fatal, but I think Taco is going to pull through just fine."

"I'm scared," I said.

"I know," Mom said.

"Is Taco going to be okay?" I whispered.

"I hope so," Mom said, even though I'd wanted her to say, "Yes, of course!" She added, "Dr. Gross is an excellent vet."

I nodded but felt like sobbing. "Is this all going to cost a lot?" I asked. I don't even know why I asked except that Mom and Dad sometimes worry about money, so I sometimes do too.

"Dr. Gross will give us a discount," Mom said. We were quiet for a moment, then she said, "You know what else he told me?"

"What?"

"He thinks having a pet has been good for me because it's given me a greater understanding of how our clients feel when they have an emergency or an end-of-life decision."

"We don't have an end-of-life decision!"

"No, I don't think we do." Mom took another peek at me even though she was driving. "But I guess I never fully understood how *attached* people get to their pets. I never had a pet growing up."

"I know," I said, then added, "I'm sorry," because I felt sad for Mom-when-she-was-a-girl.

"I really *did* want a Dalmatian puppy," Mom admitted. "My best friend's dog had a litter, and she wanted to give me one." Mom smiled a soft, sad smile. "You know, when I first started working at the clinic, I was surprised by how much everyone talks to the animals."

"What do you mean?"

"Like, just now, Dr. Gross said, 'Don't worry, Taco. You'll be your old self again soon.'"

"*You* talk to Taco."

"I know. But I never thought I would."

It was nice talking to Mom in the dark car. "When will we know for sure that we don't have an end-of-life decision?" I kind of wanted a guarantee.

"Ava, you did everything right. Taco let you know that something was wrong, and you let me know, and I let Dr. Gross know. Everything's going to be okay."

"Promise?"

"I can't promise."

"Mom, you know how cats have nine lives?" My voice cracked. "What if Taco has already used his all up?"

We were turning into our driveway, and I hated that he wasn't with us. I pictured him on the arm of the sofa, pricking up his ears, hearing our car, and heading over to greet us at the door. "Think about it!" I said. "He got attacked by a coyote, *and* he had a peeing problem—that's *two* lives in *three* weeks! What if, when he was a kitten, he fell off a roof, or picked a fight with a raccoon, or—?"

Mom drove into our garage and parked. Then she opened her arms and gave me a hug. For most moms, that's probably no big deal, but my mom is not very huggy. It's not part of her inner nature. Her mom, Nana Ethel, doesn't hug at all. She gives stiff little pat-pats that are the *opposite* of bear hugs.

I hugged Mom back and wondered if, as Dr. Gross said, Taco really was softening her up. I also wondered this: If Goldy Lox had died *now* instead of two years ago, would things have been different? Would Mom have let us give him a proper burial in the backyard instead of flushing him down the toilet?

Well, "what's done, is done," I thought, which was me quoting Dad quoting Shakespeare.

Mom and I walked in, and Dad and Pip were right there ~~dying~~ wanting to know everything. (I can't believe I wrote "dying"!!)

Mom told them that Taco had been "straining to urinate" and that I had done "everything right." She said we'd get test results soon and, if all went well, we'd get Taco back tomorrow. We'd have to give him medication and "modify his diet" and get him to drink more water. Mom said it's good Taco likes to drink from faucets since our house is heated and the air gets so dry in winter.

I asked Dad if he knew where the expression "nine lives" comes from.

He said no, but that Shakespeare used it in *Romeo and Juliet*. Then Dad found the exact lines and showed them to me (which was *very* Dad). They were in a fight scene when Romeo's friend Mercutio calls his enemy, "Good King of Cats" and says he wants one of his "nine lives."

Anyway, I hope Taco stays fast asleep at Dr. Gross's. If he wakes up in a cage, he'll be so scared. (My bigger hope is that he wakes up!)

Poor Taquito! (That's Pip's nickname for him—she says that in Spanish, adding "ito" means "little.")

AVA WITHOUT TACO

339

DEAR DIARY,

Pip said we should do another page to distract ourselves.
I didn't want to, but Pip seemed upset and I didn't feel
like fighting with her. So I wrote a W rhyme and handed
it over:

W is for witch flounder.

Some witches have cats, ride brooms, and cast spells.
These witches are fish that swim among shells.

Pip is now drawing a border with Halloween cats and witches on
brooms. She's also revising the borders from the early pages. Dad
says writers have to do revisions ("Write and rewrite till you get
it right!"), and I guess artists do too.

I could do revisions on my earlier fish poems, but number
one, I don't feel like it, and number two, Pip already illustrated
them the way they are.

I'm glad Mom told me not to worry, but I can't help but

worry. I wish Taco were here! The house feels so empty without him!

AVA, ANXIOUS

1/17
MIDDLE OF THE NIGHT

DEAR DIARY,

An X rhyme just came to me so I turned on the penlight Bea gave me and am writing it down:

> *X marks the spot where the fish swam away.*
> *What was it? Sunfish? Starfish? Moonfish? Moray?*

X-O-X

A-V-A

DEAR DIARY,

I gave Pip my middle-of-the-night masterpiece, but she said X has to stand for a fish, not a spot. I said that she could draw wavy water and make a border of suns and stars and moons. She said she did not want a page without fish in the middle of a fish book. I said, "Why not? It'd be funny." She said, "I just don't!"

Well, instead of making a new X poem, I felt like making a giant X on Pip's artwork.

I felt like shouting, "I'm sick of fish and I'm sick of collaborating, and you'll be lucky if I even write the last three rhymes!"

But I didn't feel like starting World War III, so I dashed off an "X is for x-ray tetra" poem and handed it to her. I'm *not* going to copy it in here because it's not very good and the whole thing makes me mad.

AVA, ANNOYED AND ARGUMENTATIVE BUT ATTEMPTING TO BE ADULT

PS Are Pip and I both in X-tra bad moods because we're worried about Taco?

DEAR DIARY,

Taco is back!! Dad picked him up while we were at school. Taco must have missed us too because he started purring the second I hugged him and kissed his little snout! Poor Taco! Was he afraid he would never get to see us again? I was afraid I might not get to see him again!

He greeted me by rubbing against my leg, then he jumped onto the arm of the sofa and settled in under the warm reading lamp. I petted him, and he purred, and I blinked at him, and he blinked back.

We also bought him a get-well present: a small plastic fountain with a pump so he can always have fresh running water.

I called Maybelle and told her Taco was better. She sounded happy for me.

Weird that one month ago, I hadn't even met Taco, and now I sometimes get sad or happy or scared because of him.

Weird that one month ago, I hadn't really noticed Zara, and now she affects my moods too.

I've been thinking: Zara is not a terrible person. And it's not terrible that she is *outspoken* (just like it's not terrible that Pip is *soft-spoken*). It is, however, hard to get used to Maybelle having a close friend besides me. But maybe there's enough of Maybelle to go around?

AVA, ATTEMPTING TO BE ACCEPTING

PS Since Zara messed things up with Chuck, it's not like I'm 100 percent accepting either.

Dear Diary,

Pip kept pressuring me to write the Y and Z poems. I didn't feel like it, and it's only Monday. But Pip wouldn't stop asking, so I finally wrote them. Here they are:

Y is for yellowtail.

The pretty yellowtail swims with speed and grace;
If you ran and it swam, it would be a close race.

Z is for zebrafish.

Zebrafish have stripes that are shiny and blue;
A zeal of zebras are black, white, and furry too.

I hope Jerry Valentino likes our book even though, as Dad might say, it finishes with a whimper and not a bang.

Frankly, I'm glad the English alphabet has only twenty-six letters. Pip says the Spanish alphabet is longer because of *ñ* (as in *mañana*) and *ll* (as in *llama*) and *rr* (as in *guitarra*) and *ch* (as in *mucho*). Mrs. Lemons once said that the Japanese language has *three* different alphabets.

Anyway, my part is done. Z is for zebrafish and now Z is for zzzzzs.

I wish Taco would sleep with me instead of going prowling around at night.

At least he's back home. Tonight he rolled onto his back asking for a tummy rub, so I rubbed his tummy. Fifteen seconds later, he wriggled upright as if to say, "How dare you rub my tummy?"

He definitely has a mind of his own!

Just now, I took a bath and the door creaked open. I thought it was Pip or Mom or Dad and was about to yell, "Don't come in!" but it was Taco! He put his paws on the rim of the tub and stared at me. I went to pet him, but my hand was dripping wet, so he ran away.

AVA IN A TOWEL

PS Tonight's Meatless Monday was bulgur wheat and pea pods. Worst yet!!!

DEAR DIARY,

Last night, I was almost asleep when I heard a sound in my room. What was it? Could it be? Yes! It was…Taco!! He came padding over and jumped right up onto my bed. I could hardly believe it!

At first, he stayed near my feet. I didn't want to scare him away, so I stayed stock-still. Then I drummed my fingers to invite him to come a little closer.

He crept up and stopped just above my knee where I could pet him. He was almost out of reach, but I stretched out my arm and brushed his fur with my fingertips. He crept a smidge closer and stayed there for a few minutes. I thought he might let me curl up with him, but he turned around and faced my feet—in case he wanted to make a speedy getaway.

Which he did, right as I was about to drift off.

At breakfast, I told everyone that Taco had come to visit me. I was afraid Pip or Dad or Mom would say, "He sleeps with me every night," or "I was wondering where he went." But they didn't. Mom said, "One night in a vet's cage, the next in a bedroom. He's no fool." Dad quoted Charles Dickens who said, "What greater gift than the love of a cat." And Pip just said, "You're lucky." I admitted that Taco stayed for only a few minutes, and by my knee, not in my arms. Pip said, "You're still lucky."

I know I am. Taco is a good cat—and maybe he finally realizes that I'm a good kid.

AVA, LUCKY

PS I have to hurry and get ready for school! Funny that today in the world, I'll see lots of people, but the only people Taco will see are us. We *are* his world.

RIGHT AFTER SCHOOL (USING MY TIGER PEN)

DEAR DIARY,

I decided I should try harder to talk to Chuck, so I asked if he finished the book. He looked confused. I added, "The boxer one. The one you got at the bookstore."

"Oh right," he said. "Yes, it was good." He asked if I'd been using the tiger pen I'd bought. Well, that broke the ice, and I said, "Yes," and then we both looked right at each other and smiled for, like, two seconds. Maybe even three.

I was glad that just as a bad question can mess things up, a good question can fix things up. Or start to, anyway.

"You'll appreciate this, Ava," Chuck said, opening his spelling notebook and digging out the test from last Friday. "I got a 75—but I got one of the bonus words right: 'illiterate.' So I'm *not* illiterate! I can read and write!"

I laughed.

"Is your 100s streak still going strong?" he asked.

"It is," I said, and might have blushed a little. *Do* I like Chuck a teeny bit? Or am I just relieved that we're friends again?

He showed me two words that he got wrong. He'd spelled

"sophomore" "soft more" and he spelled "self-esteem" "self a steam." I laughed, and the good thing was that he knew that I was laughing *with* him, not *at* him.

AVA, SMILING

DEAR DIARY,

I was starving, so after school, I heated up some alphabet soup.
I love alphabet soup. I always spoon out one A and eat it first.

In school, when it was time to grade our spelling tests, we
had to pick a partner. Chuck and I looked right at each other
at the exact same time and switched papers without even saying
anything. He got another 75 and I got another 100.

One of the words he got wrong was "caterpillar." In front of
the whole class, he asked Mrs. Lemons, "What are caterpillars
afraid of?" She hesitated, so he answered "*Dog*erpillars!"

Mrs. Lemons laughed. The funny thing is that our math
teacher, Miss Hamshire, never thinks Chuck is funny. She thinks
Maybelle can do no wrong and Chuck can do no right.

In the library, Pip and I gave our book to Mr. Ramirez to give
to Jerry Valentino. I hope he can help us get it published!

I wonder if Jerry Valentino has already started reading *Alphabet
Fish*. If so, I wonder what letter he is up to?

ABC AVA WITH HOPES AND DREAMS

Dear Diary,

It's still light outside because the sun is staying out longer now than it did last month. I like long summer days more than short winter ones. Maybe everyone does?

Dad made us all little Sunday sundaes. Even Taco was hanging out in the kitchen.

Mom gave Taco his last dose of medicine (she's way better at squirting it into his mouth than Dad is). Then she started taking photos of him.

Dad said, "The cat as *muse!*"

"Taco *mews!*" I said, as if we were playing the Homonym Game.

"You guys are a-*mus*-ing!" Pip chimed.

Taco pushed his forehead against my shin as if asking to be petted in return for all his posing. Mom took more photos, including one of Dad and Pip and me, and then stretched out her hand and took one of all four of us. It was not a selfie; it was a family-ie.

Question: Has Taco made us more of a family??

AVA, MUSING AND AMUSING

PS I think having Taco *has* helped us all be in a good mood. (Except on weekend mornings when Mom and Dad say he wakes them too early.)

DEAR DIARY,

In the library today, Mr. Ramirez handed me an envelope from Jerry Valentino. I have to confess: when I opened it, I was expecting something very different.

Mr. Ramirez could tell from my expression that Jerry Valentino didn't think our book was about to take the world by storm.

I'm going to staple the letter in here, even if it means I have to cut it in two. (Note: I might enjoy cutting it in two!)

Dear Ava Wren,

I was glad for the opportunity to take a look at *Alphabet Fish*, particularly because I remember meeting you at Misty Oaks Library last October and reading your unusual story about the queen bee. I am pleased to see that you are still writing and that you and your sister have been able to work together. It is clear that you both have talent and have gone to considerable effort. I applaud you for that.

If Mr. Ramirez had asked for just a quick reaction, I might have said, "Bravo!" and "Well done!" and that would be that.

But since Mr. Ramirez asked me about "the possibility of publication," I feel I should let you know that the marketplace for picture books is very tight, and most editors are not keen on rhyming books. *The Cat in the Hat* aside, successful rhymes are deceptively difficult. There's also the question of the audience for *Alphabet Fish*. Do most children care about mudskippers or queen triggerfish? Can they relate? (A stickler might question whether a jellyfish is a fish at all.)

I'm looking forward to working with your grade next Tuesday and Friday, and we will talk more about writing then. For now, Ava, think about what inspires you. Is it fish? Or might there be another subject closer to your heart? And can you come up with a real story someday, one with a beginning, middle, and end? Is there something you are ardent about?

I hope you don't find my candor discouraging. I like the way you use words, and I admire your ambition.

Respectfully yours,

Jerry Valentino

I showed the letter to Mr. Ramirez. "Aren't I too young to get a rejection letter?" I asked.

"He's an author, not an editor, so technically, it's not a rejection letter," he said, reading it. "And it's very respectful, even though, okay, he doesn't think you hit a home run your first time at bat." (Mr. Ramirez was using a baseball metaphor.) "Look, maybe he should be taking *me* to task for putting thoughts into your young heads."

"Pip *was* excited," I confessed. "And his 'candor' *is* 'discouraging.'"

"Can you break it to her gently?" Mr. Ramirez said. "Or do you want me to?"

"I will."

At home, I showed Dad the letter. He was making *ratatouille*, which is a hard spelling word as well as a gross vegetarian dish. Dad read the letter all the way through. "Publication at this stage probably wasn't a very realistic expectation," he said, putting his hand on my shoulder. "But hard work is its own reward. And you and Pip had fun doing it, right?"

"Most of the time," I said and made a face.

Dad smiled because he knows that Pip and I don't alllllllways get along any more than he and Uncle Patrick allllllllways got along. "You're talented, Ava," he said. "And you're disciplined. If you want to write a book or a play someday, I have no doubt you'll do it."

"I don't want to write a play," I said, because Dad's the playwright, not me. I almost added, "But I *do* want to write a book." I didn't though, because I'm not ready to say that out loud, not even to Dad.

"Want to slice veggies with me?" Dad asked.

"Sure," I said, and he showed me how small he wanted the pieces. I swear, sometimes it seems as if Meatless Mondays come way more than once a week!

We chopped and chopped, and when I cut into an onion, my eyes got teary, and I pretended it was because of the rejection letter.

Dad knew I was kidding, but when Pip came home, I showed her the letter, and it was obvious that she really was disappointed. She tried to hide it, but at dinner she was almost as quiet as she used to be. When I think about it, Pip *had* spent way more time on the fish drawings than I had on the rhymes.

Just now, we were brushing our teeth, and Pip said, "I wish he'd liked it."

At first I said, "What?" (Actually, I said, "Whaaa?" because my mouth was full of toothpaste.) But then I said, "Me too."

"And I wish we could reject his rejection letter," she added.

I nodded and spat and said that at least Jerry Valentino hadn't said anything bad about her illustrations, just about my words. Which was true, but also nice and unselfish of me to point out.

AVA, ALTRUISTIC (THAT MEANS NICE AND UNSELFISH)

Dear Diary,

Pip knocked on my door and said, "I might make a flower alphabet book called *Z is for Zinnia*. It could be all pictures, no rhymes."

"Great idea!" I said because I didn't want her to ask me to write twenty-six flower rhymes.

Truth is, I think Pip likes working by herself as much as she likes collaborating. In school, I often like working by myself more than doing "teamwork" or "group work" too. (Exception: I like when Chuck and I switch spelling tests.)

Anyway, I just read an Aesop fable, and it was so scary that I feel like knocking on Mom and Dad's door. But I haven't done that in a long time.

The story is called "The One-Eyed Doe" and goes like this:

A deer that had lost an eye was grazing on a high cliff near the sea. She liked grazing there because she could keep her good eye toward the land and be on the lookout for hunters, and keep her blind eye toward the sea where she assumed she was safe. One day, however, a sailor on a ship noticed how beautiful she was and took his bow and arrow and shot her dead. As she drew her last breath, she realized (and this is the moral): "Trouble can come from where you least expect it."

After reading that unhappy ending, I did *not* want to turn my light off, so I reread Jerry Valentino's letter one more time, and it got me thinking: What subjects *are* close to my heart? What *am* I "ardent" about? ("Ardent" is when you care a lot about something.)

AVA, ARDENT

1/26
FIRST THING IN THE MORNING

DEAR DIARY,

Did Taco sense that I'd gotten bad news and read a bad fable? Last night he jumped onto my bed and instead of staying by my feet or knees, he nestled right up in the crook of my arm. He didn't *face* my *face*, but he waved his tail once so that the soft white tip brushed the bottom of my chin. It tickled and was so sweet. I didn't think cats could do that.

Then he did something even sweeter: he purred! In the dark with me!

It was the first time he'd ever purred in my bed, and it made me happy—especially since that bummer letter had bummed me out and that creepy fable had given me the creeps! Everything was silent in my room except for Taco's *rumble bumble rumble bumble*. It sounded louder than ever, but also warm and comforting and peaceful and…hypnotizing.

For the first time, he also pressed his paws against my side, first one then the other, one then the other. It was like he was giving me a *massage* and a *message*. Was he saying, "I love you"?

Mom once told me that what some people call "kneading," others call "making biscuits."

Then, all of a sudden, for absolutely no reason, Taco stopped and ran off.

That's how he rolls.

Still, it was nice while it lasted!

Pip likes to go to sleep with a book, but me, I'd rather go to sleep with a cat.

AVA, ABOUT TO BE LATE TO SCHOOL

DEAR DIARY,

I don't know how much I can write tonight because we wrote a ton in school today, and there's only so much writing a *hand* can…*hand*le!

Besides, I'm not Ava the Ambidextrous—I'm Ava the Rightie. If I were ambidextrous, maybe I could switch hands whenever my writing hand got tired. (Then again, brains get tired too.)

So here's what happened:

Jerry Valentino came to our classroom. He's as tall and skinny as ever, but his straggly hair is longer than it was in October, and this time he wore it in a ponytail. I bet Principal Gupta was shocked that our school's special guest had a ponytail, but I guess there's no dress code for grown-ups.

Anyway, Mrs. Lemons introduced Jerry Valentino and lifted up our class copy of *Campfire Nights*. It had been read, reread, and *re*reread so many times that someone should have ordered a new one by now. The book is missing a corner of its cover!

Well, I was worried that Jerry Valentino might say out loud what he'd said in his letter (that my rhymes were lame and who cares about fish?). But he didn't. He just looked out at us all, including Maybelle, Zara, Chuck, Riley, and the three Emilys, and said he wanted to help us become better writers. He talked about his six best writing tips and we copied them down. Here they are:

CREATIVE WRITING TIPS

1. Write from the heart: write about what you care about.
2. Use your head: think about beginning, middle, and end.
3. Show, don't just tell: it's better to reveal than to explain.
4. Use your senses: sight, smell, sound, taste, touch.
5. Provide details: paint pictures with words.
6. Read your work aloud: listen to the rhythm and music of the words.

Next he said he was going to give us a "prompt."

"What's a prompt?" Riley asked.

Jerry Valentino said it was a word or phrase that he hoped would "spark ideas" and inspire us. He said we would write for five minutes, and afterward, we'd go around the room and share our work aloud, and everyone would say something positive.

"Only positive?" Zara asked.

"Only positive," Jerry Valentino said.

"You mean we can't hold our noses and say, 'P.U. That stinks!'?" Chuck joked.

"Chuck, please." Mrs. Lemons scowled at him. Chuck gave me a tiny smile, so I gave him a tiny smile back.

Jerry Valentino said, "Is everyone ready?"

Amir said, "Should we use lined paper?"

Mrs. Lemons said yes.

Zara said, "Can I sharpen my pencil?"

Mrs. Lemons said, "Make it quick."

Emily Jenkins said, "Can I go to the bathroom?"

Mrs. Lemons looked exasperated. "Can't you wait five minutes?"

Finally, Jerry Valentino gave us the first prompt. It was: "my grandfather's hands."

At first, everyone looked confused, but then everyone (except me) wrote and wrote and wrote until he said to stop.

Soon everyone shared their writing out loud, and he didn't let anyone apologize ahead of time even though Emily Sherman started to say she didn't get to finish.

He said she could finish at home if she wanted and not to worry because what we were doing was more like "sketching with words" than "creating polished prose."

Well, Chuck was the first to read out loud. He wrote about how his grandfather taught him to box with big brown soft gloves. I said, "That was really good" because it was.

Zara wrote that her grandfather's hands are rough and calloused and "have dirt under the fingernails." Riley said, "Dirt is a good detail."

Emily LaCasse wrote about how her grandfather used to play the piano, but now his hands have spots on them and one pinkie bends the wrong way. Jerry Valentino said, "Nice!" which was weird because it was *not* nice that his pinkie bends the wrong way and is funny-looking, but I guess Jerry Valentino meant that he liked the detail.

Maybelle wrote about how her grandfather was "a card shark" whose hands always "held an ace." Jerry Valentino said her writing was "very clever."

I wrote just one sentence saying that I'd never gotten to meet either of my grandfathers and that this was a shame. Chuck said that was sad. But Jerry Valentino said I should have asked for a different prompt.

That made me mad because how was I supposed to know? Everyone had been scribbling away, and the classroom was so pin-drop quiet that I thought I was doing the right thing by not interrupting.

Fortunately, he gave us a brand-new prompt. He said to write about something "warm and comforting."

Everyone started writing a mile a minute, including me.

Later, we went around the room again. Emily Sherman wrote about hot chicken soup after a snowball fight. Emily LaCasse wrote about how her baby blanket had been washed so many times it was "the size of a dish rag." Emily Jenkins wrote about the "gentle sound of summer rain" on the roof of her camp cabin. Riley wrote about her pony's sweaty neck. Maybelle wrote about the gingerbread her great aunt used to make, back when Maybelle used to help push her around in a wheelchair. And Chuck wrote about his stuffed animal, Buffalo Billy, and how he used to sleep with it when he was little, but it always ended up on the floor, and then he'd feel bad, so now Buffalo Billy sits on a shelf. Chuck seemed embarrassed after reading that aloud, but I said it was sweet.

Mostly everyone said good things about everyone else's words, and I think the exercise helped us all get to know each other better—even though most of us (besides Zara) had already known each other for years.

Guess what I wrote about?

Correct! Taco Cat and his warm and comforting rumbly bumbly purring!

Jerry Valentino said we'd all done "fine work" and if anyone wanted to take the prompt home and develop it into a longer story, he'd be happy to take a look on Friday. I think most people (like Chuck and Jamal) thought, "No way," because this was extra credit, not homework. But I was thinking, "Way!"

I also felt a little shift happening inside me. Or maybe a big one?

It was like, deep inside my body, for three or four seconds, everything went totally still because I was making a decision. No, I was making a *plan*. No, I was making a…*commitment*! (That's a bonus word that's like a promise.)

In his letter, Jerry Valentino had asked if there might be another subject closer to my heart. Obviously, my cat is closer to my heart than angelfish, bumblebee fish, or *cat*fish—combined. (For a while, maybe Taco really *was* my "primary topic of conversation.")

My hand shot up into the air. "Can I try to turn what I wrote into a children's book?"

"*May* I, not *can* I," he corrected. "And sure, you may."

I wanted to say, "I'm glad I *may* and I hope I *can!*" But I didn't. Besides, my brain was already busy thinking about the story I wanted to write. It kept coming up with ideas and I kept taking notes.

Now I'm yawning and yawning, so I am calling it a night.

AMBITIOUS AVA, INSPIRED BUT TIRED

PS Should I ask Pip to draw a cover for the new book? I don't think so. She might be better at fish and flowers than cats and people anyway.

1/28
BEDTIME

Dear Diary,

I didn't write in you yesterday because I'd already spent a zillion hours writing and rewriting a picture book I'm calling "The Cat Who Wouldn't Purr." I tried to use my heart and my head, to show not just tell, to use senses and details, and to think about the rhythm and music of words.

I also employed alliteration and onomatopoeia and poetic license. And I made Pip a character (sort of). I even read my work aloud before pressing print, which Dad says real writers do.

It was not easy. It was work. But it was fun work (which seems like an oxymoron but might not be).

What I mean is: I liked feeling so focused. Instead of my mind being in lots of places, it was in just one place. And I was in charge. In real life, I don't have that much control over my cat or my friends or my family, but I guess I do have control over my work, or at least what words I put on what page.

Like, you can't 100 percent count on other people, but if you do your best, maybe you can count on yourself.

Last year, Mrs. (Bright) White said that if you have talent, you "owe it to yourself and others to put it to good use."

Well, I tried anyway.

I am now stapling one copy here, and tomorrow I will give a copy to Jerry Valentino. I hope he likes it more than *Alphabet Fish*. I revised this story so many times, I don't know if this is the fifteenth draft—or *fiftieth*. I kept thinking, "Ta-da! I'm done!" but then I kept making changes.

And now, without further ado, ta-da! Here's:

The Cat Who Wouldn't Purr
by Ava Wren, Age Eleven

Once upon a time, two sisters brought home a cat.
At first, the cat was very shy and very scared.
For three days, he hid in the dark under the sofa.
On day four, he crept out, whiskers first.

He found many things he liked to do.

He liked to nibble the tops of tulips.
He liked to drink water from the faucet.
He liked to burrow in brown bags.
And he liked to nap by the fireplace.

But he would not purr.

He liked to smell shoes that came in from outside.
He liked to watch movies on TV.

He liked to chase string and ping-pong balls and
laser lights.
And he liked to nap on folded clothes, warm from
the dryer.

But he would not purr.

He liked to hunt for flies.
He liked to sprawl on books.
He liked to step on keyboards and type mmmms
and zzzzs and jwfqs.
And he liked to nap in a corner of the closet, by
the slippers.

But he would not purr.

The two sisters began to feel impatient,
But they tried to keep the faith and
Respect their cat's inner nature.
Because you can't force a cat to do anything—

Especially purr!

One morning, after nibbling and chasing and hunting,
The cat found a rhombus of sunshine on the rug.
He licked himself, yawned, and tucked in his
tail.

He put one paw over his eyes and curled up for a catnap.

Did he purr?
No, he did not.

The younger sister began to brush the cat's fur.
She brushed slowly and gently, slowly and gently.
After a while, a long, long, long while,
She heard a funny, soft sound coming from deep inside the cat:

rumble bumble rumble bumble rumble bumble

She motioned for her sister to come over.
The older sister tiptoed over and began to pet the cat.
She pet his fur slowly and gently, slowly and gently.
And she heard the same sound coming from deep inside the cat:

rumble bumble rumble bumble rumble bumble

The two sisters smiled at each other,
The cat stayed in the sunshine and did not scamper off.

He let the girls brush him and pet him.
He even let them put their ears on his soft fur to listen to his

rumble bumble rumble bumble rumble bumble
rumble bumble rumble bumble rumble bumble

And he kept right on purring and purring and purring—
Safe and sound and snug in his brand-new home.

Ava Wren, Author for Real

1/29
FRIDAY NIGHT

DEAR DIARY,

Today was ridiculously exciting!

Not only was the author Jerry Valentino in our class, but so were both librarians—Mr. Ramirez and Mrs. (Bright) White—as well as a reporter (Rebecca) and a photographer (Rafael) from the *Misty Oaks Monitor*! We were supposed to act like everything was normal, but that was impossible with so many grown-ups around.

I kept watching them watching us and observing them observing us. They were looking at our classroom walls with the stapled-up drawings and handwritten compositions and posters about good habits and how to be a model middle school kid. I wondered what they thought of Mrs. Lemons's poster of a dog with glasses saying, "Bad spelling! Poor grammar! I cannot eat this homework!" And what they thought of our nutrition poster with its pea pods saying, "Peas try me," and cheese saying, "Choose cheese." Did they think it was cheesy?

I also observed the reporter reading the sign on Mrs. Lemons's desk that says, "Teachers touch tomorrow."

Today's first prompt was "playground accident," and we all wrote for five minutes. I wrote about the time I fell off the monkey bars, but I confess, I was distracted because I'd given Jerry Valentino my "manuscript," and while we were writing, he was *reading*!

Soon, we were sharing our playground accident stories out loud. Chuck's was the funniest. His was about when he was in kindergarten and he *had an accident* during recess. He actually peed on the slide because he hadn't realized he'd needed to go to the boys' room!

The second prompt was "frostbite or sunburn." Everyone wrote and wrote, and then we shared our stories. Today's stories were even better than Tuesday's because we've learned new techniques, and as Jerry Valentino put it, we were "digging deeper."

At the end of class, Jerry Valentino asked if I'd mind if he read my picture book out loud. I said no, but to be honest, inside I felt a little shaky. I never imagined that he'd read my words aloud with his deep author voice and with grown-up strangers in the room. But he did. And you know what? I thought my words sounded good. I hoped others thought so too.

"Any comments?" he asked.

Zara was the first to say she liked it, and I saw the photographer, Rafael, take a few pictures.

I looked at Chuck and he gave me a thumbs-up.

Maybelle said she liked "the rhythm of the words."

Riley said she liked the "specific details," and that it reminded her of a cat in her barn who likes to groom himself and how afterward, the tip of his tongue sometimes sticks out. Emily Sherman said, "I liked your story too, and that's saying a lot because I'm a dog person. I have a bichon frisé and a maltipoo. Cats give me hives."

Jerry Valentino jumped in and said he admired my "vivid verbs" and "colorful details" and "suspenseful buildup," and his only suggestion was for me to cut the opening "Once upon a time," because those words were cliché and not needed.

"You can cross them out," I said. He smiled and said, "*May* I?" I said, "Yes. You *may*. Please do. Thank you." He took his pencil and crossed out the four words.

At the end of the workshop, he told us all to be aware of how much "original and evocative" writing we could do in just five minutes. He said that whether we became authors or not, *everybody* writes messages and emails and reports and thank-you notes, so we should always strive to "have something to say and to say it well." He also gave us bonus pointers like "Avoid repetition," adding, "Unless you're repeating specific words or phrases on purpose, as Ava did so effectively."

After class, I didn't want anyone to think I was a teacher's pet, so I started to zoom out the door. But Jerry Valentino asked me to stay for a moment. So I did. Then he asked what inspired me. That was funny because last time he'd asked was in October in the Misty Oaks Library. This time, instead of talking to a big audience, I told my answer just to him, Mrs. Lemons, the reporter, and the photographer.

"Taco Cat!" I said and explained that I'd convinced my

parents to let me rescue a cat, but that, at first, he'd done nothing but hide.

The reporter took notes, and the photographer asked if it would be okay to take a photo of me and my cat.

I was surprised but said, "I guess."

"Are you free today after school?"

"This could be a human interest story for the Sunday paper," Rafael explained and handed me his cell phone. "Do you want to call your parents?"

I looked at Mrs. Lemons, and she was sort of beaming, so I said, "Okay." I was hoping Dad was home and would say, "Sure."

And he was. And he did.

Next thing you know, the reporter, the photographer, and I were in our living room. Taco was mostly keeping his distance while Dad was helping us get ready for the "photo shoot." Dad was moving stacks of newspapers and plumping up cushions while I changed into a red blouse and brushed my hair. When Rafael said he was all set, I picked up Taco and sat on the sofa, and for way over a minute, Taco didn't even wriggle. It was like he was posing too. And even though nobody did my makeup or adjusted lights or said, "Action!" the whole experience made me feel kind of like a movie star. So it was easy to smile for the camera. (When Rafael said, "Say 'Cheese!'" I thought of how, when Chuck takes pictures, he says, "Say 'Boogies!'")

Rebecca called her editor at the *Misty Oaks Monitor*, and said that if the paper had our permission and "enough space," they might want to run not just the photo, but also my cat book and cat haiku.

I said, "Okay," and Dad smiled. It was exciting that everything was happening so fast!

"This will be a feel-good story, if you will," Rebecca added.

"I will," I said, because it was all making *me* feel good.

Pip might never want her picture in the paper. But me, I love attention. The more, the merrier!

AVA WREN DOES IT AGAIN!

1/30
SATURDAY AFTERNOON

DEAR DIARY,

The big news today was that Dad made his famous Irish breakfast.

Will the big news tomorrow be me me me? Will *I* wake up famous?

AVA, ANONYMOUS (A BONUS WORD THAT MEANS WHEN
PEOPLE DON'T KNOW WHO YOU ARE)

DEAR DIARY,

Dad woke me with a giant smile on his face and handed me the newspaper. He never hands me the newspaper. He and Mom sometimes hand it to each other, but it's not like I care about town hall meetings or grocery store coupons.

"Take a look," Dad said.

Well, my eyes almost popped out of my head (gross metaphor) because Taco and I were on the front page!!! In color!!! And GIANT!!! There was a big photo of me with my red blouse and Taco with his white zigzag. And we looked pretty cute, if I do say so myself. (I hope that doesn't sound conceited.)

"Whoa, Dad, I had no idea—" I started to read the article about Jerry Valentino, when I saw, right next to it, "The Cat Who Wouldn't Purr"! There they were, my very own words (minus "Once upon a time")!

Our phone, which rarely rings unless there's an emergency or, like, an election, started ringing and ringing. Maybelle called and both her parents got on. Even Mr. Ramirez called! Mom called Nana Ethel, and she said, "Congratulations!" And Dad emailed Uncle Patrick the link to the article, photo, story, and haiku, and he said it was "the cat's pajamas" (which Dad said is a compliment).

And okay, I know the *Misty Oaks Monitor* is not *The New York Times* or whatever, but it is all very exciting!

Bea called too. She said her mom had thumbtacked the article to the bulletin board in Bates Books and scribbled, "a young writer to watch."

"Really?" I asked because last fall, Bea's mom had said I was a "young writer with a lot to learn."

"Really," Bea said. "She even tacked up one of your snowflakes next to it."

"Cool," I said because it *was* cool. So cool!

AVA WREN, YOUNG WRITER TO WATCH

2/1 AFTER DINNER
(WHICH WAS COUSCOUS WITH BOK CHOY
AND SUN-DRIED TOMATOES)

DEAR DIARY,

The newspaper article was posted on the bulletin board outside Principal Gupta's office with two thumbtacks, one yellow, one green. A lot of people, from the nurse to the custodian to the lunch lady, said nice things to me. Even scary Miss Hamshire, with her googly glasses. And even Alex Gladstone, the fourth-grader who got first prize in last year's library contest for his story about Ernie the Earthworm.

Monday scrambled is *dynamo*, and I guess today was very dynamic.

It was fun to have so many people come up to me. Embarrassing too—but mostly fun.

Chuck said, "I can't believe I have a famous friend! I thought you had to rob a bank to get your picture in the paper!" He told me two jokes, one about spelling and one about cats.

Joke One:
Question: Why is Old MacDonald a bad speller?
Answer: Because he adds E I E I O to every word.

Joke Two:

Question: When is it bad luck to see a black cat?

Answer: When you're a mouse.

Both jokes made me L-O-L—but Chuck can make me laugh just by flapping his arm and making farty noises. (Which is *sophomoric*, I know.)

Anyway, all this attention made me remember a story I wrote before vacation. It was called "Invisible Girl," and Dad and Mrs. Lemons had both liked it. "Invisible Girl" was about a girl who could disappear at will. At first, she thinks it's a fun trick. Then she gets lonely and realizes she'd much rather be visible than invisible.

AVA WREN, THE OPPOSITE OF INVISIBLE

2/1
IN BED

DEAR DIARY,

Tonight Mom put beets in the salad. I don't usually like colorful things in my salad; I like my salad green. But the beets were surprisingly okay. I even tried a brussels sprout. It was *bitter*, but *better* than I thought.

At dinner, Mom said Dr. Gross's entire staff got a kick out of seeing Taco in the paper. "And seeing *you* too!" she added. "Bob, we should frame the newspaper story, don't you think?"

Dad said, "Absolutely." (They've already framed three of Pip's drawings. Not that I've counted.)

After dinner, the phone rang and I picked up. A lady named Gretchen said she'd read the article and wanted to "drop by." She said she lived in Vernon Valley, which is "twenty minutes to the north." She sounded nervous, which was weird, but said that if tomorrow at 4:30 worked for me, it worked for her.

"Will one of your parents be there?" she asked.

"Probably my dad," I said.

After we hung up, a tiny part of me wondered if she was a scout for *The Today Show*. Or if she ran a publishing company and needed a book about cats. Maybe a happy book about a girl and her cat.

I mean, there are plenty of books out there about a boy and his dog. Pip went through a pile of them. *Old Yeller* and *Where the Red Fern Grows* and *The Call of the Wild* and *Beautiful Joe.* Most had unhappy endings, and when Pip would turn the last page, she'd be in a puddle on the sofa.

Pip galloped through horse books too, like *Black Beauty* and *National Velvet* and *The Red Pony* and *Misty of Chincoteague.* And *Seabiscuit*, which is for grown-ups. They had sad or scary parts too.

Anyway, there was something strange in the lady's tone. Why had she sounded nervous when *she's* the grown-up? Kids get nervous talking to grown-ups, not the other way around. And why had I told her she could come over? What if she's a…kidnapper??

I guess I could have mentioned this to Mom or Dad, but so many people called that I forgot.

AVA, A LITTLE APPREHENSIVE (WHICH MEANS WORRIED)

2/2 Groundhog Day
(well, Groundhog Night)

Dear Diary,

I've never had a day like this and I never want to again!!

At school this morning, I mentioned to Maybelle that a stranger was dropping by and that she had sounded nervous on the phone. Maybelle offered to come over, but said she was supposed to hang out with Zara, so could they both come? I said sure. And for once, I didn't even mind.

At 4:30 sharp, the doorbell rang. Mom was at work, Dad was running errands, and Pip, Maybelle, Zara, and I were in the living room. I peeked through the keyhole and saw a tall, skinny woman with short, fluffy, white hair standing in a red coat. She looked basically normal, so I opened the door.

I wish I hadn't!!!

She said she was Gretchen Guthrie and started complimenting my "nice story" about the "nice cat." I said thank you and noticed she kept looking all around. Suddenly Taco came bounding down the stairs, his white-tipped tail high in the air. He rubbed his zigzag against her shin and began weaving in and out of her legs.

"This is Taco," I said. I didn't get why Taco was being so friendly. Did the lady have catnip in her pockets?

She stooped down to pet him.

"May I pick him up?"

"He doesn't like being picked up," I said, but she scooped him up anyway and held him close and breathed him in. And Taco didn't mind! He didn't wriggle away or bite her nose or scratch her cheek or anything.

"What a cat," she said, and her voice caught. Pip and Maybelle and Zara stood up and walked over.

"This is my sister, Pip," I said. "And these are my friends, Maybelle and Zara." The word "friends" popped right out, which Zara probably appreciated.

Gretchen introduced herself while still holding on to Taco. Pip leaned in and scratched Taco behind the ears and under his chin.

"He likes that," the lady said, which was odd. Then she asked, "Are your parents here?"

"Our dad will be back soon," Pip replied. "He's buying groceries." I'd totally forgotten to tell Dad that she was coming by.

"I'll come back." She gave Taco a kiss on his head, which bothered me (though it didn't bother Taco), and put him down.

She left, and I shut the door behind her, glad it was just us kids again.

"She's a little weird," Zara pronounced. "Don't you think?"

None of us said anything, but none of us disagreed.

Zara marched to the living room window and pulled back the

curtain. "She got back into her car, but she's just sitting there," she reported. "I changed my mind: she's not *a little* weird; she's *a lot* weird."

"*Dangerous* weird?" Pip asked. "Like, Stranger Danger, let's call nine-one-one, weird?"

"I don't think so," I answered. "She was sweet to Taco."

"Too sweet," Zara pronounced. "All snuggly-wuggly." (Note: Zara wasn't bugging me as much as usual, probably because I was agreeing with what she was saying.) "Why isn't she leaving?" she asked. "Does she have a flat tire? Is she out of gas?"

"Is her battery dead?" Pip added.

"Is *she* dead?" Zara said.

Maybelle joined Zara by the window. After a minute, Maybelle said, "Hey, Ava, your dad just pulled into the driveway."

When Dad walked in with a bag of groceries, Zara announced, "Mr. Wren, a lady came while you were gone, and she's just sitting in her car out front, across the street. She hasn't left."

"A lady?" Dad said.

Zara pointed out the window and said, "A lady who looks like a Q-tip." Now all five of us were peeking out at Gretchen. She must have seen us because she got out of her car and came walking toward our door.

"Who is she?" Dad asked, still holding the groceries.

"You know how people kept calling yesterday?" I said. "I forgot to tell you that—"

The doorbell rang.

"Do we have to let her back in?" Zara asked. "I have a bad

feeling." Zara grabbed Taco and handed him to Maybelle. Taco started squirming, but Zara said, "Maybelle, take him to Ava's room. Go! Now! NOW!"

Maybelle looked confused, but she slung Taco over her shoulder and ran upstairs, two steps at a time, following orders. Dad looked confused too, but he put down his groceries and opened the door.

A gust of wintery air blew in, and so did Q-tip Lady. She introduced herself, and Dad said, "What can we do for you?"

She said, "Hello, Mr. Wren. I'm afraid we have a situation."

"A situation?" Dad repeated.

"I'm afraid you have my cat."

I swear, I thought I was going to faint on the floor right then and there! Pip and I stared at each other, and Zara started giving the lady the evil eye.

"My sister brought me a copy of the *Monitor* because she recognized Amber on the front page. She knew my cat had gotten lost over Christmas, and that I'd posted photos on Facebook and put flyers in stores. She knew I was *beside* myself! Well, my sister recognized Amber's coloring and his little lightning rod"—she touched her own forehead—"and when she read your daughter's story, she had no doubt." She turned to me, maybe expecting me to say something. But I just stood there in total, utter shock.

"Amber was standoffish with me at first too," she continued. "He's not a natural nuzzler. But you're right. He does like to be brushed, and he likes TV." She smiled at me.

I did not smile back. It was like I'd died inside. I was hoping Dad would ask Gretchen to do an about-face and march out the door. And what was in her hand? Was it a... cat carrier??

"I'm sorry to upset you," she concluded, "but Amber is mine. He belongs to me." She was looking all around for him, expecting him to race over again. "I adopted him four years ago last November, shortly after my husband died. He was just a kitten. Well, last month, my niece came to cat-sit over the holidays, and I guess she left a window open—"

"If you're talking about the cat who was just here," Zara interrupted, "he's dead. It just happened. It's terrible. It's...tragic. We're all, um, *beside* ourselves."

I wondered if Zara had gone nuts, but apparently she was just getting warmed up. "I'm sorry to, um, upset you, but he jumped out another window. I guess he likes windows— *liked*. Only this time he didn't land on his feet, the way cats are supposed to. He landed on his...head, and he died. He's...dead."

I thought for sure Dad was going to say something, but maybe he got distracted by Zara's "improv" skills. (Dad says every actor needs improvisational skills.)

"He's dead," Zara repeated. "*Deceased*. So it doesn't even matter whose cat he was."

Dad put his hand up to shoosh Zara and turned to the lady. "Mrs. Guthrie," he began—but then we all heard a loud strange pounding from above. *Thump. Thump thump! Thump THUMP THUMP!* At first I didn't know what it was. Then I realized it was Taco hurling himself against my bedroom door! He wanted out—probably because he sensed that his "owners" were both downstairs. Gretchen looked up toward the noise, and Taco started yowling and howling. I heard my door open, and we all watched as Taco came flying downstairs.

"Oh, my mistake," Zara mumbled. "I guess he survived." She took a small step back.

"Amber!" Gretchen said. She picked him up and threw him over her shoulder like a scarf.

Taco didn't resist, but he shot me a glance, and I wondered what he was thinking.

"His name isn't Amber," Pip piped up bravely. "It's Taco."

"Taco Cat," I heard myself say. "T-A-C-O-C-A-T. It's a palindrome. Like Ava, A-V-A. And Pip, P-I-P." I gestured toward Dad. "And D-A-D, or, well, B-O-B."

Gretchen nodded. "I'm sorry, Ava." She was looking right at me. "Really, I am."

"I'm sorry too," Maybelle whispered to Zara and me. "I couldn't hold on to him. He was going crazy. He even scratched me a little, though I know he didn't mean it."

"I want to thank all of you very much," Gretchen said, "but now I am going to go ahead and take Amber home. My niece has been feeling terrible. She's going to be so relieved—"

"You can't just *take* him!" Zara practically shouted.

"Mrs. Guthrie," Dad said very calmly, "we adopted this cat on New Year's Eve from the Misty Oaks Rescue Center. We rescued him and he is ours."

"Yes, but I rescued him first," she said. "I got Amber at the ASPCA. I have papers. He was my cat. He was my *kitten*!"

I tried to picture Taco as a playful kitty with matching ears.

"I don't doubt that," Dad replied matter-of-factly. "And clearly Taco is comfortable with you. But we have papers too."

"That's right," Pip said softly.

"I'm sorry," Dad added.

I was grateful to Dad and Pip and even Zara and Maybelle, because mostly I was trying not to faint. Was this really happening? My insides were cramping up.

Gretchen said, "May I sit down?" and sat in Dad's big brown chair before Dad even said "Sure." Her whole body seemed to crumple into it.

Taco (Amber?) rubbed against her legs and jumped onto her lap. He was facing her, and she was stroking him, and watching them gave me a lump in my throat *and* a knot in my stomach. I couldn't believe everything was going so wrong so fast.

"I have years of photos right here on my cell phone." Gretchen started fumbling with her phone to prove it, then realized we weren't doubting her. "And I'm very grateful to you all for taking care of him. Really. I can see he had a rough time." She was rubbing his left ear and examining the jagged part. Taco/Amber was not even objecting.

"Our mom works for a vet," I said, speaking up at last. "He's the one who stitched Taco up. Last week, Taco had another emergency—he couldn't pee—and Dr. Gross took care of him again. And it was on a *Sunday*!" I wanted her to know that we got VIP treatment for his UTI, and we were an excellent... *foster* family?

Gretchen gave me a sad smile, stood up with Taco/Amber, and started heading toward the front door. "I'll just put him in the cat carrier," she said. "And I'll reimburse you for the veterinary expenses. I know how expensive that can be."

I didn't know whether to cry or run to my room. It didn't help that I knew we were both right: Taco was mine...but Amber was hers. I mean, I could say that Gretchen reminded me of Cruella de Vil, but she wasn't really a monster. She was a lonely widow whose cat got lost. And she loved Amber. But *I* loved Taco!!!

Gretchen started lowering Taco/Amber into her cat carrier, and again said that she was "going to take him home."

Dad and I looked at each other. Zara took a step forward and said, "Over our dead bodies!"

Dad said, "Zara, that's enough."

Zara shouted, "It's *not* enough!" and placed herself between Gretchen and our front door. For a second, I thought Zara was going to challenge Gretchen to a duel or something.

Dad ignored Zara, but then he said, "Mrs. Guthrie, you cannot just come into our home and take our cat. He was Ava's birthday present—and he's our family's first pet."

"Not counting Goldy Lox," Pip said, and I nodded.

Dad continued and said very clearly, "So I'm afraid *that* is the 'situation.' The cat belongs to us now." We all watched as Gretchen tried to stuff Taco/Amber into her cat carrier, but he wouldn't go in. He kept sticking out his nose and paws. Soon Gretchen was seeming less sure of herself. Dad softened a little and said, "If you would like to visit him from time to time, you're welcome to."

"Joint custody?!" Zara muttered.

Dad gave Zara a stern look and turned back to Gretchen, "Perhaps you could take care of him when we go on vacation…"

"We never go on vacation," I said. It just slipped out.

Taco/Amber started meowing and was shoving out his paws more and more frantically, and finally Gretchen unzipped the zipper, and he jumped out and raced off. But he came right back and started weaving between her legs *and* my legs. I was glad she didn't try to pick him up again. I didn't either.

"I need some air," Gretchen said, leaning against the wall. Maybe *she* was trying not to faint too. "But this matter has not been settled," she added.

"Yes, it has!" Zara said.

"Zara, be quiet!" Dad scolded. He doesn't usually criticize kids unless he's tutoring them (and that doesn't count because parents *pay* him to be critical).

Gretchen kneeled down to pet Taco/Amber and said, "I'm glad you found such a good family when you needed one." She looked at Dad, then Pip, then me, then back at her cat. "I was so very worried about you," she whispered. "I really, really missed you." She sort of buried her face in his fur, as if she wanted to remember how he smelled.

Well, that got me feeling bad for *her*. Her eyes were all shiny, and she looked as if she might have a breakdown right in our living room, which I hoped she wouldn't.

After that, she didn't say another word. She just gave Amber/ Taco a giant last squeeze and left our house really fast. The door clicked behind her.

"Wow," said Dad.

"Can you believe the nerve of some people?" Zara said.

"I know!" Pip agreed.

"That was crazy!" Maybelle said.

"She's crazy!" Zara said.

I looked at Taco and took a breath. "I don't know," I began. "If I went on vacation, and my niece was supposed to feed my cat, but instead she opened a window, and the cat got out, and someone *adopted* him and renamed him…I'd be upset too."

Zara shrugged. "Finders keepers, losers weepers!"

"She *did* seem like she was about to weep," Pip said.

"She did," Maybelle agreed.

"Kids, Taco is *our* cat," Dad said. "We didn't make anything up."

"But she didn't make anything up either," I said. "And it wasn't her fault that her husband died, and her niece was a bad cat-sitter, and her cat jumped out the window. Cats are naturally curious."

"It *was* her fault she named him Amber," Zara said. "She should never have done that to a boy cat!"

"It *is* a terrible name for a boy cat," Maybelle agreed.

"She could have named him Leo or Lightning or Simba or *anything* else," Zara stated.

"Lightning would have been good," Pip agreed.

"On a scale of one to ten of boy cat names," Zara said, "Amber is a two and Taco Cat is a ten."

"Exactly," Maybelle said.

Zara walked back to her spying spot. "I swear, something is seriously *wrong* with that lady! She still hasn't left! She's just sitting in her car, leaning her head on the steering wheel." Zara shook her head. "Go away!" she said into the darkness. "Why are you still here?"

I walked toward the window. "There's nothing *wrong* with her," I said. "She doesn't want to leave without her cat. I can't blame her for that. She *loves* him!"

"Ava," Pip said, "it's not *her* cat. It's *your* cat."

"He was hers first and for much longer," I said, looking at Amber/Taco, who was now pacing by the front door even though he'd never before asked to be let out. He even meowed once. "He was hers first, fair and square. For four *years*."

"And now he's *yours*, fair and square," Zara said. "He probably ran away on purpose!"

"I don't think so," I said quietly. "And it doesn't feel one hundred percent right for us to keep Amber."

"It's *not* Amber. It's Taco!" Dad said. "And, sweetie, things hardly ever feel one hundred percent right."

"I know but…" I picked up Amber/Taco, and slung him over my shoulder and tried to wear him like a scarf, but he wouldn't let me. So I held him in my arms, the regular way. "Is she still out there?"

"Yes," Zara said. "She obviously has a screw loose!"

Well, maybe *I* had a screw loose, because next thing you know, I opened the front door, holding tight to Amber/Taco.

I went down our front walk, looking both ways because Mom and Dad always say, "Better a second of your life than your life in a second." I crossed the street and approached Gretchen's car and tapped on the window. My heart was pounding! She looked startled, but rolled the window halfway down.

"Here," I said, lifting up Amber and tilting him in. He scrambled into her warm car. "He's your cat. He was yours first." My throat was tight, and my eyes started to prickle. "I guess I was… borrowing him."

Gretchen looked dumbfounded and said, "I don't know what to say."

My voice was all shaky. "Just say, 'Thank you.'" We looked at each other for what felt like a really long time, and I didn't know if I was doing the right thing or making the biggest mistake of my life. "If you go on any more trips, call us. We'll borrow him back and take really, really good care of him."

Amber settled onto Gretchen's lap, and I reached in and stroked his head. I studied him one last time, his mismatched ears and wispy whiskers and taco-colored fur. I even mumbled, "Good-bye, Taco." But he didn't look back at me. And to tell you the truth, my heart started breaking in two…then four…then a hundred little pieces.

"Thank you," Gretchen said, "Ava, thank you very much."

I was freezing. I hadn't put on my coat, and my nose and toes were tingling, and my hands were turning to ice, and my eyes were beginning to burn because I was beginning to cry. I didn't want to say, "You're welcome," and I didn't want to burst into tears, and it was too late to change my mind, so I just turned and ran home.

Inside, I shut the door behind me and went straight to Dad's big brown chair and curled up. And there, in front of Dad and Pip and Maybelle and even Zara, I started to bawl my eyes out. Big, loud, pitiful, wracking sobs. I couldn't help it.

The only one who didn't see me sobbing was Amber/Taco because he wasn't ours anymore. I'd given him away!

To be continued because I really have to pee.

AVA, ADMIRABLE BUT *ANGUISHED*

A LITTLE LATER, IN MY PAJAMAS

Mom came home, and our living room was as sad as a cemetery. We told her everything, and she said, "Oh, honey," about twelve times and handed me tissues and even offered to be on the lookout for another cat, "not right away, not this week, but soon."

Zara kept saying she didn't get it. Maybelle just sat by me because she knew I felt miserable, and when you feel miserable, it helps if your best friend is with you even if she doesn't say a single solitary word.

After Zara and Maybelle left, we had dinner, and Pip barely said anything. I could tell she was really upset, and I felt bad because I hadn't thought about how much *she* loved Taco.

Now I'm going to bed. I hope I don't have nightmares.

A

DEAR DIARY,

I'm skipping lunch and writing in you in the library. (I was afraid I might cry if I went to the lunchroom.)

I can't believe I gave Taco away! I guess I was trying to be noble or altruistic or mature or something, but really, I'm just a stupid moron. This morning Mom and Dad and Pip seemed depressed at breakfast. And of course Taco didn't come in and cheer us up and brush our legs and ask for *his* breakfast.

How could I have forgotten that even though Taco was mine, we *all* loved him?

Last night when I was trying to fall asleep, I could almost hear Taco padding into my room and almost feel him jumping onto my bed. I remembered a story from the Bible (not Aesop). It goes like this:

A bouncing baby boy was set before King Solomon, and two different women were crying and saying the baby was hers and that the other lady had stolen him. "It's my baby!" they both said. "She's lying!" King Solomon didn't know who was telling the truth, so he grabbed a sword and said, "Tell you what. Let's divide the baby in two, and you can each have half." The first lady said, "Okay, sounds fair," but the second lady started screaming bloody murder and said, "Noooo! Don't kill him! She can keep him! Just let him live!" And that's how King Solomon, who was very wise, knew the second lady was the real mother, and the first lady was a liar. He handed the baby back to his actual mom, and they lived happily ever after.

Here's what I think: Gretchen may have been Amber/Taco's first "mom," but I was his real "mom" too! Why oh why did I give him back??

Question: If I hadn't, would I have felt bad for Gretchen? Or guilty about keeping him?

Answer: Maybe. But not thaaat bad or guilty. Or maybe only at first?

Mr. Ramirez has been looking at me. I think he knows I'm upset. But he hasn't walked over because one of his rules is, "Never interrupt a person who is writing."

AVA THE IDIOT

AFTER DINNER

DEAR DIARY,

I came home after school, and even though I knew Taco wouldn't be there, I didn't know how it would feel.

Here's how it felt: awful.

Here's where Taco wasn't: He wasn't at the front door. He wasn't on Dad's brown chair. He wasn't on the armrest of the sofa. He wasn't by the fireplace. He wasn't hiding in Mom's closet. He wasn't on my bed. He wasn't anywhere.

Our house feels sad and silent and sorrowful. And more like a *house* than a *home*.

Dinner was pizza, but I could barely taste it. Mom started to tell a story about what happened at the clinic today, and some dog that had been peeing on the carpet and how the owners bought him "Tinkle Tonic." But then she stopped because she could tell none of us wanted to hear it.

AVA, CATLESS

I didn't sleep well because the second I woke up, I remembered Taco was gone, and then I couldn't get back to sleep.

AVA, EXHAUSTED

I don't know why I even opened you because I don't have anything to say.

You know the expression "at a loss for words"? That's me right now.

AVA, WORDLESS

I noticed that Dad put a photo of Taco by his desk, Mom changed her cell phone photo to a picture of us with Taco, and Pip has been sketching more cats than flowers.

Dad, Mom, Pip, and I are very different, but loving Taco was one thing we all had in common.

A

DEAR DIARY,

We had a spelling test and Chuck and I graded each other's papers and he said I'm amazing.

"I don't feel amazing," I said. "I feel sad." I told him I feel as sad as I felt on Tuesday.

"That's only three days ago," he said. "It would be weird if you didn't still feel sad." I nodded, and to be honest, that made me feel a tiny bit less sad.

Mrs. Lemons asked if I was okay. I shrugged because I couldn't bear to tell her about Taco, and besides, I was pretty sure Zara already had.

"Ava, you'll like this," Mrs. Lemons said, and wrote this on the board:

"I love cooking

my pets and

my family."

She asked our class, "What's wrong with this sentence?"

Well, I could have blurted, "It needs commas!" because on the board, it looked like the confession of a cannibal.

But I let Riley answer because I didn't want to talk about pets or family.

After school, Dad said he wanted to try a recipe for "spaghetti and wheat balls."

I said, "Please don't," and (this is embarrassing) my voice got wobbly. Dad hugged me, and I started crying a little.

He said he'd make me regular bow tie noodles, and I nodded into his chest, which got the front of his shirt damp.

Observation: When you feel sad, you want regular food, not fancy food or experimental food. Right now, if Jerry Valentino told me to write about something "warm and comforting," I might even write about bow tie noodles.

I wish I'd never written "The Cat Who Wouldn't Purr"!

Except...wait.

You know what?

That's not totally true.

Confession: (1) I liked writing it, and (2) I liked that people liked reading it.

I guess what I wish is that Gretchen Guthrie had never seen Taco's photo in the newspaper. I can't believe I gave her back her cat—*our* cat.

She loves him, that's true, but I love him too. *Loved?*

I wonder how Taco/Amber is doing.

Here's how I'm doing: bad.

A

DEAR DIARY,

I decided I had to *do something*, so I got out a piece of paper and wrote Gretchen a letter. After a few false starts and one really long, dumb practice letter, I finally settled with:

Dear Gretchen Guthrie,
I've been thinking about you and Amber (a.k.a. Taco). Can you tell him I say hi? And that my whole family misses him a lot?
　Please write back. And please send a photo that I can frame. It doesn't have to be new, but if possible, I would like it to be of him as a cat, not a kitten, because that's how I will always think of him.

Thank you.

Ava Wren

I was going to draw a cat next to my name, but instead, I folded up my letter and tucked it into an envelope. Then I knocked on

408

Pip's door and asked her to draw Taco on the back. She did. I added a cat sticker on the front and knocked on Mom and Dad's door. Mom took my decorated envelope and said she'd look up Gretchen's address and mail the letter this weekend.

A

Saturday morning, still in bed

I dreamed we got a big friendly golden retriever. He fetched sticks and chased balls and went on walks and seemed like he would never leave our side! But then he went swimming in a dark pond, and he came out and started shaking off the water. He was shaking and shaking, and suddenly he started fading away and disappearing! I tried to hug him, but he wasn't there.

I woke up crying! And now I'm the exact *opposite* of well rested.

A

DEAR DIARY,

Dad is rereading a giant book called *War and Peace*. He says he "can't put it down." It's so long and heavy, I don't know how he can pick it *up*!

He said he wishes he spoke Russian because it "probably lost something in translation."

I said, "Do books ever *gain* something in translation?"

He laughed and said he was going to have to think about that.

I was glad I made Dad laugh. And I wished I liked to read more because then I could be all involved in someone else's up-and-down life instead of just my own.

But I'm more of a writer than a reader. So far, anyway.

How long will it be until I feel better? I'm glad I have you.

AVA, STILL MOPING

Dear Diary,

Pip drove me crazy tonight. Every fifteen minutes, she said things like, "It's vanilla, but it's not chocolate."

Or "It's good, but it's not great."

Or "It's silly, but it's not clever."

Or "It's funny, but it's not amusing."

Or "It's terrible, but it's not awful."

Or "It's noodles, but it's not pasta."

Or "It's speedy, but it's not fast."

Finally I told her I didn't know what she was talking about and I was going to clobber her if she didn't cut it out. She said, "It's clobber, but it's not hit, *and* it's killing, but it's not murdering." Well, somehow, just like that, I figured out that she was doing a word game about double letters.

So I said, "It's letters, but it's not sounds, right?"

"That is indeed correct!" she said.

Not to be violent, but considering the gloomy mood I've been in, Pip is lucky I didn't hack her up into itty bitty pieces.

AVA ELLE WREN, NOT IN THE MOOD

PS I'm probably lucky Pip is even talking to me. If she'd given away our family's first real pet, I'd have a hard time forgiving her. Sometimes I do stuff that's well-meaning but boneheaded. Dad said that I'm "a little impulsive," which I think means "not thinking enough."

I asked Maybelle to come over and said she could even invite Zara if she wanted. I need to get out of my funk. These have been the longest days of my life. They've been like *forty-eight*-hour days!!

AVA, TRYING

DEAR DIARY,

Wait. Till. You. Hear. This.

Mom and Dad were running an errand, and Maybelle and Zara and Pip were playing Monopoly, and I was under a blanket on the sofa.

After her turn, Zara got up and peeked out the window. "You guys," she said, "isn't that Q-tip Lady's car?"

Maybelle and Zara and Pip smooshed against the window.

"It *is*! What the heck does she want now?" Zara said.

"Maybe to pay us for the vet bills?" Pip said.

"Why isn't she getting out?" Maybelle said.

"Yeah. Why is she just *sitting* there? It's like she's *thinking* about getting out." Zara kept narrating, so I went to look. "She opened the door but then she closed it again!" Zara made a face. "Wait, now she *is* getting out—but she's still taking her time about it!"

Maybelle said, "Should we go to her?"

Zara said, "No way!" so we all just watched as Gretchen started heading up our front walk.

"Here she comes," Pip said.

The doorbell rang, and we looked at each other, and I decided I'd be the one to let her in.

Well, get ready because here comes the Holy Moly part: Gretchen stepped inside, and instead of handing us a check, she unbuttoned her red coat. First, I heard a muffled mew. Next, I saw a furry snout. Then I saw soft whiskers and green eyes. And finally there was Taco/Amber!!!! Gretchen held him out (her eyes were a little puffy), and I stretched out my arms, and she pressed him against me, and I closed my arms around him, and she backed away. And Taco peered up at me as if to say, "Hi."

"Ava," Gretchen began, "I love this cat. I really do. But I've hardly slept a wink all week, and Amber didn't sleep through the nights either—"

"Me neither," I said although I hadn't meant to interrupt.

"I think he's been sleeping all day while I'm at work. At night, he's been running around and meowing and"—she looked at me—"asking about you."

Was she saying what I hoped she was saying?

"Ava," Gretchen continued, "I work long hours and I travel a lot for business. Even this week, I'll be away three days." She sighed. "I guess I've come to realize that I'm not around as much for…our cat as you and your family would be."

I kept petting Taco and listening as hard as I could. I could feel Pip and Maybelle and Zara staring at me, but I didn't want to look away from Taco and Gretchen.

"What I'm saying is: I'm glad he found a good home when he needed one, and that you love him as much as I do. So if you want to keep him, well, I want you to." Her voice quavered. "I know you'll take good care of him."

I held Taco tight—he was the softest, sweetest, furriest feline in the world. "For real?" I squeaked. "You're giving him back?" I wanted to be 100 percent sure before I let myself do a happy dance, even in my head.

She nodded, and I hugged Taco harder—but still gently, of course. "Yes. But if you let me, I *would* like to visit him from time to time."

Zara lunged forward and gave Gretchen a big hug. "I'm sorry I lied and said he died," she said. "Sometimes I just say stuff."

Gretchen smiled. "You were trying to help your friend."

Zara looked at me and I realized it was true, she was. Even when Zara bugged me, like when we were making paper mice, or when she talked to Chuck, or when she told Mr. Ramirez about our fish book, maybe, in her own way, she was trying to be helpful. And I couldn't really blame her for wanting to be friends with Maybelle.

Pip, Maybelle, and Zara all started petting Taco, who was still in my arms. Pip turned to Gretchen and said, "You can visit him anytime. Just call. And if you ever want to, we could go with you to the rescue center and help you pick out a new kitten."

"They have really cute ones," I said.

"You could even get a *pair* of kittens," Pip said. "That way, they could keep each other company during the day, chasing each other around and tiring each other out."

"If you take *two* kittens, it's free," I added.

Gretchen smiled at us both. "Let's take one day at a time." She buttoned her red coat back up. "Please tell your parents that I would like to stop by from time to time," she said. "And tell them they raised two very good kids."

Well, we were thanking her and saying one last good-bye, when guess who came home? Mom and Dad!

We told them everything, and they thanked Gretchen too. After a little while, Dad suddenly said, "Would you like to stay for dinner? We're having Irish stew. It's one of my signature dishes."

She hesitated for two seconds, then said, "You know what? I'd like that very much."

Dad said, "Great," so I asked if Maybelle and Zara could stay too. He said, "Sure." Maybelle called her parents, Zara called her grandparents, and Mom and Pip and I set the table for seven. We even lit candles, which we hardly ever do. And we all had a really nice dinner, grown-ups at one end, and Pip, Maybelle, Zara, and I at the other. It felt a tiny bit like Thanksgiving, but without the turkey and cranberries and stress.

We talked about a lot of things, and I asked Gretchen if she got my letter. She said no, and Mom said, "That's because I just mailed it. There's no mail on Sunday." Gretchen said she'd keep an eye out for it, and Pip mentioned that she drew a picture of Taco on the back.

Speaking of Taco, he stayed close by all during dinner. He was curled up on the sofa, fast asleep, one white paw over his face.

And I have to say: he looked right at home.

AVA WREN, HAPPY AGAIN

DEAR DIARY,

I was looking over these pages when Dad knocked on my door. "Come in," I said, halfway under the covers.

"Special delivery," Dad said and deposited Taco on my lap.

"Thank you!" I said.

"Can you believe how everything worked out?"

I nodded but didn't answer because I didn't want to scare Taco.

"You know," Dad said, "not to play the Homonym Game or anything, but, Ava, you did the *write* thing and the *right* thing."

"Last year, I did the write thing and the *wrong* thing," I whispered. It was always embarrassing to remember that I'd based "Sting of the Queen Bee" on our friend Bea.

"Well, tonight I think you should feel proud of yourself."

"You know how you and I are *both* writers?" I replied.

"Yes," he said and smiled.

"Someday I might want to write a book about a girl and a cat."

"Why not?" he said, a little too loudly.

I said "Shhh" and pointed to Taco. He was settling in by my shoulder, and for once, he was facing my face, not my feet.

"Someday," Dad said, lowering his voice, "I can see you writing that book. But right now, it's time to turn off the light." He gave me a good-night kiss and gave Taco a good-night pat.

"Dad," I said, showing him you, my diary. "Can you believe I'm almost out of pages?"

"Impressive! Maybe we can go to Bates Books tomorrow and get you a new one."

"Okay if I write for a few more minutes?"

"Okay by me," he said and left the door open a crack.

What I want to do now is scribble down a few notes for the book I might want to write someday. It could be about a girl who rescues a cat and doesn't know that the cat has *already* been rescued. When she finds out, she's very upset but also pretty mature for someone who just turned eleven, and she ends up offering the cat back to his first owner even though this makes her cry her eyes out. (She's not thaaaat mature.) Five days later, the first owner says the girl can keep the cat after all. So the story has a happy ending, which is good, since it would be for kids.

Mom just came in to say good night. She saw Taco and whispered, "Sweet dreams, Ava. You too, Taco."

I whispered, "You too, Mom."

I've been thinking. If my story were a fable, it would need a moral. Maybe something like: When you're generous, it comes back to you.

I wonder if that is true. I bet it usually is.

I also wonder how long it would take to write an *entire* book.

Rhymes and haiku (and sometimes rhyming haiku) come to me pretty fast. For instance:

Ava and Taco Cat

I like my cat and

I like to write, but now it's

time to say good night.

But a book? That would be a *lot* of work. Then again, it might be fun work—especially if I use my head and my heart and my senses.

Well, I'm going to turn off the light. I'm also going to try *not* to move a single solitary muscle—even if I get an itch—because I want Taco to stay with me as long as possible. Right now his eyes are closed, and he's purring *and* kneading. It's like he's in a trance.

I love him so much! And he loves me back—in his own skittish, cattish way.

Will he stay with me until morning? I doubt it. But I hope that tonight at least, he'll stick around long enough for me to fall asleep first.

Even if he doesn't, Taco is my *forever* cat—I'm never letting him go again!

I love the sound of his purring and purring.

What a purrfect way to end this day!

H-U-H. Maybe it's a good way to end a book too...

PALINDROMES AND BONUS PALINDROMES

How many palindromes and palindrome sentences are there? Tons! Especially if you look at other languages.

In Spanish, there's *YO SOY*, which means "I am," and *LA RUTA NATURAL*, which means "the natural route," and *ANITA LAVA LA TINA*, which means "Anita washes the tub."

In French, there's *ÉTÉ*, which is "summer," and *ÉSOPE RESTE ICI ET SE REPOSE,* which, believe it or not, means "Aesop stays here and rests."

And that's just for starters!

A total stickler might argue that true palindromes cannot have commas or colons or periods or apostrophes or accents. But Ava Wren is more of a word nerd than a stickler. And while she likes one-word palindromes, such as KOOK and BOOB and ROTATOR and REDIVIDER (not to mention WOW, XOX, YAY, and ZZZ), she loves longer ones.

Here are some of Ava's favorites, old and new, in alphabetical order:

ABLE WAS I ERE I SAW ELBA.

A DOG! A PANIC IN A PAGODA!

A MAN, A PLAN, A
CANAL: PANAMA
A NUT FOR A JAR OF
TUNA
A SANTA AT NASA!
A SANTA LIVED AS A
DEVIL AT NASA.
AS I PEE, SIR, I SEE PISA!
A TOYOTA'S A TOYOTA
BORROW OR ROB
CAIN: A MANIAC
DENNIS SINNED.
DESSERTS, I STRESSED!
DID I DO, O GOD, DID
I AS I SAID I'D DO?
GOOD, I DID!
DOG DOO? GOOD GOD!
DO GEESE SEE GOD?
DRAWN ONWARD
DRAW, O COWARD!
DUMB MOBS BOMB
MUD.
DUMB MUD
ED IS ON NO SIDE.
EVA, CAN I STAB BATS IN
A CAVE?
EVADE ME, DAVE!

EVIL OLIVE
FLEE TO ME, REMOTE
ELF!
FUN ENUF
GNU DUNG
GO HANG A SALAMI, I'M
A LASAGNA HOG!
GOLD LOG
HE DID, EH?
HE LIVED AS A DEVIL,
EH?
HE WON A TOYOTA
NOW, EH?
HOHOHOH
I DID, DID I?
I'M, ALAS, A SALAMI.
I MOAN, NAOMI!
IN WORDS, ALAS,
DROWN I.
I PREFER PI.
LION IN OIL
LIVE NOT ON EVIL!
LLAMA MALL
LONELY TYLENOL
MA IS AS SELFLESS AS I
AM.
MADAM, I'M ADAM.

MADAM, IN EDEN I'M
ADAM.
MIRROR RIM
MY GYM
NIAGARA, O ROAR
AGAIN!
NAME NOW ONE MAN.
NEIL, AN ALIEN!
NEVER ODD OR EVEN.
NO, IT IS OPPOSITION.
NO MELON, NO LEMON
NO MISS, IT IS SIMON.
NORMA IS AS SELFLESS
AS I AM, RON.
NO SIR—AWAY! A PAPAYA
WAR IS ON!
NO SIR, PREFER PRISON!
NOT A BANANA BATON!
NOT A TON
NOT SO, BOSTON!
NOW EVE, WE'RE HERE,
WE'VE WON.
NOW I WON!
NOW SIR, A WAR IS WON.
NURSES RUN.
OH WHO WAS IT I SAW,
OH WHO?

PARTY BOOBYTRAP
POP POP POP
REWARD DRAWER
RISE TO VOTE, SIR!
ROY, AM I MAYOR?
SENILE FELINES
SH! TOM SEES MOTHS.
SIR, I'M IRIS.
SO MANY DYNAMOS!
SOME MEN INTERPRET
NINE MEMOS.
SPACE CAPS
STACK CATS
STAR RATS
STAR COMEDY BY
DEMOCRATS!
STELLA WON NO
WALLETS.
STEP ON NO PETS.
SUE US.
TATTARRATTAT
TOO BAD I HID A BOOT.
TOP SPOT
TOO HOT TO HOOT
WAS IT A CAR OR A CAT I
SAW?
WONTON? NOT NOW.

YO BANANA BOY!
and
#AMMIT I'M MAD

Oh wait, here's one more:
AIBOHPHOBIA
It means the irrational fear of palindromes!

AVA
XOX

CAROL WESTON

sourcebooks
jabberwocky

For Steve Geck

2/8
BEFORE DINNER

Dear New Diary,

I'm pretty upset about what happened today.

My new friend Zara asked if I'd heard about Chuck.

"No, what about him?" I said.

"He and Kelli are going out," she said.

"How do you know?" I asked because this did *not* seem possible, and, well, Zara has kind of a big mouth.

She said Chuck was on the bus minding his own business when Kelli hopped on and sat right next to him without asking. She was wearing one of her sparkly headbands—she has about a million—and sneaking bites of banana bread even though you're not supposed to eat on the bus. She offered him a piece. And he took it.

Later, in homeroom, Kelli passed Chuck a note that said, "Do you want to go out?" Zara said it had two circles, one marked YES and one marked NO. At first Chuck didn't answer, but Kelli made a sad puppy face, so he put an X in the YES circle and passed it back.

And now they are "going out"!!

I have to say, this really bugs me.

Number one: we're only in fifth grade.

Number two: Chuck and I have been friends since the apple-picking field trip in kindergarten, and Kelli just moved here last year, and I've never once noticed him notice her.

It just doesn't seem right that they've said about five sentences to each other—total—and all of a sudden they're "going out"! How long has she even liked him? Did she start *today*?

And how can they be going out when none of us is allowed to go anywhere anyway?

Lunch was spaghetti and meatballs, which I usually love, but my insides felt like cold, stuck-together spaghetti. It didn't help that Zara and my best friend Maybelle were talking about Valentine's Day, which is Saturday.

Our grade has three Emilys, but only one Ava, one Maybelle, and one Zara, and lately the six of us have been sitting together at lunch. Well, it's usually all-girl or all-boy, but today, Kelli plunked her tray down at Chuck's table! I was in shock! The Emilys just giggled, and Emily Jenkins said, "Kelli and Chuck make a good couple." And everyone agreed!

I swear, that made me want to throw up my meatballs. (Sorry if that's gross.)

The problem is that I'm not supposed to care as much as I guess I do. Last month, Zara asked if I liked Chuck, and I said no.

Why *do* I care anyway? Chuck is sweet and funny, but I think of him as a brother.

At least I *think* I think of him as a brother.

A sweet, funny brother.

Nothing more.

We're just friends.

H-U-H. That's a weird expression, isn't it? "*Just* friends." As though years of being friends is less important than *hours* of "going out."

AVA, ANNOYED

BEDTIME

DEAR DIARY,

One thing about Kelli: she's bubbly. Very bubbly. If you poured too much bubble bath in your bathtub and forgot to turn off the water, that's how much she bubbles. She's always laughing hysterically as if the whole world is a joke and she's the only one who gets it.

She also does splits and handstands and cartwheels at random times, which is impressive but show-offy. And she talks a lot about her lake house and vacations, which isn't polite considering the rest of us have one house, not two, and we have "staycations," not fancy trips. Another thing that bothers me is when Kelli's headband and fingernail polish match. (Today, they were emerald.)

She should take it down a notch.

Or move to a different school!

Anyway, when I got home today, Dad was taking out ingredients to make a yucky, squishy squash recipe for Meatless Monday (his new-ish tradition), so I told him a vegetable riddle:

Question: What room has no windows or doors?

Answer: A mushroom!

I asked if we could go to Bates Books so I could get a new diary—you!—and he said sure. (Dad likes that we're both writers.) I was glad because I *really* needed a place to dump all my feelings—as you can see because I've *already* filled five pages!

So far in my life, I have finished two diaries and given up on six. The unfinished ones are in a dead diary graveyard underneath my underwear.

I got my coat, and we drove over, and Dad and I walked inside the bookstore, and there were hearts everywhere! Red ones and pink ones. Big ones and little ones. Flat ones and 3-D ones and ones hanging from the ceiling. There were also Valentine's Day books, cards, pins, pens, mugs, magnets, stickers, and even giant heart doilies and heart-shaped boxes of chocolate. The owners of the bookstore are my friend Bea's parents, and she says they try to sell tons of holiday knickknacks so they can afford to keep selling regular books.

Confession: the happy hearts made me sort of sad.

I just can't believe Kelli asked Chuck out! And that this aggravates me so much.

Dad offered to buy me a box of Valentine cards, but I said no thanks. I told him that in second and third grade, our whole class used to exchange valentines, but now I'm too old.

"Too old?" Dad thought that was funnier than my mushroom riddle. "How about chocolate kisses? Are you too old for chocolate kisses?" He picked up a bag of chocolate kisses wrapped in silver and set it on the counter. Fortunately, moods are contagious, and Dad's good mood was helping me shake off my bad mood.

"I am the exact right age for chocolate kisses," I said, and on the way home, I unwrapped one for each of us.

AVA, AGGRAVATED

EARLY MORNING

DEAR DIARY,

I just had the worst nightmare! I dreamed I was naked in school!! NAKED IN SCHOOL!!! I was in gym class and looked down and I wasn't wearing any clothes at all.

Not even any underwear!

Not even a…fig leaf! (That's what Adam and E-V-E wore.)

In my dream, I went racing full speed to the locker room and hid behind a shower curtain and held on tight. When I woke up, I was holding on to my *sheets* for dear life. And that's when I realized it was just a dream.

Phew!!

I think I had that dream because our gym teacher, Mrs. Kocivar, said that next year in sixth grade, girls can shower in school if they want to.

I will *never* want to!

AVA, WHO PREFERS PRIVACY

PS Mrs. Kocivar also showed us some modern dance steps and

said we should watch Kelli because she was doing it "perfectly." I made a little face and looked around to see if anyone else wanted to make a face back, but no one did. Am I the only person who doesn't think Kelli is perfectly perfect??

2/9

AFTER SCHOOL

DEAR DIARY,

Guess who I just ran into? Chuck!

Dad had to run some errands, so I went along. At the bank, I heard a crazy clinking clanking sound. I turned and there was Chuck pouring a bagful of pennies, nickels, dimes, and quarters into a giant sorting machine. When I went to say hi, it felt like my heart was beating as loudly as the machine. Which surprised me.

Since when do I feel nervous around Chuck?

Chuck said his mom said he could keep all the coins he found in their house and added, "But I bet she had *no* idea how many I would find!" He said he looked in pockets and drawers and under cushions and everywhere.

We waited together while the numbers kept going up, up, up. When they finally stopped, you know what the total was? $18.17!

"You're rich!" I teased. "What are you going to do with all that money?"

"I don't know."

"You could buy me bubblemint gum!"

He laughed and asked what my dad had cooked for "Barfy Monday." I told him squishy squash and made it sound extra gross, and then I was tempted to ask about his new girlfriend, but his mom came over and said they had to go. His mom always makes me nervous, probably because she is very tall and serious and has excellent posture.

Chuck is tall too, but he never used to make me nervous. He just made me laugh. While we were waiting for the noisy machine to count his money, for instance, he told me a joke that had a word from last Friday's spelling test: "Two *cannibals* were eating a clown, and one said to the other, 'Does this taste funny to you?'" (Hehe.)

I was glad he told it because it made things seem normal-ish between us even though I feel like they aren't.

Back home, our kitchen smelled scrumptious. Pip was baking gingerbread men (and gingerbread women and teens and kids and babies) with a seventh-grade girl named Tanya. Pip hardly ever has friends over, and I'd never met Tanya. Dad went upstairs, and I reached for a chocolate kiss, but the bowl was empty. I was about to say, "Pip, you ate *all* the chocolate kisses?!" when I realized Tanya must have helped.

If I had to describe Tanya, I guess I'd say that she is *pretty* but also *pretty* heavy. I've never really thought of this before, but Pip might be the smallest kid in seventh grade, and Tanya might be the… opposite?? It feels weird to write this down, and I don't mean that she's just a little chubby and who even cares? I mean that when she has checkups, I bet her doctor talks to her about weight and stuff.

Anyway, Tanya said that when she met our cat, she felt like she "already knew him" because of my story in the *Misty Oaks Monitor*, "The Cat Who Wouldn't Purr," which she'd "really liked."

"When did you adopt Taco Cat?"

"He was my birthday present on January 1 when I turned eleven."

She showed me two pencil sketches she'd made of him. They were both cute, and she'd even drawn in the white zigzag on his forehead and the white tip of his tail.

"You can have one," she said.

"Really?" I asked.

"Really."

I picked one and just now taped it on the rim of my mirror.

Hey, M-I-R-R-O-R-R-I-M is a palindrome! Which is funny because palindromes are sort of like words in mirrors since they're the same backward and forward.

I've never thought of M-I-R-R-O-R-R-I-M before, and trust me, I, A-V-A, sister of P-I-P, daughter of A-N-N-A and B-O-B, and owner of T-A-C-O-C-A-T, have thought of piles of palindromes.

Well, I helped Pip and Tanya take their gingerbread families out of the oven, and we let them cool. Then, minutes later, we started nibbling them, feet first, as though *we* were cannibals. Suddenly Pip said, "Whoa! We'd better save a few!" I think she realized it would have been bad if M-O-M or D-A-D walked into a yummy-smelling kitchen and found only ginger crumbs instead of ginger people.

After Tanya left, Pip told me that they were supposed to

have started their art project for Spanish but instead started baking and cutting out pastel hearts for a Valentine collage for Pip's boyfriend.

Sometimes I can hardly believe that Pip, who used to be so shy, has a real live valentine. And that he's *Ben Bates*, *Bea's Big Brother* (*al*literation *al*ert).

I can't imagine having a valentine.

(Or can I??)

AVA, AMBIVALENT (THAT'S WHEN YOU'RE NOT SURE)

BEFORE DINNER

DEAR DIARY,

Fifth grade is more complicated than fourth grade. Not just the math. *Everything*. It used to be that Maybelle was my best friend, and Chuck was my best guy friend, and that was that. Now Maybelle hangs out with Zara, and Chuck hangs out with Kelli, and I'm supposed to be okay with it all.

Even gym is complicated because some girls are "developing" and some aren't (like me). I think everyone is a little freaked out. The "mature" kids whose bodies are changing, and the other kids whose bodies are just sitting there. (Or standing or walking or running or whatever.)

Tomorrow we're starting a new class called FLASH. It stands for *F*amily *L*ife *A*nd *S*ocial *H*ealth. The funny thing is that our health teacher's name is Ms. *Sick*le. (Get it?)

It meets every Thursday.

My favorite class, of course, is English. Today Mrs. Lemons showed us something she'd printed from the Internet:

1 2 3 4 5 6 7 8 9 10 11 12 13 14 15
Re-post when you find the mitsake.

I kept looking and looking and was about to say, "I don't see any mistake" when I noticed it was a *spelling* "mitsake"—not a numbers one!

After class, Chuck and I started walking out the door together, the way we always used to, but there was Kelli waiting for him on the other side! I couldn't believe she came to meet him!! You might call that friendly, but I call it stalker-y! (Not that stalkers usually wear sparkly headbands.)

Chuck walked off with Kelli, and Zara looked at me like she could tell I was mad and sad.

Which I was.

Both.

I even mumbled, "I don't get what Chuck sees in her."

Without waiting a single solitary second, Zara said, "Well, she is pretty. And she's popular."

Popular? I've never really thought about popularity. Or maybe I thought popularity was something we didn't *have* to think about until puberty, which is something else I don't like to think about.

"And she's a good dancer," Zara continued. "And she's good at sports. And—"

Was Zara just getting warmed up? I put my hand in the air as if to say, "Stop!" Then I mentioned that in the girls' room, Kelli had applied lip gloss and announced that she likes "the natural look," and I'd wanted to say, "If you want to look natural, why wear makeup at all?"

Zara laughed, so I added, "I just hope Chuck doesn't get his feelings hurt."

Zara looked at me sideways as though she wasn't one hundred percent convinced this was my biggest concern.

AVA, CONCERNED

DEAR DIARY,

I just reread the Aesop's fable "Dog in the Manger." It goes like this:

A dog spends all afternoon napping on a pile of hay in a manger that belongs to an ox. At dusk, the ox comes home, and the dog wakes up. But he doesn't leave; he just stays there and barks and barks. At first, the hungry ox is patient, but finally he says, "Dog, since you aren't even eating my hay, why won't you let me have some?"

The moral: "Don't begrudge others what you yourself are not enjoying." Which means: don't be a selfish nincompoop for no good reason.

Am I being selfish about the Chuck-and-Kelli thing? It's not like Chuck and I were boyfriend-girlfriend, so why should I care who he goes out with?

Then again, I do care, whether I'm supposed to or not. Whenever I see Chuck, my insides lurch a little.

I went into Pip's room to talk, but she said, "Ava! Look!" and showed me the giant Valentine card she'd just finished for Ben.

She'd drawn HAPPY VALENTINE'S DAY in big balloon letters, and inside each, she'd glued the cut-out pastel hearts, and inside each of those, she'd written in tiny block letters "BE TRUE" and "YOU & ME" and "CUTIE PIE" and "CUPCAKE" and "SWEET TALK" and even "FIRST KISS."

She said she used the actual sayings from Sweethearts "conversation hearts"—but did *not* include "TRUE LOVE" because she didn't want to go overboard.

"Ben's going to love it!" I said and tried to feel happy for her instead of bad for me.

Then I wrote AVA and PIP and ANNA and BOB on a piece of paper and held it up to her mirror. "Look!"

"What?"

"My name is the coolest palindrome in our family because it's the only one that looks identical even in the mirror."

Pip studied the reflected words but shrugged as if it was no big deal, even though it kind of was. "Who cares?" she said.

"I do," I said and pointed out that WOW is a perfect palindrome too.

Pip shrugged and picked up the novel she was reading and said, "I have only three pages left." I knew that was code for "See you later, Alligator." So I took the hint and tried to find Taco because I felt a teeny bit lonely.

I thought of calling Maybelle, but it was too late, and besides, I haven't even told her that I am not happy about Chuck + Kelli. And maybe I shouldn't say anything because it seems like Maybelle + Kelli are becoming friends now too.

I guess everyone is falling under Kelli's sparkly spell—even the new science teacher. We did a unit on space and Kelli told our whole class all about a lunar eclipse she saw on one of her fancy vacations. And the teacher was just beaming.

AVA + TACO

PS Petting Taco helped…until he ran away.

PPS I bet it would be nice to like a boy who liked you back.

PPPS I wish I liked reading as much as Pip does. Whenever she wants to take her mind off things, she can enter a whole new world without even putting her shoes on. I'm a word nerd too, but I like writing more than reading, so the only world I ever hang out in is Misty Oaks.

IN THE LIBRARY

DEAR DIARY,

At breakfast, Mom asked us to sign a Valentine's card to go with a present for Nana Ethel. In my best handwriting, I wrote:

The Wren Family would like to say:

Happy Happy Valentine's Day!

Pip decorated it with flowers (mostly azaleas) and birds (mostly wrens).

We all four signed, and Pip added a paw print for Taco, and I added an XOX for kiss hug kiss. (Another perfect palindrome.)

Mom said, "Great job!"

But it was *not* a J-O-B. It was a J-O-Y.

Observation: one little letter can make a BIG difference!

I put the card in an envelope and asked if I should tape it on the present. Mom said, "No, tie it on," and handed me some ribbon.

"Is *that* a palindrome?" I asked and wrote it down: N-O-T-I-E-I-T-O-N. "Whoa! It is!" I announced and showed everyone.

"W-O-W," Mom said, so I showed her how WOW and MOM and AVA all look the exact same in the mirror, whereas

PIP and SIS and DAD do not. She smiled and said, "H-U-H, so they're symmetrical."

"Cool, right?" I said.

She nodded, and Dad said, "Do you ladies think Dr. Seuss was a word nerd?"

Pip said, "Definitely."

"Aha!" Dad continued in a teasing way. "But do you think he had Seuss issues?"

Mom and Pip looked puzzled, but I got it and said, "He definitely had Seuss issues! He had serious S-E-U-S-S-I-S-S-U-E-S!!"

Mom laughed and Dad high-fived me.

A-V-A, SYMMETRICAL

DEAR DIARY,

Obviously, I believe in girl power and think girls should dream big and go after their goals, just like boys. But today Kelli wore a bright-pink Girl Power sweatshirt to school, and it bugs me that she acts all *entitled* and as if she *expects* to get whatever she wants.

Emily Sherman said that in third grade, Kelli's mom let her have a party at the Pampered Princess, an hour away. Everyone got manicures and pedicures and facials!

"What's a facial?" I asked.

"It's when someone rubs cream on your cheeks and puts cucumber slices on your eyelids to help you relax."

"Oh." I tried to remember third grade. Did I need creams and cucumbers to relax? I'm pretty sure I could relax by jumping rope or watching videos or hanging out with Pip or Maybelle or…Chuck.

Speaking of, at lunch, Kelli sat at a table near ours, and when Chuck walked by, she said, "Chuck! I saved you a seat!" So he sat down with her.

Confession: it took away my appetite.

Zara says Kelli's been saving him a seat on the bus home from school every day too.

Does Chuck even *want* to sit next to Kelli all the time?

Should I ask him?

And why do I care as much as I obviously do? *Do* I like-like my friend Chuck??

In FLASH, Ms. Sickle said feelings can be messy.

I think she's right. It would be easier if when you liked a person, that person liked you back the exact same amount in the exact same way, and that was that.

Ms. Sickle broke us into groups and had us flip through women's magazines. She said we should look for pages that show "mixed and contradictory messages." At first we didn't know what she meant. But then it was "eye-opening" because the magazines had ads for candy bars and recipes of gooey desserts *right next* to articles on how to "shed pounds fast." Ms. Sickle said it's hard to "live mindfully" in a world full of temptations, but it's important to try.

AVA, OPEN-EYED?

2/11
TWENTY MINUTES LATER

DEAR DIARY,

There's something I didn't tell you, and now I'm almost embarrassed to, even though you're my private diary. But writing helps, so here goes:

At the end of the day, I had to pee, so I went to the girls' room and dashed in and out and didn't notice that I'd stepped on a piece of toilet paper. I ran to where Pip usually meets me after school, and two older kids were pointing at my feet and smirking. One was Loudmouth Lacey, that girl who wears thick eyeliner and used to pick on Pip. The other was an eighth grader named Rorie who everyone says is mean. (She looks like she could beat people up without even trying.)

Chuck must have noticed, because he came over and mumbled, "TP alert."

"Huh?" I said. (I did not spell it out.)

He pointed at my left boot, and I glanced down and saw the tissue trail and thought, *OMG! TP?* I mumbled thanks and stepped on the tissue with my right boot. The TP came off, but so did what was left of my *dignity*.

When I looked up, Chuck was gone—probably already on the bus next to Kelli, who would never be caught dead dragging TP around. (Not that *I* was *literally* "caught dead." I mean, I'm still breathing.)

Anyway, Pip showed up with Tanya, and my face must have been toilet-paper white, because Pip said, "What's the matter?"

All I could say was, "Nothing."

AVA, NOTHING

PS One of tomorrow's spelling test words is *humiliated*.

2/11
BEDTIME

Dear Diary,

After school, Tanya and Pip worked on their homework poster. So I made a poster too. I made mine for Bates Books, and in my best handwriting, I wrote: "Books are gifts you can open again and again." I even added, "Buy Local," because Bea said it drives her parents crazy when people browse for books at their store and then order them online. Mrs. Bates says she wishes they'd worry about "saving their community," not just "saving every dollar." She also says bookstores give towns "character," which is funny since bookstores are full of books that are full of characters.

Anyway, we made popcorn, but Tanya melted half a stick of butter and poured it all over the top, and it ended up *too* buttery.

After Tanya left, I told Pip about the toilet paper, and she said, "That's happened to everybody," which made me feel better. Then Pip told me what *she* is worrying about. It's way bigger than tagalong TP.

Last week, Pip's Spanish class got divided up into pairs, and one kid from each pair had to reach into a hat and pick out a name of an artist from a Spanish-speaking country. "One kid got Picasso," Pip said. "Another got Goya. Another got Frida Kahlo. Another got El Greco. Another got Velázquez. And Tanya picked for us and got Botero." (I had to look up those spellings.)

Pip said each pair of kids is supposed to give a short talk and make a poster of one of their artist's paintings.

"So? What's the *problema*?" (That's "problem" in Spanish.)

"We have to do our presentations during an assembly in front of the whole middle school!"

"But in English, right?"

"Duh."

"And for kids, not parents, right?"

"Right."

"You can do it, Pip!" I said, because Pip really has come out of the shell she used to be all scrunched up inside.

Then again, it was still hard to picture Pip talking in front of such a big group.

"It's not just me. It's Tanya." Pip lowered her voice as if she didn't even want to say what she was about to say. "We were talking about height and weight, and she…she…told me she wears size XXXL."

I waited. Pip is not the kind of person who judges people on their appearance. She doesn't even judge books by their covers.

Pip pushed her art book toward me. "Look."

I looked, and it was open to the Botero paintings. Well, it turns out that Botero has a very particular style. Someone could probably walk right into a museum and say, "I bet Botero painted that!" He paints all his subjects larger than life. There was a big round king, and a big round princess, and a big round dancer, and a big round bullfighter. Suddenly I understood the *problema*. Botero paints big people, and Tanya is…not small.

"Oh," I said.

"I just hope no one says anything," Pip said. "Tanya's pretty insecure. One of her cousins makes fun of her."

"That's terrible," I said.

Pip showed me the poster that they'd finished drawing and coloring. They'd done a really good job copying the *Mona Lisa*. But it was not the *Mona Lisa* that Leonardo da Vinci painted hundreds of years ago. It was a *Mona Lisa* that Botero painted much more recently.

Oh, I'll just come out and say it. Botero's *Mona Lisa* is… *chubby*. Instead of an oval, her face is a circle. Her cheeks and chin and neck are big, and her eyes and nose and mouth are small.

We were both quiet, and I got an idea. "Pip, I could make Tanya a valentine, an anonymous one."

"Like from a secret admirer?"

"Not lovey-dovey, just nice. And unsigned. Maybe it would boost her confidence?"

"I don't think it's that easy. But sure, if you want." Pip went back to her homework, and I made a heart-shaped valentine for Tanya that I'm going to sneak into her locker tomorrow. It says:

Happy Valentine's Day to a very sweet person!

I decorated it with red balloons and red lollipops—though I'm not sure you can tell which are which.

AVA, MORE ALTRUISTIC THAN ARTISTIC (*ALTRUISTIC* MEANS WANTING TO HELP)

MORNING, STILL IN BED

DEAR DIARY,

I dreamed I made a valentine for Chuck but was too embarrassed to give it to him.

Question one: Do boys ever dream about girls?

Question two: Do I wish Chuck were *my* valentine?

Since you are my diary and no one else will ever read this, I guess I will admit that I think I do.

Okay, yes, I do.

I do.

I *do* like Chuck.

Wait, all those "I do's" make it sound like we're getting married!!

All I mean is that I realize that when I think about Chuck, I *keep thinking* about him. He doesn't just cross my mind; he finds a chair and sits right down!

And usually that's okay, because thinking about him makes me smile. Lately, though, it makes me frown.

Is he telling Kelli jokes and making her laugh? Does he think about her as much as I think about him?

AVA :-(

Dear Diary,

After homeroom, I went to the bathroom and was about to come out of the stall when I recognized Kelli's and Zara's voices. Kelli said, "Isn't Chuck soooo cute? Do you think he's the tallest boy in fifth grade?"

Zara said, "Maybe. Or maybe tied with Jamal?"

"I can't wait for my party!" Kelli said. "Should I invite the whole grade?"

Zara said, "If your parents will let you, why not?"

"Oh, there are a few kids I could do without!" She laughed, and I wondered who she meant. Did she mean *me*? I don't like her, but does she not like *me*? And if so, is it because Chuck and I are...friends?

Well, I couldn't just poke my head out, so I had to stay hidden until the coast was clear. And it was awkward sitting there, trapped. Plus, Mrs. Hamshire gets mad if you're even two seconds "tardy."

Finally Zara and Kelli must have had to pee, because they went into the stalls on either side of me. The second they closed the doors, I made a run for it—and a beeline to math class.

At lunch, Kelli announced that she was having a Valentine's party, and now that's all anybody can talk about. It's our grade's *first* boy-girl party—if you don't count all the ones we had when we were little.

I wish the party weren't at Kelli's.

I also wish I had the guts to give Chuck a card—or collage.

But he's *not* my valentine, so that would be *inappropriate*!

AVA, APPROPRIATE

Dear Diary,

Taco Cat and I were on the sofa, and Pip was on the floor working on her new book, *Z Is for Zinnia*. She's made three pages: A is for azalea, B is for buttercup, and C is for chrysanthemum. (Note: *chrysanthemum* is a hard spelling word, which is one reason most people just say "mum.")

Anyway, P-I-P was filling in the petals of her M-U-M and making them R-E-D-D-E-R and R-E-D-D-E-R (palindrome alert!), and I asked if Tanya had said anything about getting a valentine.

Pip said, "No, but she did ask me a personal question."

"What?"

"She said, 'Didn't you used to be shy? Like *really* shy?'" Pip looked at me. "I didn't answer right away, but she kept asking how I got less shy, so I ended up telling her the whole story about how you and Bea made those five Pip Pointers to help me get braver."

"You told her about the five Pip Pointers??"

"Yes. And you know what she said? She said she wished she

had ten Tanya Tips to help her lose weight because she knows she's not 'the prettiest flower in the garden.'"

"She *said* that?" I made a sad little "Oh" sound. It just came out. "What did you say?"

"I didn't know *what* to say! I objected and everything. But Tanya said that all her relatives—except her grandmother—used to say, 'Look how big you are!' like it was a compliment, and then one day she noticed that, without any warning, that sentence went from being a good thing to a bad thing."

"That's awful!"

"I know. So I said I'd ask you."

"*Me?*"

"You and Bea."

I scrunched my face and pointed out that Bea and I don't know anything about losing weight. "Bea only knew about shyness because her brother Ben used to be shy."

"He's not anymore," Pip said and smiled to herself. Then she added, "Oh, c'mon, Ava. You told me Bea wants to be an advice columnist."

"Yeah, but someone who *wants* to be a pilot can't fly an airplane," I protested. "And someone who *wants* to be a doctor can't perform an operation. And someone who *wants* to be a boxer can't—"

"Can't you and Bea just give it a try?" Pip asked, interrupting. "I bet it took a lot of guts for Tanya to ask."

"Let me think about it," I said.

AVA, CORNERED

2/12
BEDTIME

DEAR DIARY,

At dinner, I told Mom and Dad that I got another 100 on our Friday spelling test. Dad said, "Way to go!" and Mom said, "Good for you!" (They used to forget to say things like that.)

What I didn't say out loud is that when we graded the tests, Chuck and I traded papers—and this was the highlight of my whole day.

One of the words was *handkerchief*, and Chuck wrote *Kleenex*. I thought that was really creative and he should get at least partial credit. But Mrs. Lemons said to mark it wrong. He also got *earnest* and *sincere* wrong. Another word was *palindrome*, which of course I know backward and forward. Another was *afterthought*, which I sometimes used to feel like at home back when Mom and Dad were always worrying about Pip. One last word was *valentine*.

When Chuck gave me back my test, he drew a big star around the 100. When I gave back his, I did not circle the 70, but I did whisper, "You got *palindrome* and *valentine* right."

He whispered, "Did you hear about Kelli's party this weekend?"

I nodded.

He said, "You going?"

I nodded again.

He said, "Me too."

Maybe I should have left well enough alone, but I didn't. I whispered, "Are you and Kelli really going out?" I could *not* believe I said that!

He looked like he couldn't either. His eyes went wide, and he turned a little pink. "Sort of."

Mrs. Lemons said, "No talking." She looked right at us and added, "Or whispering."

I passed Chuck a note: "Sort of?"

He turned the note over, scribbled on it, and pushed it back to me. It said, "1. I'm not aloud to go out." (He wrote "aloud," but I knew he meant *allowed*.)

Then he ripped a second strip of paper from his notebook and wrote "2." He was about to scribble something else, but the bell rang, and You-Know-Who was already peeking in the little window in the door. (If you don't know, I'll give you a hint: she was wearing a sparkly sunshine-yellow headband.)

AVA, NOTE PASSER

PS What was Chuck going to write in his second note??

2/13
SATURDAY MORNING

DEAR DIARY,

There's no school on Monday because of Abraham Lincoln's and George Washington's birthdays. I cannot tell a lie: I love three-day weekends!

Y-A-Y presidents!

I also like that it's not getting dark quite so early. But it's still icy cold out. Today I went outside to bring in the newspaper, and I could see my breath.

Valentine's Day is tomorrow, and the whole grade is going to Kelli's. She said all the girls should wear red or pink. I don't own anything pink, but Pip has a top I can borrow that is not too girlie-girlie.

This morning Pip asked me if I'd talked to Bea yet, and I had to admit that I hadn't. She said I should and handed me her cell phone, with the number already pressed in.

Bea answered, and I said hi, and she said, "What's up?"

"The ceiling," I replied, but then felt immature since Bea is two years older than me. So I just went ahead and told her that Pip talked to Tanya about the Pip Pointers and now Tanya wants us to come up with Tanya Tips—but about weight loss. I thought Bea might say, "Tanya's weight is not my problem" or "What do I know?" But Bea said Tanya was one of the first kids who was nice to her when she moved to Misty Oaks and added, "I didn't know her weight bothered her."

"Want to come over?" I asked.

"One sec," Bea said, and I heard a muffled conversation. Then she said, "Or you and Pip can come to the bookshop. Ben and I are about to go there."

I ran that idea by Pip, and she liked it and jumped in the shower. Now she's drying her hair with a blow-dryer and just asked loudly, "Should I give Ben the valentine I made?"

"Definitely," I shouted back, Little Miss Love Expert.

"Think he'll have one for me?" she shouted.

"I don't know if boys are as into Valentine's Day as girls," I shouted back. "But he could always grab one from the card rack."

Pip shouted, "That's real romantic."

I rolled up my poster and put it in my backpack and mumbled, "At least you're giving your valentine to a boy. I'm giving mine to a store."

Ava, Whose Crush Is Someone Else's Valentine

PS I didn't mean to write "CRUSH," but it was like my hand had a mind of its own. (Wait. Can *hands* have *minds*?)

DEAR DIARY,

We entered the bookstore, and Mrs. Bates put my poster by the register, which made me feel good.

Bea and Ben came over, and we went to the back and put our coats and hats and scarves and gloves in a big clothes puddle in the corner. Then Pip gave Ben her handmade valentine, and he handed her a great big red envelope! It *was* romantic! Especially since Bates Books is practically polka-dotted with hearts.

Ben and Pip stayed in the kids' section, and Bea and I walked to a grown-up section. Meow Meow, their friendly Creamsicle-colored cat, followed us, his tail high in the air.

I have to say: I'd never noticed how many books are in Bates Books. I guess I'd always hung out in the kids' area, but there are shelves and shelves of books for grown-ups.

Mrs. Lemons once told us about genres—like mysteries and sci-fi and fantasy and graphic novels and historical fiction and realistic fiction (my favorite). But most books are nonfiction. And a lot of them have to do with food.

I'm not kidding. Bates Books sells hundreds of cookbooks.

Some explain how to cook French or Italian or Greek or Mexican or Indian or Chinese meals. Some explain how to cook soup or fish or meat or vegetables or dessert. Some are for beginners, some are for experts, some are for people with allergies. And they're all bursting with recipes and photos! They're like picture books for grown-ups.

Right next to the cookbooks are diet books. Tons of them! There are almost as many books about *not* eating as there are about eating! It made me think of when Ms. Sickles had us look for "mixed and contradictory messages." Bea said they have books about eating disorders too, like when people eat so much, they make themselves sick, or starve themselves and have to go to the hospital.

"I think Tanya wants just general suggestions," I said.

We sat on the floor and started looking at self-help books on "wellness," and I started writing down tips. Bea said her mom and dad don't like it when kids treat the bookstore as if it's a "lending library," but they don't mind if *she* does.

I told her that if we come up with a good list for Tanya, I might make a poster for FLASH class. I also told her that Ms. Sickle just put up a poster with a giant B+ and, underneath, the words: "*Be positive.*"

Bea smiled, and Meow Meow rubbed up against my knee and hopped onto my lap and started purring and purring like there was no place he'd rather be. (Taco never does that.) "He's such a good cat," I said.

"I know," Bea said.

We kept leafing through books and talking, and I took notes like: "If you drink sugary soda, try to switch to water." And "If you tend to eat fast, try to put down your fork between some bites." And "Leave the ice cream in the grocery store because it's much easier to resist temptation *once* in a store than all day long at home." I also wrote "Use smaller plates," and "Take the stairs not the elevator," and "Go places by bike, not car," which is exactly what Pip and I had just done even though it had meant bundling up with hats, scarves, and gloves.

Besides all the practical tips, Bea said her aunt—the psychotherapist—would say to think "big picture."

"Big picture?"

"Like, picture yourself in better shape so you're 'visualizing success,' rather than just 'feeling deprived.'"

I nodded, and Bea kept dictating tips like, "Avoid high-fructose corn syrup." And "Don't expect to drop pounds over-night." And "Give yourself lots of credit for trying to take better care of yourself."

It was fun to be working with Bea again. Interesting too, because I'd never thought about *c*arbs, *c*alories, or *c*orn syrup.

It reminded me of when we made the Pip Pointers, back when Pip could hardly say hi to people.

I guess we all have different strengths and weaknesses.

One of my strengths is spelling. I can spell *carbohydrate* even though I'm not exactly sure what it means.

One of my weaknesses is math. I wish I could remember numbers the way I can remember letters. But everyone's brain is different. Chuck once joked: "There are *three* kinds of people in this world—those who can count and those who can't."

One of Pip's strengths is drawing and another is concentration. When she reads, she's in another world. Sirens could be blaring all around, and she wouldn't hear them. Another strength is her sense of direction. The only place *she* gets lost is inside books!

Well, this might be another one of my weaknesses (or maybe it's normal?), but once something starts to bother me, it's hard for me to stop thinking about it every single second. So another nice thing about being with Bea was that it got my mind off Kelli and her sparkly headbands and perfect backflips and princess parties and how she stole Chuck away from me (even though he was never mine in the first place and she probably didn't know I liked him, since *I* barely knew).

After a while, Meow Meow jumped off my lap and climbed onto the pile of clothes to take a catnap while Bea and I put all the books back. I thought about asking Bea what to do if you have a crush on a boy who is "taken" *and* who used to be your best guy friend. But I didn't.

When you hang out with older kids, it's better not to remind them of how immature you are.

On the bike ride home, Pip led the way but seemed upset, which was weird because she'd been so happy an hour earlier.

"What's wrong?" I shouted.

She didn't say, "Nothing," which meant, "Something." When we got home, she went straight to her room and closed the door.

I went into my room and spent a little time with my stuffed

animals. Sometimes I worry that I'm neglecting them. But now that I'm eleven, I guess it makes sense that I don't play with Winnie the Pooh all day.

H-U-H. I just thought of something. If Winnie owned a hula hoop, it would be Pooh's hoop or P-O-O-H-S-H-O-O-P.

I wonder what's bugging P-I-P anyway.

A-V-A, L-I-L S-I-S

ALMOST DINNERTIME

DEAR DIARY,

I got a haircut today. A bob (B-O-B)!

Maybelle is about to come over for a sleepover. Y-A-Y for BFFs!

Dad showed me some words that come out funny if you rearrange their letters, so I'm taping in my favorites:

WORDS	SAME WORDS WITH REARRANGED LETTERS
THE EYES	THEY SEE
ASTRONOMER	MOON STARER
SNOOZE ALARMS	ALAS NO MORE Z'S
A DECIMAL POINT	I'M A DOT IN PLACE
THE MORSE CODE	HERE COME DOTS
DORMITORY	DIRTY ROOM
LISTEN	SILENT

I started looking for words inside AVA ELLE WREN and found lots, like EVER and NEVER and REVEAL and ALL NEW.

AVA ELLE WREN, ALL NEW

PS You know what TACO is scrambled? COAT. And you know what TACO CAT scrambled is? CAT COAT or...fur!

PAST MY BEDTIME

Dear Diary,

Maybelle conked out (maybe because she does a lot of sports all week), but I couldn't fall asleep, so I'm writing in you with the light-up pen that Bea gave me last year.

It's funny. A lot of people like to read at night, but I like to write at night.

Anyway, dinner was chicken potpie, and Pip was as quiet as in the olden days. The rest of us started talking about pen names or *pseudonyms*. Like Mark Twain's real name was Samuel Clemens. And Lewis Carroll's real name was Charles Dodgson. And Lemony Snicket's is Daniel Handler.

Mom also talked about a cat with kidney failure that Dr. Gross had to "put down." She said their office always sends out a condolence note after a pet dies, but today's made her sad because the lady was eighty-six and the cat's name was Valentine.

Dad changed the subject away from dead pets and asked Maybelle about soccer and Mathletes. Maybelle answered, then said she'd brought us each a box of "conversation hearts"—and me a bag of gummy bears.

Next thing you know, Mom and Dad both found a heart that said "MARRY ME," and gave them to each other, which was pretty…sweet.

Maybelle said the Sweethearts company makes two *billion* hearts a year.

Mom and Dad seemed impressed, but Pip just shrugged.

After dinner, Pip, Maybelle, and I went upstairs, so I said, "Pip, you should show Maybelle the valentine Ben gave you!"

Pip said, "That's the last thing I want to do."

"Oh, come on!"

"No way!"

"Yes way! Why not?"

"Because!"

"Because what?"

Maybelle began to squirm. She's an only child and doesn't get that sister fights are not that big a deal. Personally, I think Pip *wanted* to show us but also wanted me to beg. I wasn't even surprised when, two minutes later, she said, "Oh fine. Come in, but close the door behind you."

We went into her room, and Taco scurried in too. He sniffed Maybelle's socks but did not climb onto her lap and start purring up a storm, like Meow Meow.

Pip took out the valentine. The envelope was even bigger than I remembered! It was giant, and the card inside was shaped like a bouquet of roses!

"Whoa," Maybelle said.

"So what's the matter?" I asked. I can tell when my sister is upset. I've known her since the day I was born. (She was two years, two months, and two weeks old when she met me—not that either of us remembers.)

"Read what he wrote," she said. We did. And it did not take long at all because what Ben wrote was just three words (four if you count his name).

After I read the words, I said, "Oh."

Maybelle read the words aloud: "I love you." She looked from me to Pip and didn't seem to get what the problem was. But I did. Obviously, D-A-D, M-O-M, P-I-P, and I take words (not just palindromes) very seriously, and LOVE is a very serious word!

For instance, I think about Chuck a lot (too much?), but I'd never, ever write "I love you" on a valentine!

I guess it can be tricky to put feelings into words. Maybe that's why so many Valentine cards mostly have pictures of kittens (and puppies and bunnies and ducklings) that make you melt and go "Awww."

"So what *did* you say?" I asked.

"I thanked him for the card," Pip said.

"You didn't say it back?" Maybelle asked.

Pip shook her head sadly.

"Did he notice that you didn't?" I asked.

"I think so."

"*Do* you love him?" I asked really quietly.

Pip squinted. "Isn't love for when we're older?"

"Ben *is* in eighth grade," Maybelle pointed out.

"Well, I didn't feel right saying it. So I didn't."

Maybelle and I stayed silent. Taco put his head under his paw.

"But I guess I should say...something," Pip added.

"Want us to talk to him for you?" I asked. "I could tell Bea to tell Ben—"

"NO!" Pip shouted before even I realized that this was a moronic idea.

Taco darted out the door, and I mumbled, "Just trying to help."

"I know," Pip said. "But, Ava, you have to be careful! It's not enough to have good intentions." Obviously she was referring to the boneheaded "Sting of the Queen Bee" story I wrote last fall when I felt bad for Pip after her birthday party got canceled. (Bea had thrown a huge boy-girl party on the same day that Pip was having her slumber party—but Bea hadn't done it on purpose.) "And don't tell Mom and Dad!"

"I won't."

"I don't want them worrying that Ben and I are getting too serious. Because we aren't!"

"Okay!" I said a little huffily.

"Think I should text him?" Pip asked.

"*Maybe*," *Maybe*lle said.

Pip sighed as if she couldn't believe she was asking fifth graders for advice on her love life—or *not-love* life.

She took a breath, picked up her cell phone, and started to type. Then she showed us what she wrote: "Dear Ben, I ♥ you but I don't feel ready to use the L word. I hope that's okay. Please don't take it personally because I like you as much as I've ever liked any boy. Happy Valentine's Day!"

"That's good," I said and tried to imagine texting Chuck something like that someday. (Not that I even have a cell phone!)

"Should I press Send?" she asked.

We nodded and…she did.

Then we all sat there and stared at her phone.

Nothing happened.

"He might be playing video games," Maybelle said after a minute.

"Or at a movie," I said.

"Or eating dinner with his parents," Maybelle said.

"Or doing homework," I added.

Pip looked worried and reread the text she'd sent. To distract her, I said, "You should show Maybelle *Z Is for Zinnia*!"

Pip nodded and got out her book project. Since I'd last seen it, she had drawn F is for foxglove, G is for geranium, H is for hollyhock, and I is for iris.

"You're such a good artist!" Maybelle gushed, so Pip got out the Botero poster and showed it to her too.

Maybelle took one look and laughed out loud. "Hahaha! That's hysterical! A tubby *Mona Lisa*!"

Pip snatched back the poster, rolled it up, and said, "It's not supposed to be 'hysterical.'"

Maybelle looked at me, confused, and apologized to Pip.

I felt bad for both of them.

Soon Maybelle and I went downstairs and made P-O-P P-O-P P-O-P popcorn. I told her that Pip is nervous because in three days, she and Tanya have to talk in front of the whole middle school.

"Who's Tanya?" Maybelle asked, and I described her. "Oh, I know! Chubby, but a pretty face, right?"

I nodded and wondered if Tanya knew that this was probably how most people described her. *Nice* people, anyway. Who knows what not-nice people said? (Poor Tanya!)

I watched as Maybelle attempted to pour the popcorn equally into two bowls. She was taking a long time, so I teased, "You could count the kernels."

She threw a piece of popcorn at me, and I tossed it up in the air and tried to catch it in my mouth, but I missed.

"Do you think people ever love each other the exact same amount?" I asked as I picked up the piece of popcorn.

"I don't think love is something you can quantify," she answered.

We both laughed because that was such a Maybelle thing to say. (Math is one of her strengths!)

But *is* love lopsided? Is it like an out-of-balance seesaw? Does one person always like the other one more?

And will tomorrow's Valentine's Day party be fun?

AVA, ASKING

DEAR DIARY,

Maybelle is still asleep, and I'm still awake, so I got Bea's light-up pen back out because I wanted to write down a joke Dad told me:

Question: Why should you never use a dull pencil?

Answer: Because it's pointless.

H-O-H-O-H-O-H

AVA, AWAKE

PS I can't believe I'm still awake. Am I nervous about the party? Is my crush *pointless*?

Dear Diary,

Maybelle's mom picked her up early, so I hung out in the kitchen with Dad, and we made heart-shaped pancakes while Mom and Pip slept in. I framed each stack with sliced strawberries and set the table with red cloth napkins. Dad sizzled eight strips of bacon to perfection, and I called, "Breakfast!"

Mom came downstairs and said, "Mmm, smells good." She was right. The kitchen smelled of bacon and maple syrup.

Pip came down next and brought her cell phone with her. I guess she's still hoping Ben will text back. But what if his feelings got hurt? He's probably never written "I love you" to anyone. He was probably hoping she'd just say it back and that would be that. (Observation: when Kelli asked Chuck to go out, he didn't leave her hanging; he said yes back, and that *was* that. Stupid Kelli!)

When we were all sitting down, I looked at Mom and Dad and asked, "Do you guys love each other the same amount?"

Mom looked startled, and Pip glared at me, but Dad put down his coffee and said, "Great question." Then he said, "Love means different things to different people. But I think we do. Mind you, Mom likes to hold her cards close to the chest."

Pip looked confused and said, "H-U-H?" (Funny how my family really does spell out H-U-H when we're talking to each other. It's like a weird inside joke.)

"It's an expression," Dad said. "If you're playing poker and don't want people to know if you have a royal flush—or a pair of deuces—you hold your cards close to your chest."

"Deuces?" I asked.

"Twos," Dad replied.

"What Dad means," Mom said, "is that I don't go on and on as much as some people."

I realized that this was true. Like Dad might say, "This book is pure genius!" but Mom never would. If Mom and Dad were teachers, Dad would be a much easier grader.

"Which of you said 'I love you' first?" I asked. Pip kicked me under the table. But I wasn't talking about Ben and Pip. I was talking about Mom and Dad.

Dad said, "That's pretty personal, sweetie, but I'll tell you. In college, when I was a senior and Mom was a sophomore, I told her I loved her on our third date. I meant it too. She didn't say it back for *months*. I wasn't worried though. I knew she found me irresistible!"

He smiled at Mom, and she giggled as though they were still in college. She even tossed her napkin at Dad, which was funny. They don't usually throw stuff at each other.

AVA, WHO ASKED

PS Do Chuck and Kelli like each other the same amount?
PPS Do *I* like Chuck and Taco both more than they like me?
PPPS Will Kelli's Valentine's Day party be *aw*esome or *aw*ful?

2/14
A LITTLE LATER

DEAR DIARY,

Pip was working on her Spanish homework and suddenly said, "Ava, I just learned a Spanish palindrome."

"What?" I asked.

"*O-S-O.*"

"What does it mean?"

She told me.

"*Bare?*" I asked. "Like *bare* naked?"

"No. B-E-A-R. Like *bear* hug."

"Oh," I said.

"Oh-so," she said, because that's how you pronounce *oso*.

"Want to hear a bear joke?" I asked.

"Sure," she said but rolled her eyes to show that fifth-grade humor is beneath her.

"What do you call a bear with no teeth?" I asked.

"What?"

"A *gummy bear!*" I said. Before she could groan, I ran into my room and grabbed her a few gummy bears.

"Aw, thanks," she said.

"For Valentine's Day," I said.

O-X-O (WHICH IS HUG KISS HUG)

AVA THE SWEET

PS I wonder what age people are supposed to be before they can give each other bear hugs.

Dear Diary,

Pip's cell phone rang, and she jumped and read it and smiled big-time. It was a text from Ben, and soon they were texting back and forth. Later Pip showed me what they wrote—which was lucky because otherwise I might have been tempted to sneak a peek while she was in the shower!

He texted: "It's OK. We can just ♥ each other."

She texted a pink heart emoticon.

He texted: "PS My battery was dead and I couldn't find the charger. Sorry!"

She texted another pink heart.

He texted: "What are you doing later?"

She texted "idk" which means "I don't know." And then he called! And they made a plan to go skating! Today! On Valentine's Day!

I wonder if they will hold hands. Like whoever skates better can make sure the other one doesn't fall? Or maybe they'll skate and skate and not touch at all? (A rhyme!)

I can allllllllmost picture myself skating with Chuck. But I can't picture us holding hands.

Kelli's party starts in an hour. I don't know if I'm ready for a real boy-girl party, especially at Kelli's. And especially since, as I confessed, I ♥ Chuck a little even though I'm not supposed to.

AVA, INAPPROPRIATE

DEAR DIARY,

Why *do* I ♥ Chuck anyway? Sometimes he is gross. For example, here's a joke he told me that I can't get out of my head:

Question: What do people who eat lots and lots of alphabet soup have?

Answer: Vowel movements.

At first I didn't get it. Then I said, "Ewww!"

I just told that joke to Pip and asked if she thought it was funny or disgusting. She said, "Both," and explained that a lot of middle school boys have sick senses of humor. She said that last week, a boy in her science class said, "It's better to be 'pissed off' than 'pissed on.'"

"Ugh!" I said, shocked by the joke and the fact that Pip knows so much about middle school boys.

She also said, "What's the difference between roast beef and pea soup?"

"What?" I asked.

"Anyone can roast beef," she said.

I said "Ewww!" again and rolled my eyes.

Then I asked if she was still nervous about her presentation in the assembly next week. She said yes but added that she was *not* going to think about it on Valentine's Day. I asked if I could borrow her pink top and she said sure.

AVA IN PINK

PS It's not that I like all of Chuck's jokes. What I like is that he picks them out just for me. Or he used to anyway.

Valentine's Day Night

Dear Diary,

When I walked into Kelli's big modern house, the whole place smelled like pizza. A lady in a uniform took my coat and put it in Kelli's room, and a younger blond lady said, "Come in! Come in!" I figured she was Kelli's mother.

All the girls in my grade were wearing pink or red except Emily Jenkins, who forgot. I'm glad I didn't forget. I would not have wanted to be wearing yellow if everyone else was wearing pink and red.

I looked around and did not see Chuck anywhere.

Kelli was wearing a white top with red hearts and golden heart earrings. (She's one of the only girls in our class with pierced ears.) Her headband was red with shiny sequins. Even her dog had little red bows. She's a goldendoodle, which is a golden retriever and poodle mix. Her name is Snuggles and she's hypoallergenic, which means she doesn't make Kelli's father sneeze as much as a regular dog would.

I hope it's not weird that I'm about to write what I'm about to write, but I also noticed that Kelli was wearing a bra. It would have been impossible *not* to notice, because her shirt was thin and her shoulder straps were peeking out.

Most girls in our class do NOT wear bras!

I doubt I'll ever *need* a bra, to tell you the truth. (Hey, the initials of "to tell you the truth" are T-T-Y-T-T!) But who knows? Pip and Kelli are growing up—so maybe I am too and just can't tell?

Anyway, the lady in the uniform, Mrs. Atkins, kept asking what kind of pizza we all wanted and offering different toppings, from *pepper*s to *pepper*oni. I asked for a plain slice because my stomach was full of butterflies, and I wasn't sure if pizza and butterflies mix.

Well, I was in the middle of a bite when Chuck walked in. He wasn't dressed up (maybe boys dress up only for Halloween?), but he did look extra handsome.

Kelli bounded over and handed him a card. "Open it!" she said, all excited. I hoped no one was watching me watch them, but I leaned forward so I could see the card. On it, a pair of honeybees were saying, "BEE MINE!"

Chuck had a card for her too! It had a picture of a bright-green dinosaur and the words, "You're DINOmite." Even though it was misspelled, when I read that, all the butterflies in my stomach flapped their wings one last time and...died. Every single one.

Is this what jealousy feels like? If so, it is terrible!

I didn't want to be looking at them looking at each other, but I couldn't turn away. I wished he'd handed *me* the DINOmite card. But he hadn't, so it was like tiny sticks of dynamite were exploding in my head. It's just so hard to believe that they are each other's valentine.

I was standing there trying not to feel sorry for myself when Kelli flicked the lights on and off and announced it was time to play limbo. "I did it every day on vacation in Trinidad," she added. (That's an island. I looked it up.) We followed her to her family's giant "rec room" where she had set up two vertical poles with a three-foot pole between them. She said we would all take turns trying to dance under the horizontal pole without knocking into it or falling down.

A few kids looked confused, so she said, "I'll go first. Watch." Then she put on Caribbean music, leaned back so she was facing the ceiling, and with her knees forward, managed to step-step-step under the pole without knocking it over or landing on her butt.

Confession: I *wanted* Kelli to land on her butt!

"Who's next?" she asked.

Jamal said, "I'll go." But his shoulder bumped the pole, so he got eliminated.

Ethan said, "I'll try." But his chest bumped into the bar, so he got eliminated too.

"It isn't easy!" Kelli exclaimed with a lip-glossy smile. I thought that was obnoxious. Obviously, it *was* easy for her because of her gymnastics lessons and fancy vacation.

Grace, Olivia, Abigail, Aiden, Namira, Conner, Zara, Riley, Maham (whose name is a palindrome, M-A-H-A-M), and a bunch of others all went. Some made it under; some didn't.

"I'll try," Maybelle said. She leaned back, inched forward, and scooted under the pole.

I decided to get my turn over with, so I leaned back, stuck out my knees, and moved to the drumbeat. And I made it!

Chuck said, "I'll go," and made it look like it was a piece of cake, which we all knew it wasn't.

But here's what I have to tell you: when Chuck was practically horizontal to the floor, something fell out of his jacket pocket. A pack of bubblemint gum! When he stood up, he grabbed it really fast and jammed it back into his pocket. Then he looked at me, and I looked at him, and we kept looking at each other for a few really long seconds. (I know seconds all last the same amount, but some definitely feel longer than others.)

And I couldn't help wondering: Was that bubblemint gum for me? Part of me thought, *No, why would it be?* But another part of me was chock-full of hope.

"Who's next?" Kelli bubbled.

Emily J. bumped the pole with her tummy.

Emily S. bumped it with her chin.

Emily L. bumped it with her forehead.

Kelli kept saying, "How low can you go? How low can you go?" and kids kept getting eliminated. After each round, Kelli lowered the pole a smidge so it got even harder to slither under.

On my third turn, I lost my balance—splat!—so that was that. I was out. It made me mad that Kelli had invited us all to play a game she's so good at. Limbo is easy-peasy for her. She's been practicing. Her parents probably hired a limbo coach. (She really does have a homework helper who comes to her house every week, which I don't think is fair!)

Question: Did I lose my balance because I'm only so-so at limbo or because thinking about the mystery gum had made me dizzy?

Anyway, soon it was down to just Chuck and Kelli. Of course I was rooting for Chuck, but I have to say, they were both *naturals*, if that's the word. I guess Chuck and Kelli have limbo in common. But one difference is that every time she made it under, she seemed all proud of herself, and every time *he* did, he just looked relieved.

One good thing is that whenever it was his turn, I could look right at him without thinking twice about it, because everyone else was looking at him too. (I wish I didn't like looking at him as much as I do like looking at him.)

After two more rounds, Kelli whispered in his ear, he nodded, and they called it a tie. We all clapped, and Kelli's mom rushed over and took a million photos of the Limbo King and Queen. I wondered if she was going to post them or frame them—or both! Right when I was sick to death of clapping, Kelli's mom brought out pink mini cupcakes from Angel Cakes, the fanciest bakery in Misty Oaks. And Mrs. Atkins brought out chocolate-covered strawberries!

Soon parents started coming, and Kelli stepped outside to say good-bye to everyone.

I went to Kelli's bedroom to get my coat. Her room is pink and has a private bathroom with a lavender shower curtain dotted with bunnies. Part of me wanted to roll my eyes, but if I had my own private bathroom, I might not mind having a lavender shower curtain dotted with bunnies either.

I grabbed my coat and was about to scoot out the door when Chuck said, "Ava."

We hadn't said two words to each other all night.

"Yes," I said quietly.

"Remember at the bank, you said I could buy—?"

"I was kidding..." I interrupted, because I didn't want to say, "Of course I remember! I even wrote the conversation down in my diary!"

He reached into his pocket and handed me the pack of gum.

And I took it.

I took it!

And I know a pack of gum is *not* the same as a Valentine card with honeybees or dinosaurs or red roses or cutout letters. But bubblemint *is* sweet and so is Chuck.

I couldn't help smiling as I pictured him going to a store for gum and paying for it with his own money and knowing the whole time he was going to give it to me, me, me.

"Thank you," I said, and we looked at each other. I was feeling nervous but happy-nervous.

Just then, Kelli burst back in. Her blond hair was staticky and her cheeks were pink, and she saw us smiling. "Wasn't that super fun?" she asked.

I felt like she'd caught us breaking some rule, but she said, "Chuck, you're really great at limbo! I bet you're a great dancer too!"

"I've never really danced," he replied.

"I take classes every Thursday," she said, maybe hoping he'd sign up and they could learn cool new dance moves together.

He nodded, and I put the pack of gum into my pocket and touched it with my fingertips. It felt like a secret, and I made a decision: I might never even chew it. I might just *keep* it forever.

AVA, WITH A SECRET

Dear Diary,

When Pip came home, I asked about her date, and she said it went great. I said, "*Date* and *great* rhyme."

She ignored me and said, "But I'm starting to get really worried about the assembly."

"What do you mean?"

"Do you think Tanya and I should pick a different artist?"

"Why?"

"Well, when Maybelle saw our *Mona Lisa*, she laughed. Remember?"

"She didn't *mean* to be *mean*," I said, defending my best friend.

"I know, but maybe I should email Señor Sánchez and say we want to switch."

I thought about all the time Pip and Tanya had put into their project. "You already worked pretty hard on Botero."

"I know."

"And it's normal to be nervous, right?"

"I guess."

"It'll go great," I said because I was trying to be supportive.

"I hope so."
And I hoped I was giving her good advice.

AVA, ADVISING

DEAR DIARY,

I just put the bubblemint gum in the drawer of my bedside table and I felt really happy. But then I started wondering if Chuck bought me the gum at the same time as he bought Kelli the dino card. And if he did, which did he buy first?

Or let me put it this way: Why did he go to the store? Did he go to buy Kelli a card or to buy me the gum? Was one of us an *afterthought*?

AVA, AFTERTHOUGHT?

Dear Diary,

I've been thinking about the Aesop fable "The Fox and the Stork":

A fox invites a stork for dinner. The stork arrives hungry, and the fox sets out a yummy broth in a shallow dish. The fox laps it up, but all the stork can do is moisten the tip of his long bill. The fox says, "What's the matter? Did I make it too spicy?" The stork says no and invites the fox to come to his house. The following week, the fox sees that the stork has prepared a tasty fish soup, which he serves in a tall jar with a narrow neck. The stork eats it cheerfully, but all the fox can do is sniff it. So this time the fox is the one who goes home hungry.

The moral? "Beware of neighbors who play tricks."

I don't think Kelli was *tricking* us with the limbo party. But then again, I can't imagine inviting the whole grade over to play Boggle or do word scrambles or have a spelling bee. Just because you are good at something doesn't mean you should be a show-off about it!

Speaking of neighbors, the twins, Carmen and Lucia, who live next door and are in fourth grade, invited Pip and me over. We decided to dress in the same color since that's what *they* always do. (We picked green.) Pip is taking her Spanish homework with her so she can ask them a question. Funny that the twins can be homework helpers in Spanish even though they're years younger. Their parents are from Peru and always speak with them in *español*. I wonder if they'll think it's funny that we "copied" them by dressing in the same color.

AVA (AND AESOP)

Dear Diary,

When Carmen and Lucia answered their door, they were wearing green too, so we took selfies of all four of us in matching *verde* (that's green in *español*). Then the twins did something immature. They stuck tennis balls under their shirts so it would look like they had B-O-O-Bs. Lucia said she knows a secret code where A=B and B=C and C=D, and if you write out the whole alphabet that way, our mom's name, ANNA, spells something inappropriate.

"What?" I asked.

"BOOB!" Lucia answered and cracked up. I laughed too. I couldn't help it.

One fun thing about hanging out with the twins is that we can all act silly sometimes. I mean, fifth grade can be very serious.

Back home, in Pip's room, I picked up Otto, the stuffed orange fish that stays on her pillow, and pointed out that OTTO inside out is TOOT.

Pip said, "*Inside out?* Ava, that's nuts."

I said, "NUTS backward is STUN."

Pip said, "Stop!"

I said, "POTS."

Pip said, "I'm not in the mood!"

I said, "DOOM."

Pip said, "Leave!"

I wanted to say, "EVIL," but that's not how you spell "leave" backward, so I just stuck out my tongue and left. I'd wanted to ask Pip for some big-sister advice, but I could tell she was not in the MOOD.

BWB (THAT'S AVA IN CODE)

PS If you decode DIVDL, guess what you get?

2/15
EVENING

Dear Diary,

Since there was no school today, I asked Dad if we could take a holiday from Meatless Mondays.

He said no. He says he likes having a weekly excuse to come up with a new vegetarian dish, and besides, Americans eat too much meat, and we should all eat more plants and nuts. I was going to say, "*That's* nuts," but I didn't.

Instead I helped Dad slice the cauliflower, onions, and Brussels sprouts, and toss them into a bowl with salt, pepper, olive oil, and a spice called cumin. Then we put the vegetables on a cookie sheet and roasted them in a very hot oven until they were practically burned up.

Maybe I was starving, but to tell you the truth (T-T-Y-T-T), dinner tasted way better than it looked. It was actually pretty good. If it were a P-O-P quiz, I'd give it an 85.

While Dad and I were cooking and Taco was sleeping in a block of sunshine, I told Dad that in FLASH, Ms. Sickle said that one out of *three* American kids is overweight or obese, and that this was "dangerous" because obesity is linked with serious health issues.

Dad said that it takes a lot of money and time to make salads and good-for-you dinners, "whereas fast food places are everywhere and you can buy junk food in every convenience store."

"You mean junk food is almost *too* convenient?"

"Exactly."

He also said even most juices have too much sugar in them, but supermarkets are not really in business to provide people with "healthful food"—they're in business to make money.

"I never thought of it that way," I admitted.

AVA, NAIVE?

PS Dad also told me a funny sentence. Ready?

"You can tune a piano but you can't tunafish." Hehe.

PPS It's weird that Brussels sprouts has a capital B. I mean, you don't write "Lima beans," and Lima is a city too. (There's a Lima in Peru and in Ohio.)

DEAR DIARY,

Last night I looked online for more tips for Tanya. There's a lot of dumb stuff about miracle pills that can help you drop twenty pounds in a week (which doesn't sound safe or possible). And sites that say that eating bacon can reverse diabetes (which can't be true).

But there are also good suggestions. Like: "When you go to the movies, order a small bag of popcorn, not a tub." And: "Don't weigh yourself every day." And: "Avoid late-night snacks."

All the experts say to eat less and exercise more and that vegetables are good for you (and not just on Monday).

Bea would say that common sense is good for you—and not just on Monday!

Anyway, I worked on the tips and wrote some rhymes, and when I went to bed, I was cold, so I kept my socks on. Taco jumped up and joined me. I should have left him well enough alone, but I tried to get him to go inside the covers, and he ran away. And after that, he wouldn't come back at all.

This made me think of a metaphor: feelings are like cats. You can't always control them.

Example: I never meant for my best guy friend to become my hush-hush crush, but that's what happened.

AVA, WITH CONFUSING FEELINGS

PS I want to ask Maybelle or Pip or even Dad or Mom about this, but I feel a little bad about liking someone else's boyfriend. PPS Then again, I don't feel thaaaat bad. Should I feel worse? Or should I feel bad about not feeling thaaaat bad??

11:50 A.M. IN THE LIBRARY

DEAR DIARY,

Last night after dinner, Pip practiced her Botero talk once for Mom and twice for her mirror. She's obviously anxious. The presentation is seventh period, so on the way to school, I let her practice it again for me.

Now I'm in the library. Two eighth graders, Rorie and Valeria, are at the next table. I know who they are because Valeria is in choir and Rorie is the one who is big and scary and friends with Loudmouth Lacey.

Both girls are staring at their cell phones, and Rorie just said, "Did you like the photo?"

Valeria said, "Not really."

Rorie said, "*Hello!* I don't care if you *like* it. I want you to *Like* it!"

Valeria mumbled, "Oh. Okay. I Liked it."

"What about this one?" Rorie said. "Should I post it?"

Valeria said, "Sure."

Rorie said, "You'd tell me if I looked fat, right?"

Valeria looked too afraid to tell Rorie anything, but she nodded.

Rorie said, "Okay. It's posted. Now Like it."

Valeria touched her screen.

Rorie said, "Last night when I posted the picture of all of us, everybody Liked it *except* you."

Val searched in her cell phone. "This picture?"

Rorie sneered. "Duh."

Valeria said, "Okay. I just Liked it."

"About time!" Rorie glanced over and saw *me*! She gave me a nasty glare and said, "What are you staring at?"

"Nothing," I mumbled. I could feel her eyes burning a hole in my head, so I went back to writing in you and decided not to even look up at all until they both left…

Which they…

finally…

finally…

did.

Confession: I'm glad I'm not on Facebook or Instagram or anything. Face-to-face life is hard enough! Plus, my neck would hurt if I looked down at my phone all day.

I "Like" that when I write in you, it's just for me.

AVA, EAVESDROPPER

Dear Diary,

Brace yourself.

Remember how I told Pip her presentation would go great?

It did *not* go great!

It went *terribly*!

The entire middle school filed into the auditorium, and I sat in the third row between Maybelle and Zara. I was right behind Kelli, who walked in front of a bunch of people so she could scoot in next to Chuck. I was tempted to say something about the silvery sequins on her headband, but I didn't. (I may *think* rude things, but I rarely say them out loud. And yes, I know I sometimes *write* mean things in you, but that's different, because I'm the only one who ever sees them.)

Anyway, the seventh-grade French students went first. Two by two, they talked about artists and showed their homemade posters and other paintings. We saw kids by Renoir, lilies by Monet, and a circus made of dots by Seurat.

Next, two boys talked about Manet and showed a painting called *Luncheon on the Grass*. Well, that made everyone laugh.

Why? Because it was of people on a picnic, and one of the women was totally naked. And that's the *naked* truth! (Get it?) I was shocked that the teachers let us see this, but maybe some art is supposed to be shocking?

I also noticed that MONET and MANET are spelled the same except for one little vowel.

After the French teacher said, "*Merci*," the Spanish students took their turn.

Isabel and Nadifa showed a poster of melting clocks based on a Salvador Dalí painting. Bea and another girl showed a poster of a deer with a woman's face based on a Frida Kahlo painting. Two boys showed a poster of Aesop (looking old and tired) based on a painting by Velázquez.

Finally it was Pip and Tanya's turn. Pip talked too quietly into the microphone, but last fall, she would not have been able to talk in public at all, so I was proud of her. She was talking about Botero's life and saying he was born in Colombia and lived in lots of countries and got married three times.

Tanya went next, and her job was to talk about Botero's *art*. And everything was going fine until they showed their poster and some of Botero's famous paintings.

Maybe by then, everyone had been sitting for too long. Or maybe people thought it was okay to laugh because they'd laughed at Manet's picnic painting. Or maybe middle school kids just aren't good at being mature. (*I'm* not that good at being mature.)

Anyway, when the fifth, sixth, seventh, and eighth graders saw Pip and Tanya's chubby *Mona Lisa* and Botero's chubby *Mona*

Lisa, chubby king, chubby dancer, chubby bullfighter, chubby cat, and chubby dog, they burst out laughing. They didn't even try to hold it in.

What really got them was Botero's painting of a naked lady from behind. You could see her...*behind*! And it was *jiggly*!

It didn't help that Tanya was going on and on about Botero's "passion" for "volume and proportion and corpulence."

One boy yelled, "Just say it. He likes FAT PEOPLE!"

"And BIG FAT BUTTS!" another boy added.

A third boy made piggy sounds and said softly, "Like yours!"

I couldn't believe he said that!

A fourth shouted, "WIGGLE WIGGLE WIGGLE!" which is a line from an annoying but catchy song.

Everyone started *losing* it! Everyone except Pip and Tanya. They just stood there *frozen*.

Should Señor Sánchez have seen this coming? He *is* the teacher. But it's his first year. And what was he supposed to have said? "Tanya, given your size, perhaps you shouldn't present Botero"? He *couldn't* say that, could he? If he had, her mom might have called the school to complain—or sue! I guess he could have *removed* Botero's name from the hat, but would it be right if *nobody* at Misty Oaks School ever got to learn about Botero?

Should *I* have seen this coming? I now realize that Pip was right to have worried, and I was wrong to have encouraged her not to switch artists. I was trying to be nice, but would it have been better if I'd kept my big mouth shut?

While Pip and Tanya stood there mute, more and more kids

were laughing. Not Maybelle or Chuck. But it makes my blood boil to report that even though Kelli was in the second row, she was giggling. She was also elbowing Chuck, and I heard her whisper, "Tanya could *model* for Botero! Wiggle wiggle wiggle!" Chuck didn't answer, but here's the awful part: Tanya heard every word.

Her eyes got shiny, and I could tell Pip had no idea what to do. Fortunately, Señor Sánchez raced onto the stage and nudged Pip and Tanya to the right. Then he turned to us and said, "*¡Basta!* Enough! Presenters, *muchas gracias.* Students, please exit in a quiet orderly fashion and report to your eighth-period class. Now! Now!!" His eyes flashed with rage.

Tanya was trying to hold back tears. And she was doing pretty well. But then all of a sudden, she wasn't. She was crying—just *crying.* It was like she was having a mini breakdown.

I was glad they were off to the side, but to be honest, it wasn't the quietest mini breakdown anyone had ever had, and I felt terrible for her, because I think a lot of other kids heard her too.

Pip was talking to Tanya—probably trying to convince her that people were laughing at the *paintings,* not at *them.*

But Tanya wasn't buying it, I could tell.

She was hurt.

No. Worse.

She was *devastated.*

AVA, ANGRY AND ANGUISHED

2/16
BEDTIME

DEAR DIARY,

At dinner, Mom asked Pip how the presentation went.

Pip stared right at me and said, "Okay."

I got the message and stayed M-U-M.

"Did people like your poster?" Dad asked.

Pip said the posters would be on display outside the language classes.

"How was *your* day, Mom?" I asked, because I knew that if I asked them a question, it would take the spotlight off us. Well, Mom started talking about a Dachshund that had "tangled" with a porcupine and ended up with quills in its snout. She also told us about a Manx cat (Manx cats have no tails) that had bitten a toad and was foaming at the mouth because the toad was a little poisonous, but not in a lasting way.

Later when Pip and I were brushing our teeth (and foaming at the mouth, but not in a lasting way), I asked, "Why didn't you tell Mom and Dad?"

Pip said, "I just didn't."

"I'm sorry I told you everything would be fine."

She spat into the sink and shrugged. "I should have talked to Señor Sánchez."

"Tanya was so upset," I said.

"Can you blame her? She didn't deserve that! I'm about to text her to make sure she's okay."

I nodded. "You know the saying, 'Sticks and stones can break my bones, but words will never hurt me'?" I asked. "That's the dumbest thing ever."

"True," Pip said. "Some words are sharper than knives."

I did not ask if this was a simile or a metaphor.

I also did not ask: "Why did Kelli say that Tanya could model for Botero? And how can Chuck like her??"

Instead, I decided to be positive (B+) and try to B helpful. I'd felt humiliated because of tagalong toilet paper. Tanya must be feeling so much worse!

Pip might have been thinking the same thing, because she asked if Bea and I had finished the Tanya Tips.

"Not quite," I said. "You sure she still wants them?"

Pip nodded. "Yes. She told me she wants to lose weight but doesn't know how."

"Okay," I said and used Pip's cell to call Bea. We set up a time to meet. And I told Pip that our tips would be worth the wait.

AVA, ADAMANT (THAT'S LIKE "DETERMINED")

DEAR DIARY,

This morning, I asked Pip if Tanya had texted her back. She said no. I said, "Maybe her battery died, like Ben's?"

Pip shrugged. "Maybe. But Tanya is also not one of those people who checks her phone every five seconds."

Just now, Bea and I looked at what we have so far. Bea liked my poems and said she had called her aunt, the psychotherapist, for last-minute ideas.

We worked and worked and finally finished a list for me to copy over. I told Bea I might write them out on a piece of paper for Tanya and on a poster for my FLASH class.

In English, Mrs. Lemons always says we should revise our work before handing it in. "You check yourself in the mirror before you leave home, right? It's just as important to check your work." Well, tonight I will check, double-check, and triple-check our list.

I'll also try to come up with a catchy title.

AVA, POSTER GIRL

DEAR DIARY,

I copied the tips for Tanya, and Pip decorated the page with lark-spur, morning glories, and petunias. (She's already up to Q in *Z Is for Zinnia*.)

I also copied them onto a poster, which I'll give to Ms. Sickle tomorrow morning. I'm pretty happy with it all. I feel like while Kelli made Tanya feel worse, I'm trying to help her feel better.

Oh, on the poster, on top of the tips, I wrote FIT OR FAT in big bubble letters.

FIT and FAT are another pair of words that are spelled exactly the same except for one powerful little letter that changes everything! (Like JOY and JOB. And MONET and MANET. And BABBLE and BUBBLE. And TOP and TIP.)

After I finished, Pip took a photo of my poster with her cell phone and printed it out. I'm now going to tape it in my diary.

I hope Tanya likes our tips. I put them in an envelope, and on it, I wrote: *Your friend, Ava.*

YOUR FRIEND, AVA THE WISE

FIT OR FAT

Want to lose weight?
What's on your plate?
Also try to think
About what you drink.

Ava and Bea's Top Ten Tips

1. Drink H_2O—it's free and has zero calories.

2. Eat less—but don't obsess. (That's a rhyme!)

3. Exercise more than you did before. (Another rhyme!)

4. Slow down when you eat. It takes twenty minutes for your brain to figure out what your mouth has been up to.

5. Watch your *S*'s. Cut back on Seconds, Sweets, Snacks, and Sugary Sodas.

6. Watch your *O*'s. Cut back on
   FritOs, CheetOs, DoritOs,
   TostitOs, and OreOs.

7. Be colorful. Enjoy red, orange,
   yellow, green, and purple
   vegetables and fruits.

8. When you get tempted to overeat
   or binge on junk food, brush your
   teeth, chew sugarless gum, or
   nibble on fruit, veggies, or
   unbuttered popcorn.

9. Find a workout buddy or go on
   walk-and-talks. You can also do
   sports or walk a dog.

10. Congratulate yourself for taking
    care of yourself, one day at
    a time. Y-A-Y YOU!

IN THE LIBRARY

DEAR DIARY,

I ran into Tanya in the girls' room and told her I liked her presentation—but she looked like I'd hit her with a pillow. "I was about to put this in your locker," I said and handed her the envelope. I hoped Pip was right and that Tanya knew I was trying to be helpful.

"Thanks," she said and skimmed the list. It was awkward. I guess it's one thing to tell your quiet new friend that you wish you could lose weight and another to have her little sister show up with actual suggestions after you've been laughed at in front of the whole middle school. But Tanya *had* asked for tips. And to be honest, ever since Bea and I made the Pip Pointers, I'd kind of wanted to do another good D-E-E-D.

I'd also been thinking that if I ever do get to write kids' books someday (my new answer to "What do you want to do when you grow up?"), maybe I could write one called *Ava Wren Does It Again*. Or I could make a series called *Ava and Bea* about two girls who go around solving problems the way detectives solve mysteries…

Tanya studied the handwriting on the envelope and looked up. "Whoa, Ava. *You're* the one who gave me that valentine?"

"Sorry," I mumbled guiltily. I hadn't even thought about disguising my handwriting. I'd forgotten that you can recognize people by their handwriting just as you can by their voice or haircut or…posture. I hoped Tanya didn't feel tricked.

She frowned. "It's okay. At first, I guess I was hoping it was from a guy. But then I thought someone was making fun of me."

"No one would make fun of you!" I almost blurted, but, well, we both knew that wasn't true.

Some people really are *mean*. You know the saying, "He doesn't have a mean bone in his body"? Some people have mean *skeletons*. Some could give lessons in mean. Kelli has a few mean ribs in her rib cage. And Rorie, that scary eighth grader, probably has a whole mean spine!

I looked at Tanya in the mirror and what I *did* say was, "Tanya, don't let those dumdums get you down."

She gave me a soft smile and said, "My grandmother says, 'Don't let the *turkeys* get you down.'"

I mumbled, "Gobble, gobble," which I knew was immature the second it came out.

But Tanya laughed and said, "Gobble, gobble" back. Then three other girls came in, so we left.

After that, I went to find Ms. Sickle. I showed her my poster and asked if I could put it up in the hallway. She said, "Sure," and complimented my handwriting. I would have preferred if she'd complimented the words themselves, but I could tell she was busy.

I hope people like it as much as they liked "The Cat Who Wouldn't Purr."

AVA, ATTEMPTING TO AID AND ASSIST

DEAR DIARY,

At lunch, Kelli was sitting next to Chuck, showing him photos of her goldendoodle, Snuggles. I wished I were sitting next to Chuck talking to him about my yellow tabby rescue cat, Taco. (I also kept sneaking peeks at the back of his head and then telling myself not to.)

After lunch, Tanya came by my locker. "I didn't know you were making a poster," she said. "I thought you made the tips just for me."

I didn't know what to say. It was true that Tanya had inspired us, but after Bea and I spent so much time on the tips, we (I?) thought it would be okay to share them with other people too. Especially since I want to be a writer and Bea wants to be an advice columnist.

"Does it matter?" I asked. I didn't want Tanya to be upset.

She looked down. "I guess not."

"No one knows you had anything to do with it," I said, in case that was her worry. "Ms. Sickle has been doing a unit on 'health and body image.'"

Tanya shrugged. "I just kind of liked the idea that you two made the list for me, special."

"We did," I said. "We mostly did."

She nodded. "It's okay. Never mind." She went to her next class, and I did too, but I have to say, the whole conversation made me feel a little upside down.

AVA (THAT'S AVA UPSIDE DOWN)

DEAR DIARY,

I read an Aesop fable and told it to Pip:

A conceited ass was braying insulting things about a lion. At first, the lion was upset, and he started to growl and roar and bare his teeth. But then he looked more closely and realized the insults were coming from a silly ass, so he decided to just go his merry way and not pay any attention.

"What's the moral?" Pip asked.

"If the person insulting you is a dumdum, try not to care too much," I said, and told her that I gave the tips to Tanya.

"Yeah, but it's easier to ignore one dumb donkey—or dumdum," Pip said, "than to pretend you don't care about a whole assembly full of them, you know?"

"I know," I said and felt sad for Tanya. It seems like school is just easier for some kids (like Kelli and even me) than others (like Tanya and even Pip).

A.

AFTER SCHOOL WITH TACO BY MY SIDE

DEAR DIARY,

Today was the worst **worst WORST**.

I don't even want to tell *you* what happened! It was so awful that in English, I barely said a single syllable (even to Chuck), and I was shaky during the spelling test, which, by the way, included the word *nightmare*. Chuck kept looking at me like he could tell something was wrong, but I couldn't talk about it. Not in front of everyone!

After class, Mrs. Lemons asked if I was okay, so I waited until the very last person left and then I started to *cry*! Which I hardly ever do in school! It was embarrassing, even though Mrs. Lemons was nice and gave me a hug.

Here's what happened.

(Actually, I still don't want to write it down, because then it will feel real.)

Okay, I got to lunch late because I'd gone by our FLASH room to check on my poster. It wasn't there! Ms. Sickle wasn't either, so I decided I'd ask her about it later. By the time I got to the cafeteria, Maybelle's table was full. Chuck was with You-Know-Who. And even Pip was with friends. I figured I'd put my tray down at a corner table by myself, and someone nice would come join me.

That is *not* what happened.

That big scary eighth grader, Rorie, sat down. Then Valeria sat down. Then Loudmouth Lacey sat down. So did Rorie's seventh-grade friend Jayda, who has red hair. And so did Mackie, an eighth-grade girl whose dog recently ate a rubber ducky. (Dr. Gross had to operate.) For one stupid second, I thought, *W-O-W. All these older kids are sitting with me.* I even wondered if they liked my new poster.

Then I noticed that not one of them was smiling.

Maybe I'm better at reading faces than books, because suddenly it was crystal clear that these girls had it in for me. I was getting…ambushed.

Rorie spoke first. "One question, Ava," she said. "Who made you queen of the world?"

"Yeah," Lacey said. "You get your picture in the paper, and now you're like an *authority* on everything?" She crinkled her eyes like a snake.

"'Fit or Fat'? *Really?*" Jayda asked. "Who says it's either/or! There are plenty of overweight people who are fit. And plenty of skinny people who are wimps."

"How strong are *you*, anyway?" Lacey asked. She shoved my shoulder, and the others laughed. I knew I should stand up and run, but I felt stuck. Powerless. It was as if I'd wandered into a movie—a *horror* movie.

Rorie said, "You're lucky you're in fifth grade. Otherwise we'd be having this conversation *outside*."

Lacey cackled. "Little toothpick thinks she's the body police." She gave me a push to see if I'd fight back.

Rorie looked at Valeria, and Valeria said, "Yeah. We don't appreciate you telling people what they should or shouldn't eat. Or how they should or shouldn't look." Rorie nodded. "No one gets to tell us how to live our lives."

"It's a free country," Jayda added. "If I want to eat a pack of Oreos, it's none of your business! No one asked you!"

I wanted to shout, "That's not true!" because Tanya *had* asked me. But I also wanted to leave Tanya out of this. She had enough to worry about. I wished I could defend myself the way I'd defended Pip last year when Lacey made fun of her. But I couldn't. I was crumpling before their very eyes. If we were outside, would they be beating me up?

"You know how some girls eat two peas and a lettuce leaf and call it lunch?" Jayda said. "*That's* what's really bad! That and the girls who throw up on purpose." She studied my face. "And just so you know, I'm *fine* with how I look." She put one hand behind her head in a sassy way. "In fact, I'm so *fine*, I could be a plus-size model!" Mackie high-fived her.

Rorie said, "Oh, and if you're looking for that nasty poster you made with your buddy Bea, it's in the trash, okay? We don't need twigs like you going around telling everyone they should be a size zero. You got that?"

I might have nodded. Or my face might have gone up and down. But really, I don't think "I" had anything to do with it. It was like I was *watching* this scene, not living it.

Rorie gave Lacey a look, and Lacey added, "And for your information, some people gain weight more easily than others. So watch how you throw around the word 'fat,' okay?"

The girls were all staring at me, and I wished I'd never titled my poster "FIT OR FAT." To be honest, I mostly just liked how the words "fat" and "fit" *looked* together.

Stupid, stupid me!

"And some boys *like* girls with curves," Jayda said.

That cracked everyone up, but to me, it seemed really random, because what did boys have to do with *any* of this?

Mackie spoke up for the first time. She's the one who knows my mom because her dog ate the duck. "Ava," she said, "you've probably heard about sexism and racism. Well, there's such a thing as sizism too. So you need to think about that."

Sizism? Is that even a word? How could I be a sizist? I am not a sizist! I made that list because Tanya asked me to and because Ms. Sickles had said obesity is *dangerous*.

Rorie jumped in again. "Here's the thing: you may think it's bad to be fat, but we think it's worse to be a shallow little *zero*!"

Mackie looked at me and added more softly. "Ava, the point is that it's not good to judge people's insides by their *out*sides."

I wanted to say, "I wasn't! I don't!" but my nose was tingling, and I knew that if I said *anything*, I'd burst into tears.

"People come in all sizes," Mackie continued. "Some are big and some are small, and so what? It's not what you look like—it's who you are that counts."

She glanced at Rorie as if to say, "Enough already."

Rorie shrugged, then turned to me and said, "Okay, we're done. But we don't need you judging us. So why don't you get out of here and let us have our lunch in peace?"

"And while you're at it, grow up!" Lacey threw in.

I wanted to say that I was *trying* to grow up, but instead I ran out of the lunchroom even though I hadn't eaten a single bite. I didn't see Maybelle or Pip or Chuck, but I did see Kelli. She was staring at me. And I bet she knew exactly what had just happened.

AVA, ZERO

2/19
AN HOUR LATER

DEAR DIARY,

I phoned Maybelle, but she was on her way to Kelli's for a sleepover with Zara. That made me feel even worse!

I told Dad what a horrible mess I was in and how in my head, I'd gone from hero to zero without passing Go. He said he and Mom already knew about it, because after I'd told Mrs. Lemons, she'd told Principal Gupta, and she'd told Dad, and Dad had told Mom. Now there's going to be a special assembly for the whole middle school on bullying and health and I don't know what else.

There was supposed to be a P-E-P rally next Tuesday, but it got postponed because of me. Kids like rallies more than assemblies, and I wonder how many people will know it's my fault it got postponed.

Probably everyone.

I never want to go to school again.

I wonder if I can fake being sick until summer vacation.

AVA IN AGONY

5:30 P.M. IN THE LIVING ROOM

DEAR DIARY,

Dad asked if I wanted to go to the Great Wall or the Kahiki. I said I'd rather stay home with Taco, and could we order in tacos? Dad said sure and sat down next to me on the sofa.

"Thanks, though," I said, and Dad patted my knee as if I were seven. He also said he had a cat joke for me:

Question: What's the difference between a cat and a comma?

Answer: A cat has claws at the end of its paws, and a comma means a pause at the end of a clause.

I tried to smile, but I couldn't, partly because the joke wasn't very funny and partly because I'm feeling too mopey.

Kelli once said her family likes to dine out on Friday, and what if I ran into Maybelle and Zara and Kelli in a restaurant, having a great time without me? I couldn't take it.

AVA, AILING

PS I thought I was Ava the Wise, but I am…other*wise*.

Dear Diary,

At dinner, while we ate takeout tacos, Pip said that *her* poster got ruined too—and so did Bea's! Someone gave *Mona Lisa* a beard and wrote "Wiggle Wiggle Wiggle" on her chest! And someone drew inappropriate private parts on Bea's deer! And boogies under the deer's nose! And someone gave Aesop sunglasses and a goatee!

I said the art poster vandals probably weren't the same girls who ripped down my FLASH poster because those girls would never have written "Wiggle Wiggle Wiggle" on *Mona Lisa*.

Pip said, "So true, Nancy Drew!" which she used to say back when she was reading an old series about a girl detective. (Now she's reading a series about a lady detective. It starts with *A Is for Alibi* and *B Is for Burglar*, and there's a new book for every letter.)

We talked about who might have written on the posters.

We did *not* talk about stupid Kelli's stupid sleepover.

Are Maybelle and Zara and Kelli hanging out in Kelli's pink room? Are they eating chocolate-covered strawberries? Are they talking about Chuck? Are they talking about *me*?

I wish *I* were having the sleepover.

And I wish Chuck weren't Kelli's boyfriend, because if he weren't taken, maybe I could call him and he could help me feel better. I keep thinking about Rorie, and I do get some of what she and those girls were saying. But did they have to gang up on me five to one???

A Is for Alone

TWENTY MINUTES LATER

DEAR DIARY,

I wanted to talk, so I walked into Pip's room and said, "Life is not fair."

Pip said, "Number one, you should learn to knock. Number two, I'm on the phone with Ben. And number three, life is *fairly fair* for you and me. We have food and shelter, and you should have more *perspective*."

I made a face and left. She didn't used to have *any* perspective, so who is she to criticize?

Writing things down usually helps, but tonight I also wanted to *talk*. I'm only human. And only eleven.

AVA, ARRRGGGH

PS I wish I'd never written those Tanya Tips. I'm having a hard time not giving myself a hard time!

2/20
MORNING, SQUEAKY CLEAN

Dear Diary,

I'm glad it's Saturday. I don't have it in me to even think about going back to school yet.

I don't even feel like writing in you.

I feel like soaking in a hot bath until it's not hot anymore, then draining out the water, turning the hot water back on, and taking an even longer bath.

But I already did that! I took the world's longest bath! By the time I got out, my fingers and toes were crinkly. (I'm lucky Pip didn't want to shower right after me, because when I use up all the hot water, she loses *all* perspective.)

The thing is, it's upsetting to have people upset with me. I wish I could wash away the bad feelings!

And it's hard to have "perspective," because I mostly see things through my own two eyes. Doesn't everyone?

Yesterday at school, it felt like all eyes were on me. Like I was at the eye of a storm.

A-V-A, E-Y-E?

LATE AFTERNOON

DEAR DIARY,

Dad made his famous Irish breakfast, and Pip told us she dreamed that *Z Is for Zinnia* won an award. I said I dreamed that some big kids were about to beat me up.

"Oh, honey," Mom said.

Later I went to Maybelle's, and we watched a Disney movie. That helped take my mind off my troubles—except for the part in *Beauty and the Beast* when the whole town just assumes that Beast is terrible when he isn't.

I decided to ask Maybelle about her sleepover with Kelli and Zara.

She said it was fun. At least she didn't say, "It was sooooo much fun!" Maybelle knows it hasn't been easy for me to watch her become friends with Zara, and now with Zara's friend Kelli—a.k.a. my...enemy? My *rival*?

"What did you guys do?" I asked.

"We watched a movie and went to the Great Wall," she said. (That made me extra glad that my family didn't go!) Maybelle looked up and added, "I will say this: Kelli's mom is a little—"

"A little what?"

Maybelle hesitated. "Well, let's just say she let us watch a movie that our parents and Zara's grandparents would *never* have let us watch. It was about a teenage girl who likes a boy who is a *bad* influence. And Kelli's mother, Candi—"

"Candy?"

"Candi with an *i*!"

"Go on."

"She watched part of it with us and acted…inappropriate."

"What do you mean? You have to tell me!"

"She said when she was our age, she wanted to be bigger, you know, up top. And she showed us this exercise she used to do with her friends. They'd kick back their arms and chant, 'We must, we must, we must build up the bust. The bigger, the better, the tighter the sweater, the boys will look at us!'"

"Omigod!"

"I know!"

"What did you and Zara do?"

"What could we do?"

"Didn't Kelli make her stop? Or tell her she was being, I don't know, sexist and sizist and…weird?"

"I don't think Kelli realized how weird it was. All she said was, 'Did it work?'"

"What did her mom say?"

"Of course not."

"Do *you* call her Candi?"

"Of course not!" Maybelle repeated.

I nodded and thought, *My mom may not be the huggiest mom in the world, but at least she's not embarrassing with a capital E.*

Back home, Mom was reading in bed and said, "Come in," so I did. I even got in next to her. She asked me what had caused "all the fuss" at school. So I told her that Tanya got laughed at in assembly, and I got *ostracized* (spelling word) in the cafeteria. She asked me to show her the Tanya Tips, so I did, explaining that I hadn't called anyone "fat," and Rorie had taken everything personally.

Mom nodded, and for a second, I wished she would give me a big hug and say all the right words like TV moms do. But Mom isn't like that. Her mom, Nana Ethel, isn't either.

Here's what Mom did say: "People get very sensitive about this subject. It's a minefield. Even Dr. Gross has to be super-careful when he tells clients that their cats or dogs need to lose weight." She looked at me. "He avoids saying 'fat' because it's such a loaded word."

"Like a loaded gun?"

"Well, not *that* dangerous." She met my eyes. "And not as dangerous as a real minefield either."

I pointed out that the word *diet* has the word *die* in it.

Mom chuckled. "Even for animals," she said, "losing weight is harder than you'd think. It's mostly up to the owner to buy special foods, provide exercise, and hold back on table scraps. No one wants to hear that their pet should go on a diet, but if an owner wants a pet to live a good, long life…"

Just then, Taco nudged the door open with his head, padded

toward us, and jumped onto the bed. Mom and I started petting him, and after a moment, Taco started purring.

I like how sweet Mom is with Taco. I sometimes forget that he's not only *my* first real pet, he's *Mom's* first real pet too!

"Taco's not a fat cat, right?" I whispered.

"Right," Mom replied.

"But he's not as scrawny as he was when we rescued him, right?"

"Right," she repeated.

"He's purr-fect," I said, and Mom agreed. I kissed Taco on his white zigzag.

"He's at a healthy weight for an adult indoor male," she added.

"You know the expression 'puppy love'? There should be a term 'kitty love.'"

Mom laughed. "You're right. There should."

AVA, RIGHT *NOT* WRONG

PS What I feel about Chuck may not be "true love," but it's more than "puppy love."

2/21
BEDTIME

DEAR DIARY,

I just read an Aesop fable that I wish I hadn't. Its moral is the opposite of the one for "The Lion and the Mouse."

That's the famous fable about the lion who gets really mad at the mouse who wakes him from a nap. The mouse begs the lion to spare him, and the lion says okay, and later, when hunters throw a net over the lion, the mouse sees him and starts gnawing away at the ropes and saves the lion's life. The moral? "No good deed is ever wasted."

Well, *this* fable, the one I just read, is called "The Frog and the Scorpion," and its moral is "No good deed goes unpunished." It starts out with a scorpion who begs a frog to ferry him to the other side of a stream:

"How do I know you won't sting me?" asks the frog.

"If I do, I will die too, because I can't swim," says the scorpion.

"How do I know you won't sting me when we get to the other side?" asks the frog.

"I would never do that!" says the scorpion.

The frog says, "Okay, fine," and the scorpion crawls onto the frog's back, and they start across the water. In the middle, the scorpion stings the frog! His poison paralyzes the frog, and suddenly they are both about to drown.

"Why did you sting me?" the frog says. "Now we're both going to die!"

"It's who I am," the scorpion says. "I couldn't help it."

Worst. Fable. Ever.

I mean, I like how Aesop sometimes tells different stories to make different points. And I get that the world is complicated.

But still. "No good deed goes unpunished" is a terrible moral.

(Even if it might sometimes be a teeny-tiny, itty-bitty bit true.)

AVA, STUNG

2/22 (A PALINDROME DATE)
AFTER SCHOOL

DEAR DIARY,

Observation: when things are bad, you can tell who your friends are. Today a lot of people were *looking at* me, and a few were *looking out for* me.

Not Rorie. If looks could kill, I'd be dead as a doornail! She and her gang got detentions because they "harassed" me, and I bet she's blaming me for that—which is totally not fair. I also saw Lacey today, and she stared at me in a way that made me *want* to go hide in a bathroom stall!

Maybelle was extra sweet all day.

Zara was *too*.

And Bea was...*three*. In the hallway, she even said that those older girls had had no right to "dump on me," and there was "nothing wrong with our list." I was glad she didn't add, "Except your title," since *I* was the one who'd idiotically called it "FIT OR FAT."

Tanya actually left a note in my locker. It said, "Don't let the turkeys get you down. (Not easy, I know.) Gobble, gobble." She even sketched an excellent turkey with a droopy wattle and trusting eyes. An hour later, I left a note in her locker that said "Thanks!" and drew the only turkey I know how to draw, which is the kind you trace with your five fingers, the way we learned in first grade.

At lunch, Alla, a sixth grader whose name is a palindrome (A-L-L-A), told me that some of those same girls picked on her when she moved here from Russia. She also said that at her bus stop this morning, Tanya told her that her whole family is giving up soda.

"They are?" I asked.

Alla nodded and added that Tanya had asked her if she wanted to start taking walks after school.

"What did you say?"

"I said sure. So we're going to try to walk on Thursdays."

Okay, I am now about to tell you the best part. One other person was really nice to me today. Can you guess who?

Chuck! Yes, Chuck!

He and I got to English before anyone else, so we were alone for about one minute, maybe two. He said, "I heard what happened." I looked right at him, and my nose got tingly and my eyes got hot. "I wish I could help," he said.

"Maybe I'm just not cut out to be a writer," I said. I didn't expect to say that, but sometimes with Chuck, all I can be is honest. And after all, my writing *does* keep causing trouble, whether I write about a queen bee or rescue cat or weight loss. "I probably shouldn't be trusted with a pen."

"Ava, don't say that! You're a great writer! The S rule was funny. So was the O rule." He met my eyes.

"Wait! You saw the poster before they took it down?" Had Chuck read what I wrote about Seconds, Sweets, Snacks, and Sugary Soda? And Fritos, Cheetos, Doritos, Tostitos, and Oreos?

"I recognized your handwriting, so I read it on Friday morning."

"You didn't think it was bossy and offensive? Or that I was acting like the 'body police'?"

He shook his head. "I thought it was *sincere* and *earnest*." He smiled because those were recent spelling words. "And brave," he added. "And…sweet."

He kept looking at me, and maybe this is all in my imagination, but it felt like he was thinking "…like you." And that he could tell I was thinking this.

It was as if we could read each other's minds.

"Chuck," I said, meeting his eyes, "you said you wished you could help, and I think you just did."

AVA, FEELING A BIT BETTER

DEAR DIARY,

For Meatless Monday, Dad made kale quiche and a salad with fava beans, avocado, radishes, and quinoa. If I had to grade dinner, I'd give it a 75.

I don't get why quinoa is so popular, but maybe I don't understand popularity.

After dinner, I opened the drawer by my bed because I wanted to take a peek at my pack of gum. The one Chuck gave me. I thought it would make me feel warm. And calm. And happy.

Well, I opened the drawer and…the pack was opened! There were two crinkled wrappers and two missing pieces!

I barged into Pip's room without even knocking. "PIP!" I screamed. "What did you do?"

She was under the covers reading *I Is for Innocent*. "What?"

"That was *my gum*!" I said loudly.

She looked confused.

"You opened my pack of GUM!"

She stared at me. "Since when is that a federal crime?"

This might sound stupid, but since you are my diary and you

can't laugh or tell anyone, I will tell you what I did next: I started to cry. To *bawl.*

"Whoa, whoa, Ava, I can buy you a new pack," Pip offered.

"Chuck gave me *that pack*," I said, gulping. "You can't just replace it. It was special. It was"—I looked up at Ben's card on her bulletin board—"like a valentine."

"Chuck?" Pip asked, wide-eyed. "Chuck-Chuck?"

I nodded and felt like an idiot.

"You should have told me."

I shrugged, because what was I supposed to have told her? That I had a crush on my best guy friend since kindergarten, but he was going out with Headband Kelli? Or that Chuck gave me a pack of gum, and it felt like a present. And a secret. A secret present.

I hadn't told anyone. Not even Maybelle!

Some things are so private, I can only tell *you.*

What I *did* say was, "Pip, I have secrets too."

"I'm sorry, Ava, I didn't know," she said softly.

I nodded and finally said, "It's all right." I liked that lately Pip has been acting more like a big sister. "But *don't* take *any* more pieces!"

"Of course not!"

"Pinkie promise?"

"Pinkie promise," she said, and we hooked pinkies. And now I'm going to sleep because I'm tired as can be.

AVA, A TO *ZZZZ*

Dear Diary,

I asked Dad if I could stay home from school instead of going to the emergency assembly. He said no but offered to sit in the back if I wanted. I was about to say sure, but then I pictured Rorie and Lacey and Valeria and Jayda and Mackie making fun of me for having my "daddy" there to protect me. So I said, "It's okay." The words came out funny, because each one had to get around the lump in my throat. And because it was *not* okay.

Pip and I walked to school, and on the way, I asked if she knew who Kelli was. She said, "The pretty blond girl who's kind of full of herself?"

"Yes," I said. But then I thought: Aren't we all full of ourselves? Who else could we be full of?

AVA, TRYING TO HAVE PERSPECTIVE

PS Then again, I still don't get why Chuck even likes her. Does he truly like-like her? Why did she ever have to move to Misty Oaks anyway?

IN THE LIBRARY AFTER LUNCH BUT BEFORE THE ASSEMBLY

Dear Diary,

It feels like everyone keeps looking at me. I think everyone heard that a group of older kids ganged up on a fifth grader and "defaced her property." But I think everyone also heard that the kid was an insensitive smarty-pants know-it-all who was so full of herself that she'd probably tell Santa to go on a diet. And I think everyone knows exactly who's who and thinks it's my fault the P-E-P rally got postponed. Which I guess it is.

Still, here's why it doesn't really feel fair:

1. I would *never* tell Santa to go on a diet.
2. I'm not insensitive. If anything, I'm *too* sensitive.
3. If Tanya hadn't *asked* for tips, I would never have come up with the list.

All I *mean* is, *well*, I'm not a *mean* person; I'm a *well-mean*ing person.

Since you're my diary, I will admit two things. Number one, I guess I'd been hoping that people would like our tips and Bea and I might even get a little recognition. (Is that a crime?) And number two, I did say something mean out loud today at lunch. I told Zara that I thought Kelli's rainbow headband was stupid-looking. I couldn't help it. It just popped out.

Instead of agreeing, Zara said, "But, Ava, why do you care so much? Maham wears colorful hijabs, and I bet you don't think twice about it." I looked at Maham, and it was true: today the hijab covering her head and neck is peacock blue, and other days she wears other colors, and I barely notice. (I used to, back when she first came to school.) And believe me, I realize that a head *scarf* has nothing to with a head*band*. But I could see Zara's point.

Then again, what did Zara expect me to say? *"I care about Kelli because I care about Chuck, and Chuck and Kelli care about each other."* Not a chance! And anyway, Zara may have halfway figured this all out.

The other reason why I've been obsessing extra is that I saw this on Kelli's notebook:

C

H

U

C

K E L L I

Maybe I'm a K-O-O-K, but I don't like that Chuck and Kelli have the letter K in common. He and I don't have any letters in common. Let alone limbo. Or sports.

AVA, MISUNDERSTOOD

Dear Diary,

Usually when we sit down for an assembly, all you hear is everyone talking. Well, today, while we were finding our seats, Mr. Ramirez put on a catchy song called "Respect." When he turned it off, he told us that the singer was Aretha Franklin and asked us to spell out the word. So we did: "R.E.S.P.E.C.T."

"I can't hear you," he said, which was funny because as a librarian, he's usually shushing us.

"R.E.S.P.E.C.T.," we repeated.

"And what's that spell?"

"Respect!" we shouted.

"I can't hear you!" he said.

"RESPECT!" we shouted even more loudly.

"I still can't hear you!" he said, cupping his ear.

"RESPECT!" we yelled at the top of our lungs.

"That's right. And from now on, I want you to be more respectful of your classmates, yourselves, and other people's work. Is that clear?"

"Yes."

"Is it?"

"YES!"

No one snickered, and by now Mr. Ramirez sounded so serious, it made me wonder if *he* had ever been disrespected.

Next Principal Gupta stepped up and introduced the two speakers.

The first was a therapist in a suit and bow tie. He talked about *b*ullying and *b*ystanders and *b*oundaries, *b*ut he was *b*oring. Also, one of his pants' legs was twisted into his sock, which was distracting.

The second was a young nurse *practi*tioner whose advice was more *practi*cal and who had lots of twisty braids wrapped around her head.

"Your parents used to take care of you," she began. "Now you're learning to take care of yourselves." She said that chips and cookies have "empty" or "useless" calories, and we should eat real food and read labels and buy products with ingredients our "grandparents would recognize." She said little treats are fine, but if you get in the habit of "double desserts" and "emotional eating," you'll "jeopardize" your "long-term health" because obesity is linked to diabetes and heart and liver troubles.

"I'm not blaming or shaming," she said, "just sharing vital info. When it comes to weight, there's no magic pill, no one-size-fits-all advice." She said that kids have different body types and grow at different rates, and that some have "an easier relationship" with food than others, but we should all cut back on meat and sugar. She also said what Dad had said: that it doesn't help that food that is good for you costs more than food that is bad for you.

Soon it was time for questions, but I kept my head down, because the last thing I wanted was for more people to look at me.

A girl asked about anorexia, and the nurse practitioner said it is a serious disease, because if you don't eat enough, you can literally starve to death. She said bulimia is "life-threatening" too, because if you barf up your food, it can mess up your whole system, "even the back of your teeth." (She didn't say "barf"; she said "purge.") A sixth grader asked about skipping lunch, and she said, "It's better to have a glass of milk and a piece of whole wheat bread than nothing at all.

"Listen," she said, looking out at us. "I get that this can be tricky. Adults can say, 'Don't smoke' and 'Don't do drugs,' but no one can say, 'Don't eat.' You *need* to eat! So you have to learn to be *sensible* about it. If you need help, get help."

The therapist with the hitched-up pant leg took back the mike again. "I want to add that there's *not* a 'fine line' between *under-weight* or *overweight*. The majority of kids are in the middle." He looked out at us and nodded as if proving his own point. "And the goal is *not* to be thin—it's to be healthy and active and self-accepting."

I thought that was the end, but he said, "By the way, your principal told me you've been studying Botero." I could feel myself tensing up, and the whole room got a little extra quiet. Why was he reminding us of last week's disaster—not that anyone had forgotten? "Well, you might find it interesting that centuries ago," he continued, "if someone was curvy, that was prestigious. It was a sign of wealth! It meant that person wasn't going hungry. The painting *The Three Graces* by Rubens shows three very full-figured women."

For a second, I wondered if he was going to whip out a naked ladies art poster. But he didn't, and soon Principal Gupta hopped up and thanked both speakers. We all clapped, and as we filed out, Mr. Ramirez put the "Respect" song back on.

I bet I'll be spelling that word in my head for a long time.

A.V.A.W.R.E.N.

PS After school, I saw Lacey by the buses. She did not look at me *respect*fully. She gave me what Uncle Patrick calls "the hairy eyeball." So I tried to ignore her. Like the lion in the fable did to the a_ _.

BEDTIME

Dear Diary,

Maybelle called, and we talked about the assembly. She said, "Maybe I'm lucky, but I don't really get tempted to eat way too little or way too much."

"Same," I said. "Except on Halloween. Or when a tray of cookies is coming out of the oven."

"Kelli said her mom is a 'fitness nut,'" Maybelle said. "She spends *entire* mornings or afternoons at the gym—and she's not a professional athlete or anything."

I tried to picture Candi running on a treadmill for hours on end.

Maybelle continued. "My parents say, 'Everything in moderation, including moderation.'"

"I like that," I said. And then I *allllll*most told her I also like Chuck—but I didn't.

Ava the Moderate

Dear Diary,

Dad showed me a funny sentence on his computer: "English is weird. It can be understood through tough thorough thought, though." I asked him to print it out so I could show it to Mrs. Lemons.

We started talking about all the ways to pronounce *ough* and about silent letters in general. Like the *d* in *handsome*, or *b* in *dumb*, or *l* in *salmon*, or *t* in *castle*.

Or the *g* in *gnat* and *gnu* and *gnaw*.

Or the *k* in *knife* or *knickknacks* and *knock-knock* jokes.

I wanted to tell Dad a knock-knock joke, but I couldn't think of one because, well, I haven't heard any new ones in a while.

AVA WREN (WITH A SILENT W)

DEAR DIARY,

Dad needed eggs, so I went with him to the grocery store. I grabbed some cans of chicken soup, but then I read the label, and there was so much sodium (salt) and so many strange-sounding chemicals that the ingredients sounded like a practice list for a spelling bee.

I put the cans back and picked out a different brand.

We were about to leave when I saw Chuck in the produce aisle! He was with his mom, so at first, I kept my distance. But then his very tall mom started talking to the very short butcher, so I gave Chuck a wave, and he walked over.

I felt a little nervous and blurted, "I have a joke," even though he's usually the one with the jokes. "What word becomes shorter when you add two letters to it?"

"What do you mean?"

"What word becomes *shorter* when you add two letters to it?" I repeated.

After a few seconds, he said, "I give up."

"Short! Get it? SHORT + ER = SHORTER!"

He laughed, and we talked about yesterday's assembly.

Suddenly my heart started beating. "Chuck?" I said. "Speaking of R-E-S-P-E-C-T, when Kelli told you that Tanya could model for that Botero guy, that wasn't very nice. And Tanya was *right there*."

Chuck didn't say anything.

"Do you really like her?" I asked softly. "Like *like-like*?" I couldn't believe I was asking him this. It's one thing for me to ask this question over and over in my head, but another to ask him out loud. "You two have been going out for sixteen days."

Omigod!! Now he knew I'd been counting!! I wanted to stay quiet, but more words came flying out. I wondered if I was putting my cards on the table (instead of holding them close to my chest). "I know it's none of my business," I said, "but not minding my own business might be one of my weaknesses. And I'm still sort of surprised that you two are boyfriend-girlfriend."

Part of me wanted to go racing down the aisle and dive behind the display of organic pancake mix. But another part wanted to hear his answer.

"Me too," he mumbled.

"Wait. *You're* sort of surprised that you two are going out?"

He nodded.

"I don't get it."

"Me neither," he said. "It all happened so fast!"

"Wait. What?"

"Everything! One minute, I was on the bus, starving because I'd overslept. The next, Kelli offered me banana bread, so I took some. And suddenly we were in homeroom, and she was asking if I wanted to go out, and I don't know… I think I checked the circle because I didn't want to hurt her feelings."

He was looking at his sneakers, but I was looking at his face, his cheeks and nose and eyelashes. If I were older, I probably would have given him a hug or something.

"But what about *your* feelings?"

He gave a tiny nod. "She does call our house a lot. Like twice a day. My mom doesn't like it." He looked over at his mom. "I tell her it's about homework—but sometimes I just say, 'Mom, don't pick up,' because I don't always want to talk." He looked back at me and added, "Kelli *always* wants to talk. Especially about her dog."

"Snuggles," I offered.

"Snuggles," Chuck repeated. His eyes were soft and brown. "And she always wants us to sit together. Like every chance there is."

He was frowning, but I wanted to do a happy dance right there in front of the lemons and limes. If I knew how to juggle, I might have been tempted to juggle the lemons and limes and clementines, all while balancing on a watermelon.

"Maybe you could tell Kelli that your mom figured out that her calls weren't about homework, and she got mad and she's making you break up?" *Omigod*, I thought. *Did I really just say that?*

"I don't know," Chuck mumbled.

"All I mean is, you checked a circle. You didn't sign a contract in blood."

"True." He looked like he was considering this. "Ava, you know what you said about not minding your own business?"

"Yeah."

"I don't think that's a weakness."

"You don't?"

"Maybe sometimes it's the opposite. Maybe sometimes, it's a…strength."

I almost said that STRENGTH is a cool word because it has eight letters and only one is a vowel. Instead I told *that* part of my brain to SHUT UP. "Chuck," I said, "just remember that *your* feelings count too."

I hoped it wasn't dumb of me to be giving advice when I'm not a psychotherapist and my advice isn't always right.

Then again, what are "friends" for?

Just then, his very tall mom came over with her cart, so I said hello—and good-bye.

AVA, OUTSPOKEN?

BARELY AWAKE

DEAR DIARY,

Did that conversation really happen? Or was it a dream? I *think* it really happened, but I also feel like I dreamed it...

Oh. Wait. Now I remember. I dreamed that Chuck and I were at a bank! We were laughing and putting coins in a sorting machine, but it was more like a vending machine, and packs of *gum* and *gum*my bears (!) kept flying out.

Dreams are funny, right?

G-T-G. Got to go to school!

AVA, DREAMY

IN THE LIBRARY

DEAR DIARY,

After FLASH, Ms. Sickle said, "That assembly stirred up an important conversation," and asked if I had another copy of my tips.

"Right here," I replied and pointed to the page in my diary.

"Great!" she said, reaching for my diary. "I can type it for you if you like."

"I'll copy it over!" I said, because I was *not* about to hand her my diary.

"Even better," she said and gave me poster board and a Sharpie. I said I'd do it in the library during study hall.

"And maybe just leave off the title this time?" she suggested.

Duh! I thought, but said, "Okay." I did not add that I'd probably never use the word *fat* again for the rest of my life. I'd probably never even say "bacon fat."

I'm now in the library making some changes to my list. I even decided to add a new tip: "Try to be positive and not let other people make you feel bad." Mr. Ramirez peeked over my shoulder, so I asked him if he thought I should add that.

"Sure." He smiled. "Ava, I wish I'd had this list when I was a kid."

"Really?" I asked.

He nodded. "My aunt called me 'Chunky.' A few kids at school called me 'Fatty' and 'Fatso.' It was bad. I was glad when I finally figured out that for me, doughnuts and McDonald's weren't worth it. And also when I figured out I should steer clear of idiots and start hanging out with the people who were interested in what I was interested in."

I noticed that Mr. Ramirez wasn't skinny, just regular. Or, as that bow tie guy put it, "in the middle."

"When's your wedding?" I asked, because we're all excited that he and his boyfriend are "tying the knot."

"End of the school year. June 19."

"Cool," I said. "I bet it will be fun."

He smiled. "We're going over lots of details right now. The menu, the band, the flowers, the rings."

I nodded, even though I'd never thought about the work behind a wedding.

"Mr. Ramirez, do you think I might be a little bit sizist?"

"Sizist?"

"Mackie said that's when you judge people by how much they weigh."

He considered this. "I suppose a lot of people are judgmental about one thing or another. But with obesity, it's almost not fair."

"What's not fair?"

"Well, many people have secret problems, like addiction or gambling, and you'd never know it just by looking at them.

Obesity is there for the whole world to see. But it doesn't help when someone wags a finger."

"Wags a finger?"

"Scolds, reprimands, criticizes." He put on a fake frown and wagged his finger up and down, which made us both laugh. "Anyway, Ava, I know you realize it isn't 'fat' versus 'skinny'—it's *healthy* versus *unhealthy*."

I like that Mr. Ramirez talks to me like we are two thinking people, not one smart grown-up and one dumb kid. But I might be dumber than he thinks.

I reread my list and was about to write "Weight Loss Tips" at the top. But what if a girl had an eating disorder and was starving herself? Telling her to drink zero-calorie water and to eat less would be horrible advice. I was beginning to see why there were so many books on this subject. And so many contradictory messages!

I made a few more changes and finally finished the new version and copied it over. On the top, I wrote "Take Care of Yourself." I rolled up the poster and shoved it in my backpack. It stuck out a little, but that didn't matter, because I was about to hand it to Ms. Sickle.

AVA, NOT A REAL *AUTHOR* OR *AUTHORITY* (BUT NOT A BAD PERSON EITHER)

PS I'm going to ask Pip to take a photo of it so I can print it out and tape it in here.

TAKE CARE OF YOURSELF

Want to feel great?
What's on your plate?
Also try to think
About what you drink.

1. Drink H_2O—it's free and is good for you.

2. Exercise more than you did before. (A rhyme!)

3. Be colorful. Enjoy red, orange, yellow, green, and purple vegetables and fruits.

4. Slow down when you eat. It takes twenty minutes for your brain to figure out what your mouth has been up to.

5. Watch your *S*'s. Cut back on Seconds, Sweets, junky Snacks, and Sugary Sodas.

6. Watch your *O*'s. Cut back on FritOs, CheetOs, DoritOs, TostitOs, and OreOs.

7. If you get tempted to overeat or binge on *S*'s or *O*'s, brush your teeth, chew sugarless gum, or nibble on fruit, veggies, or unbuttered popcorn.

8. Find a workout buddy or go on walk-and-talks. You can also do sports or walk a dog.

9. Try to be positive and not let other people make you feel bad.

10. Congratulate yourself for taking care of yourself, one day at a time. Y-A-Y YOU!

DEAR DIARY,

At dinner, Dad said he had a new palindrome for us: "As I pee, sir, I see Pisa." (A-S-I-P-E-E-S-I-R-I-S-E-E-P-I-S-A). Pip laughed, and I pictured a tourist boy looking up at the Leaning Tower of Pisa.

Mom scowled as if she didn't think this was proper dinner conversation, but talking about sick or hurt pets might not be either, and she does that.

Just last week, she told us about a cat that had diarrhea, and how the owner had to bring in a "fecal sample." Pip said, "Frozen P-O-O-P?" and Dad said, "Let's change the subject, shall we?"

I think one of the nice things about when it's just our family is that it *is* okay to talk about absolutely everything. Like revised posters or frozen P-O-O-P or even forbidden crushes. (Not that I've talked to M-O-M or D-A-D about my *new* feelings for my *old* friend!)

ABSOLUTELY AVA

PS I wonder if Chuck is going to break up with Kelli. I wonder if it's bad that I spend a lot of time wondering this.

PPS Pip just came in and said, "Nothing is impossible," and showed me that if you add a space and an apostrophe, you can change "IMPOSSIBLE" to "I'M POSSIBLE." I said, "H-U-H" and then I said that some things *feel* impossible.

DEAR DIARY,

Last night, Taco jumped onto my bed for a long purring session. He usually acts tough and independent, but sometimes even he likes to cuddle and be comforted.

Question: Do tough *people* have soft sides too?

Pip has lots of sides, and I see all of them. Before bed, I asked her if she had any art books with Rubens paintings. She said no but googled *The Three Graces* and up popped an oil painting of three large naked ladies.

Pip read about the painting and said that Rubens painted it in 1639, and the women were supposed to be Zeus's daughters, and the three graces are charm, beauty, and creativity.

"H-U-H," I said and told Pip that I'm not going to use the word *fat* ever again.

"A nicer word is 'zaftig.'"

"Zaftig?"

"Zaftig," she repeated. "You can also say 'Rubenesque.' Think you can spell that?"

I thought about it, then got it right. Pip said "W-O-W."

AVA ELLE, WHO CAN SPELL QUITE WELL

DEAR DIARY,

In English, Chuck said he saw my poster. "It was as *earnest* and *sincere* as last time."

"And it's *not* judgmental," I said, because I liked my new title and because *judgmental* was about to be on our spelling test. Then I showed Chuck that the "preferred" spelling of *judgmental* has only one *e*, not two. "Same as *acknowledgments*. No *e* after the *dg*." I wrote both words out.

Guess what? We took our test, and he got both words right! So he got an 80!

We traded papers, and I put a big star around his grade and handed his back. He looked right into my eyes and said, "Thanks."

I didn't know whether the "Thanks" was for the grade or the star or the spelling lesson or just because. But I smiled and was glad that Kelli wasn't there, because I didn't even try to look away.

AVA, HONEST

PS Maybelle was absent today because she has a bug (weird expression) and was home sick. (Not "homesick"!)

SATURDAY AFTERNOON

DEAR DIARY,

I put on my coat and snow boots and went to Maybelle's to give her the schoolwork she had missed, including a "brain teaser" from our math teacher Miss Hamshire (a.k.a. Miss Hamster). This is it:

"*A bat and a ball together cost $1.10. The bat costs a dollar more than the ball. What is the price of the ball?*"

"Easy!" I said. "Ten cents!"

"No," Maybelle said. "Five."

"No," I insisted, though I should have known better than to argue with Maybelle about math. But maybe she was dizzy from being sick? "It's ten!" I said.

"No," she replied patiently. "Let's say the ball is a nickel. If the bat costs a dollar more, then the bat costs $1.05. Right?"

"I guess…"

"Well, there you go. If you buy a five-cent ball, and also a bat that costs $1.05, you've spent your $1.10. So the ball costs five cents."

"Oh." I changed the subject because my head was spinning. "What'd you do yesterday?"

"Mostly slept and watched TV," Maybelle said. "But can I tell you something really personal?"

I hoped she wasn't going to say that she got her period. Or that she realized that she has a major crush on Chuck. Or that she and Zara and Kelli are going to start a club.

"Sure," I said.

"I found three little hairs under my arms."

I tried to hide my shock. "What are you going to do?"

"Shave, I guess? I mean, maybe someday? I think I'm going to ask my mom."

I nodded as if any minute now, I too expected to find private hairs in surprising places and would consult my mom.

Maybelle also said that last night, after she was feeling better, she convinced her parents to let her look at the stars because it was really clear out. (Maybelle is the only person I know who thinks about nighttime weather as much as daytime weather.)

"And?"

"It was beautiful! All the constellations! And the Milky Way! Do you know that the Earth travels through space at 67,000 miles per hour?"

"No."

"But it travels *silently*! There's no sound in space!"

"Why not?"

"There's no air, so the molecules can't vibrate."

I didn't know what she was talking about, and she could tell.

"Ava, isn't it weird? We're just dots in the universe! Our whole solar system is miniscule when you think about all the other stars and galaxies out there."

"Maybe," I said. "But I still get all worked up about stuff."

Maybelle smiled.

Anyway, I am now home, and I can't believe I'm writing in you, my diary, about the universe and my BFF's armpit hair. But I am.

Funny, it feels like I'm sitting completely still at my desk, but when you consider how fast the Earth travels and how fast everyone is growing up, maybe I'm not sitting *still* at all.

AVA, DOT

Dear Diary,

I raised both my arms in front of the mirror, and I definitely do not have any armpit hair.

But you know what? I think Pip *has* started to shave. I noticed a pink razor in the back of the bathroom drawer! How long has it been there? Days? Weeks? Months?

AVA, ANALYZING

2/27
SATURDAY NIGHT

DEAR DIARY,

Pip finished *Z Is for Zinnia* and showed it to me. My favorite new pages are Q is for Queen Anne's lace, S is for snapdragon, and U is for umbrella plant.

"You know what I'm looking forward to now?" Pip asked.

"Getting it published?"

"No. *Real* flowers. Spring."

"Spring?" I repeated.

"*Spring!* Crocuses and daffodils! Purples and yellows!"

I looked out at our lawn, and it was brown with dirty clumps of unmelted snow that were gray and shiny on top.

"Hey, how are things with Chuck?" Pip asked.

"Better." I didn't say anything else because I don't know what's going on between him and Kelli. Then I asked her about Ben.

"His mom might let me work at the bookstore," she said.

"For real? For money?"

"No, not for money. But she said she can give me advance reading copies of YA books and I can write reviews for their website."

"W-O-W," I said, because that sounded perfect for Pip. (Not

for me. I would *not* want to have to read young adult books or write bonus book reports.) I lowered my voice. "Have you and Ben…" I began, "…kissed on the lips?" It just popped out.

"Ava!" she said but did not kick me out of her room. "Not yet," she finally answered. "But he did kiss me on the cheek."

My eyes went wide.

"And that's our secret, okay?" she added.

"Okay," I said, glad we had sister secrets.

A B C = Ava in Bed with Cat

PS When a boy and a girl kiss for the first time, how can they be sure they won't bump noses or do it wrong?

2/28
BEDTIME

Dear Diary,

This is *not* a leap year, so today was the last day in February.

This morning, the twins next door, Carmen and Lucia, came over in pink jackets. Pip and I were in our pajamas, but we got dressed, and I told them about playing limbo two weeks ago. They thought that sounded fun, so we took turns holding up a broomstick while one person tried to scoot under it. I started talking about how my friend Chuck is great at limbo. (I think I just like saying—and writing—his name.)

Carmen said, "Is he your *boy*friend?" and I answered, "NO!" a little too loudly. Lucia dared me to invite him over, and I said "NO!" even louder.

Well, Tanya texted Pip and asked if she wanted to go for a walk, so next thing you know, all five of us were in the park playing Frisbee. The sun was shining and the snow had melted, and I'd forgotten how good it feels to run around and not be bundled up.

I thought of a baseball joke that Chuck had told me and told it to them:

"Once there was a boy who kept wondering why a baseball was growing larger and larger…and then it hit him!"

Everyone laughed.

Tanya ended up staying for dinner (a first) and helped us make roasted vegetables with shrimp. While we were cooking, Tanya told Dad that thanks to me, her whole family has been trying to eat better.

"Really?" Dad asked.

"Yes," Tanya said. "I asked my mom to stop buying Pepsi and Oreos, and she thought that was a good idea and would save us money too. My little brother is mad because he's not heavy, but my mom said it's better for all of us." Dad nodded. "She even put Ava's tips on our fridge."

"With a refrigerator magnet?" I asked, trying to picture it.

Tanya nodded. She turned back to Dad. "Mr. Wren, Ava's gotten the whole school talking!"

"About me?" I asked, suddenly paranoid.

"No! About soda and vegetables and 'paying attention' and stuff."

Taco brushed against my leg to remind me that it was his dinnertime and I should pay attention to him too.

AVA, ATTENTIVE

IN THE LIBRARY

DEAR DIARY,

You know how some people are hard-hearted? When it comes to Chuck, I might be *softhearted.*

I got to lunch early, and so did Chuck, and he put his tray down next to mine, which he never does. I looked around for Kelli but didn't see her.

"Hi," I said.

"Hi," he said, and our eyes locked a little. (Can eyes lock a little? I just mean that I tried to look away but couldn't.)

I told him that Pip and the twins and I had played limbo over the weekend, and it was fun, but nobody was as good at limbo as he was. (Was that flirting? I did *not* giggle or anything!)

Our eyes locked again. They just did. It felt like there was something more we wanted to say to each other.

But the world of school came rushing in when Maybelle and Zara and all three Emilys came and sat down. Jamal too. (Do he and Zara like each other??) It was like our old "lunch bunch," but with...boys. T-T-Y-T-T, it was a little awkward.

I remembered that Dad had printed out a riddle for me,

and I'd stuck it in my backpack. "You guys, I have a riddle! Are you ready?"

Everyone leaned in, and to be funny, the three Emilys said, "Ready." "Ready." "Ready."

"Okay," I said. "I am the beginning of the end, and the end of time, and I am essential to creation, and I surround every place."

They guessed "air" and "God" and "infinity" and "life" and "death" and even "love." "Wrong!" I said. "It's the letter *e*!"

I showed them the paper and pointed to all the *e*'s.

After a while, Chuck said, "I have a joke about a kayak."

Zara said, "K-A-Y-A-K is a palindrome!"

"I know," Chuck said and smiled at me. I smiled back, and our eyes locked again, and I totally had to *force* myself to look away. "Two people were in a kayak," he began. "It was freezing cold, so they built a little fire in the bottom of the boat. But the kayak started burning up, and the people sank and drowned."

"I don't get it," said Emily J.

"That's not funny," said Emily S.

"That's sad," said Emily L.

"Let me get to the punch line!" Chuck said and pronounced, "So it just goes to show: you can't have your *kayak* and *heat* it too."

Everyone laughed except Kelli, who suddenly appeared holding a chair and wormed her way between me and Chuck. "Can you tell it again?" she said.

Chuck frowned a tiny bit but repeated the joke. She still didn't get it and said she'd never heard the expression "You can't have your cake and eat it too." Well, Chuck explained it, and she finally laughed, and I wondered if maybe some rich people *can* because they can buy two cakes, and then, when they eat one, still have one?

Lunch was *not* as fun with Headband Kelli there, so I said I had to go to the library. I knew that being here alone—well, alone with you—would help me relax.

Funny. Writing and petting Taco help me relax. Reading and drawing help Pip relax. Reading and cooking help Dad. And maybe what helps Kelli is prancing around with headbands on her head and putting cucumber slices on her eyes and calling Chuck's house and sitting next to him even though I was there first.

AVA AT SCHOOL

AT DR. GROSS'S WAITING FOR MOM TO FINISH WORK

DEAR DIARY,

I went to Dr. Gross's after school because Pip and Dad both had plans and I'm not allowed to "go home to an empty house." Soon I might be. Mom said that when she was eleven, she used to *get paid* to babysit for her neighbors.

I said that I like when I come home and, for instance, Dad is cooking, even when it's a Meatless Monday (like today). I also said I'm glad Taco is always home now too.

Anyway, I was doing my math in Dr. Gross's waiting room, and I was asking Penny at the desk about her three cats (one has just one eye) and her partner (whose name is Henny, which is pretty funny, since Penny rhymes with Henny). I was also noticing the containers of dog biscuits and cat treats and Dr. Gross's framed diploma from vet school. (He went to Cornell.) Well, guess who walked through on her way out the door? Mackie and BowWow!

I thought about pretending I didn't see them, but it's a small waiting room. I thought about pretending I didn't remember she was one of the girls who ganged up on me, but how could I forget? And then *she* said, "Hi."

I said hi back and even asked if BowWow had eaten any more rubber duckies.

"No," she said. "And it's a good thing! My dad said that operation cost a fortune!"

I didn't know what to say, because it's not like I'm the one who makes up the price for rubber duck removal surgery.

"He's been eating everything else in sight though," Mackie said. "Dr. Gross said he's too sedentary, and I should take him for a thirty-minute walk every day."

I know how to spell *sedentary* and that it means being a "couch potato" (or, in the case of a dog, maybe "floor potato"). But I was *not* about to comment on BowWow's physique.

No way.

No. Way.

No. Way. José.

While I sat there M-U-M, Mackie said, "You know what? It'll probably do me good to have to walk my overweight dog." Suddenly Penny went to the back to check on something which meant Mackie and I were alone. She looked right at me. "Ava," she said. "I feel bad about the other day."

I stayed quiet.

"I should have told Rorie to chill," she continued. "I swear, that girl has anger management issues. She knows she has to get in shape. She can barely walk up two flights of stairs! She had no business dragging the rest of *us* into it."

I couldn't disagree. (Double negative.) So I mumbled, "She always makes me nervous."

Mackie laughed. "She makes everyone nervous!"

BowWow started licking my fingers, which tickled, and was half nice, half gross.

"BowWow! Stop!" Mackie said.

"It's okay," I said, because it was.

"Rorie made it sound like you were going around saying that you have to be skinny to be happy," Mackie continued. "She said you'd crossed a line, and we needed to put you in your place. And yeah, you're pretty young to be dispensing advice, but I read your tips today and they weren't malicious. They were basically no big deal."

I was glad Mackie said that, but I also felt bad for my tips. Were they "basically no big deal"? I'd worked hard on them!

"Anyway, I probably should have thought about it a little more before I piled on."

"Thanks," I said quietly. "I probably should have thought about it a little more before I made that poster."

She sized me up and seemed to notice for the first time that I'm just a harmless fifth grader.

"You're a good kid," she said.

"I know," I said, even though I hadn't meant to agree out loud.

Mackie laughed and said, "Brave too." That was funny because people sometimes say that about me, but I never feel brave.

Mackie dug into her backpack for her cap, and out came a little bag of Wise potato chips. She put the cap on and said, "I may regret this the second I do it, but let's consider it a science experiment." She dropped the bag onto the floor. BowWow looked at her, confused.

I was confused too. I looked down the hallway and hoped Penny wasn't coming back right away.

"Five, four, three, two, one," Mackie said, then stomped on the bag with her boot.

The bag popped, BowWow barked, and Mackie laughed.

"It worked!" she said. "I thought that mostly just air would come out, but I wasn't totally sure. Of course if all the chips *had* gone flying, BowWow would have licked them up. Still, that would have been a lousy way for him to start his 'weight loss regime.'"

"An un*wise* way," I said. The word slipped out, and I was relieved when Mackie laughed.

She tossed the smashed bag into a garbage can. "Well, no backsies. The real test now will be if I can pass the 7-Eleven on the way home and *not* buy a new bag."

I almost said, "You can," but I kept my mouth shut.

AVA AFTER SCHOOL

DEAR DIARY,

We just had a Meatless Monday dinner, and it was *really* good. I'd give it a 95. If vegetarian food were always that yummy, I would actually look forward to Mondays!

Dad and I made it together. It was eggplant parmesan, and my main job was to peel and slice the eggplants. The skin was beautiful, shiny, and sort of midnight purple. Dad said the French word for the color—*and* vegetable—is *aubergine* and asked me to try to spell it. I hesitated because foreign words can be hard, but I got it right. Dad high-fived me.

Then he started talking about how he used to cook with his father.

"Back then, not many fathers cooked," he said. "Let alone fathers and sons."

He told me his dad started the tradition of Irish breakfasts and Sunday sundaes. "He loved a good meal," he said.

Dad doesn't talk about his dad very often, and I kept peeling because I wanted him to keep talking. All I really knew about my grandfather is that he died at age sixty, before I was born. And that everybody loved him. And that his hair was red, like Pip's. And that he was good with words and liked to come up with limericks and funny toasts.

"My father would have loved you, Ava. You and Pip." Dad put down his knife and wiped his tomato-y hands on his apron. "He'd have taken you to plays and ball games and maybe even Ireland. I just wish he'd...taken better care of himself physically. His heart was in the right place, but it had to work too hard to sustain his body."

"What do you mean?" I asked quietly.

"Well, it's possible my dad would have died at sixty of a heart attack anyway. But maybe if he'd taken the time to exercise a little more back then, he could have had a little more time now. And since *I'm* not as young as I used to be, I want to do what I can to take care of myself and of you three." He smiled. "That's why *my* Sunday sundaes aren't as big as his were. And that's why when we have cake, we have slivers, not slices."

"You're still pretty young, Dad," I said. "Maybelle's dad has gray hair." Then I added, "I wish I could have met your father," because that was less shallow. And just as true.

"He was the original word nerd of the family, you know."

"I know," I said.

Dad showed me how to dip the slices of peeled eggplant into a bowl of beaten eggs, coat them with bread crumbs, and fry them, turning them each over once. Next we made layers: tomato sauce, eggplant, ricotta, and mozzarella, over and over again until we ran out.

"You're becoming more adventurous with food," Dad said.

I said, "Thanks." And then I added, "And thanks for taking care of us."

AVA, ADVENTUROUS AND APPRECIATIVE

RIGHT BEFORE BED

DEAR DIARY,

I just reread an Aesop fable called "The Bundle of Sticks." It goes like this:

An old man who was about to die summons his sons to give them parting advice. He orders his servants to bring in a bundle of sticks, and he says to his eldest son, "Break it." The son tries and tries with all his might, but he cannot break the bundle. The other sons also try and try, but they can't either. "Okay, now untie the bundle," says the father, "and each of you take one stick." They do, and the father says, "Break it." Each son breaks the stick, no problem. "You see," says their father. "Union gives strength."

I've been thinking about the moral, and sometimes it's good to *unite*, but sometimes it's better to *untie*.

For instance, Rorie is *trouble*. Her clique is "strong," but in a bad way. They're "strong" and *wrong*. And I get that it's hard to say no to someone like Rorie—I guess it was hard for Chuck to say no to Kelli. But Mackie ended up feeling bad that she went along with Rorie, and Chuck doesn't like getting stuck on the phone talking about Kelli's goldendoodle.

So maybe when you say yes to someone you *should* have said no to, you sometimes wish you'd just plain said no in the first place. Like, it might be better to be alone than with someone you don't like.

AVA, ASTUTE

PS Pip told me a joke. Why can't a bicycle stand alone? It's two tired. (Teehee.)

3/2
IN STUDY HALL

DEAR DIARY,

First thing this morning, Zara came up to my locker and said, "Did you hear about Chuck?"

"What about him?" I asked

"I think he and Kelli broke up."

"Why do you think that?"

"Because on the bus just now, Kelli walked right by him and sat next to Max. And she and Max started sharing a sticky bun and laughing."

"Did Chuck seem upset?"

"Not at all." Zara gave me a smile.

I couldn't help it. I smiled back.

AVA :)

DEAR DIARY,

I sort of avoided Chuck today because I didn't want to say anything stupid. Of course, now I realize that avoiding him was stupid!

AVA, AWKWARD

IN BED FIRST THING IN THE MORNING

Dear Diary,

Today is March Fourth, which, if I were playing the homonym game, sounds like March Forth.

Right now, right this second, I think I am *marching forth* into my future and that I am slowly but surely going from being a kid to being a *teen*.

Little by *little*, I'm getting less *little*.

Question: Are things between Chuck and me going to keep changing? Should I tell him that I know things changed with Kelli?

I don't want to ruin our friendship, because I like our friendship. But I'm also (I admit it!) curious and excited to see what might happen next.

I think this means I'm growing up. But is anyone ever really all "grown-up"? Are all grown-ups *all grown-up*?

AVA IN BETWEEN, AGE ELEVEN YEARS, TWO MONTHS, AND THREE DAYS

ON THE LIVING ROOM SOFA WITH TACO

DEAR DIARY,

Pip said that she likes to make *to-do* lists, but then likes to check everything off and turn them into *ta-da* lists.

She also said that Ben heard a funny palindrome on YouTube by a comedian named Weird Al: oozy rat in a sanitary zoo. (O-O-Z-Y-R-A-T-I-N-A-S-A-N-I-T-A-R-Y-Z-O-O.)

Here's another surprising palindrome: Dr. Awkward. (D-R-A-W-K-W-A-R-D.)

AVA, AMUSED

PS Today Chuck had a doctor's appointment so he missed English. You know what? I missed him!

DEAR DIARY,

We had our Friday spelling test, and I got another 100 and Chuck got another 80, and we both drew giant stars around each other's grades. He said my spelling brains must be rubbing off on him, which is a gross image, but I liked how his eyes smiled when he said it.

I didn't want to pass him a note and ask him out, but what if someone *else* asks him out? What if someone asks him out this weekend?

None of the Emilys like-like him, do they?

Confession: I can't imagine why *every girl* in our class—and in our grade—doesn't have a crush on him.

AVA, ANXIOUS

DEAR DIARY,

I don't know what got into Mom, but we were all four in the living room (all five if you count Taco), and out of the blue, Mom said that if Pip and I wanted to invite some girls to sleep over, that would be fine.

"Like a slumber party?" I said. The last time we'd planned a slumber party, it had *not* gone well.

"More like a sister sleepover," Mom said. "You could each invite a couple of girls."

Pip was so deep into her new detective novel, *J Is for Judgment*, that she did not even hear us talking. Mom and I both called her name, but Pip did not react. Taco did. He was looking down at us from on top of a bookshelf—which was funny. He keeps finding new places to sit and perch. And sometimes they are way up high—as if he wants to be sure to stay out of the way of any random dogs or coyotes.

Well, Dad winked at us and said, "Watch." Then he called Pip's cell phone. It rang, and she looked startled but picked up.

Dad said "Hello!" and Mom and I laughed. Pip didn't. In fact, she was about to get mad when I told her Mom's idea. Next thing you know, we were inviting Maybelle, Zara, Bea, and Tanya over.

Guess what? They're all coming—with sleeping bags! We're going to have a camp-out in our living room! I've never had a slumber party with older girls before.

AVA IN ANTICIPATION

PS Should I ask the girls about Chuck? Would that be a *terri*fic idea or a *terri*ble idea?

Sunday afternoon

Dear Diary,

We did not slumber much at our slumber party.

We played Pictionary (Pip and Tanya were the best) and charades (Bea and Zara were the best) and we tried to hold a séance with a Ouija board (but it didn't work).

After Mom and Dad went to bed, we raided the refrigerator and ate grapes, Twizzlers, and M&Ms. Mom and Dad must have *expected* us to, because they were the ones who bought the snacks, but it was still fun to be sneaky.

At ten p.m., Bea made up a game called Secrets. First everyone had to write out a personal question on a strip of paper and put it in a bag. Then everyone had to pick out a random question, answer it, and choose someone else to answer it. Then that person picked the next question—and next person.

I'm about to tape all six questions in here. We didn't tell which question we wrote, but *I* wrote the first one, and I will write down my guesses about who wrote the others. (Note: I was going to write, "Have you ever kissed a boy?" but I didn't want Pip to kill me if she picked it.)

QUESTIONS

WHEN WAS THE LAST TIME YOU CRIED? (AVA)

WOULD YOU WANT TO BE FAMOUS? WHY OR WHY NOT AND FOR WHAT? (PIP)

DO YOU HAVE A CRUSH, AND IF SO, ON WHO? (MAYBELLE)

WHO IS YOUR FAVORITE (OR LEAST) FAVORITE RELATIVE, AND WHY? (BEA)

IF YOU COULD CHANGE ONE THING ABOUT YOUR BODY, WHAT WOULD IT BE? (ZARA)

WHAT DO YOU FEEL GUILTY ABOUT? (TANYA)

We started, and I picked my own question (the one about crying), so I read it aloud then said, "At school right in front of Mrs. Lemons." Everyone nodded sympathetically. Then I chose Zara. She said she cried when her mom said she had to live with her grandparents. We stayed quiet in case she wanted to say more, but she didn't.

Zara picked the crush question and admitted that she likes Jamal! (Observation: when you like—or dislike—someone, it's pretty hard to hide.) I thought Zara might choose me, but she chose Pip, and Pip said, "Ben used to be my crush, but now he's my boyfriend!"

Pip picked the body question and said, "I wouldn't mind being taller than my *little* sister." She stuck her tongue out at me in a nice-ish way, so I quoted Dr. Seuss to her: "A person's a person no matter how small." Pip gave Tanya a questioning look, and Tanya nodded, so Pip picked her. I guess Pip thought it wouldn't be toooo awkward, because it was just us girls and we already knew what Tanya might say.

What she said was, "My goal is to lose twenty-five pounds, and I'm proud of myself because I've already lost four." We said encouraging things, and Tanya added, "I'm big-boned, like my mom, so I'll never wear a small or a medium. But maybe someday I can shop where you all do, instead of in special sections."

Next Tanya picked the favorite relative question. If Pip or I had picked it, we might have said that our Nana Ethel is *not* "one of those Hallmark grandmothers" and explained that she gives pat-pats instead of hugs and rarely sends gifts or asks about Taco or anything. But then we might have felt disloyal. So I was glad Tanya got that question. Tanya said her favorite relative is her grandmother, "because she always makes me feel beautiful."

Then she pointed to Bea, who, of course, said her favorite relative was her aunt the psychotherapist.

Bea picked the famous question and said she wants to be an advice columnist. (I now realize that I would *not* want to—too much responsibility and too easy to mess up!) Bea chose Maybelle, who said she wouldn't mind being an astronaut or the president of the Hayden Planetarium but added, "I also wouldn't mind being a regular math teacher."

Maybelle picked the very last question ("What do you feel guilty about?"), and since the other girls had already answered two questions each, I knew that I would also have to answer it too. Maybelle said she still felt guilty about the terrible haircut she gave me last year. I said I'd gotten two real haircuts since then and not to worry.

When it was my final turn, I looked at Bea and said that I still felt bad about writing "Sting of the Queen Bee," that contest story that had hurt her feelings. She said, "It's water under the bridge," which is an expression.

Well, I'd had a moment to think about guilt, so I decided to give some bonus answers. I looked at Pip and said I felt bad about practically giving away Taco last month without asking her and also about telling her the presentation would go fine when what did I know? I looked at Bea and said, "And I shouldn't have written 'FIT OR FAT' on our tips." I looked at Zara and said I could have been nicer when we started becoming friends. I looked at Tanya and said I was sorry I hadn't told her that I'd planned to turn her private letter into a public poster. Then I looked at

Maybelle, my BFF, and since I *still* hadn't told her about Chuck, I decided this was an excellent time to announce right then and there, out loud, to everybody, that I was ready to make a big confession. So I said that.

Everyone got quiet, and my heart was racing, and my mouth went dry, and I wondered if this was dumb. After all, I hadn't even *gotten* the crush question! But I made myself be brave and take a risk and just plain say it. So I took a breath and declared, "I have a crush on Chuck."

Instead of gasping in astonishment, they all looked at each other and cracked up. For a second, I felt like an idiot.

Zara smiled and said, "I think we all kind of knew that."

Bea said that I wasn't the first person to have a crush on a friend and that I shouldn't feel bad about *anything*. "Let yourself off the hook," she added. "That's what my aunt would say."

Tanya said, "Ava, I just hope he likes you back. He should."

AVA, SLUMBER PARTY GIRL

3/7

AN HOUR LATER

DEAR DIARY,

This morning, after Bea and Tanya left, Maybelle and Zara and I made breakfast snacks of banana slices topped with dabs of peanut butter.

Maybelle said that next Sunday is Pi Day and she might ask her mom if she can have a party too.

"A slumber party?" I asked.

"A *boy-girl party*," Maybelle said.

Zara liked that idea but asked, "What's Pi Day?"

"March 14," Maybelle said. "My family always celebrates by making pies."

"I don't get it," Zara said.

"Pi is 3.14159…" Maybelle began and then *kept going* until Zara and I, even though we were impressed, said, "Stopppp!" (And then, "Jinx!!")

Maybelle said, "Pi is a number that never stops. Every year, people celebrate it on 3/14—which happens to be Albert Einstein's birthday."

She explained that it's a letter in the Greek alphabet and drew the symbol π on a piece of paper for us.

"It looks like the three poles you need for limbo," I said.

"It does!" Zara agreed.

Maybelle laughed. "The point is we can have a party and make pies."

"What kind of pies?" I asked.

"Cherry, apple, coconut, banana cream. Whatever kind you like!"

I asked Maybelle if she was going to invite Kelli, and she said yes, but that she'd invite Max too. I said, "Good, because if she flirts with Chuck, I will throw a pie in her face."

Zara said, "I dare you."

"Ava," Maybelle said, "Kelli is not one hundred percent bad. Don't forget that you didn't like Bea right away either."

Zara added, "Or even me."

My mouth flopped open, but I realized I couldn't deny this, because I had been mad when she and Maybelle went to the circus and started hanging out. So I just looked at Zara and mumbled, "Sorry."

"It's okay." Zara laughed. "It's…water under the bridge!"

I thought about how Kelli had told Chuck that Tanya could model for Botero, "Wiggle Wiggle Wiggle," and added, "Okay, maybe I won't throw a pie in her face, but Kelli and I will never ever become besties!"

AVA, AT TIMES APOLOGETIC AND AT TIMES NOT

3/8
BEDTIME

DEAR DIARY,

At lunch today, I did something I've never done before: I sat next to Chuck! Emily LaCasse saw us and said, "Can I join you guys?" We had to say yes, but fortunately, she put down her backpack then went to get in line. So Chuck and I had about three minutes, just us.

"How's it going?" I asked.

"Good," he answered.

"Is that a new shirt?" I asked.

"Yes," he said.

I knew I should say, "It looks good" or "I like it" or something, but I couldn't and instead just stared at my chicken rice soup.

He took a peek at Kelli, who was wearing a short fuzzy white dress and sitting with Max three tables over. I peeked too. Max had two straws sticking out of his nose and looked like a moronic walrus, and Kelli was laughing hysterically. I wasn't sure if she was trying to make Chuck jealous or if she thought a boy with straws in his nose was the funniest thing on the planet.

"Is she still calling your house to talk about her goldendoodle?" I asked, then hoped that wasn't too rude or direct.

"No."

"Do you wish she were?"

"No."

"Am I asking too many questions?"

"No."

We both laughed, but not as hard as Kelli and Max. And I don't think it's because Kelli and Max were having much more fun at their table than we were at ours. I think it's because they are both just very loud. Maybe even *exuberant* (bonus spelling word). Come to think of it, maybe *they* make a good couple.

Suddenly Chuck leaned forward. "Ava, you were right," he said. "I should never have checked that circle. I didn't want to have a girlfriend. I mean, maybe when I'm in high school. Or *college*."

I nodded, waiting. This was not exactly the way I pictured this conversation going. Did he really *not* want a girlfriend until *college*?

He put down his fork. "Last Monday, she called three times in one day, so I finally told her that I didn't want to go out anymore. I tried to be polite, and maybe I should have done it in person? At least I didn't break up by text."

I half nodded.

"Anyway," he continued, "I did what you suggested: I blamed my mom and said she thinks I'm too young to go out."

I sat there, frozen. Whoa. Had I *suggested* that? Maybe I kind of had.

"Kelli and I don't have much in common," he added. "And we have totally different senses of humor."

I was *not* about to argue, *You're both good at sports! And limbo! And you both have a K in your name!*

The lunchroom was loud and so was my heartbeat. "But, Ava," Chuck continued, "if I *did* want to have a girlfriend"—he dropped his voice and I had to lean in—"I'd want it to be you."

At first I stayed silent. Then, when I knew I had to say something, I said, "Chuck, I don't want a boyfriend now either. But if I did…" Suddenly I stopped. I wasn't brave enough to finish that sentence! Not then and there anyway. So I started a new one. "Chuck," I said. "Maybe we can both *not* go out, but, like, *not* go out *together*. Like, we could be *not-going-out together*."

He nodded as though he understood what I meant even though it didn't really make sense. Then he said, "Maybe we can," and we both started laughing—but not hysterically or anything.

The Emilys came over, and Chuck made room by moving his chair closer to mine. Soon Maybelle, Jamal, Zara, Aiden, and Ryan sat down too. And just like that, we had an official boy-girl table, and it didn't even feel that weird.

"What's so funny?" Jamal asked, because Chuck and I must have been looking at each other as if we had a secret. (Which we sort of do.)

Without missing a beat, Chuck said, "I just told Ava the world's dumbest joke. Want to hear?"

"Sure," Zara answered for everybody.

Chuck gave me a smile and said, "There were two hats hanging on a hat rack in the hallway. One hat said to the other, 'You stay here—I'll go on a head.'"

Everyone half laughed half groaned (if you can half laugh half groan), and Bea walked by with Tanya and gave me a little thumbs-up, which, thank heavens, I don't think anyone else saw.

Now I'm home, and Taco is with me, and Mom and Dad and Pip are in their rooms, and I'm going to write down the words Chuck said to me, because I want to play them over in my mind. Like a song lyric.

Wait, I'm going to get my magic pen for this, the one Dad bought me at the Dublin Writers Museum.

Okay. Got it.

Here is what Chuck said:

"If I did want to have a girlfriend, I'd want it to be you."

We're both just eleven, and who knows about the future. But I'm glad that today we admitted that we like each other. Not that there's any big hurry to go public or get mushy or use the L word or think about *X*'s or *O*'s or *anything*. But still, I can't stop smiling.

XOX

AVA

PS After dinner, I checked to make sure my pack of gum was safe and sound. It was. It is. (Even though it will always be missing two pieces.)

BEDTIME

DEAR DIARY,

I can't believe I've almost filled up another whole diary! Neither can Mom or Dad. If diaries counted as books, I'd be *prolific* (spelling word alert).

Dad said he'd take me to Bates Books tomorrow to buy a new one. Since Dad is Irish, I teased, "You just want an excuse to see all the shamrocks."

He laughed. "Busted!"

Yesterday, Pip helped Ben and Mrs. Bates decorate the bookstore, and they hung shiny green clovers everywhere to get ready for St. Patrick's Day—which is March 17. Pip also helped two kids pick out books—*The Story of Ferdinand* and *A Fish Out of Water*. To thank her, Mrs. Bates gave her a magnet that says YAY! BOOKS!

When I grow up, if I do get to write books for kids, I might want to write a love story about two kids who are too young for real love.

Or maybe I can write about a girl who tries to do a good D-E-E-D, and at first it backfires, but then things work out, and she learns that what people say and how they say it both matter.

Speaking of, I hope Tanya keeps liking our tips and also that she can keep caring *about* herself enough to keep taking care *of* herself, if that makes sense.

Dad came to tuck me in, and we started talking about writing, and I said that one good thing about kids' novels is that they have happy endings.

"What do you mean?"

"Didn't you once tell me that plays sometimes end unhappily?"

"Did I?"

"Yes. You said that in Shakespeare plays, sometimes everyone ends up dead all over the stage. You said *Hamlet* ends up with a pile of bodies. And Romeo and Juliet don't get to go on a honeymoon or anything."

Dad laughed. "True. Until Disney came along, a lot of fairy tales had sad endings too. The way Hans Christian Andersen wrote it, the little mermaid turns into sea foam."

"Some Aesop fables have sad endings," I said. "The boy who cries wolf gets eaten up."

"Nom, nom, nom," Dad said as if he were a hungry wolf. He even *ululated*, which is a fancy word for howled.

"Stop!" I said, and he stopped. "You know something else about books?"

"What?" he asked.

"When an author writes a book, and someone buys it, the author still gets to *keep* the book. For artists, it's worse."

"What do you mean?"

"Like if Botero or Picasso or even Pip or Tanya sold a painting,"

I began, "they'd have to give up the original." Dad nodded. "Or take your plays. When the actors take the final bow, it's over. You can't play it again live in your office."

"Ah, but I can play it over in my mind. And when you write for the *stage* instead of the *page*," he said, making a rhyme, "you get to hear the audience laugh. Novelists don't usually get to hear readers' reactions."

"How's your new play coming?" I asked. I sometimes forget that not only do kids have ups and downs, but so do parents. (And elevators.)

"Pretty well," Dad said. "I have a new draft, and we're going to have a table read this month."

"A *first* draft?"

"More like a *tenth* draft!"

"What's this one called?"

"I haven't told you?" He looked surprised. "*First Love.*"

"Is it autobiographical?"

"All writing is a mix of imagination, observation, and memory."

"H-U-H." Dad had once told me that success was a mix of *t*alent, *t*iming, and *t*enacity—I remember because it was an alliteration. "Has Mom read it?"

"Mom loves this play! And as you know, Mom can be a tough cookie."

"Can *I* read it?"

"Let me keep polishing it," he said. "Besides, you'll like it more when you're older." (Note: that's parent code for "You're too young.")

"Do the people in the play like each other the same amount?" I asked.

"Not right away," Dad replied.

"But it has a happy ending?"

Dad laughed. "It does."

"Are there any rivals?" I asked.

"Rivals?" Dad repeated, surprised. "I guess there are, actually. 'The course of true love never did run smooth.'" Dad smiled. "That's Shakespeare. Now lights out, okay?"

"Okay," I said, but then *negotiated* (spelling word) for five more minutes so I could write in you.

AVA...ALMOST...ASLEEP...

DEAR DIARY,

This is the last page of this diary. I'm about to put you on my bookshelf next to the other two diaries I finished.

Sorry I won't be able to tell you about the Pi Day party. It's in four days, and *everyone* is talking about it. Chuck and I have agreed to be pie-making partners, which, I confess, is about all I can think about.

Back in kindergarten, he and I were *assigned* to be apple-picking partners. This time, we *chose* each other. On purpose.

Funny. When I started this diary, I didn't even know I liked Chuck. Now we both know that we both like each other.

And the thing is: that feels like sort of enough.

For now, anyway.

Someday I might be ready for lip gloss and texting and phone calls and holding hands. But not yet.

At least not quite yet.

Oh wait. I just thought of something. This diary doesn't have a happy ending. What it has is (drum roll, please) a happy *beginning*…

AVA WREN, ON HER WAY

About the Author

Carol Weston kept diaries as a girl. Her parents were word nerds in the best way. Her first book, *Girltalk: All the Stuff Your Sister Never Told You*, was published in a dozen languages and has been in print since 1985. Her next fourteen books include *The Diary of Melanie Martin* and three other Melanie Martin novels, as well as *Ava and Pip* and *Ava and Taco Cat*. Carol studied French and Spanish comparative literature at Yale, graduating summa cum laude. She has an MA in Spanish from Middlebury. Since 1994, she has been the "Dear Carol" advice columnist at *Girls' Life* magazine, and has made many YouTube videos for kids and parents. Carol and her husband, playwright Rob Ackerman, met as students in Madrid and live in Manhattan. They have two daughters and one cat. Carol's next novel is *The Speed of Life*. Find out more at carolweston.com.